TAROU: THE FALL

Praise for *Tarou: The Fall*

"Sometimes a novel reminds me why I love to read epic fantasy. That's the case with the beautifully wrought *Tarou: The Fall* … It's Dungeons and Dragons. It's sword and sorcery. It's as dark as it is bright … with a sensibility and mystique all its own. Don't miss this!"

—James Rollins,
#1 *New York Times* bestselling author of
A Dragon of Black Glass

"Fredsti and Fitzgerald have created a magnificently complex world with a meaty plot and a great set of characters, all three of which will captivate and compel you. Do check it out!"

—Keith R.A. DeCandido,
USA Today bestselling author of
Supernatural Crimes Unit: NYPD

"A richly layered, high-action tale of courage and comradery … These quirky, ragtag characters are the heroes we all need right now. A startling metaphor for our times."

—Lee Murray,
five-time Bram Stoker® Award-winning
author of *Grotesque: Monster Stories*

"*Tarou: The Fall* has intriguing and meticulous world-building, a cast of quirky and engaging characters, and lavish prose. It reminds me of the classic works of Fritz Leiber and Clark Ashton Smith."

—Kevin J. Anderson,
New York Times bestselling author of
Dune: House Atreides and *Nether Station*

"*Tarou: The Fall* is a wild mix of ancient magic, flashing swords, and complex characters! Dana Fredsti and David Fitzgerald weave real sorcery with this new fantasy thriller!"

—Jonathan Maberry,
New York Times bestselling author of
Kagen the Damned and *NecroTek*

BOOKS BY DANA FREDSTI AND DAVID FITZGERALD

THE TIME SHARDS SERIES
Time Shards
Shatter War
Tempus Fury

STANDALONE NOVELS
Tarou: The Fall

BOOKS BY DANA FREDSTI

THE ASHLEY PARKER SERIES
Plague Town
Plague Nation
Plague World
Pinky Swear

THE LILITH SERIES
The Spawn of Lilith
Blood Ink
Hollywood Monsters

COLLECTIONS
Darling of Decay
Z Resurrected
Shifting, Swirling HERitage (edited by D. J. Stevenson)
Joe Ledger: Unbreakable (edited by Jonathan Maberry and Bryan Thomas Schmidt)
Weird Tales: 100 Years of Weird (edited by Jonathan Maberry)

NOVELLAS
A Man's Gotta Eat What a Man's Gotta Eat

BOOKS BY DAVID FITZGERALD

NONFICTION
Nailed: Ten Christian Myths That Show Jesus Never Existed at All
The Mormons
Jesus: Mything In Action, Volumes I–III
Playing God: An Evolutionary History of World Religion, Volumes I–III

COLLECTIONS (AS KILT KILPATRICK)
Under the Kilt: The Best Stories by Kilt Kilpatrick

TAROT: THE FALL

DANA FREDSTI & DAVID FITZGERALD

Tarou: The Fall

Cover illustration/design, interior design by Jeff Wong.
Tarou map by Dana Fredsti, David Fitzgerald, and Jeff Wong.
Interior illustrations by Pamela Colman Smith (1909 Rider-Waite tarot deck).

Published by *Weird Tales*® Presents and Blackstone Publishing.

www.WeirdTales.com
www.BlackstonePublishing.com

Blackstone Publishing
31 Mistletoe Road
Ashland, Oregon 97520

ISBN: 979-8-212-56372-7
Fiction/Science Fiction/General

Printed in the United States of America

First Edition: 2025

10 9 8 7 6 5 4 3 2 1

For Jonathan Maberry, who continues to bring positivity, creativity, and much-appreciated humor to our lives.

TAROU

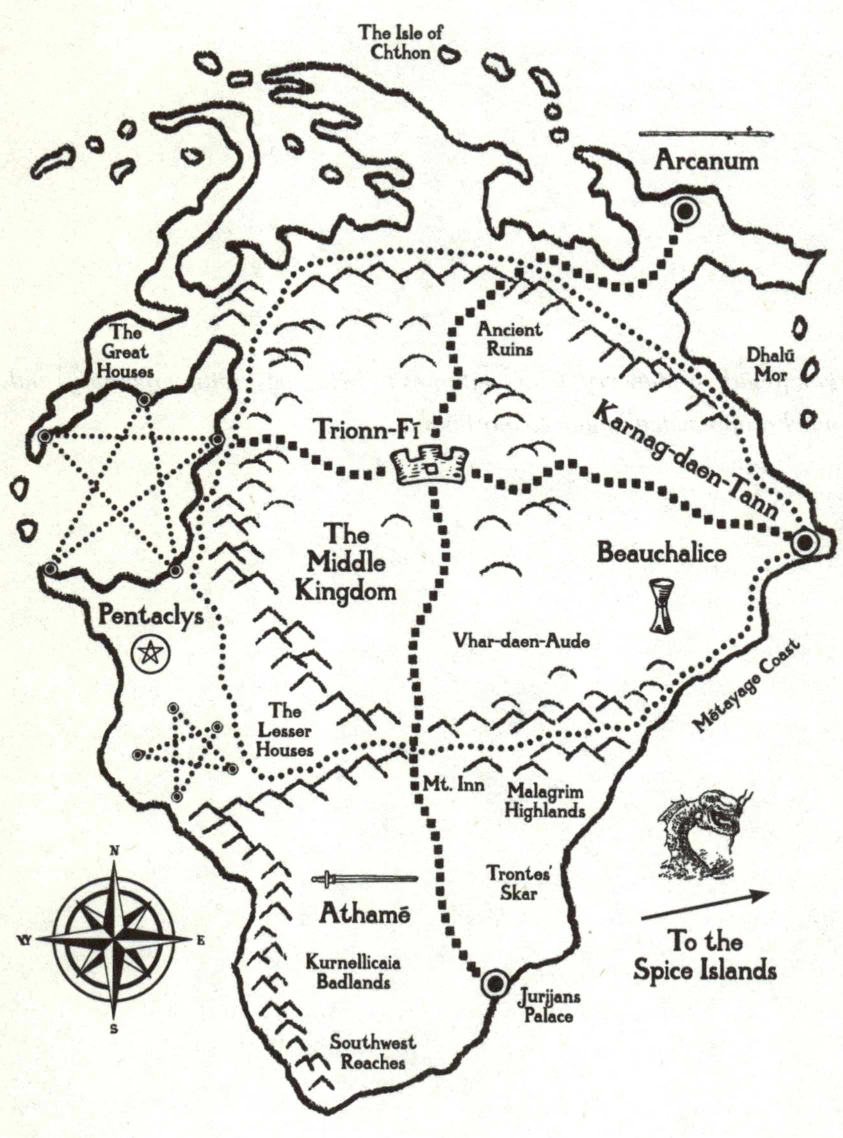

Ring Road ●●●●●●●●●●●

High Roads ■■■■■■■■

Prologue

Arrayed in splendor and sophistication, the magnificent empire of Tarou is a panoply of dreams and wonder, the envy of the world. Its ships rule the seas and air, its magics and science bring forth new learning, and its tutelary gods smile upon all the many peoples and cultures of its shining lands.

For decades the imperial capital of Trionn-Fí, nestled deep within the central mountains of the continent, has been the glittering aristocratic crown jewel of the empire, supported by its four surrounding provinces, each with its own riches and strength. The warrior-ranks of Athamé—the harsh province of Swords—give Tarou its martial might, its gold and steel, and the most precious of gems and minerals. The entire realm rejoices in the lush and fertile vineyards, farmlands, and pasturelands of Beauchalice, the province of Cups. Avaricious merchant princes of Pentaclys, the province of Coins, prosper amid the many guilds of traders, craftsmen, and artisans. Meanwhile, the sorcerers, mages, and thaumaturges of Arcanum—the mysterious fourth province of Wands—work miraculous wonders, even as they delve into dark secrets and tap into powers undreamed of by outsiders …

Until now.

Tarou is doomed.

III
THE EMPRESS.

IV
THE EMPEROR.

II
B
J
THE HIGH PRIESTESS

V
THE HIEROPHANT

Trionn-Fí

One Year Ago

There were no defensive outer walls to the city of Trionn-Fí—the capital had been conceived and constructed in a triumphant time of peace and unity. Instead, to enter the city, the High Road crossed over a grand canal—so large it was really more of a lake—that encircled the outermost limits of the city along with a ring of mercantile warehouses, fishing boats and fish markets, berths for pleasure boats and gondola taxis, terraces of waterside taverns and eating houses.

Behind them lay the wide circle that formed the greater part of the city, all shot through with traceries of roads and bridges, aqueducts and canals. Within its mazelike districts could be found every manner of artisans, tradesmen, working-class wizards, merchants, market bazaars, schools, libraries, and guildhalls. Here, too, could be found the hippodromes and circuses, barracks and guardhouses of the city watch, and the landing fields and hangars housing the ships of the sky navy.

A ring of multistoried mansions, each within its own walled-off private estate, made up the de facto line of division between the wider outer ring of the city and the inner ring of the sumptuous Noble Quarter, with its manors, pleasure gardens, fountains, opera houses, theaters, salons, and all the finest shops and restaurants, divided by wide boulevards and romantic waterways.

But the innermost and most glorious heart of the capital lay within the circular space enclosing the palace and the palatial grounds. If the city of Trionn-Fí was envisioned as the triple crown—as its architects intended—then the Imperial Palace's unearthly beautiful Aurichalcum Tower formed the central adornment of the imperial diadem.

No castle hewn from stone, no iron-banded fortress, could ever hope to rival the palace. The impossibilities of its construction were multiple. First, its appearance. Rather than an assemblage of masonry and brickwork, its broad spire resembled the teardrop of an exquisite azure gemstone—an impossibly gigantic sapphire carved from a mountain.

The lines of its soaring strands of stained glass windows—which made the whole edifice gleam like the facets of a jewel—were a second impossibility. The tower seemed composed more of windows than walls, surely impossible to stand under its own weight. And while it towered impossibly high over the city, it also defied gravity with unbelievable grace, for it was not rooted to the ground, but—impossibly—suspended in the air, upheld by the strongest sorceries, which made it seem to be tethered to the earth by a sweeping filigree of flying buttresses and walkways, all slender as silver strands, and that the entire immense structure might float serenely away at any moment.

The monumental crown formed by the palatial complex's encircling walls held a second adornment. This was the smaller—none would dare say a *lesser*—palace of the *Cathedralis Geminae,* the Twin Seat of Trionn-Fí's Holy See, where the High Priestess and the Hierophant held sway. Ensconced along the innermost ring enclosing the palatial estate, it stood opposite the Imperial Palace—in more ways than one.

TAROU: THE FALL

Within the heart of the palace and its overwhelming splendor, Her Most Imperial Majesty, Rheanna, Empress of Tarou and the Five Realms, was bored, though her regal demeanor would never betray the fact. Whenever she was seated on the throne before the court, she was at all times a highly trained and most skilled expert in maintaining composure and serenity—as was His Most Imperial Majesty, her husband, the Emperor.

The high-waisted gown she wore on this particular occasion was of the finest Chalicean silk—this one a sky-blue and diamond-dusted fabric that evoked the skies of spring and matched the pale blue of her eyes. On her crown of gleaming white gold, twelve starbursts rose over a band of stylized woodlands, mountains, and fertile fields, three for each of the four original realms of the empire. Beneath it, her lustrous auburn hair hung in a long, thick regal braid tied with blue-and-white jewels that shone like stars.

Beside her, Patrokleos, her husband and Emperor, was even more resplendent in his ceremonial armor and robes of crimson, holding the imperial scepter. Upon his golden chest plate blazed a sun design, as bright as the eagle's head and wings that formed his crown. The cool amber fire of the eagle's eyes matched his own. She never grew tired of gazing upon him.

All the regular denizens of the imperial court—and scores more besides—filled the throne room under the watchful eyes of the towering statues of spearmen lining the walls. There were perhaps a hundred in all, armored with breastplates and high-crested helmets. Their long-limbed bodies were not entirely human, each topped with the stylized horsehead of a chess piece. Every marble sentry stood four times the height of an average man, bearing a spear half again that long. The Empress often took comfort in knowing that even if some enemy force managed to slay every man and woman of the Imperial Guard, with but a single word of command from her or the Emperor, the massive stone giants would come to life in defense of the throne.

All observers said the Aurichalcum Tower's outer appearance was bejeweled, but Rheanna felt its interior was no less breathtaking or beautiful. A thousand tiny dancing points of were-light floated in the cavernous space overhead, making myriad constellations to illuminate the throne room in glorious day, no matter what hour of night. The finest artisans of the Five Realms had created the famous cathedral-length windows that completely ringed the walls of the soaring, high-ceilinged throne room. Each delicate multicolored panel of stained and ruby glass was intricately wired in slender lines and tiny loops of aurichalcum—and electrum, silver, and gold. And though the precious artwork had never known war, the most powerful enchanters of Arcanum had ensured that every pane was strong enough to repel a lightning bolt or a boulder from a siege engine.

Gazing out upon the throng of nobles, the Empress casually and automatically took note of the faces of friends, allies, sycophants, and enemies. Through both subtle magics and cunning architectural design, the great throne room of the Aurichalcum Tower could not only host an audience of a thousand with ease but also allow every courtier, visitor, and servant to clearly hear the voices of the imperial couple.

At the moment the court was politely tolerating a highly technical debate on Modern Thaumaturgy and Evocation between two factions of apparitor-magicians—the ambitious, so-called "soul-traveling" Psychidions, and their more cautious rival faction, the Antrean Exiles. Because this second group of dour killjoys opposed their grand plans, the Psychidion faction had given them the nickname "Anti-Exultationists," and so the name Antexultationists had stuck.

Both delegations had come prepared to make lengthy presentations of their respective cases. After a spirited back-and-forth for the better part of four hours, Málach, the steely-eyed leader of the Psychidion faction, with a most distracting set of flared muttonchop whiskers, was—at last—making his final arguments.

"In closing, Your Imperial Highness, having demonstrated the superlative excellence of our most gracious Imperial Majesties' devoted schools of sorcery, our total mastery of the elementals, indeed, all the mighty achievements brought forth on behalf of our beloved sovereigns, we extend our most humble and subservient gratitude.

"Of course I scarcely need remind our Imperial Majesties, yet to all the worthies of the imperial court gathered here, let me speak simply, without obfuscation or fear of repudiation from those who would gainsay, to wit—the magical might of the Taroutian Empire has conquered everything under the sun and moon. Now we but ask your imperial patronage to go beyond them. Indeed, beyond the very stars themselves."

Ah. Now we are getting somewhere.

That last line regained the attention of the Empress. Her Highness already had her suspicions about where the Psychidion's spokesman was headed with their request for funding from the Crown. She was not unfamiliar with the science—her education was, after all, the finest—and she knew the scholars of Arcanum had long since recognized that though their own kingdom was renowned for sorcery, in truth it was here in the middle kingdom that the metaphysical ley lines of the continent aligned. They delineated those points where, at the proper times, the dimensional membrane between worlds was thinnest, and there were those who could sense the power lying beyond that veil.

Cutting through his bloviation, at last she discerned the faction's aim—they were asking for support from the imperial coffers to assemble the necessary arcane equipment and aligned sorcerous structures to pierce the veil and so tap into the eldritch energies of another dimension.

She listened more intently.

"... the costs of such a construction, though considerable, would soon prove to be trifling and should not dissuade us in the least regard," he was saying. "Imagine the unprecedented power—for what else could be worthy of our sovereigns' imperial magnificence?" he asked, arms spread outward in a grand gesture.

"It is *not* unprecedented, noble Málach," called out his adversary. Aneirin, the speaker for the Antexultationist minority, stepped forward. "In ages past, others have foreseen the potential that our colleagues have dreamt of—and indeed, it *would* seem the mark of wisdom to pursue such plans, for so magnificent a reward—if we did not know better." He gestured to his apprentice, who hastened to his master's side bearing a heavy leather-bound codex.

"One such was the Circle of the Passelekites, on the lost isle of Dhalú Mor. Our archives speak of their efforts. We know the names of seven—seven!—of their school's conjurers and evokers who went mad, one after another, before the island itself sank under mysterious circumstances. Indeed, it is suspected that the unusually vile sea monsters that have long plagued those cursed waters first sprang forth from this misbegotten and infelicitous endeavor."

His opponent quickly cut in. "Their ancient methods were primitive and unsophisticated, their sorcerous powers weak and ill-understood! We know we can succeed where they failed! We—"

"Hah! The very words of Hallam, your own disgraced colleague," Aneirin called out, turning to the rest of the court. "Or, as we now know him, Hallam the Mad! Hallam the Damned!"

"Unfair," Málach shouted. "You know Hallam has been cast out of our order! He—"

The Emperor raised his hand, instantly silencing the mage before he could launch into any further harangue.

"We thank you both, worthy mages," he spoke, bringing a merciful end to the deliberations. The two leaders bowed and withdrew, each to their respective retinue.

"What word from Chthon?" the Emperor asked, turning his gaze to the court. A representative of the Oracle School came forward at once, scroll in hand, to present to their Majesties. The imperial couple had, of course, seen the divination as soon as it had arrived that morning and had analyzed it at length in a private session with their advisers. Nevertheless, as the Arcane envoy cleared his throat and spoke the message aloud, they bestowed their full attention, as though hearing it for the first time:

Farewell
The wheel, the world—all turn
Eyes look up
The hand outreached will touch another
The gift sought is great; the gift received is greater still
The hand stretched forth is not the hand that grasps it
Eyes look down
The world, the wheel—all change
Farewell

"Here ends the divination, Your Imperial Majesties," the representative said with a final bow before taking his leave. Murmurs of wonder rippled through the courtly audience at the prognostication—even though it was more cryptic than might have been hoped for.

With the slightest of glances, the Emperor gauged his spouse's opinion. By careful placement of the fingers of her right hand and a subtle tilt to her head, she clearly signaled to him and him alone her disapproval of the Psychidion position. He signaled back his acknowledgment and his own agreement with a thoughtful stroke of his beard and two unobtrusive twists of the imperial scepter.

The Empress was relieved that she and her husband were of the same mind. Time then, to debate the matter with their opponents. She maintained her poise as she watched him take a moment to silently prepare for his attack. Then he spoke again, throwing down the gauntlet.

"This is a weighty matter," the Emperor said in an even tone. "We would hear the wise counsel of Their Holiness, our Most Sacred Hierophant and our Reverend High Priestess." The two stepped forward from their entourages. The High Priestess was a tall woman with fined boned features, dressed in robes of a shade of blue so dark they were near black, spangled with a dusting of starry gemstones. Her eyes were shaded by a silken veil beneath a silver crescent headdress.

As the High Priestess's garments evoked the moon, the Hierophant's vestments of white and gold did the same for the sun, as did his gilded miter. The pair drew near and raised their open hands in a beneficent gesture, bestowing their blessings upon the imperial couple.

The High Priestess crossed her hands over her heart and bowed her head, speaking first. "Imperial Highness, Beloved Chosen Servant of the Gods, Their Most Faithful Defender of Truth and the Right. Our Most Gracious Empress, upon whom the Gods have bestowed every blessing and virtue."

The Empress graciously lowered her gaze and bowed her head in acknowledgment. The High Priestess spoke again. "We who rejoice in the service of the Heavenly Host, we fear no mortal endeavor. As it is written in the Holy Scriptures:

For that which is in the hands of the Gods cannot be wrested from them, nor is there any knowledge unknown to them, no secret that can stay hidden from their sight.

Therefore, let not our hearts be troubled, and be assured that the Gods shall grant success as it please them."

So it was to be a yes to the Psychidions from the High Priestess, the Empress mused, unsurprised and already contemplating the best countermove.

The Hierophant lifted up his eyes. "Oh people of Tarou, happily we join together to praise the Gods in whose sunlight we bask. For is there any blessing they have withheld from us? Foremost, a wise Emperor and Empress, to reign in splendor and execute all justice, even as they themselves submit in regal humility to the will of the Gods. And being so blest, what greater need have we? What other power need we chase? As the Panegyricist tells us: *To the faithful king, the crown is a yoke; to the faithful servant, the yoke is a crown.* So, following the noble example set by our divinely appointed sovereign majesties, let us then show contentment in our hearts with that which the Gods have so generously bestowed upon us—and therefore cease any other vain pursuits out of pride or avarice."

A no from the Hierophant? Interesting. This was a pleasant surprise.

As for the High Priestess, she gave away no sign of any surprise on her part either, but only raised her head skyward and outstretched her open arms to receive a new divine revelation. "Doubts are cast aside in the presence of the Gods. Let those who love wisdom take comfort in their arms—and reach no further for refuge. We are secure, as we have ever been, wanting for nothing more, but content in the many blessings they have bestowed. Praise be unto all the Gods and blessed are their servants."

The Empress admired the speed with which the High Priestess pulled such an elegant about-face. *And just like that, the ecclesiastic authorities are of one mind again.* So there was not going to be a second debate with their rivals after all. A refreshing change.

On cue, she turned her loving gaze upon her Emperor, who thanked the pair of High Ecclesiarches and now feigned to be taking in this new guidance and carefully deliberating the issue. After a swift but suitable time of reflection, he addressed the entire imperial court.

"We commend all our splendid schools of magic, who have brought forth so many marvelous achievements from the misty shores and isles of Arcanum to the benefit of all the realms. Furthermore, as their sovereign, we do charge them to continue steadfast in their duties and studies, for which they have long earned so much rightful acclaim."

Having given the spoon of honey, he followed with the bitter pill. "So that all these worthy efforts may continue without distraction, let your hearts be untroubled by thoughts of any such new endeavor. It is our will that the faction known as the Psychidions return to more fruitful labors alongside their brothers and sisters."

Everyone in the courtly audience understood the meaning perfectly—there would be no support from the imperial treasury for any further pursuit along these lines. As one, the delegations of mages bowed in obedience, were dismissed, and took their leave—crestfallen Psychidions and victorious Antexultationists alike.

The Empress permitted herself an almost imperceptible sigh of relief. The Gods alone knew what future catastrophe they may have just avoided by curtailing wizardly meddling with such dangerous, unpredictable, and potentially calamitous magics.

Málach and his despondent retinue had scarcely departed the palace grounds when a furtive man in the drab clothing of a low-level servant approached.

"My Lord Mage, a moment, please."

Despite his dress, the man's voice and manner seemed too fine for a mere beggar or a hawking street seller. He bent his head closer and spoke in a soft voice as to not be overheard.

"Their Holinesses the High Priestess and Hierophant bid me counsel you not to despair—you shall have their patronage for your endeavor. Tell no one."

PART ONE

THE DAY BEFORE THE FESTIVAL

Chapter One

In the Foothills of the Athaméan Borderlands

Alia ducked as a blade slashed at her eyes, shifting to one side at the same time and sweeping her own finely honed steel across her assailant's torso. It skidded off the bandit's boiled leather jerkin, and an ugly grin split his already ugly face. He growled in triumph, but the growl turned into a gurgle as Alia backslashed his throat. The bandit fell to the ground, blood spilling out over the dusty road to pool with that of three of his fellows who'd been cut down before him, part of a pack of scruffy mountain brigands hoping to catch stragglers traveling to the Imperial Festival off guard.

Spinning around, Alia parried the downward blow that would've split her head in two, threw off the blade, and smashed the pommel of her sword into her new opponent's face—this one even uglier than the man she'd just killed. He howled in pain, nose shattering. Alia ended his misery with a sidelong cut that nearly decapitated him.

A yell to her right caught her attention—*Callan!*

She turned to see a hulking bandit in a mismatch of stolen armor smash the blade of her fiancé aside with one brutal blow of an iron club, sending him sprawling onto his back with a kick to the stomach. The bandit raised his club with the intent of caving in Callan's skull, but Alia covered the ground between them with a diving roll, rising to her knees between the two men and driving the point of her sword up into the underside of the bandit's chin. His club dropped to the ground, followed shortly by the would-be assassin.

Before she could dislodge her sword from the dead man, another bandit—this one a wiry, feral-looking woman in leather pants and tunic—launched herself at Alia with a shriek of fury, the promise of death in her eyes and in the blade that she swung in a vertical cut at Alia's face. Her sword still embedded in the man's throat, Alia grasped its hilt with both hands and pivoted, the movement jerking the corpse around like a grotesque puppet. The female bandit's blade bit deep into the thick leather scales of the man's spaulder, wedging itself. Alia shoved the corpse with one foot, pulling her own blade free at the same time. The body fell on the woman, knocking her to the ground and tangling her in dead limbs. A quick thrust to the heart dispatched her.

Alia dropped into a low guard, glancing over her shoulder to make sure she hadn't missed any of the bandits. A half dozen or so bodies sprawled on the road, the coppery smell of blood mixing with the thicker stink of human waste. Then she turned to her fiancé, who was getting to his feet.

There was no doubt that he was pleasing to look at. Callan was the Pentan ideal of male beauty. Thick, dark, wavy hair the color of dark oily coffee beans. Light olive complexion. Oval hazel eyes framed by dark lashes and finely drawn brows. Now, however, his full lips were pressed together in a thin line.

She put an anxious hand on his arm.

"Callan, are you hurt?"

He didn't reply, his attention focused on the sleeve of his doublet as he brushed dirt off the sapphire-blue velvet. Perhaps he hadn't heard her … ?

Before she could pursue the matter, Raff, the captain of the escort, clapped a hand on her shoulder. "That was one of the clumsier ambushes I've experienced." Shoulder-length black hair worn in multiple braids to keep it out of his face, Raff towered above her by a good foot and some change. He bore a wicked scar across the right side of his face, cutting from the corner of his eye past his mouth. Alia thought it added character to his otherwise ordinary features.

"They moved through the trees like three-legged pachyderms," Alia replied. "It's a wonder they haven't been arrested or killed long before now."

"And only an idiot counts on the weather to hide the glint of metal." Raff shook his head in disgust.

The bandits had chosen their place of ambush well, taking advantage of the densely forested foothills just before the road angled up into the mountains. But a stray shaft of sunlight cutting through heavy gray clouds had glinted off something in the trees—a metal fastener perhaps, or an unsheathed blade—alerting one of the sharp-eyed Athaméan soldiers to the ambush even before they heard them blundering through the undergrowth. By the time the bandits burst from the thick trees lining the road, they were howling bloodthirsty battle cries. But if they hoped to strike fear into their targets, they were in for disappointment—the caravan's armed escort had already drawn their own weapons and met the attack on the offensive.

The soldiers wiped their blades on the clothes of the dead bandits, the fresh blood blending in with older stains and untold layers of grime. Alia did the same, filled with the satisfaction that a good fight brought her. Then she saw her fiancé's frown as his attention finally turned to her, and her pleasure shriveled beneath the weight of his disapproval.

She knew what he was going to say. Sadly, she was not disappointed.

"Why can you not let our escort do their job, Alia?" Callan's tone, even in the lively staccato of the Pentan accent, was frosty. "It is not proper for my betrothed to take up a weapon when there are armed soldiers on hand for that very purpose."

"But … Callan, you joined the fight and—" She stopped herself from adding, *and see how well that worked for you before I intervened.* Some things, once said, could not be taken back or forgiven. Especially if those words happened to be the truth.

"It is not the same thing at all," he snapped. "Not where I come from."

In that instant, she saw the humiliation at the root of his anger and knew that he might never forgive her for saving his life. That who she was—her very identity as a warrior of Athamé—would always displease him. What had been intriguing, even appealing to him during several weeks of courtship was now an anathema.

His about-face had manifested after a broken axle had delayed their caravan on their way to the Imperial Festival—a fortnight of feasting, games, and celebration at Trionn-Fí, where the Emperor and Empress held court. Thousands of celebrants traveled up the High Road to Trionn-Fí for the annual event, and most had already reached their destination.

Now, so close to the last leg to the capital city of Tarou, she caught herself and swallowed her anger, then tried to put together an answer that would, if not please Callan, might at least placate him for the time being.

"I am truly sorry, Callan," she said, striving to hide her irritation under a placating tone. "But I *am* a member of the guard." *And would still be captain of it had I not agreed to marry you*, she thought.

He arched one eyebrow and shook his head. "Do you really think so much of your skills that you believe you alone could turn the tide of battle? Or do you think so little of your soldiers that they could not handle a few scruffy, starving bandits without your help?"

Alia's face flamed with an unaccustomed flush of rage and shame—rage at being spoken to in such a demeaning way after fighting to defend his life as well as her own, and shame because a small part of her *did* believe she was indispensable no matter how skilled the soldiers might be. Rage quickly won out, though—she would not apologize for doing her job.

She opened her mouth, unsure of what she was going to say but determined to defend her choices even if it ended her marriage before it began.

"What do you want to do with this, Captain?"

Dari's interruption could have not, in Alia's mind, have been better timed. Raff's second-in-command, a solidly built woman in her thirties with raven-black hair shorn close to her skull, held a wriggling child in her grip—although whether a girl or a boy was difficult to tell under the layers of dirt and a body made sexless by malnutrition. Alia thought it was a girl, but either way an unprepossessing specimen.

Crooked teeth in shades of yellow and browns. Ice-gray eyes staring out from under greasy bangs so covered in grime that the color could have been anything from blond to deep brown. The noises coming out of the child's mouth were more suited to a wolverine than a human—and not anything like the plaintive cries of distress that had caused the caravan to pause in its journey in the first place.

Raff gave an uncomfortable shrug and scratched his head.

Alia knew he had a soft heart. She didn't like the idea of killing a child either, but the offspring of bandit tribes were widely considered vermin to be extinguished. As soon as they were old enough to walk—and sometimes even before that—these children were trained to do just what this one had done—act as bait. An argument could be made that this girl and her ilk considered the travelers they preyed upon to be less human than the other predators with which they shared the heavily forested foothills.

"What's it to be, Captain?" Dari gave her captive a sharp shake to emphasize her words.

Before Raff could reply, the child sunk sharp teeth into Dari's hand, wriggled out of her grasp, and darted off into the trees.

Dari swore as the child vanished as if by magic into a thick undergrowth of blackberry brambles just as the mist increased to an annoying drizzle that threatened to turn into rain.

"You'll want to clean that sooner rather than later," Alia said, looking over Dari's shoulder at the blood dripping from a vicious bite mark on the pad of flesh below her left thumb. "I don't even want to think about the diseases that little forest rat is probably carrying."

Dari swore again, squeezing more blood from the wound to prevent infection. The blood mixed with the rain, dripping onto the ground.

Callan exhaled, more impatience in that small sound than was reasonable under the circumstances. "And this can't wait until we reach Trionn-Fí? We'll arrive too late for the opening festivities as is, thanks to all the delays."

"We can't risk the possibility of infection, sir." Raff's diffident tone was on the razor's edge of insincere and Alia could easily read his mind; the unspoken words *jack* and *ass* clearly audible, at least to her.

"Fine then. Take my horse—I'm going to ride in the carriage." Shoving his horse's reins into one of his men-at-arms's hands, Callan turned and stalked away toward the carriage, turning the collar of his greatcoat up against now spattering raindrops. He was met by his manservant, Ermo, who immediately started fussing over his master's state of disarray.

Alia stared after him, anger and depression warring for dominance. She patted her horse, Vigo, on his neck and sighed. "Do you think people can change?"

Raff gave Alia a sympathetic look. "Only if they want to."

Chapter Two
Trionn-Fī

A Dodgy Alley in the Outer City

Boisterous song echoed off the cobblestones as the trio of Athaméan swordsmiths emerged from the drinking house. Even before it had officially begun, the festival had already proved worthwhile, and they had celebrated their early sales with gusto. Now, like corks floating in a tub, they bobbled their merry way through the crowds back toward their inn for the night.

Though their purses were heavy, they strode through even the worst-lit alleys with no fear of being set upon by ruffians. Even in their cups, the burly trio were formidable fighters, with blades or without. So they took little notice of the festivalgoer who bumped into one of them—a mousey little man in a drab brown cloak who immediately broke into a nervous apology for his clumsiness and then quickly scurried away.

"Hey!" A bespectacled clerk hurried up to the trio and tugged on the arm of the same swordsmith. "I just saw that one there make off with your coin pouch!" He pointed to the fellow in brown, who looked back in alarm.

The burly smith felt for his missing purse, then bared his teeth and stared daggers at the little man. "You're dead, thief!" he roared. As one, the Athaméans took off after the wide-eyed culprit, who turned and ran for his life through the crowded thoroughfare.

The clerk allowed himself to enjoy watching a little of the pursuit, then turned the other way and sauntered off, whistling a happy tune. He jangled the swordsmith's purse in his hand for a moment before slipping it back into his pocket, pleased with his catch.

In truth he wasn't a clerk, though he certainly looked the part. He went by many names, but those few who knew him well—not friends, exactly, as he had very few of those—called him the Magpie. He had tried his hand at many professions and was blessed with many hidden talents.

Magpie was not handsome enough to tread the boards at the Imperial Theater, but he was a consummate actor in his own right. He had the face of an innocent angel, forgettable but affable, bespectacled and cherub-cheeked.

From his days as a young apprentice in the Arcane Isles, before he'd left for the sunnier climes of Beauchalice, he picked up a smattering of magical basics. He knew many of the runes and sigils, and while he could draw them well enough, he could not charge them with any real power. On a good day, he might manage a minor cantrip—but more often, no more than make his fingers give a hint of sparkling lights without any further effect. And that was as far as his best efforts could take him.

Luckily, his skill at sleight of hand bordered on the magical. In fact, *that* was his real magic—he had far better luck posing as a mage when he relied solely on legerdemain instead of any sorcerous expertise.

Since his failed apprentice days, he had bounced around from province to province, never staying in any one place or at any one job for long. If you wanted to be kind, you could call him a jack-of-all-trades. A less charitable person might say he was an interesting failure.

But what he was, in fact, was a thief.

Chapter Three
Arcanum

Isle of Chthon—the Oracle School

Long before humanity came to the continent, the province of Arcanum and all its islands had been, for better or worse, a realm of magic. Its primordial inhabitants were unknown, inhuman races whose existence long ago could only be guessed by the eerie and eldritch traces fossilized in the oldest faces of sea cliffs. Forgotten millennia later, in the age of stone and ice, giants, ogres, and stranger monsters reigned supreme, raising colossal megaliths and hunting great shaggy beasts now long extinct.

The first people to reach the isles were warlocks, shapeshifters, sorceresses, and witch-kings, drawn to the raw mystic power so pervasive among the misty islands. They left behind circles of standing stones, and the magic residue of their dark experiments, schemes, and wars.

In the four thousand years since, pioneering hedge-wizards, thaumaturges, and other upstart dabbler-magicians had eventually tamed the ancient and magic-drenched wilderness as much as any mere human mage could ever hope to. For centuries, the

Arcane mainland and isles had been dotted with great schools, expanding knowledge of the craft and the supernatural world, and nurturing and tutoring generations of spellcasters in the arts and mastery of every kind of magic.

Each island's school tended to specialize in its own brand of sorcery. Chthon, a small, rocky isle at the farthest reaches of its own chain of islands, housed the venerable Oracle School of Divination. It had always been home to the best seers.

In the heart of the school's great house, a woman crowned with snow-white hair shot with silver lay still and feverish on her bed. The school's physicker, another woman whose silver strands were just starting to appear in her own auburn hair, sat beside her, dabbing her brow with a soft wet cloth. The pair was ringed by a trio of students acting as nurses. The patient they attended to was Eluned, the High Seeress of Arcanum, and therefore of all Tarou. Her current fever dream had lasted all week.

Close at hand, a thin, ginger-haired man stood in the doorway, watching and worrying. His name was Casander, and he had served as the Seeress's personal amanuensis of many years. Nearly every day of that service, he had taken notes while his mistress was entranced for hours, her eyes fluttering or wide open in alarm, her body held stock-still or swaying to some unheard rhythm.

But never had he seen her overtaken by such a force as the sickness that held her now. He had made his own attempts at divining what the final outcome of this ailment would be, but the answers were ambiguous at best. The Seeress had never groomed a successor, and there were none on the island who could come anywhere near to her level of expertise.

With every new day that passed without her recovery, his worries had grown. If they lost her now, what would become of the school? Indeed, what would become of the realm without her guidance?

That eventide, he sat in his quarters supping indifferently on a plate of turnips and pease porridge, when a knock on the door broke his train of anxious thoughts. It was one of the young students serving as Eluned's nurse. He took a deep breath before he answered the door.

"Yes?"

The boy broke into a smile. "Her fever has broken. She's awake."

The Seeress still lay in bed, but now her attendants were buoyant, making the chamber feel more like a party than a wake. Eluned's eyes lit up at the arrival of her personal secretary, but she remained stately and reserved.

"Seeress," he said, recognizing her with a slight bow as always. He, too, retained his composure, but his heart swelled to see her awake again.

"Casander. I will have work for you soon."

"Wonderful news. I look forward to it."

She seemed strangely quiet in response, and looked at him with an odd expression, as though she were seeing right through him and the walls of the school, out somewhere leagues beyond …

After several days and nights of enduring a brain-addled fugue, Eluned felt a certain amount of relief to be clearheaded once more. But she did not want to talk to her charges about what she had gone through. Her precognitive art entailed sending her consciousness through time itself, a voyage that sometimes involved circuitous routes through very hazardous waters. And sometimes the visions made the journey to her instead, unbidden and at times unwelcome. Like now—when all she could see in her mind's eye were the ley lines of the earth, burning with an eldritch fire …

Chapter Four

The Mountain Borderlands of Athamé

The rain increased to a steady downpour, and the bitter chill grew still worse over the course of a half hour. Alia thought they might see snow before the night was out. She was tempted to join Callan in the carriage—both for warmth and to try and make peace with him.

Even prepared for the lower temperatures of the mountains, those members of the caravan who were natives of Athamé shivered uncomfortably, pulling dark green–oiled silk cloaks over their hauberks and brigandine armor. The Pentan contingent didn't fare much better—their province's climate rarely dipped low enough to require more than a light overcoat.

"How much farther to the High Road?"

Raff, who had done more than a few escorts to the annual festival, shrugged. "If the weather was fair, I would say two more hours. But as it's not, and given that we were attacked while the sun was still high, I would wager there's more than one opportunistic pack of bandits waiting for stragglers like us."

"In other words," Alia prodded gently, "you're suggesting we don't try to go any further tonight."

Raff shot a dark look in Callan's direction. "At the risk of offending your affianced, precisely."

"I've offended him so many times in the last day alone that I hardly think it matters at this point," Alia said, trying to hide how forlorn she felt. "No doubt he'll complain about not arriving in time for the opening festivities tomorrow morning, but he would complain far more loudly if we were ambushed again."

"Unless bandits slit his privileged throat." Raff looked as if the thought brought him some pleasure.

Alia smacked him on the arm. "That's not nice."

He grinned at her. "It wasn't meant to be."

"It's settled then. There is an inn somewhere on this road, isn't there?"

Raff nodded. "Another mile or so up the way. It's the last inn before we reach the High Road."

"Tell the rest of the escort that we will be stopping." Alia straightened her shoulders. "I'll inform Callan that we will not be continuing to Trionn-Fí until tomorrow morning."

The High Road was broad, well-traveled, and well-maintained, but it still wound around and through increasingly steep mountains with sheer drops that fell hundreds of feet to jagged rocks below. Better to sleep on threadbare mattresses than risk a deadly misstep by a tired mount.

"Their beer isn't half bad," Raff assured Alia as they pulled up to the roadside inn.

The inn lay at the juncture of the middle and high roads, a good two hours past the point where the foothills gave way to mountains, and the scattered copses of oak and maple became supplanted by pines. Worries of bandits eased as their forest camouflage grew sparse.

On the craggy mountain slopes, granite outcroppings thrust out between the scrub, the drop-off alongside their narrow path becoming steeper with each step.

Just before the road curved sharply uphill, a cluster of evergreens stood guard with their backs to the mountain. Tucked inside the little grove stood a nameless inn of lesser regard. Being the only hostel for miles, the inn had no need of a name, though some referred to it as the Mountain Lodge, and some local wags called it the Last Tavern, not only because it was the last way station on this route where weary travelers could find food and shelter until they reached the capital—but because it was the last a traveler would ever *want* to see.

Rock walls rose up in a horseshoe around the inn and its outbuildings, creating a welcome break from the increasingly frigid wind. Two were-light lanterns hung from iron hooks that flanked the heavy wooden front door, swaying precariously in the wind. In their glow, the two-story wooden structure's oaken beams were a uniform weathered gray, the windows shuttered tight against the pelting rain, which blew sideways in icy gusts.

The weary, waterlogged caravan approached it gratefully, ready to get out of the downpour. All but Callan, who had argued bitterly to press on through the dark and bad weather to Trionn-Fí before begrudgingly accepting the decision to stay the night at the unimpressive hostel.

"Will our horses be safe here?" he asked, his tone equal parts doubt and disdain.

"We've sheltered here more than once, sir, and our mounts have yet to come to harm." Raff used the overly deferential tone that was his default when addressing Callan. It skirted the edge of irreverence, subtle enough that someone with a lack of self-awareness wouldn't notice the disrespect.

"Very well. See to it that the horses are stabled and a guard is set to watch the goods." Callan turned on his heel and stalked off to the front door of the inn, manservant on his heels. He did not wait to see if Alia followed him.

The Athaméan guards looked after him with expressions varying from anger to disgust to contempt. Geffi, a sharp-featured soldier in her twenties, spat with great accuracy where Callan had stepped. Her twin brother, Soren, followed suit. They were both slight of build—deceptively so—wiry, strong, fast, and deadly.

Alia's glare, however, was the sharpest of all.

"Try not to kill him," Dari said in a low voice. "Unless you really feel the need. I'll help you hide his body."

"He has no business treating Athaméan soldiers like servants!" Alia had trained and fought alongside these soldiers all her life. They were more like family than retainers.

Dari gave a crooked smile. "What do you expect from a Pentan nobleman?"

"I'm sorry to burden you all," Alia said glumly.

"Don't be," Dari replied. "It's not your fault that your father betrothed you to a preening Pentan twat."

Raff nodded. "I'd like to think Lord Irkhanan didn't realize what an ornamental peacock he was sticking you with."

"He's not bad with a sword," Alia said, wishing she didn't feel obligated to stick up for both her fiancé and her father's chosen son-in-law. She knew that her father's reasons for sacrificing his daughter on the marital altar had less to do with Callan's martial skills than the Tozzo name.

Raff shot her a look. "The difference between 'not bad' and 'good' nearly got him killed before you saved his fool life."

"Ugh." Alia shook her head vigorously as if trying to dislodge all the unpleasant thoughts swirling around inside. It didn't work. "Let's go see what this place has to offer in the way of beer. I need a drink."

Chapter Five
Trionn-Fī

An Open-Air Market in the Outer City

Festivals always had the potential to be lucrative for an enterprising individual of the Magpie's talents—as long as he was never recognized. Fortunately, his looks were bland and easily ignored. His inoffensive baby face would neither catch a maiden's eye nor intimidate a foe, but he could effortlessly blend into a crowd—and he always looked completely trustworthy.

The morning before, when he was running lighter on funds, he had snatched a lower priest's modest cassock right off the laundry line first thing in the morning, so he looked especially respectable as he made his way through one of the outer city's open-air markets in search of some breakfast.

One booth tempted him with neat stacks of pomegranates, lovely but pricey. He admired them discreetly until the instant the fruit seller's attention was diverted, and then swiftly slipped a nice one up his sleeve. He turned to quietly make his escape—only to see a small boy glaring up at him.

"You stole that!" the lad said in a low growl, unimpressed with Magpie's priestly garb.

"What's that, now?" asked the fruit seller.

Magpie wasted no time, seizing the boy by the ear and theatrically producing the purloined fruit in his upraised hand.

"Not so fast, you young rascal!" Magpie called out with dramatic flair. "My good man, I just caught this little scamp filching your wares!" The boy howled in a blend of moral outrage and pain, struggling to break free—but Father Magpie's grip on his poor pinched ear was unbreakable.

"You scoundrel!" the vendor yelled.

"No need for a reward; it is my duty to thwart wickedness," Magpie said in a soothing priestly voice, getting into his role. "But now, do let us show mercy to this orphaned waif."

"*Mercy*? To this *orphaned waif*?" The seller stared at them both in incredulous rage. "Why, I'll—"

The boy cried out again as Magpie gave his hapless victim's ear another twist to keep him from speaking further.

"Easy now, my dear man! This miserable urchin cannot help he was raised on the streets. I'll be off now, but I'll see to it that he learns his lesson." This did not satisfy the fruit seller, who only seemed to be growing more apoplectic by the moment.

"Bring him back here this instant!" the man demanded.

"Have no fear," Magpie assured him as he turned to leave with his kicking, wailing prisoner in tow. "He'll not escape his just deserts. He's in for a good thrashing! Believe me—he'll curse the father who left him without proper moral guidance."

But none of this was good enough to assuage the fruit vendor, more enraged than ever. With a roar, he came out from behind the stall after them, red-faced and furious, so sputtering mad he could barely speak.

"*You*!" he bellowed at the pair, grabbing the boy's arm.

Magpie feared he might have overplayed his hand. "Sir! I insist you unhand the lad at once!"

The seller jabbed a finger in Magpie's face. "*You*!" he repeated through gritted teeth. "*You* unhand *my son*—or I'll bash your teeth in right now!"

Magpie froze. And then turned and ran for it. The fruit seller scooped up the boy in his arms.

"And you an acolyte of the Holy Church!" he yelled at Magpie's swiftly disappearing backside. "And come back with that pomegranate!"

Chapter Six
Athamēan Border
THE MOUNTAIN INN

The inside was no better and no worse than many another inn had to offer. A captive *salamandre*—a fire elemental—blazed in a stone hearth against the far wall, giving welcome heat against the cold. Another roasted the side of a pig on the spit in the open kitchen. Some long-dead artist had painted hunting scenes in an effort to add some gaiety and color to the drab walls, but with age, the faded images only made the inn look like an ancient tomb.

The common room was not crowded. Around a baker's dozen, most sitting at long wooden trestle tables while others conferred in one of several booths against one wall or took a stool at the bar, made of a rough-topped length of pine.

The occupants looked to be made up of hired help and fellow travelers, the latter a mixed bag representing the different provinces of Tarou. There was a brief pause in the low hum of conversation when Alia and the rest of her group walked in the front door, but everyone quickly went back to their own business when they saw nothing more than a group of waterlogged, weary Athaméan soldiers.

A few seats away, a small contingent of Pentan men clad in breeches and velvet doublets in bright scarlets, rich crimsons, tawny golds, and cobalt blues clinked copper goblets in sloppy toasts and spilled red wine onto the table. One of them, all white teeth and bright gold hair, his skin several shades darker than his fellows, glanced up and gave Alia a lazy grin, raising his goblet and winking at her.

Dari nudged her. "That one's not bad-looking. If things don't work out with Sir Shit Don't Stink ..."

"If things don't work out, I'm going to make Father let me rejoin the guards," Alia retorted as she continued to scan the room.

"We'd be happy to have you." This was Raff, coming up behind them. "Horses stabled, guards posted on the wagon."

Dari nodded toward the stocky Pentan. "Check out the chubby one's cock cover."

Alia glanced over and her jaw dropped. "Oh my." She tried not to stare, but it was impossible *not* to stare at the man's truly remarkable codpiece, crafted in the shape of an ornate, rampant golden dragon with jeweled ruby-red eyes.

"That is quite ... impressive," she finally managed. "Where do you suppose he got it?"

"The Emperor no doubt bestowed it upon him for bravery," Dari replied, a wicked gleam in her eyes.

"I think he's a pirate and pulled it off the roof of some foreign temple in the Spice Islands," Raff said.

Dari elbowed him in the side. "I dare you to go up and scratch it with your knife—if it's anything more than cheap gilt and glass, I'll eat his floppy hat."

Neither Raff nor Alia took her bet.

"Looks big enough to store a mackerel in there," Raff mused.

Dari snickered. "I'll wager there's no more than a minnow swimming around in that dragon's belly."

Alia started to reply but her gaze fell on Callan, already seated at one of the booths, dimly lit by a flickering candle in a copper sconce. He was offering a pleasant if aloof smile to the cheerfully plain barmaid leaning over the table to take his order, her low-cut tan bodice displaying her ample cleavage like meat on a platter. At least he wasn't showing interest in what she was offering.

"I can make this work," Alia muttered more to herself than to her friends. She headed toward his table with a smile, hoping it didn't look forced.

Callan glanced up briefly as Alia approached. Then turned back to the barmaid without further acknowledgment of his fiancée.

Face burning with mortification, Alia changed course and joined Raff and Dari at the bar. The two made room between them. Without a word Dari handed her a tankard brimming with dark beer and signaled to the bartender for another. Alia took it gratefully, taking a deep draught. It was just cold enough and tasted of bittersweet chocolate and spices. "Gods, that's good." She took another long swallow, feeling the knotted muscles in her shoulders relax as the strong ale did its magic.

Before she knew it, her tankard was empty and her head spun just enough to remind her that she hadn't eaten anything other than an early breakfast of oat cakes and dried apricots, along with a few pieces of jerky on the road. Alia wiped foam from her upper lip and turned to Raff. "I could eat an entire roast lamb by myself. But first …" She slammed her tankard on the bar. "Get me a gods-damned beer."

Chapter Seven
Athamēan Border

THE MOUNTAIN INN

Jezel Mirèlha looked at her reflection in the cheap metal mirror and frowned. Her complexion—normally as translucent as the finest porcelain—appeared muddy, almost green. Thick curly hair, the rich, glossy brown of the finest sable, had a dull sheen to it. Huge eyes, the dark blue of sapphires, seemed to have shrunk in their fine-boned sockets, her high cheekbones gaunt. Even the jeweled hues of her clothing seemed faded in the flickering light of a cheap tallow candle set in a sconce above the mirror. And while Jezel knew it wasn't an accurate reflection, it still undermined her confidence. Not an easy thing to accept as one of the most sought-after courtesans in Beauchalice.

She blamed the long, exhausting journey. It had been a week on rough roads in a rickety coach meant for four passengers shared by five instead—one of them *quite* portly and none of them wealthy enough to be worth her time—to save money. Surely it was that and not any lessening of her beauty.

Jezel tried not to dwell on the blow to her self-esteem she'd taken when Oreste, her current benefactor, had released her from their contract a full two years earlier than was agreed upon so he could enter into an engagement with a girl of suitable social status. He'd paid the hefty penalty for breaking the contract's original timeline without any fuss, which told Jezel that money was not as important as freeing himself from their agreement. And regardless of the reason, being thrust aside reduced her value—and her desirability—in the eyes of potential benefactors. Hence the trip to the festival at Trionn-Fí—a fresh hunting ground with some of the wealthiest people in Tarou in attendance.

The delay caused by the foul weather meant missing the opening festivities—an unexpected irritation. She wanted first pick, and who knew what other ambitious courtesans she might have to compete against to be noticed? Her own beauty usually was enough to reassure her, but tonight she found it wanting. Having Bellamy down with travel sickness was really too much—what good was a lady's maid who couldn't stray more than a few feet from the chamber pot? Also, though she barely admitted it to herself, Jezel worried about the young girl. She was sweet, biddable, and talented when it came to dressing her mistress's hair and making sure Jezel was always dressed just so.

The sound of vomiting from the tiny servant's room connected to hers and the pelting of rain on the roof, combined with the unpleasant pong of cheap melted tallow, underscored her gloom. Was this a portent of what her future held?

"A pox on everything," she muttered. But an especially virulent one on Oreste. She hoped he passed it on to his child bride on their wedding night.

Resisting the temptation to cast yet one more dissatisfied glance in the mirror, Jezel pushed back the rickety wooden stool that served as a seat for the room's shabby vanity and rose gracefully to her feet. Drawing the knowledge of her beauty around her like a cloak, she left the room to see if there was anyone worth bringing to her feet—even if it was only for an hour or so. If not, she'd have food and drink sent to her room and retire for the night. The door to her room had a lock on it, albeit a flimsy one, but she could put the single chair against it for added security.

Harbalorio drained the last drops of wine from his goblet, slamming it down on the sturdy wooden tabletop. "Damn fine wine."

"Has to be from the Métayage coast," Birnardus opined with drunken wisdom, pushing a hank of limp brown hair out of his flushed face. Fair-skinned and overweight, the alcohol made his plump cheeks shine like rosy beacons.

Jakobi nodded in equally soused agreement. "Say what you will of Beauchalice—even their bad wines are quaffable."

"And they never let you forget it!" Birnardus quipped, provoking laughter round the table. Picking up the half-empty bottle of surprisingly decent red plonk, he divided its contents between the three men. "This is the last of it, friends."

"Another bottle for the table!" Harbalorio looked around at his two traveling companions and business partners. "Whose turn is it to buy?"

"I paid for the last one," said Birnardus.

"And I the first," Jakobi added. Both men looked expectantly at Harbalorio, who reluctantly reached into the tooled leather pouch on his belt and extracted a coin from his uncomfortably light purse.

He looked around for the barmaid who'd brought the three rowdy Pentans their first two bottles. She was currently displaying her charms for a fellow countryman seated by himself at one of the booths. Harbalorio and his friends had hailed the man when he'd first entered the inn, inviting him to join them for a drink, but he'd excused himself with dismissive courtesy before sitting down alone. Judging by his clothes and demeanor, Harbalorio decided that he was of the wealthier merchant class of Pentaclys and too much of a snob to share a bottle with a trio of lowly traders.

A damn shame, he thought. Some of his more lucrative business dealings had happened in inns and taverns. No matter. He and his partners had bigger fish to fry in Trionn-Fí.

Damn, but the man was taking his sweet time giving his order to the wench, who was doing her best to keep his attention. A man could die of thirst!

While the Pentans waited for another bottle of wine, they pulled out and filled their long-stemmed clay pipes. Jakobi rose and strode over to the inglenook to grab the small pair of tongs hanging there. He fished around in the hearth for a stray ember to light his pipe, taking care not to bait the sullen fire elemental holding court there, like a dragon sprawled out on his horde of gold. Once his pipe was lit, he handed the tongs to Birnardus, who had joined him.

For his part, Harbolio kept his seat and waved off the offer of a light. Instead he reached into his doublet's inner pocket for a compact metal item about the size of a chess piece, shaped much like a miniature incense burner or hanging lantern. Although he kept his face nonchalant, he made a show of opening its little metal doors to reveal what was housed within—the tiniest of flame spirits, no bigger than an elegant lady's fingernail, but bright as a ray of sunlight. It was a cherished family heirloom—his grandfather's personal pipe lighter.

The tiny salamandre yawned and then stretched out its arm to rustle around in the bowl of Harbalorio's pipe, igniting the tobacco within. The Pentan pretended he was unaware of everyone's attention as he carried out the ritual and then returned the trinket to his pocket.

The front door opened to admit a small group of armored Athaméan men-at-arms, along with a gust of frigid wind and icy rain, before one of the soldiers slammed the door shut behind them. Harbalorio eyed one of them with interest, a tall girl with dusky skin and a thick braid of coppery-blond hair falling to her hips. Her hauberk was as well-worn as the other Athaméan warriors, but she also had a torque of white gold studded with emeralds encircling her neck.

Not a common soldier then, he surmised, even as he mocked himself for reaching such an obvious conclusion. She carried herself with the assurance of a seasoned warrior, but he guessed she was at most twenty years old, if even that. Of course, in Athamé, they started training as soon as they could walk.

Birnardus smacked him on the shoulder with the same hand that held his goblet, sloshing wine over Harbalorio's scarlet velvet doublet. It was not the first wine spilled since they'd started drinking.

"A beauty, eh?" Birnardus nodded toward the same young woman Harbalorio had spotted. "Almost as comely as the skirt from Beauchalice sharing our coach."

"Hopefully warmer than that cold fish," Jakobi added with a sullen scowl. He'd been quite taken by their female coachmate, an undeniably beautiful woman who'd made it clear none of her fellow passengers were of any interest to her. And she hadn't spared any feelings doing so—although she hadn't discouraged her lady's maid from flirting. Probably happy to have someone to distract them from her own precious self.

Harbalorio suspected the beauty was on the hunt for someone with more wealth and status than any of them had. She'd vanished upstairs as soon as they'd arrived and hadn't yet reappeared.

"A toast to beauty!" Birnardus shouted, raising his goblet. The other two followed suit, clanking goblets in an enthusiastic toast that slopped yet more wine on the table and their clothes.

As the lovely Athaméan girl walked by their table, Harbalorio grinned at her and winked. She ignored him, but her female companion—a stocky woman with short dark hair, obvious muscles, and at least a half dozen scars that said she meant business—nudged her friend with a grin and nodded in his direction. The copper-haired girl's eye roll notwithstanding, Harbolio took this as a favorable portent for the near future and hollered for the barmaid so they could continue toasting the good fortune certain to come.

The front door blew open as another traveler came in, seeking refuge from the elements.

Chapter Eight
Athamēan Border

The Mountain Inn

Harbalorio gave a cry of dismay at the rude blast of cold. "Close the door, man!"

Icy rain splattered the floor before the shivering newcomer shut the door again. The rest of the common room grew quiet, conversations pausing as those inside took in the new arrival. He pulled back the hood of his drenched traveling cloak, revealing a dark-haired man in his twenties with the spare features of an ascetic. He took a moment to warm himself by the fire and wipe the excess water from his face. Then he spoke.

"I need to get to Trionn-Fí," he said to no one in particular.

"Don't we all?" a red-faced drinker in the back shouted back, provoking laughter among the tables. The young man's face remained unchanged.

"I need to get to Trionn-Fí *tonight*," he said again, louder, his voice firm. Heads shook while sneers and light chuckles rippled through the smoky room.

"What's your hurry?" someone shouted.

"Yeah, the festival don't really get going until tomorrow, anyway," another patron chimed in.

"The beer's just as tasty here, me handsome, and cheaper to boot!" the barmaid called out merrily.

Another man slapped her on her generous backside. "So is she!"

The common room erupted in raucous guffaws, whistles, and hoots.

The stranger whispered a word that sent all the were-lights quivering in their cressets, plunging the inn into near darkness. Then, with a twist of his wrist and a subtle hand gesture, the salamandre suddenly rose up from the hearth like a roaring tiger ordered to stand by a circus lion tamer, until its crackling limbs licked at the ceiling and all those nearest to the fireplace, including the three Pentans, hurriedly backed away from the heat.

Pushing back his cloak, the stranger revealed the dark green embroidered cowl of a mage from Arcanum. "This is more important than the damned festival!" the mage snapped, firelight gleaming in his eyes. "I'm not drunk and I'm not joking—*and I need to get to the capital at once*!" The salamandre gave another roar, flames licking out and away from the hearth.

"Peace! Peace now, please!" the innkeeper called out, hands raised to placate him, then turned to the noisy crowd. "Show some respect, you cackling bunch of turnip-headed louts!" he hollered. "Beg your pardon, Master Mage, but take no offense at these harmless clodhoppers. And if you could gentle down that old salamander of mine before you set the whole place ablaze, I'd be much obliged."

The mage gave another subtle wave of his hand. The elemental shrank down and returned to its hearth; the were-lights once again provided their cozy glow. The innkeeper gave him a grateful smile.

"The truth of it is, son," he continued in an avuncular tone, "there's no going any further tonight in this weather, even if any of us had a spare horse to sell you. Look here, the rain and wind have already soaked you to the bones and half frozen you outright, and on a night as foul as this, what with the road all icy and slick as it is, not even a mountain goat with a moonstone could make it up to the High Road—not without taking a nasty slip and tumble in the dark, right off the cliffside."

The fierceness in the young mage's eyes softened, though he seemed no happier. He nodded and turned his back on the rest of the room, seemingly content to warm himself by the fire in silence.

Harbalorio felt for the loner. *A wizard in Athamé, a warrior in Arcanum,* as the old saying went about such fish out of water. The three Pentans exchanged looks, and then came to a silent agreement. Harbalorio joined the mage at the fire.

"Listen," he said, clearing his throat. "We can all see you're in a hurry to get to the festival—"

"I don't give a tinker's damn about the festival."

"Right, right, I meant you're eager to get to the capital, and I can see by the look in your eyes you're getting ready to buck up and head out again on foot in this rain." The mage gave no reply. "Well, our host is right about your slim chances of getting off the mountain alive. If you don't mind me saying so, you don't exactly appear to be a weather-worker." He chuckled, to let the mage know he was joking, but it made no impact. Harbalorio soldiered on. "But look, my companions and I leave for it first thing in the morning. We would be happy to sell you a seat in our coach—"

"I haven't got any money." The mage continued to warm his hands at the fire, back to the Pentan.

"Ah." An unexpected turn of events, to be sure. *Still, you had to appreciate a man with so much audacity traveling around with so little coin,* Harbalorio thought. Turning to Birnardus and Jakobi, who were unabashedly eavesdropping on the conversation, he raised his eyebrows in a question. They shrugged, so he continued. "Well, we'd be happy to have you join us as a guest in our coach. You'll get there faster than on foot, and you'll be better rested. And drier."

It appeared to be Harbalorio's turn to work some magic. After a thoughtful pause, the taciturn mage turned to the Pentan and nodded once.

"We'll have to hope that will be soon enough."

Not exactly the gratitude the Pentan was hoping for either, but he took it. "So it's settled. It will be good to have you traveling with us." He introduced himself and pointed out Jakobi and Birnardus, who gave curt nods in acknowledgment. "And you are … ?" He let the question hang in the air.

"My name is Keth." And with that, the mage excused himself and went to the bar to go speak to the innkeeper.

Harbalorio's friends rejoined him at the hearth.

"So, our scintillating new friend is joining us on our trip!" Jakobi said, clapping his hands in faux glee. "How wonderful! Now we have *two* cold fish to share a cramped coach with! Maybe next festival, they'll be married! And then they can bring along their cold-fish children for all the festivals to come!"

Birnardus nodded. "Honestly, I don't know why you're giving away free seats to *anyone*, let alone that drip."

"Save your jests, you two," Harbalorio said with a wry smile. "I think it might be good to have a mage with us."

"A mage who can't conjure an umbrella," muttered Birnardus.

"So he's not a weather mage—you saw how easily he handled that salamandre."

"There's another thing, though," Birnardus lowered his voice. "Did you mark the sigil on the collar of his cowl? Looks a bit like a bird on the wing, facing the sky."

"What do you take me for, a runesmith?" Harbalorio retorted. "And since when did *you* take up the Arcane arts?"

"I recognize it, I tell you! Remember? It's the symbol of that faction that got into hot water with the Emperor last year for trying to delve into forbidden magics."

"Wait now, I *do* remember that. Didn't one of them go crazy or something?"

"That's them! It was quite the scandal. What *were* they called again? Psyche, Psyche-something."

"Cyclones?" Jakobi said helpfully. The other two scowled at his idiocy.

"Don't be daft. Anyway, they were taken down a peg for some skul or another. So if our new friend here"—Birnardus shot a wary glance over his shoulder—"*is* one of them, we may be biting off more trouble than we can chew."

Harbalorio considered his friend's words. "You may have a point. Still, I did offer him a seat with us, so I can hardly go back on my word now. We'll just have to keep a careful eye on him." The other two only nodded, but it was clear both were now even less thrilled about the new travel arrangements.

"All right then," Jakobi said reluctantly, "but it's *you* who's going to break the news to that Chalicean woman." He gave an emphatic if sloppy poke to Harbalorio's chest and poured more wine for the three of them.

Birnardus took another draw on his pipe and nodded to himself. This young magician had to be up to no good, whatever caused him to be out on such a stormy night with so little luggage. The mage was carrying no more than a small satchel and a modest leather cylinder tied to it. It looked like a map case, but surely that was too innocuous. Maybe a case to hold magic scrolls? It was too short to be a scabbard, and clearly not made to sheath a hand weapon—unless it housed some weird battle-mage's secret weapon …

And Harbalorio had invited the man to share their coach.

Whatever this suspicious mage was carrying in there, Birnardus resolved to find out.

Chapter Nine
Trionn-Fī

THE INNER CITY—THE GRAND HOTEL IMPERIAL TRIONN-FÍ

The unpleasant business with the fruit seller required an immediate change of both clothes and scenery, and Magpie had beaten a hasty retreat into another district. Beneath one of the outer city's many bridges, he stopped to swap out his stolen cassock for a stolen boatman's shirt, and later that afternoon he supplemented it with a swiped frock coat that lent him a more respectable look—a student or a clerk, perhaps.

By nightfall he had helped himself to enough pockets and purses to enjoy a filling breakfast, an afternoon meal, and to indulge in a bit of shopping in some of the finer shops. Thanks largely to the Athaméan's hefty purse, he was able to purchase a nice silk cravat and a jaunty oak walking stick topped with a lion's-head handle of silver brass. Freshly outfitted, he felt confident enough to go try his luck in the more rewarding noble quarters of the Inner City.

He resisted the urge to risk picking pockets in the street, and instead spent a pleasing evening in the sumptuous restaurant of the grand hotel Imperial Trionn-Fí, conspicuously feasting on oysters, mushrooms, parboiled lamb's feet in white sauce, quinces in pastry, and an assortment of other Chalicean delicacies. Although enjoying himself, he did not lose sight of why he was there, keeping a sharp eye out for likely prospects. Soon enough, a fine one landed right in his lap.

"Master Lanzo?" A young blond gentleman, well-dressed in powder-blue silk, approached his table. "My name is Audoin. You must forgive me for interrupting your dinner, sir, but our waiter happened to mention to us that you are a renowned Athamaéan gem dealer, and I wonder if I might entreat you for a few moments of your time—for a business matter."

Magpie picked up on the man's Pentan accent and adopted the same. "Actually, I am from Pentaclys, Mister Audoin—but Athamaéan gems are my specialty. Do you need something appraised?"

"Indeed. I've been looking for a suitable gift for a special lady friend of mine. Today I was able to acquire some lovely stones at a bargain, but I—"

"You wish to ensure you weren't gulled by some shyster." The young gentleman blushed, and Magpie patted his hand. "Very prudent of you, young man. Do you have them on you?"

"I do, but I wouldn't want to bother you at your supper. If you would be good enough to tell me where your shop is, I'll be happy to bring them by tomorrow."

"Certainly!" Then he paused, seeming to reconsider, and steered the conversation away from his nonexistent shop. "Oh, but then the festival will be in full swing, and the streets will be maddening to navigate. Why don't we just take a look at them right now?"

Audoin brightened. "Well, if you really don't mind …"

"Not at all! Please, join me!" He called for another bottle, ordering a fine Pentan vintage this time. When the waiter brought it, Magpie slipped him two gold coins for passing on the helpful information to Audoin earlier.

The young man gratefully took a seat next to him but did not bring forth any jewels. Instead, to Magpie's chagrin, he waved over a pair of equally well-dressed but far more intimidating bodyguards. Like their master, both men were in expensive quilted gambesons, but while his clothes made him look cheery and festive, theirs—in grim shades of black and silver—made them look more like undertakers or executioners. He also looked relaxed in his finery, while the two fit their garments like hulking mastiffs dressed up in suits. Audoin introduced the two stone-faced giants as Volker and Tord.

Magpie's hackles raised, though he fought to keep his demeanor relaxed. He had an inkling of how the gentle youth was able to get gemstones—and anything else he had his eye on—at such a bargain. If young Audoin was a scion of one of the Pentan Great Houses, it would be safer just to cut and run now. But another, more reckless part of him could not resist playing with fire.

At a nod from Audoin, Volker, the taller of his men, pulled a velvet pouch of deep magenta from his jacket pocket and carefully emptied it upon the tablecloth, spilling out a pair of rubies, a perfect square-cut emerald, and a single flawless diamond the size of a pea. Neither man took their eyes off Magpie for an instant. They regarded him, steely, unblinking, and utterly without sympathy, as if they expected their next task would be to escort him outside and slit his throat in some dark alley.

Magpie pretended not to notice their barely concealed surliness and instead sunk into his latest role. From his belt pouch he pulled out a small jeweler's loop—he always carried on him a few helpful tools for these occasions—and carefully examined the lineup.

"Fine tone on these matching rubies here … not too dark, not too light … a good rosy glow, no blemishes. A very nice set." His knowledge was questionable and his expertise almost entirely pretense, but the Magpie had a true knack for patter, jargon, and dialect, whether he was playing the part of a jewel appraiser in Athamé, a journeyman runesmith in Arcanum, a gourmand in Beauchalice, or a customs inspector in Pentaclys. He turned next to the emerald, holding it up to the table's bottled were-light.

"Not a garnet or a beryl ..." He peered at it closer with the loop. "Good clean edges, a few flaws, but very few ..." He pulled the loop away and returned the green stone to the table. "Yes, a very nice piece. From the Malagrim Highlands, if I'm not mistaken." His client smiled, pleased. "And now, the diamond."

He could feel the heat from the unyielding gaze of Audoin's thugs while he removed his cravat and cleaned the lens of his jeweler's loop as well as the diamond itself before proceeding. As he admired its perfection between his thumb and forefinger, the light from the table lamp drew out tiny streaking gleams of color from its depth, red and blue and yellow. He returned the loop to his eye and peered intently, continuing to speak as he did so.

"With diamonds, we look for several things. The cuts should be razor sharp, no chipping or scuffing, of course. The luster should be very bright ... and there should be fire inside, a bit of the rainbow in it ..." He paused and looked up again, setting down the loop and the gem. He reached for the bottle of wine, as if preparing to pour a toast to Audoin's good fortune. "And most of all, a true diamond should have strength."

Without warning, he slammed the heavy bottle down upon the gemstone like a hammer, once, twice, three times. Those three sharp blows crushed it into a scattering of tiny glittering crumbs. Audoin cried out in alarm, and his two bruisers lunged for Magpie, the tall one seizing him by the throat.

Magpie fought to remain calm. "Just paste ..." he managed to squeeze the words out. "No need to get so upset over a bit of flint glass." Their young employer called them off with a word, as if commanding attack dogs to stand down. Volker relaxed his grip at once, gently straightening Magpie's cravat with a completely unconvincing smile before letting him go.

Breathing easy again, Magpie gave Audoin an avuncular smile. "I'm sorry, young man. Don't be too hard on yourself. Whoever forged that diamond did a truly masterful job. And take heart—

the rubies and emerald are real enough, and I'm sure will make your lady's heart swoon."

With that, Master Lanzo announced it was time for him to retire for the evening, though he invited Audoin and his gallant companions to stay and finish the last bottle of wine. He refused the young man's insistent offer to pay for his expert appraisal several times, before at last reluctantly accepting a token sum—more than double the amount he had expected to receive.

The delighted Audoin promised to come patronize Master Lanzo's jewelry shop soon, and Magpie thanked him warmly, providing the vaguest of directions on where he could find it. And with that, the Magpie took his leave of the wealthy young man and his pair of imposing companions, strolling most casually through the marble lobby before then departing with great rapidity once he exited the grand hotel.

Only when he was several blocks and many twists and turns away did he stop to make sure Audoin's thugs had not followed him. And it was not until he was in a private corner of a high-end drinking house—well-lit and filled with newly arrived merrymakers kicking off the night before the festival—that he dared risk another peek at the spectacular and irresistible diamond he had surreptitiously swapped out for one of the cheap imitation paste gemstones he always carried for when funds ran low.

A very fruitful evening indeed—and he had one more stop before the night was finished.

Chapter Ten
Athamēan Border

The Mountain Inn

After barging in so dramatically, Keth's demeanor was, if not exactly meek and mild, considerably subdued as he went up to the bar to discuss food and lodging for the night.

"In like a lion and out like a lamb, eh?" The innkeeper chuckled at the young mage's change of attitude. "Lording over were-lights and *salamandrae* is one thing, but paying for your supper and a roof over your head is another. Seems like money is the real magic, at the end of the day—and you don't have any. So what now, Master Mage?"

Keth pointed to the roof beams. "The storm is pounding tonight. I can touch up the runes and wards against leaks and rot. Would that be worth a room, a meal, and a tankard or two?"

"Throw in the windowsills, and I'll give you dinner, drink, and a straw tick in the common room. Best I can do, I'm afraid. As you can see, we're full up. That company of Athaméans alone has taken nearly every room I have."

The young mage readily agreed, and once he was finished with the work, the barmaid brought him a tankard of stout and a full platter by way of payment. It was a modest but filling supper—a hearty beef stew, hunks of cheese, and freshly baked brown bread.

He nodded his thanks and took a moment of deliberation. The seats closest to the door and windows were too drafty, prey to the wind and rain. Choosing a seat at the end of one of the three long tables seemed safe enough and certainly less gloomy than the shadowed booths against the far wall.

Keth was haunted by enough shadows as it was.

He settled on a seat at the far end of one of the trestle tables and hunched over his meal, doing his best to ignore everyone around him. Even used to the necessity of concentrating amid distraction, the barrage of toasts from his unwanted tablemates were enough to drive Keth to thoughts of murder. Still, between the noise from the local jackasses and the drunken Pentan merchants, he was tempted to attempt a sleep spell on the entire room. Not that he would ever misuse his power that way, even if he thought he could pull off the spellcasting. Though as the night went on and grew more raucous, he briefly considered afflicting a few there with a short case of laryngitis.

And then there was the hard-drinking warrior band with the striking female soldier. *Athaméans*, he thought in disdain even as he admired the copper-haired woman. Devoting their lives, their very culture, to the arts of war and weaponry. He would be happier still when he was back in the north.

Keth tried instead to focus on his supper. Filling as it was, his meal was a small consolation against what was at stake. The enormity of what he faced nearly robbed him of his appetite.

That, coupled with the exhaustion of the journey thus far, made it impossible to concentrate or relax—his brain kept running the same thoughts in increasingly frustrating circles. Years of meditational discipline fell away as if he was the greenest of students.

Shaking his head in disgust, he ate another bite of crusty brown bread and soft cheese, washing it down with beer. Normally he stayed away from alcohol, not liking the way it dulled his senses, but tonight he'd had one tankard of strong dark stout with his supper and was considering a second. What could it hurt now? There was, after all, nothing he could do to influence the situation until he reached Trionn-Fí.

Assuming it wasn't already too late.

PART TWO

FESTIVAL EVE NIGHT

Chapter Eleven
Trionn-Fī

THE NOBLE QUARTER—THE SILKEN MOON

Silken Moon House was as magnificent a salon as any other edifice in the Noble Quarter, though not easy to find. The tree-lined streets surrounding it were ideal for noblemen's carriages to park quite unobtrusively nearby, as well as allowing any visitors on foot to make their arrival most discreetly. For years, the Magpie had longed to pay a visit there but had never dreamt he would actually have the necessary funds to make it through those fabled doors.

Until tonight.

The doorman, a lean, dark-haired gentleman, was well-dressed in an elegant black greatcoat. He had a formal but not unsociable voice, a serious smile, and a gaze that missed little. He politely took Magpie's walking stick and allowed him into the foyer, a dimly lit space dominated by a pair of life-sized stone lions on short columns. Not mere statues, but finely carved, manicured earth elementals, *gēnomi*, or "gnomes," as the lower classes called them—pulling double service as decor and security, no doubt.

The entrance fee would have been prohibitive on any other occasion, but Magpie nonchalantly handed over every last coin he had as though it were a trifling sum. It elicited an approving smile from the house's commissionaire as he opened the inner door and bid him welcome to the spacious parlor inside.

For a moment he thought he'd stepped into a costume party, although only half the guests were in costume. Serving girls and boys bore silver trays about the room, offering exquisite hors d'oeuvres and flutes of sparkling amber wine. All around the party, a number of well-heeled gentlemen clients and a handful of adventurous ladies enjoyed the company of nearly naked dancing girls and musicians, erotic contortionists and acrobats, rubbing elbows—and other body parts—with pagan fertility goddesses, fairy princesses, and shepherd girls, and even a stern but strangely alluring priestess.

Sirens and mermaids in sequined fishtails beached themselves on chaise longues, while mesmerizing witches cast love spells with their eyes alone. Haughty Athaméan warrior women strutted about in scanty and exciting—but thoroughly impractical—armor. Chambermaids in the frilliest of uniforms waited upon their mistresses hand and foot.

Most of the female clients, along with a few confirmed bachelors, were attended to by handsome princes, lusty sailors, and fey, dewy-eyed page boys. Throughout the parlor, couples and the occasional trio were peeling off from the party to go get to know one another in private.

The Magpie had been to the red-light district of the outer city a few times, but those bawdy houses were drab, spartan affairs compared to the delights of this mansion.

A young forest nymph approached him and shyly suggested he take her up to a room where they could talk about nature—but then a schoolmistress pulled him aside and whispered in his ear that he was a very naughty boy and she needed to discipline him firmly. He made his apologies and extricated himself from them both, tempting as they were. Though there were a bevy of charming potential companions available, tonight he had a very specific tryst in mind.

At last he spotted the woman he wanted to find—a striking lady of a certain age, her long hair a bewitching blend of lavender and silver that hung down to the back of her thighs. She wore an Arcanum-style gown of flowing ivory-colored silk. Her skin was smooth and golden, and she had the almond eyes of the Spice Islands. She was introducing a client to a trio of courtesans, who promptly took the man by the arm and led him away for a business discussion. Magpie took the opening to approach her.

"You are the house mother, I take it?"

"Madam Yaislinn, at your service. And you are … ?"

Magpie bowed. "Enchanted, My Dame. I am Séverin Perig, of Karnag-daen-Tann." Her eyes lit up and she clapped her hands.

"Oh, a Chalicean! I absolutely adore Beauchalice; you *Chalicécois* have such appreciation for the finer things in life. Now let me guess …" She tapped a finger against her lips thoughtfully. "You have the look of a sommelier, I think—or no, a fine arts importer."

He raised his eyebrows in rakish surprise. "However could you know that? I do think people have been bandying my name about in certain circles."

"Not at all, My Sir! You may dress simply, but I quite see through your disguise. You have the unmistakable bearing of a man of distinction and means, and I do hope we shall enjoy more of your company at my modest abode."

"I will make it my business to ensure that you do, My Dame," he replied, kissing her hand.

"Splendid! And have any of my charges caught your eye tonight? If you wish, I would be happy to offer my personal recommendations."

"You are very kind, My Dame. In point of fact, I was hoping to speak to your concierge about one of your house's rumored special services."

"Ah! Indeed a man of rare tastes! I would expect nothing less. And what, may I ask, may we provide you with this evening?"

"I have heard tales of … I believe it's referred to as 'the Eternity Suite.'"

She raised an eyebrow, impressed. "I applaud your appetites, My Sir. Forgive me, but I trust you understand that is our most expensive suite, my dear Séverin."

"I had hoped that this payment might prove sufficient." Magpie proffered Audoin's diamond.

Yaislinn immediately turned and called to one of her servants. "Luan."

A shaven-headed older man hurried over from behind the bar. After he bent down to examine the diamond closely with a jeweler's loop of his own, he nodded to her, satisfied.

"Séverin, you do not disappoint. You are certainly most welcome to our very finest tonight." She plucked the gem from his palm, leaned over, and whispered quickly to her servant before handing him the diamond. He nodded and swiftly left the room. Madam Yaislinn took Magpie's hand and kissed him on both cheeks.

"A true pleasure to make your acquaintance, My Sir Séverin Perig of Karnag-daen-Tann." She waved over the courtesan dressed as a priestess. "Now then, the Reverend Sister Acantha will see you off to your rendezvous!"

Magpie was surprised that the frosty priestess did not lead him up the ornate staircase that the rest of the clientele had taken. Instead, she led him through a side passage off the main salon. The hallway was not as finely appointed as the rest of the mansion—actually, he found it rather off-putting. The darkened passage was constructed solely of stone walls, unadorned by doors or windows, and unlit except for a solitary candle—not were-light, but a real candle—burning in an alcove at the entrance.

Sister Acantha took the taper, pulled up her skirt with the other hand, and silently bade him to follow her. He realized that beneath her priestess's robes she was wearing high-heeled boots and thigh-high black stockings, the clack of her heels on the stone floor accenting the sway of her hips. A confusing tangle of emotions from lust to anxiety competed for his mind. In the candle's bobbing wash of ocher light, he could not see their destination—it appeared she was leading him to a dead end.

No, wait, there was someone up ahead, awaiting him in the dark. The figure was taller and more fearsome than a mere man.

It was the Devil.

It towered over them, its piercing glare baleful, bare-naked torso beefy as a bull's, with outstretched bat wings and the triangular, ornately horned head of a man-goat. Its lower body, bestial and covered in coarse black fur, perched upon a black square column, clinging to it with great taloned feet. Chained to the black stone were two smaller figures, a man and a woman, both nude, both horned.

Magpie felt foolish for his instant of fear; after all, it was only a colored bas-relief, albeit a particularly vivid one. Sister Acantha allowed herself the barest hint of a sardonic smile at his expense and took hold of the dangling member of the nude man. With a quick tug, she released a hidden trigger point and the entire panel swung open, revealing a descending spiral staircase, lit by some infernal glow far below. Moans, shrieks, and cries echoed up from the depths, but it was impossible to tell if they were from pleasure or pain—or some unholy combination of the two.

The priestess stepped aside to allow his entry. He saw now that she had completely unbuttoned her habit, revealing her bare flesh, enhanced by silken undergarments. She favored him with another smile.

"Down, sinner," she commanded him.

Descending the stone stairwell into the catacombs below with Sister Acantha following just behind him, Magpie's mix of lust and trepidation continued to marinate as the pleas and groans became louder. The lower level opened onto a dungeon. On either side of the passageway were sturdy ironbound oaken doors, each with a barred window allowing a voyeur's view of the delicious tortures being carried out within.

There were several of Acantha's profane sister priestesses at work down here in the various cells. Some applied whips or paddles or tickling feathers without mercy. Some victims were chained to posts or fettered to the walls, and some were made to kneel, others pulled by leashes until they were bent over wooden trestles or stretched out upon tables, awaiting the further indignities to come.

And the passing glimpses of what was unfolding in still other cells shocked him to his core. There were already some gentlemen and ladies there who had paid for the pleasure of observing the torments within firsthand—they grinned conspiratorially at Magpie and the priestess as they passed.

He wondered which cell was to be his, but Sister Acantha did not stop, only prodding him forward until they came to one final door, solid and ironbound, at the very end of the corridor.

"Stop. This is yours. Now strip."

"What?"

"You heard me. You enter the Eternity Suite naked. Now off with your clothes."

Titillated, he nodded and quickly did as she commanded, and she kicked each one to the side. When he was completely disrobed, he took a deep breath and reached for the door handle.

She slapped his hand away.

"Wait for your damnation, impudent wretch! There is one matter more." From inside her habit she pulled out a metal necklace, adorned with a pendant of dark brass. He recognized the sigil against flame engraved upon it.

"Bow your head," she ordered him. He obeyed her and she cinched it up snug and tight around his neck, then seized his face and pulled him in close. "Now listen to me. This is your slave collar of the damned. You will never remove it. Nor will you allow anyone else to do so."

She moved closer still and whispered in his ear, her voice uncharacteristically gentle but urgent. "This part is no game. If you take your collar off, you *will* die, most horribly and quickly, but not quickly enough for your liking—and there is absolutely nothing that I or anyone else can do to save you. Do you understand what I'm telling you?"

"Yes," he murmured, rattled.

"I said, *do you understand*?" she yelled in his face.

"Yes! Yes, Sister Priestess!"

She took his face by the chin again, kissed him hard, and then slapped him for emphasis.

"Good. And when you are done, I will need that necklace back." She pulled the heavy door wide open. A furnace blast of hot air came from within. "Now down you go. I consign your wretched soul to the abyss."

Shaken, Magpie took the last rocky steps to the Eternity Suite. The steps here led down to a true cavern—the stalactites and stalagmites made it seem like he was being swallowed up by the tooth-filled open maw of some monstrous chthonic deity. The dark netherworld ambience was offset by the angry glow coming from what looked like a very real pool of lava. Blue-and-gold flames danced openly upon its surface. The waves of heat coming off it were palpable, rippling the air of the subterranean chamber.

As he stood there, overwhelmed and uncertain of what to do next, he thought he caught sight of movement within the pool. Shapes were stirring within.

And then they emerged.

There were six of them. They rose from the glowing depths like naiads, rising wet and lovely from a cool woodland spring—but rather than shaking off drops of water, these beautiful, unearthly maidens shook off sparks and a fine spray of white-hot magma. He had never seen salamandrae so pleasingly feminine. In Arcanum they called redheads "fire-haired," but with these houris it was literally true. Their perfect nude bodies danced just as one would expect from flames come to life.

Magpie could not be sure if they could speak human language, though they laughed playfully, cooing and waving as they tried to coax him to join them in their bath—but he was not convinced it was safe. The flame maidens enticed him with wordless pleas and outstretched, entreating arms until finally two of them came up the steps to take him by the hands and gently lead him down to the waiting lava pit.

He flinched at their burning touch, but there was no pain, no searing, only a delicious tickling sensation as their fingers traced lines and curves of flame along his arms and shoulders, causing his skin to prickle and hum beneath their caresses. All thanks to the protection of the enchanted collar he wore, which the flame maidens took pains to avoid touching, as it seemed to sting them like ice. He let them pull him into the lava as if it were no more threatening than a tub of warm bathwater, and their eager sisters quickly joined in to welcome him with tender caresses of their own … and licks, and love bites, and fiery kisses …

Chapter Twelve
Athamēan Border

The Mountain Inn

Jezel paused at the doorway at the bottom of the stairs, looked into the common room, and almost went back to her room. The same trio of Pentan traders she'd been forced to travel with were well into their cups. With strictly professional interest, she scanned the room for any interesting newcomers. One dour-looking youth kept to himself. Just as well he was being standoffish. He was good-looking enough in a severe sort of way, she supposed, but from the collar of his cowl, she could see he was a mage from Arcanum. Too much trouble.

Who'd ever want to be the mistress of a mage anyway? she thought scornfully. They spent all their money on the gods-knew-what to work their magic—she doubted any one of them would give so much as a gold ring to keep a woman happy.

Her critical gaze skimmed over a scattered contingent of Athaméan soldiers and what looked to be a manservant—Pentan by the looks of his clothing. And where there was a manservant …

Jezel smiled as her gaze lit upon the man sitting by himself in one of the booths. Young. Handsome. *Very* handsome. Obviously wealthy—even across the room her practiced eye could tell the brooch on his rich brown velvet doublet was a real sapphire, not glass. At the very least he could buy her supper and provide more stimulating conversation than her erstwhile traveling companions.

After quickly downing a mug and a half of very good—and very strong—dark beer at the bar with Dari and Raff, and gaining courage from the drink, Alia decided to try to approach Callan again. She'd kept watch on him out of the corner of her eye and knew he'd had at least one, if not two, goblets of wine; perhaps the alcohol had mellowed his mood as well. She hoped so—she didn't want her first Imperial Festival to be ruined by a series of pointless arguments.

Alia didn't let herself think about the possibility that the journey was a sad preview of what life would be like when she and Callan were married.

"Another one?" The bartender nodded at the trio.

Before Alia could refuse, Raff nodded and grinned at Alia. "This round's on you."

Picking up her mug, she drained its contents, slapped down some coins, and said, "I'll skip this round."

"Hell with that," Dari said. "I'll drink hers."

Smiling, Alia pushed away from the bar and started toward the booth where Callan sat. She stopped mid-step when she saw he was no longer alone. The woman sitting across from him, sipping from a goblet with a plate of food in front of her, was stunning—dark glossy hair done up in an arrangement of curls, tendrils falling artlessly across a smooth forehead and temples. Flawless skin the color of fresh cream even under the flickering light of the copper sconce. Eyes … well, Alia couldn't really see what color they were at this distance, but the woman was using them to great effect—if she was to judge by her fiancé's smile.

She should have been happy to see him smile, but Alia hadn't seen that expression since they left her family's estate three days earlier. And now that he was, it was because of some random woman in a ramshackle roadside inn. Some *beautiful* random woman, which made it that much more mortifying.

She, Alia, had saved Callan's life and had been met with nothing but resentment. This bit of Beauchalice fluff had only to flirt with him, bat her undoubtedly long eyelashes, and he was all but drooling.

The question now was what to do about it?

"Are the rains always so fierce this time of year?" Jezel asked, toying with a stray curl in a way that caught the light of the candle. It was a seemingly artless gesture that had drawn many into her net of seduction. So many little things that could capture a man—or a woman's—attention. Jezel was second to none when it came to making someone desire her, even love her. She knew how to make her lovers feel as though they were wrapped in a soft, silken blanket of luxury. The best foods, the finest wines, and her ability to listen for hours without feeling the need to fill any empty spaces with her own words beyond those to help smooth the way to whatever she wanted to happen next.

"The weather-mages make sure that the skies above Trionn-Fí are clear for the festival," Callan replied self-importantly, almost as if he himself were capable of moving the clouds. "It's our misfortune that the rainy season came early this year and the winds were predisposed to blow the storms in our direction south."

"I've heard that when the weather is tampered with thusly, it increases the severity of the storms. Is this true?"

Jezel hid a smile as the Pentan lord appeared to ponder the question—she suspected he had no idea what the answer might be, so she decided to take pity on him.

"Thank you for your generous hospitality," Jezel raised her goblet, her voice a husky purr that very few men—if any—had been able to resist. Callan was no exception.

She'd played up the role of a woman traveling to Trionn-Fí on her own but for the company of her lady's maid—too ill to accompany her to the common room—and he'd responded with flattering alacrity. It had taken her all of a minute to procure an invitation to share his table—and what was at least his second bottle of wine. She'd briefly debated whether or not to take the bolder approach and sit next to him but discretion had won—she didn't want to come across as desperate. If she had, he might have turned a cold shoulder and wouldn't have offered her a seat, let alone supper.

The barmaid, resigned that any chance of winning the handsome Pentan's interest was nil, set a wooden platter of sliced meats, cheese, and freshly baked bread on the table, along with utensils and wooden plates. Jezel hid a smile as the woman dropped her plate an inch above the tabletop so it clattered just enough to vent her displeasure at the new arrival without being obvious. Smiling sweetly up at the barmaid, Jezel thanked her. Both women knew she didn't mean it.

"No need for that," Callan said when the barmaid left to tend to other patrons. "It is her job, after all."

Jezel offered him a smile more sultry than sweet. "It costs nothing for me to thank those who serve me."

"Indeed," he replied with a raised eyebrow. "It costs you nothing, as you are my guest."

Jezel chose to treat this as a compliment. "And I'm grateful for your hospitality." Raising her goblet, she offered him a toast. "To new acquaintances."

His smile broadened, and he touched his goblet to hers across the table, letting his fingertips graze hers. "And perhaps more."

A shadow fell over their goblets. "May I join you?"

Alia pasted on a smile she didn't feel as she looked down at her fiancé and the ridiculously beautiful woman sitting across from him. Candlelight glimmered off the gold and crimson silk of the woman's high-waisted gown and the rounded flesh of her cleavage. "Hello," she said with as much of a smile as she could muster. "I'm Alia Irkhanan of Trontes' Skar."

"Jezel Mirèlha of Vhar-daen-Aude." Her husky voice was wrapped in the soft vowels and consonants of Beauchalice. Jezel held out a languid hand with perfectly polished half-crescent nails. Alia pressed it briefly, all too aware of the dirt and dried blood under her own nails—she really should have taken the time to clean up. The contrast was no doubt apparent to both Jezel and Callan.

"Alia Irkhanan, meet Jezel Mirèlha," Callan drawled, sounding as though he'd had more than a little wine. "Alia, my love, are you sure you can take the time away from your soldiers-at-arms to spend with your fiancé?"

"Fiancé?"

The look of surprise on Jezel's face was almost worth the hurt that Callan's drunken words inflicted.

"Yes." Alia kept her tone neutral. "We're to be married in Pentaclys after the festival."

"Congratulations are in order then." The woman had the temerity to raise her goblet in a toast. "To the happy couple."

Callan clinked his goblet against hers, sloshing wine on the table, then drained its contents and carefully set it down. Then he slid out of the booth, getting unsteadily to his feet, and sketched a small bow first toward Jezel and then a more exaggerated one to Alia.

"Please excuse me, ladies. I'll be back shortly." With that, he vanished into a hallway at the back of the common room.

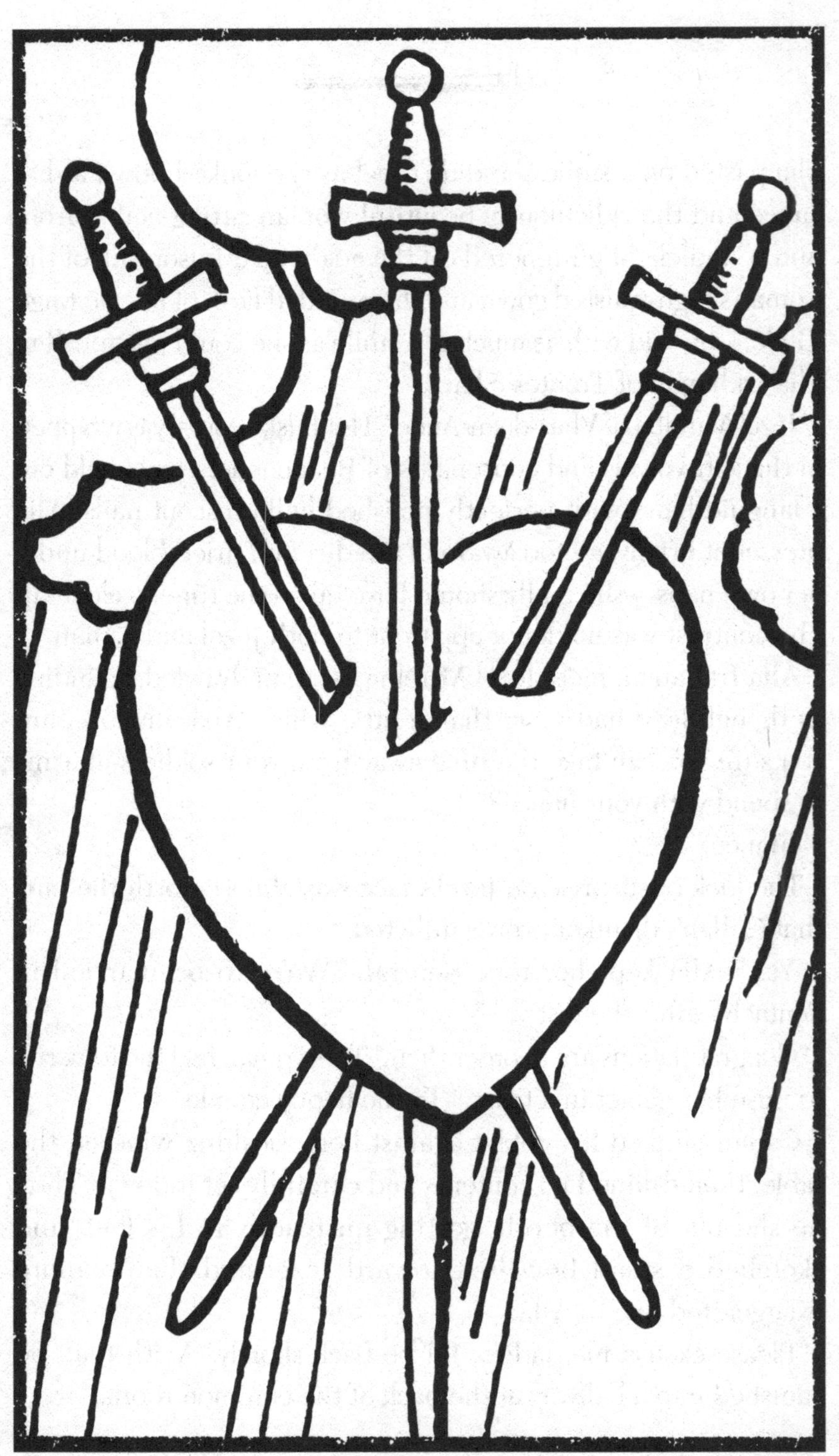

Chapter Thirteen
Athamēan Border

The Mountain Inn

Harbalorio watched the young lordling make his way across the room, leaving the two women alone. Some sort of relationship drama was obviously bubbling between the three and, under normal circumstances, he'd do his best to suss it out—he loved gossip. But in this case, his instinct—even a few sheets to the wind—told him to mind his own business.

Still, the women were both beautiful in very different ways—the courtesan from Beauchalice was everything a female trained to be pleasing and appealing should be, while the warrior woman was all golden-skinned limbs and the confidence that came with noble birth. Well, he'd be hard-pressed to choose one over the other.

He wasn't here, however, for romance or even a quick tumble under the sheets, although he wouldn't say no if one—or both, should the Gods above answer his fantasies—snuck into his bed. No, he was going to Trionn-Fí to find investors for his various enterprises, and unless one of these beauties could finance him, he would not spend his energy in their direction.

At least not *too* much.

Alia looked after Callan as he wove his way through the common room, wondering how things had soured so badly between them in so short a time.

She sank into the seat he'd vacated, grabbed the bottle of wine, and emptied its contents into his abandoned goblet, taking a deep draught before looking across the table at Jezel.

"You're traveling to the Imperial Festival?"

"Like all the other travelers staying here, yes."

"Of course." Alia hated herself for feeling intimidated by the woman's cool poise. "Will you be staying with friends?"

Jezel shrugged. "That remains to be seen. The festival is a time of opportunity as well as celebration."

"I see," Alia replied, even though she didn't.

"And you and your … fiancé. That is your destination too, yes?"

Alia nodded. "Yes. And then on to Pentaclys for—"

"For your wedding, yes." Her voice ever so slightly clipped.

"Yes."

"Tell me," Jezel said after a brief pause. "Is it for love or for money?"

Alia found herself at a loss for words. Both because she was shocked that the woman would be so rude as to ask the question and because she didn't want to think about the answer. She'd thought Callan had grown to love her over the three months of courtship, weapons training, and fighting alongside her. But now she could only conclude that her family's emerald mines were the only real attraction.

And she hated this *Chalicécois* slut for rubbing her face in it.

Instead of answering Jezel's question, Alia posed one of her own. "Is it customary in Beauchalice to try and seduce another woman's betrothed?"

"I had no idea he was taken." Jezel toyed with her wine goblet, smiling at Alia over the rim. "But make no mistake, darling. If I were really trying to seduce him, you wouldn't stand a chance."

Alia had had enough. "Pray, excuse me."

Rising from the table, she picked up Callan's goblet and, without another glance in Jezel's direction, made her way to the back of the room to hunt down her fiancé. The Pentan with the gilt-gold hair shot her another overly friendly smile and patted the seat next to him. She ignored him—she had neither time nor energy to waste on a drunken fool.

She passed the serious-looking Arcanum mage at the end of the table, his attention still focused on his supper. He was either a very slow eater or had ordered enough food for two. She briefly wondered why he was there—he didn't look the type that would enjoy anything as frivolous as the festival.

Then she was in a dimly lit hallway leading to what she assumed was the privy. A half dozen rustic iron sconces lined either side of the walls, several candles at the far end extinguished. A door at the end of the hallway opened and a gust of icy wind and rain blew in, putting out another candle.

Callan stumbled in, soaked to the skin. He didn't look good—Alia guessed he'd vomited during his trip to the privy. She'd ask the innkeeper to put an extra chamber pot in his room. It was the least she could do.

"Callan … ?" She spoke tentatively.

Looking up at the sound of his name, he wiped a hand across his mouth, propping himself up against the wall with his other. "How sweet of you to check on me." His drunken tone implied otherwise.

"Are you feeling well?"

Callan snorted, the sound turning into a cough, which turned into a spatter of wine-colored vomit against the wall, dripping down onto the floor. Alia immediately went to his side, put an arm around his shoulders, and said, "Let me help you to your room. It's late and we'll want to make an early start."

To her relief—and surprise—he didn't argue, just gave a brief nod and let her help him back down the hallway to the stairs that led up to their rooms. But before they could ascend them, his body went limp and Alia stumbled under his weight.

"Can we help?"

Alia looked up in relief at Raff and Dari.

"Oh, please."

The two soldiers took the now-unconscious Callan between them.

"By Athamé's blade," Dari swore. "How much did he drink?"

"Maybe a bottle of wine or two." Alia shrugged. "I don't know how much he had to eat beforehand." A pause, then she added bitterly, "I was not his chosen companion for supper."

"And if that was his first fight earlier," Raff interjected, "and I suspect it was, then the heat of battle probably played merry havoc with our lordling's head for alcohol."

After Alia checked with the innkeeper to find out which room was her fiancé's, Raff and Dari navigated the stairs with him, Alia trailing behind in case one or the other should trip and Callan should fall. They didn't, making it safely to Callan's room on the third floor.

"Would you help me get him out of his clothes?" Alia asked.

"Really?" Dari gave her a hard stare. "Let him learn what it's like to wake up to the smell of his own vomit."

"I'll warrant it's not the first time," muttered Raff. "Go down and find that weedy little manservant of his—what's his name, Wurmo?"

"Ermo," Dari corrected him.

Raff waved a dismissive hand. "Whatever his name is, this is his job, the worthless slug."

"Please." Alia put a hand on Raff's arm. His jaw hardened and he wouldn't look at her. "Please," she repeated, glancing at Dari as well. Neither of her friends looked happy but they both complied, stripping off Callan's boots and vomit-splattered clothing while she poured a glass of water from a cheerful blue ceramic pitcher on the wooden night table.

After Callan had been muscled onto the bed, linen sheet and two wool blankets pulled up to his shoulders, Raff and Daria left, leaving Alia alone with her fiancé. She sat next to him on the bed and held the glass to his mouth. After taking a few sips, Callan pushed the glass away, nearly knocking it from her hand. She gave a sharp exclamation as cold water spilled on her lap.

"Ahhhh, I'm sorry, Alia." Callan reached out and grasped her arm. "I'm a clumsy fool." His words were slurred, his expression slack and remorseful. "I've treated you badly these past few days. I'm sorry."

Alia lowered her gaze, as embarrassed by his drunken apology as she'd been by his insults. "Callan—" she began uncomfortably, but he cut her off.

"Can you forgive me?" He slid his hand down her arm to her hand, holding it tightly. "I vow I will be a good husband. His grip on her hand tightened just short of pain. "I ask only that you put aside your soldier's ways and adapt the gentler arts more suited to a lady of Pentaclys."

Even though she'd expected this, his words still hit her like a kick to the chest. "It is what I was raised to be." Her voice was nearly a whisper.

"I know," he murmured. "But if you love me … you'll change. And if you change, we'll be happy together." His eyes closed as his hand fell away from her arm, and his breathing thickened with sleep.

Alia sat as still as a stone for a minute, then got up and left the room.

Jezel waited another half hour. Sipped her wine. Nibbled on the last of the food. Finally she accepted that Callan would not be returning to the table nor would there be any sort of negotiations between the two of them that evening, or any other.

No matter. If he truly was going to marry the Athaméan, it had to be for money, no matter how beautiful or young she might be. In her experience, Pentan nobles didn't wed outside their circle if they didn't need an infusion of wealth. Which meant he didn't have much of his own.

She only hoped he had already paid for the food and drink.

With that thought in mind, Jezel rose from the table and went back to her room.

Chapter Fourteen
Athamēan Border

THE MOUNTAIN INN

It had taken Alia a long time to fall asleep after her last conversation with Callan. She'd briefly gone back downstairs to bid Raff and Dari goodnight. They were sleeping in the dormitory space behind the common room, close to the privies—both a blessing and a curse, according to Raff.

In her own room, still sleepless two hours later, Alia smiled at the memory. Wishing not for the first time that her childhood friend was of noble birth instead of a common soldier. They'd be happy together, she knew it—friendship was a far more lasting kind of love than infatuation. And had her family not fallen into disfavor with the Emperor and Empress, perhaps her father would have allowed the match—Athaméans were less fixated on family lineage than accomplishments, especially of a martial nature. After all, Raff was one of the best soldiers and finest swordsmen in Athamé. She'd been so lucky to train with him in their youth—his skills and her own competitive nature had inspired her to train harder. Her resulting reputation as a warrior would have seen her in command of her own unit if not for the value she held as a bargaining chip to restore her family to imperial favor.

Alia had known what her father expected from Callan's visit, and what needed to be done—and *should* not be done—to fulfill those expectations. She had, however, hoped for more from the man who had traveled across the empire to court her.

And so she would wed Callan. He didn't care about her heritage or her skills. To make him happy—for him to consider her a good wife and therefore to earn his affection—she'd have to give up most of the things she loved. The things that defined her. All that concerned Callan was the dowry brought by her family's diamond and emerald mines and the rich veins of various ores and minerals that riddled their lands. And, she supposed, to a lesser degree, her beauty. Although with the fortune she brought to the union, she'd no doubt he'd marry her even if she was one-eyed, obese, and suffering from a bad case of Dragon Skin.

Chapter Fifteen
Arcanum

ISLE OF CHTHON—THE ORACLE SCHOOL

"Casander! Wake up!"

The anxious young maid tugged at his sleeve, jolting him awake. He sat up, frowning, not from irritation at his interrupted sleep so much as from concern over what prompted it. Outside the window, the moon's arc cut through the clouds. He judged it was shortly after midnight.

"Is she all right?"

"She's left her bedchambers, without a word to anyone. The other girls fear she's in a trance!"

He rose from bed and swiftly threw on a heavy cloak over his sleeping clothes. "Where is she now?"

"Two of the younger housemaids said they heard her leave the great house and go outside. We think she must have been on her way to the sacred grove—oh, but what if she's gone sleepwalking to the sea cave—or along the cliffs? I'm scared, Casander!"

"She'll be fine, I'm sure," he replied, keeping his voice calm. "You and the others go back to bed. I think I know where she's gone." He said it with much more certainty than he felt.

In a moment he was out the door into the chill night air. He could see his breath as he gently spoke a summoning spell for wild were-light, and moments later a half dozen of them came streaking through the night sky toward him in a shower of falling stars.

Now the question was which way to go? Divination was not an exact science, but he hazarded a spell anyway. Snapping a hazel twig off the garden hedgerow, he took a minute to cast the spell and slowly turned in a circle, dowsing for her presence. The twig gave three indications—the great house itself, of course, and then wavered between the direction of the sacred grove and the path that followed the cliffside.

Knowing her as he did, the grove did seem to be a logical choice, so he headed off along the path of stepping stones leading to it. Bright as torchlight, the will-o'-the-wisps danced and whirled around him like gamboling puppies, illuminating his route.

The grove was one of the most ancient in Arcanum, a small forest of elms and oaks, along with a mix of yew, ash, and hazel. At its heart was a small clearing, housing a natural pool where moonlight liked to go bathing on nights like this. But there was no sign of Eluned.

Hurrying now, he backtracked out of the trees and headed for the cliffside trail—a popular hike during the daytime, but a foolish risk to take in the dark. His anxiety grew as he approached the edge where land abruptly ended in air and sea—and craggy rocks.

For a moment, he regretted telling everyone to go back to bed. Then again, perhaps the last thing he needed was to have a bunch of excitable young students bumbling about in the dark, especially along the edge of the cliffs.

Fearing the worst, he carefully walked the treacherous path for over two hours, sending search parties of were-lights up ahead and down among the tide-swept stones below, hoping he would not catch sight of her fallen body dashed among them.

His spirits were mixed when he reached the point without finding her walking along the path. Though greatly relieved she hadn't fallen, that also meant she could have gone anywhere on the island. He cursed and turned around to head back and keep searching … when he caught a glimpse of light through a break in the fog—lights in the window of the highest part of the school's tower.

Casander was huffing for breath when he reached the top of the stairwell leading up to the school's scriptorium and threw open the door. In the daytime, its skylight windows let in enough light that often there was no need to rely on were-light at all, but now the chamber was lit up bright enough to serve as a lighthouse. With a deep exhalation, he was at last able to let his annoyance and fear wash away at the sight of his mistress, safe and sound and hard at work. He was surprised to see her at the writing table, normally his place, and alarmed at her being reduced to doing his job.

"Mistress? You're here! Are you all right?"

She nodded but did not look up from her writing. Flustered, he continued, "My divinations seemed to tell me you were at the grove, or walking along the cliffside—" *Or, of course, the third option I foolishly neglected to follow*, he thought, *right here.*

"Your spell did not fail you. I was at the grove, and at the point. But leave me now—I have important portents to set down." She had taken the full roll of their biggest parchment, the size they normally only used for cartography and other large-scale projects, and was busy filling the oversized space with one column after another, writing at a frantic pace.

"Seeress, you needn't do all this yourself. Please, let me assist you." She looked up at last, but only to throw an empty inkwell at him.

"I said, begone! Leave me to this!"

Rattled, he could say nothing, but only stared mouth agape before he turned and ran out lest she hurl anything else in his direction.

PART THREE

FESTIVAL DAY

Chapter Sixteen
Arcanum

THE ISLE OF CHTHON—ORACLE SCHOOL

She's gone mad.

Casander had returned to his own bed but couldn't get back to sleep after seeing his mistress in such a state. He had never known the Seeress to act so erratically. She had not died of the fever, but he couldn't shake the terrible fear that they had lost her all the same.

Twice more he got up during the night, slipping quietly up the stairs to the scriptorium to check on her. He didn't dare risk opening the door again, but both times he could hear her scribbling away, muttering to herself, before he crept back down again, resolving to go speak to the physicker if things hadn't improved by morning.

Before the first light of dawn finally came, with the night sky still twilight-colored, he dragged himself out of bed once more. He had finally given up on sleep, feeling more exhausted than when he had first laid down his head the night before. He went to the kitchens and had the cooks put together a plate of the

Seeress's favorite breakfast—cabbage hash, figgy pudding, and a wooden tankard of small ale to wash it down.

Carefully balancing the tray, he ascended the stairwell again and knocked gently on the door. There was no reply. After a moment's debate, he opened the door quietly.

"Good morning, Seeress," he said, in that cautiously cheerful voice reserved for those who might still be sleeping or hungover. She was still hunched over the desk, still scribbling furiously, as she had been doing throughout the entire night. She ignored him.

"I've brought you breakfast," he added hopefully. Suddenly she snapped a look his way, glaring at his intrusion. She stared daggers at the tray as she would a basketful of snakes and toads.

"Get out! Take it away!"

He backed through the door quickly, shutting it behind him before she reached for anything to lob at him. But he hadn't gone more than a few steps before the door flew open again, the shock nearly causing him to drop the tray altogether.

"And bring me more ink! And more quills! Hurry!"

"Yes, Seeress," he answered, but she had already slammed the door.

Chapter Seventeen
Trionn-Fī

THE SILKEN MOON—ETERNITY SUITE

"Good morning."

Luxuriating in the afterglow, the Magpie looked up from his cozy reverie, nestled like banked embers in the ample bosom of an affectionate flame maiden. Sister Acantha awaited him at the foot of the steps, standing primly with hands clasped, her habit buttoned up modestly again. His own clothes and walking stick lay in a neatly folded stack at her feet.

What a rude awakening …

"Morning? So soon? Impossible!"

"I assure you it most certainly is not. In fact, it is a beautiful day and the morning's festivities are about to begin in earnest. Your hair is smoldering a bit, but apart from that, you don't look any worse for wear. I trust the night was to your satisfaction?"

"Well, yes, as far as that goes—" He tickled the cheek of the nearest flame maiden, provoking a giggle, merry as a crackling fire.

"I'm pleased to hear it. Sadly, I'm afraid it's time you take your leave of our ladies." She snapped her fingers, and all his attentive fire-nymphs instantly abandoned him, plunging down into the depths of the pool like startled mermaids. "That is, unless you wish to purchase another session?"

"Yes indeed! Put it on my tab!"

"Ah. I was informed you don't yet have one, but kindly come with me, and our house mother will be happy to make all the necessary arrangements. Oh, and I will need that collar back. But not until you come out of the lava."

The priestess led Magpie's lost soul—and the rest of him—back up from the abyss. At every step, his mind raced furiously to come up with the best course of action to take with Madam Yaislinn. His overriding instinct for survival urged him to take the better part of valor—make a quick excuse and slip out quietly without engaging with the house mother any further.

Still … perhaps she would be inclined to extend him a line of credit? Or would she suspect, rightly, that a man who paid for services with a gemstone did so because that was all he had at his disposal? In any case, the odds were sadly high that he would never have such a run of good fortune again to splurge on a return visit to the Silken Moon. No, better to cut and run without making a fuss, and allow Madam Yaislinn to forget all about—

"Séverin Perig! My dear Chalicean gentleman!"

Magpie quickly masked his inner debate and greeted his hostess. "My Dame Yaislinn! All the reports of your fabled house's hospitality paled to the actual experience! A thousand thanks!"

"Too kind, My Sir! I do hope you return again soon!"

"Oh, Mister Perig is quite eager to purchase a second visit immediately, House Mother," Sister Acantha chimed in. "He wishes to put it on his tab."

Madam Yaislinn raised an eyebrow.

"Is that true, Séverin dear? If so, we must arrange it for you at once. The flame maidens will be so delighted!" For an instant, Magpie's thoughts irresistibly flicked back to the captivating bevy awaiting him at the lowermost level, but his financial reality quickly burst that bubble.

"The good sister is quite right. Indeed I do, and I will at first opportunity! However, I have just now recalled some urgent matters I must attend to first. So, with a heavy heart I return to Beauchalice, and I look forward to my soonest return." He bowed to kiss the madam's hand—and so he did not see the trio of clients coming down the stairs.

But they saw him.

"Good morning, Madam! And good morning, Master! What a lovely surprise!" Audoin hailed them cheerfully. Volker and Tord remained their usual surly selves. Magpie froze, stunned speechless. Madam Yaislinn gave a look of surprise.

"Oh! You two gentlemen are already acquainted?"

"Yes, Madam. Master Lanza is a countryman of mine from Pentaclys." He shook Magpie's hand, who stood paralyzed, with a sickly smile hanging askew on his face.

"And who is Master Lanza?" she asked, her brow furrowed in confusion.

"Why, this fine gentleman—he exposed a sham diamond some swindler foisted on me!"

"A … sham diamond, you say? How very interesting …" Her tone took on a hint of frost. She shot a look at Luan, who snapped his fingers and signaled for two more servants to attend to their mistress. She turned her attention to Magpie.

"My Sir Perig, has this young man mistaken you for a Pentan—or have I mistaken you for a *Chalicécois*?" Now Audoin looked confused as well. Behind him, Volker and Tord seemed to sense blood in the water and edged closer to their prey. Even Sister Acantha was closing in, circling him along with Luan and the other two manservants. Magpie gulped.

"You know, this is, this is a—a quite humorous story," he sputtered. "I have a cousin, you see—that is, an identical twin, actually, though we were raised apart, so he's more like a cousin to me, mind you, he in Pentaclys and I in Beauchali—"

"Audoin," Madam Yaislinn interrupted. "Did I tell you how Séverin—or is it Lanza?—paid us for his night of pleasure? With a diamond of his own! What a remarkable coincidence! Would you like to see it?" Luan handed her a small lacquer box. She opened it, revealing the perfect diamond sitting on a bed of velvet. Audoin looked at it in shock.

"But—this is the very same diamond I bought yesterday! The one you said was false—and smashed to bits! I saw you do it with my own eyes!"

"Dear Audoin, I think your Master Lanza is an accomplished magician. And liar." All eyes were on Magpie, who seemed to be crumbling beneath the intensity of their gaze.

"Wait," he croaked. "I—I ..." His eyelids fluttered, his body wavered, and for a moment, it appeared he was about to faint dead away—and then he snatched the diamond and ran for it. He dove between the two manservants. As they tried to grab him, he struck one in the shins with his walking stick and tripped up the other, whose legs took the cane with him as he went tumbling to the ground. Audoin's henchmen followed in hot pursuit.

Frantic, his path zigzagged through the wide salon like a cyclone, sending chairs and trays of drinks crashing everywhere. Moving faster than even he thought possible, he reached the door to the foyer, flung it open, and barreled past the doorman, knocking him to the floor and nearly trampling him in his haste to get through the front entrance.

Chapter Eighteen
Trionn-Fī

A Tenement in the Outer City

"Is it time yet?"

Lally cast an impatient glance at her little brother. At eight years of age, Pax was just old enough to be annoying yet not old enough to be an entertaining companion for a twelve-year-old. She often wished she could trade Pax for a little sister, preferably three or four years older than him, but since this wasn't a possibility, Lally did her best to put up with him.

He tugged on her arm. Not hard, just making sure he had her attention. Looking into Pax's wide brown eyes staring up at her with trust and adoration, Lally felt her irritation melt away in a sudden rush of affection. All annoyance aside, she loved her little brother with the fierce protectiveness of a mother lion.

"It's not time yet, but it will be soon," she said, ruffling his curly blond hair, so much like her own. The sun was still hidden and would take longer yet to rise above the tenement houses of their neighborhood, but she could tell the dawn sky was just beginning to brighten. "If we leave now, we'll have time to look at the vendors before the regatta starts."

Pax nodded, resting his head against Lally's arm. "Can we buy pies?"

Their mother had always made sure that each Imperial Festival was celebrated in style—they didn't have a lot of money to spare, but she had made each year special. Even if that meant just enough extra coins to buy Lally and Pax something special. Velvet hair ribbons. Sweets. Carved toys and minor magical trinkets. Breakfast pies stuffed with eggs, apples, and bacon. Dessert pies filled with sugared cherries or plums, figs and ginger, or apples and almonds.

Pax especially loved those pies and the fact that last festival their father had spent all his extra coins on beer and spirits … well, looking at her little brother's confused and forlorn expression when she'd told him they couldn't afford to buy any pies that year had nearly broken Lally's heart.

"As many as you want." She mentally counted the coins in her pouch, saved from months of odd jobs here and there. She had done her best to earn what she could because she knew their father wouldn't have put anything aside for his children. Now she had plenty. "As many as you want," she repeated, pushing the unwanted memories of the last year out of her head.

Taking Pax's hand, Lally led him out of their ramshackle common lodging house in one of the poorer districts, down the maze of alleys that reeked of fish and leather tanning, and into the crowds already on the streets, a constant moving river of people.

"Where are we going?" Pax asked.

"After we get pies? To Crown Province Park. I've heard it has the best view of the airships in all of Trionn-Fí."

"Really?"

"Best in the capital!" Lally assured him.

He looked at her doubtfully. "But we're not supposed to go there."

"Not normally, but this is a special occasion." Lally crossed her fingers behind her back as she continued. "As long as we don't cause any disturbances, no one will bother us."

Lally hoped this was true. Anyone passing into the various gates to the Inner City or, the Gods forbid, the circular palatial grounds between the Aurichalcum Tower and the *Cathedralis Geminae*, had to pass the guard's approval, which could sometimes require showing the papers proving they had business there.

But during the festival, the capital guards were not as strict at enforcing the gatekeeping—this was a time for celebrating, and at least in theory, all were welcome. Besides, even though they would still chase off any obvious ruffians, hooligans, or beggars, many of the guards were half drunk by the afternoon of the first day. There hadn't been a truly serious disturbance at the Imperial Festival in recent memory—who would want to destroy the peace and prosperity that ruled over Tarou? And if two poor and unattended children should sneak into one of the parks usually reserved for the wealthy residents and visitors to observe the regatta, surely it wouldn't be met with more than a slap on the wrist—wouldn't it?

"Come on." Lally took Pax by the hand and led him through the crowds.

Chapter Nineteen
Trionn-Fī

Outside the Silken Moon

Outside the Silken Moon, several carriages were parked. Their drivers were a knot nearby, talking together while each waited for the return of their passengers. Magpie wasted no time sprinting for a little two-wheeled cabriolet carriage whose single horse looked speedy, scarcely noticing the driver's shout of alarm when he saw Magpie race up to his conveyance.

With a loud boom, the house's front door flew open again. The great stone lions let out deep, stony roars and launched after him. He let out a fearful shriek and threw himself into the seat of the little carriage, grabbing the reins and sending the already-startled beast into a full gallop. Its driver ran behind, yelling and waving his fists in a rage.

Any passersby would have been treated to another unusual sight—a crowd of scantily clad courtesans staring from the door of the great house, including a priestess in full habit, angrily shouting out after the fleeing carriage.

"You pasty-faced little pudding! We'll throw you to the flame maidens and then you'll see how they show their love to worthless thieves and cheats! They'll roast you like a suckling pig with their bare hands and devour you!"

Magpie did not need the whip to get his horse to run—it was already terrified of the lions closing in on them. He risked a look back. The bouncing two-wheeler was only just ahead of their craggy, snapping jaws. And behind them, an even worse sight—Volker and Tord were commandeering another carriage to join in the chase.

Hunters and prey careened and thundered down the elegant streets of the Silken Moon's secluded neighborhood, both carriages juddering over the cobblestones, the heavy stone lions drawing sparks on them, every footfall like hammer blows. In no time at all, Magpie's stolen carriage reached one of the main boulevards, already crowded with cheering festivalgoers. His steed balked at the surging wall of people, spooked by all the waving pennants, blowing horns, beating drums, and enthusiastic shouts of revelry.

Despite his best efforts, he could not keep control of the horse. Whinnying in fright, it bolted to the right, and then right again, turning around in a blind panic. The maneuver made the cabriolet jerk up on one wheel and nearly tossed Magpie out of the carriage completely—but it pulled them out of the path of the onrushing lion-shaped gēnomi, whose heavy stone bodies could not accommodate the abrupt change of direction. They skidded to a clumsy halt with no more grace than an avalanche, and fought their way back up to speed again, chasing them back the way they had come.

Now Magpie's little cabriolet was on a collision course with Volker and Tord. The two thugs were leaning out of their own carriage on either side, each hanging on with one hand and brandishing a weapon in the other. Volker had a knife; Tord, the driver's own horsewhip. Like jousters, the two carriages sped at one another. Magpie's horse ran straight on, only slipping to the side at the last second, forcing him to duck as Volker slashed out with his blade.

Volker's flashing knife only just missed his face, but it cut clean through the cabriolet's canvas hood, leaving its ragged edges flapping like bat wings. Magpie cursed as the tattered halves of black cloth slapped at his face and fought to fold the cover back down. Now he could see the bigger carriage turning around after them. The implacable stone lions were behind it, but now they thundered past, coming straight for the little cabriolet.

Sister Acantha and the cabriolet's erstwhile driver hurled more venom at Magpie as his stolen carriage rattled past the House of the Silken Moon once more, the lions and Volker and Tord coming up fast. The speedy little two-wheeler was faster and more maneuverable than the lions—but they were untiring and unstoppable, and how long could his panicked mount keep up the pace? Desperate as he was, a plan occurred to him.

Instead of turning on the next block, he urged the horse straight forward, off the cobblestone road and in through the open gate of one of the Noble Quarter's more secluded and exclusive gardens. The gate, like the estate grounds itself, was meant for foot traffic. His little two-wheeler barely squeaked through, and the twin lions bounded through with ease, but Volker and Tord's fatter carriage was completely shut out.

Now his driving skills—or more accurately, his horse's—were put to the test, as it pulled the cabriolet bounding over grassy knolls and tearing through lovingly tended flower gardens, making crazy twists and turns to avoid statuary, fountains, and shrubbery—to say nothing of screaming picnickers and interrupted lovers on romantic strolls.

The lions cared nothing for any of these niceties, leaping over whatever they couldn't trample, and so were making surprisingly good ground until Magpie saw his chance to take a calculated risk. Reasserting some control of the reins, he managed to pull the steed's attention toward a dainty wooden footbridge spanning a broad koi pond.

The structure was somewhat precious, built more for romantic views than load bearing. Magpie had half an instant to wonder if it would hold up under the cabriolet's weight before his mad horse clattered up and across it, the wheels of the carriage only just fitting within the little bridge's width. Magpie peeked behind them—the lion-shaped earth elementals were nearly upon them, snapping at the back of the cabriolet, dangerously close to chomping clean through the axle of the two-wheeler in a single bite …

And then like magic, both lions suddenly disappeared—crunching through the bridge like unlucky skaters crashing through ice—plunging instantly into the pond. Magpie hooted with joy to see them sink like the stones they were. But his elation was short-lived.

Chapter Twenty
Trionn-Fí

THE UPPER CITY

Trionn-Fí, while always a festive city, never saw such a celebration as during the Imperial Festival. Merchants, vendors, and artisans from across the continent showed their wares, and the odors of dishes from all four provinces scented the streets—boiled pea pods with butter and salt, savory herb tarts, shortbread knots, and honeyed fritters. And all manner of meats—venison, poultry, pork, mutton, geese, rabbit, eels and fish, oysters and mussels, prepared in any number of ways—spiced, stewed, fried, roasted on a spit, and baked in buttery pastry crusts.

Citizens wore their finest outfits during the four days of the festival—silks, satins, and velvets for the wealthy; linens and gaily dyed cottons for the working class. Everyone had something special to wear for the occasion, even if it was just a velvet or silk hair ribbon.

Already, taverns spilled over with drunken patrons as beer, wine, cider, and spirits flowed freely. The first night was always a bacchanal, no matter that the festival wouldn't officially begin until the next morning, when the regatta flew overhead and landed, and the many dignitaries on board disembarked.

First, Lally and Pax stopped for pies, little handheld delicacies stuffed with different fillings, both sweet and savory. Pax's favorite was egg and bacon, while Lally preferred the smoked salmon and goat cheese. They both liked the thistleberry pies as well, a slightly sour berry sweetened with brown sugar and spices, so Lally bought one of those for them to share along with one of each of their favorites.

They wandered through the vendors, merchants selling all manner of goods—handcrafted leather belts, purses, and bags dyed in vibrant shades. Hats and bonnets made of felt and wool, decorated with plumes, silk flowers, and gems. Artisans selling jewelry and hair ornaments made of bronze, gold, and silver, some studded with precious or semiprecious stones. A booth selling swords and daggers of Athaméan steel. Clothing of silk, velvet, cotton … so many fabrics and so many rich colors that Lally felt overwhelmed by it all—overwhelmed and envious of the festivalgoers who were shelling out coins and purchasing these glorious items. She caught Pax staring longingly at a marvelous little toy dragon. Its eyes glowed with were-light, its wings flapped, and on the toymaker's command, it let out a roar and breathed faux-fire.

Someday, she thought. She would have the money to buy this for her little brother … and more. Whatever he wanted.

Chapter Twenty-One
Trionn-Fí

THE NOBLE QUARTER

Their little joyride had attracted more attention than Magpie wanted. All over the grounds, visitors were screaming at the cabriolet running amok and he struggled to get his horse to avoid them. Looking about in desperation, he spotted a stream of frightened parkgoers fleeing for their lives, heading out through—another gate! He reined in further and tried to urge the horse toward the exit. Luckily, his horse seemed open to the idea too.

But before they could follow the flow of evacuees out of the gardens, there were new arrivals to deal with—troopers of the city watch, drawn by the shrieks and brandishing polearms. A squad of six came through the gate and took up formation, pikes out to bar his escape. He could hear their sergeant ordering him to halt in the name of the law. He could also hear calls for crossbowmen and mages.

"Turn around, damn you!" he yelled at his reckless steed while pulling up on the reins—but then its thrashings yanked them right out of his hands. He let out an inarticulate squawk of dismay as the lines fell on either side of his mount, dragging along on the ground, well out of his reach. The crazed horse was running the show now.

Magpie blanched as it charged straight ahead, dragging him directly toward the bristling pikes with suicidal abandon. He could see the steely gaze of the fighters, see the color of their determined eyes. Their long steel spearheads gleamed like the sharpest of kitchen knives.

Then his cunning mount pulled to the left just before it would have impaled itself and jerked the cabriolet into another crazy turn. It rocked the carriage up onto one wheel again and had Magpie clinging for dear life to keep from being thrown right out of the seat and straight onto their pikes. Then the wheel crashed down again and the out-of-control horse-and-buggy continued its reign of terror, scattering those stragglers still left in the park.

Something small and impossibly fast crossed their path, skimming his horse's streaming black mane. Then another—whistling just past Magpie's head. Crossbow bolts. He ducked as low as he could, kneeling on the platform, his white knuckles keeping a death grip on the seat.

The horse seemed determined to gallop through the rest of the entire park as fast as it could, somehow both utterly fearless and completely terrified. It ignored the barrage of crossbow bolts and chased anyone in sight. But then it would jump and bolt at the sight of scary things, like a monster-hiding shrubbery or a horse-eating water fountain. Magpie was so busy trying to keep his grip on the twisting, bouncing carriage, he could barely watch any of it going by. And then, with yet another frenzied turn, he lost his grip. And his carriage.

For a moment he was tumbling head over heels through the air. When he came to his senses again, he found himself suspended in the open mouth of a topiary crocodile. The cabriolet bumbled along without him, faster than ever now that the wily horse had rid itself of the deadweight. The city watch continued after it.

With some awkwardness, Magpie extricated himself from the leafy green jaws, looked around to see if he had been spotted, and carefully made his way to freedom. When he was satisfied the coast was clear, he pulled himself over the curling, wrought iron fence onto a side street and from there, onto another busy thoroughfare, bustling with happy festival celebrants.

A wave of relief came washing over him as he slipped into the crowd, wrapped in anonymity again. *Better.* He felt like a fish who had avoided being snapped up by sea eagles and found refuge in a little forest of kelp. Sadly, two bigger fish joined him almost immediately. Volker and Tord had followed him. Without a word, as usual, they seized him and strong-armed him away from the safety of the cheering, distracted throng.

Chapter Twenty-Two
Trionn-Fī

THE INNER CITY

"We'd better hurry," Lally finally said after they'd wandered through rows and rows of vendors. "We don't want to miss the regatta," she hastened to add when Pax started to protest.

Taking his hand, they wove their way through the crowds to join the throng heading to the Inner City. Lally chose a family with three children and stuck close to them, hoping no one would notice that two of their children wore threadbare clothing. It worked—the guards at the Inner Gate barely glanced at them.

Once they were inside the Inner Circle, Lally pulled Pax away from their temporary family and into a narrow alleyway between fancy houses. It was crowded but not as packed as the streets and thoroughfares most people were using. Lally tried to hurry her little brother along without tiring him too much—his legs were short and he could only go so fast.

Still, by the time they reached the end of the alley, Pax was huffing and puffing, clutching Lally's hand like a lifeline.

"When we get the park," she soothed him, "we'll eat our thistleberry pie. And later, we'll have lemonade."

Pax nodded, giving his sister a tired yet happy smile that went straight to her heart. *Someday*, she thought again.

Bending down, she kissed Pax on the top of his head. "Hold tight to my hand," she said. With that, she and Pax left the alleyway and entered the river of humanity that made its way up the pink marble-paved street toward the park.

Chapter Twenty-Three
Arcanum

THE ISLE OF CHTHON—ORACLE SCHOOL

Casander was used to being the one to hand over a finished scroll of fresh divinations—the Oracle School did not favor the term *prophecies*, as it sounded unreliable and not scientific enough—to the team of scribes the school employed.

So it was frustrating for him to come down to the dormitory common room where all of them were at breakfast, waiting on the delivery so they could go to work, making a copy for the school's library, then turning the raw notes into the most exquisite calligraphic text, illuminating it with gold, silver, and the richest of colored inks, and adding art until it was worthy of the Emperor's gaze.

Fortunately, he didn't need to wait long before a flashing were-light came flying into the common room and made orbits around Casander—the Seeress's usual signal to summon him. He hurried up the tower once again and rapped on the scriptorium door.

"Shall I bring up the scribes, Seeress?" he asked. She opened the door almost before he finished the question.

"Send the scribes away. There will be no copying or calligraphy for this one. But summon the flier—this must be in the hands of the Emperor and Empress within the hour." And with that, she slammed the door again.

Chapter Twenty-Four
Trionn-Fī

Cathedralis Geminae—Inner Chamber of the Council of Ecclesiarchs

It was not like the High Ecclesiarchs to break tradition, and this year's Imperial Festival was no exception. However, the Hierophant and High Priestess had announced the addition of a special ceremony on top of the calendar of regular observances. This was to be a sacred hour of reflection and prayer for those festival attendants who wished for a brief break from the boisterous antics of the revels.

While the faithful would gather in the plaza outside the *Cathedralis Geminae*, within the Holy See itself, the highest spiritual leaders of Tarou would come together for their own sacred conclave of reflection—the High Priestess and her vestal virgins, together with the Hierophant and his most trusted high officials.

By coincidence, the Psychidion faction of mages had quietly scheduled a private assembly of their own members at the same time, at a location not announced to the general public, for some undisclosed purpose.

It was a most unusual synod. Normally, the Inner Chamber of the Council of Ecclesiarchs was kept immaculately clean, and the meetings held there were most somber affairs, governed by strict and time-honored protocol. But today the council tables had been cleared away to make room for the ant's nest of excited activity now unfolding. An anxious crowd of Psychidion mages and their harried apprentices hurried about, busying themselves with preparations.

The meeting room's milky white floor—of the finest unblemished Pentan marble—was being covered in intricate cabalistic patterns by master runesmiths with keen eyes and deft, practiced hands, their ranks of glyphs and sigils carefully laid out with delicate precision in metallic inks of jet and gold. Around the periphery, other experts were in place, tending to a multitude of sorcerous instruments.

Taking up the center of the chamber was a massive pair of gēnomi—earth elementals—both shaped into mechano-magical servitors. One stony *gēnomos* took the rough form of a minotaur, the other a lion-man. Their eyes burned with the ruddy heat of magma. Under the directions of their handler mage, they raised up an enormous cylindrical shape whose height nearly reached to the top of the dome ceiling, and then slowly retreated out of the way with a heavy tread that echoed off the marble floor like distant thunder.

The structure they lifted up might have been the war weapon of a god. It resembled a giant twelve-flanged mace constructed out of sleek blue-black crystal. It would take the reach of three men to encircle the haft, which was engraved with lines of still more sorcerous markings. Deep within its depths, a sullen green glow smoldered.

Seated on their thrones, the High Priestess and Hierophant watched all this with great interest. Behind them, their own entourages were visibly disturbed at this circus of Arcane spellcasters wreaking such havoc upon the venerable chamber, gasping at every new indignity. Even the normally implacable cathedral guards around the edges of the room seemed ill at ease. But none dared voice any complaint.

For their part, the Holy Pair paid no mind whatsoever to any damage to the chamber floor—even if all this commotion meant replacing the priceless marble. After all, priceless was a trivial price to pay for what they stood to gain. Their patience, on the other hand, was a vanishing commodity.

At last, the High Priestess spoke. “Is all in readiness, Magician?” Her tone was cold.

Startled, the normally unflappable leader of the Psychidions turned at once from directing his subordinates.

“Indeed, very soon, Reverend High Priestess,” he said, quickly bowing with open arms. “And we have your gracious Holinesses to thank for enabling and inspiring our humble—”

“Speak directly, Málach,” the Hierophant cut him off. “We are neither in the Emperor’s court nor sermonizing to the faithful. Flowery speech and flattery will only irritate.”

The mage gave a curt nod. “Of course, Holiness.”

He extended his hand to the towering crystalline structure dominating the room. “This is the Abraxas Scepter. The inner glow you see within comes not from anything in our world, but from the energy vortex we have sensed beyond the veil. Our world and all we know—from the deepest abysses in the earth and the bottom of the ocean, to the blackness swirling the stars about—think of it all as but a single chamber in an unthinkably vast palace.

“Using our magics, we have conducted many experiments, and divined the warmth, if you will, coming from the wall between our room—that is, our world—and the adjoining one. In this way, we know there is a wealth of raw power on the other side. However, we have not simply discovered a powerful new source of energy—with this mighty device, we can draw upon that energy for ourselves.”

Again, the High Priestess and Hierophant grew impatient. Both already well knew the metaphysics behind the theory of extradimensional transverse, as well as the full potential of the Psychidions' sorcerous apparatus—in fact, they were counting upon it. But for now they pretended ignorance, content to let him believe they were learning the finer points of all this for the first time. The Psychidion leader had no idea that, in actuality, Tallas, one of the journeyman mages at his side, was in their employ and had been sending regular, detailed updates on their progress to the Holy Pair for the past twelve months.

Nor did Málach realize his very life was hanging by a most slender thread. Even now, concealed within the folds of his jacket, the High Priestess's turncoat had a freshly envenomed dagger in a hidden sheath, ready to plunge into the small of Málach's back upon her signal. If he proved false, gave any hint that he was seizing the power for himself, she would dispatch him as instantly as she would swat a stinging insect, and with as little remorse.

Oblivious to his mortal circumstances, Málach continued his demonstration. He nodded to the scry-seer standing off to his side, who raised her hands and promptly invoked a shimmering vision in the air between them—an overlapping profusion of curvilinear lines. "With this," Málach said, "we see the matrix of the ley lines which converge here in the High Kingdom, in the center of the continent. From the power contained in these lines all sorcerous activity ultimately stems."

He turned his attention back to the giant structure.

"Once we have pierced beyond the veil between worlds and tapped into the power which lies there, it will flow into our world through Abraxas and energize our ley lines as never before. But there is more." He paused with the timing of a showman, dark eyes gleaming. "Once it has absorbed these new mystical forces, our device will not only manifestly increase the power of our ley lines, but it will also be formidable enough that one may employ it to then restrict or encourage the flow of magic anywhere along their courses ..."

"Effectively taking control of the network of ley lines," the Hierophant said, finishing the thought. "And subsequently, all major forms of sorcery." At last he seemed impressed with the presentation.

"Just so, Your Holiness," Málach said humbly, his eyes downturned. "The Abraxas Scepter will make Your Reverend Highnesses the supreme—and should your Holiness wish it, the *only*—sorcerous power on the planet." This revelation drew sudden gasps and murmurs of stunned disbelief from the respective entourages of the Holy Pair. With mastery over the flow of all sorcery in their hands, nothing could stop the Holy See from wresting control from the Emperor and Empress and turning Tarou into a *holy* empire, under the direct control of the Gods—and themselves. The excitement in the chamber was thrilling and palpable.

The Archmage and the Ecclesiarchs smiled at one another, all sharing the same thought: *When we seize control over the ley lines, we alone will be the most powerful entity on the planet. And then we will swiftly dispense with these fools …*

Behind the whispering vestal virgins and the ashen-faced members of the Hierophant's inner circle, one of the *Cathedralis* palace guards unobtrusively slipped into a side corridor, and from there into a stairway.

He ascended swiftly and moved up to a small window, opening it partway before fishing out a small item from a pouch on the belt of his tabard. It was a dragonfly, crafted from jade, with exquisite wings of silver wire mesh. The guard spoke the word that brought it to life and quickly reported what he had just seen and heard, then lifted his palm to the open window. The jade insect flew away, straight toward the Aurichalcum Tower, while the guard made haste to return to his post.

None were the wiser. No one had noticed either his departure or return—all eyes were upon the ranks of chanting mages encircling the giant mace of darkened crystal. The ritual to activate the Abraxas had begun.

Deeper than the mystic chants from the summoner-mages, the great crystal flanges atop the pillar began to produce a low rumbling drone that slowly grew and filled the council chamber, echoing off the marble floors and resonating in the breastbones and teeth of the onlookers. Darkness also seemed to be emanating from the device, making the illumination from the cressets of were-light quaver, as though the encaged will-o'-the-wisp spirits within were trembling in fear.

"We are receiving energies from beyond the veil, My Lord Málach," reported one of the mages, looking up from the magical instruments at his station.

"Excellent!" Málach replied, pleased.

As if stealing the strength of the were-lights, the luminescence lurking deep within the pulsating column grew steadily stronger even as the rest of the room grew dimmer, until the only remaining light was the glow from the scryer's display of amber-tinged ley lines, the banked embers in the cressets, the eyes of the gēnomi, and the eerie sea-green glow from Abraxas itself, which bathed the entire chamber in an eldritch emerald cast.

First one by one, then in a rush all along its rune-carved surface, the scepter's magical glyphs began to blaze. "Power surges along all ley lines," the scryer called out, and all could see the ley lines blazing like fresh-forged saber blades, glowing white-hot where they began to converge on the outskirts of Trionn-Fí. Cheers arose from the mages and apprentices, as well as the other onlookers—even the famously inscrutable High Priestess and Hierophant could not hide their pleasure. Málach beamed at his subordinates, exultant with pride.

And then the wheel of their fortune turned.

As the echoing applause died down, it became clear that the blue-black pillar's deep, sonorous drone was also dying down, retreating before an eerie and indescribable new sound—faint at first, but rising inexorably in volume, as though drawing nearer.

Málach raised an eyebrow but caught himself before his expression gave away any other signs of confusion. The gaffe did not go unnoticed by the Ecclesiarchs, however, who struggled to contain their own puzzlement and mounting unease.

The scryer pointed to her ley line display hanging in the air. "My Lord, there is a surge building along the conjunctions to the north of us."

Face tight, Málach strode closer to see the telltale glow for himself and waved two of the older masters over to come confer quickly with him. He pointed to a position at the center of the inner city.

"Should not the influx of power be manifesting *here*, where we now stand?" he demanded, his voice low but strained. His colleagues, equally bewildered, could only stare.

"It would appear, My Lord," one of them spoke up timidly, venturing the obvious, "that the Abraxas has indeed succeeded in breaching the veil."

"And yet, the focus of the materialization is not centered with us here," the second chimed in, brows furrowed. "But as our scrying-sister rightly says, somewhere just to the north of us."

"Keep your voices down!" Málach hissed. Just north of them was, of course, the Imperial Palace. "Are you saying the power is flowing directly into the *Aurichalcum Tower*?" he asked in a harsh whisper. The trio blanched at the thought. If the Emperor was somehow directly intercepting their influx of extradimensional sorcerous energies, then all was lost and they would all soon be losing their heads—if they were lucky.

"The surge is *not* originating in the palace," the scryer reassured them, peering carefully at her map. "I would place it just a few leagues outside of Trionn-Fí. But see here," she added, tracing with her finger as the spot of brightness at that particular conjunction began to drip down a ley line. "It *is* moving toward us."

"*What* is moving toward us?" Málach exclaimed. Tallas, the High Priestess's pawn, was already standing close at hand to the master mage, but now he edged closer still, hand in his jacket, trying to remain inconspicuous as he waited for any signal from the High Priestess to strike.

In a terrible moment of clarity, the Psychidions' leader realized what was happening. Yes, the Abraxas had successfully gone through the veil to tap into the adjoining dimension, like a mosquito biting a neck through a wisp of lace collar—but *now something from the other side was ripping an even greater hole into their own world.* And not a mere pinprick but cutting through like a razor-sharp blade.

And the blade's point was coming toward them.

"What *is* it, Málach?" the furious Hierophant demanded in a querulous tone.

But *it* was the wrong term. Not it. *Them.*

There were many of them. And they were drawing nearer.

A swirling visual cacophony—bright sparks and shimmering, pearlescent orbs—filled the chamber, tiny at first, but growing larger and brighter with each passing moment. The eerie sound of their coming was marked by unearthly—and strangely beautiful—tones. Something almost—almost—bordering on music . . .

All around the chamber, the sparkling lights and iridescent globules teemed about, capering like the dancing stars a fighter sees when struck on the head. As the awed spectators watched them jostle madly about, the strange lights seemed to be observing them as well. After a few moments of this stalemate, their movements slowed, steadied, and then they began to amass together in a single large swarm—but a curiously well-ordered one.

The unearthly music became more like the agitated hum of a stirred-up wasp hive as they formed into the shape of an oval, all the sparks and pearly shapes pulling together and aligning themselves in rows as though trying to mimic the compound eye of some monstrous gigantic insect, or spider.

Low moans of dread began to ripple through the crowd below.

As if bloodred wine was being poured into it, the beaded sphere coalesced into a single baleful eye, all scarlet except for a single black pupil, more fitting for a demon. The nightmare vision filled the dome above their heads, staring down with a horrid alien fixation at their upturned, terrified faces. Its gaze seemed particularly fixed upon the solitary figure of the head Psychidion mage quailing beneath it.

As it maintained its terrible gaze, the bloodred eye transformed from a bloated red sun into another form—the face of Málach himself. First, the reflection wavered and rippled, distorting Málach's face like some huge fish-eye mirror before capturing his terrified visage more accurately. Its mouth opened in a silent scream, its implacable eyes burned into his, and its hair and flaring sideburns streamed out like phantom tendrils.

For a few awkward moments, the two Málachs exchanged wordless stares at one another. Then the giant reflection grew suddenly agitated and morphed again, as if dissatisfied with its new look—or simply unable to hang on to its borrowed human form. Boils of varying size bubbled up all over the face and forehead. Some split open to form glaring eyeballs, while others blossomed into gaping mouths that began to shriek and wail in an unholy chorus, its skin sloughing away, melting and bubbling as it slid off its face.

Below, the real Málach joined in with a howl of his own. Clutching his pendant of authority in one fist and extending his other arm, the mage shouted a word of power to release a blinding white bolt of eldritch lightning at the mocking specter looming over him. The deafening roar of its thunder shook the chamber and everyone in it—but did nothing to the horror above him.

Instead, the lightning strike passed through the open mouth and vanished into its blackness. In return, the giant head slowly descended and engulfed the mage in its open maw. Málach seemed to both burst into flame and fall away screaming into a dark void, spiraling into a black oblivion like a moth that had flown through a torch.

Screams reverberated and reached a fever pitch as the chamber erupted in terror. While those trapped inside the chamber struggled to escape, the thing's hair sprouted into a thick mane of gigantic tentacles that began snatching the shrieking morsels, tossing them crying and flailing into the black vortex that was its primary mouth.

Then the glowing shape of the Abraxas Scepter caught its attention.

Like rooting fingers, its tentacles stretched out to seize the Abraxas in their grasp. The crystalline pillar shuddered with the contact, violet chains of energy crackling to life where the alien limbs laid hold of it. In one sudden burst, all the were-lights in the chamber broke free, scattering away like a startled flock of birds. As if in collusion with them, the two gēnomi suddenly let out earthen roars of outrage and went berserk, smashing into the crowd as they struggled and fought one another to flee the chaos.

The High Priestess and Hierophant remained unmoved on their thrones, transfixed with horror. Only when the gigantic abomination finally turned its hungry gaze toward them and slowly, implacably, closed in while they stared back with quavering lips and eyes grown wide with madness, did their screaming begin.

Chapter Twenty-Five
Trionn-Fī

Above the Inner City

With the entire capital city packed with celebrants for the festival, there was a distinct lack of good locations to carry out a murder in broad daylight. A more reckless pair of killers might have just knifed their victim in hopes that the press of the crowd would hide the crime. But unlike Magpie, Audoin's thugs were not the blend-in type, so they had to find other arrangements.

There *was* one place nearby in the Noble Quarter that wasn't packed with cheering festivalgoers—one of the old aqueducts that rose about a hundred feet above a stretch of neighboring rose gardens. No one but city workers ever entered the little maintenance shed that opened onto its heights, so it was a simple matter to pick the lock and slip through unobserved.

Magpie had spent the short walk to his death trying to talk his way out of his fate, explaining, bargaining, and finally pleading—but he would have had better luck getting a response from a stone. The two thugs opened the door and unceremoniously pushed Magpie out onto the uncomfortably narrow walkway of the aqueduct. The height was dizzying, and under happier circumstances he might have thrilled to see the rings of the city spread out before him, its streets and canals filled with throngs, its towers and spires decked out with lines of festive pennants. Above him, the bright, clear sky was filled with the aerial fleet. As it was, he had to ignore the incredible vista and fight to keep his balance, his arms windmilling, the tails of his frock coat snapping like flags in the stiff breeze.

If Volker and Tord were afraid of heights, they didn't show it. They watched his struggles with mild interest, as if they had a bet going whether they would have to throw him off—or if the mix of vertigo, wind, and his own clumsiness would do the job for them.

Magpie managed to crouch down in a more or less stable position, though the wind kept tugging at him to come join it. His fevered mind considered desperate options. Could he just run the length of the aqueduct and escape—*without* falling? Or just jump in the canal and swim away? He peered down the length of the elevated channel. It ended in a waterfall, dropping down onto a shallow stone fountain, as he recalled. He could only think of one chance left.

He turned to his would-be murderers. "Looks like if you want me, you're going to have to come over and get me!" he said with a sneer of faux bravado. He suddenly dropped to his knees and reached into the water, splashing it liberally on the stone walkway between them. "Ha! Still feel so sure-footed now?"

Neither man answered or took a step closer, but Tord reached into the fold of his gambeson and pulled out his stolen coach driver's whip—not some little riding crop, but a true bullwhip, seven feet long. Casually, he played it out to its full length, and then gave it a few gentle preliminary twists of his wrist, snaking it back behind him. His unflinching gaze never left Magpie.

Then his arm snapped up, sending the lash to crack just over Magpie's head. The hapless thief yelped and pulled back to avoid the strike, winding up on his backside, crab walking precariously down the narrow stone ledge to try and get away. He couldn't. Tord took two confident strides forward and pulled his arm back for another swing. Magpie raised a hand to ward off the blow.

No further than an arm's reach away, a large bird plunged past them both, straight toward the ground. Both men turned in surprise to watch it fall. The great bird did not pull out of its dive but crashed with a sickening crunch among the thorny roses far below. Now all three men looked down over the edge at the sight. It was no bird. It was the body of a sailor.

Tord and Volker turned to each other in puzzlement, the first human emotion Magpie had seen either of them display. Then the moment passed, and by some unspoken agreement, Tord turned back to the task at hand. He drew his arm back and snapped the lash forward to tear Magpie's face into an ugly red wound—or would have, if a piece of ship's rigging hadn't tumbled out of the sky that very moment.

A heavy pulley block and its iron hook struck Tord, swatting him off the ledge so instantaneously it was as if he had never been there at all. Its trailing tail of ropes and chains took half a moment longer to entangle Volker and drag him screaming to the ground. *So Volker could talk, after all,* Magpie thought. He sat there, trying to catch his breath.

"This must be my lucky day."

W

Chapter Twenty-Six
Trionn-Fí

THE INNER CITY—CROWN PROVINCE PARK

Crown Province Park was packed by the time they reached it, people spread out over the large expanse of grass on picnic blankets, with food and drink in abundance. It was laid out in a pattern of four outer circles surrounding a central one, representing the four provinces of Tarou united by the capital. Each circle encompassed ever-luxuriant lawns and beds of vibrantly colored flowers: flame lilies for Athamé; sweet olive for Pentaclys; passion flowers for Beauchalice; vervain and daffodils for Arcanum; and for Trionn-Fí, the finest red roses, their scent heady and pervasive.

"Where shall we go?" Lally asked her little brother. "Would you like to see a fountain? It's famous—and it has *undines*!"

"Yes!" Pax exclaimed. He loved elementals. She was happy to have the chance to humor him, and just as excited to see the rose gardens and the great big fountain at the park's center. They had never before been so close to the Imperial Palace, which overlooked the park. Lally's mother had described it to her, though, and she was thrilled to see the giant azure jewel of the Aurichalcum Tower and the walls enclosing the palace estate that formed the innermost ring of the architectural triple crown that was Trionn-Fí.

Street performers were everywhere—jugglers shared space with dancers and musicians, hats and jars overflowing with tips. Magicians conjured little miracles to entertain the crowds. The sheer number of people packed into the space, which took up four city blocks, was overwhelming. The large fountain in the center, the water jetting twenty feet or more into the sky, held a veritable circus of undines pantomiming rearing sea serpents and leaping dolphins, or performing acrobatics, their tumbling shapes changing with each impossible maneuver.

Lally felt a brief stab of sadness—she missed her mother. It was an ache that never truly went away and seemed especially bad during happy occasions. Sometimes it occurred to her that maybe this same ache was why their father no longer had time for them. Reminders hurt.

Stuffing those thoughts away, she focused on the sheer wonderment in Pax's eyes as he watched the undines do their endless acrobatics, the water shifting shapes and colors in the air, sunlight reflecting off the spray, creating jewel-toned prisms.

"Look, Lally!" he cried. "It's a butterfly!" Before she could reply, the crowd broke into cheers as the regatta suddenly appeared on the horizon, swooping in over the Aurichalcum Tower.

Pax's hand clutched hers as he stared in awe at the dozens and dozens of airships above. The sky was filled with them—they almost blocked out the sun with their numbers. The view was better than any place down in the outer ring of the city, and the excitement of the onlookers was palpable, almost something Lally could taste.

Pax will remember this for the rest of his life, she thought. *And so will I.*

At first Lally didn't realize there was anything wrong.

She was distracted by the sounds of boos, followed by gasps. A nearby mage's petty conjurings suddenly fizzled out in the middle of his act, and then he reeled and collapsed to the grass. And he was not the only one. *All* the street mages in the park were falling over—as if they were a field of marionettes and some ghostly, unseen scythe had swept through and severed all their strings in one blow.

The undines in the fountain seemed to sense the change as well. They paused in their acrobatics, water backwashing with a splash into the tiled pool and overflowing onto the festivalgoers closest to it, provoking both laughter and shrieks of outraged surprise. Instead of splashing harmlessly off the onlookers, however, the water wrapped around them as the undines enclosed each person they touched.

In no more than an instant, the elementals joined up to suddenly form a waterspout, slowly at first, then picking up speed, lifting their victims into the air, spinning them round and round, tossing them like juggling balls. The waterspout was translucent at first but then ... but then ... the water turned red. Nervous cries morphed into screams of mortal agony. Skin flayed off by water turning hard as crystal. Flesh and blood flying into the air, while many in the crowd still wondered what had just happened.

What was still happening.

Without warning the ground shook with a sudden violence that threw Lally to the ground, wrenching her baby brother's hand out of hers.

"Pax!" Lally screamed his name as the world crumbled around them.

He gave a shrill scream of fright as the grass heaved and bucked, throwing him into the fountain. Water immediately enveloped the boy as the undines drew him into the air to join the rest of their victims. His screams rang in Lally's ears.

And then the sky began to fall.

Chapter Twenty-Seven
Arcanum

THE ISLE OF CHTHON—ORACLE SCHOOL

The *Arrow* was well-named. A slender, single-pilot vessel made for speed, with only enough additional space to carry a minimum of cargo, usually no more than a single scrollcase, to be delivered with the greatest swiftness and urgency. Its narrow airfoils were almost translucent, and it relied on a team of just four dedicated *sylphs* to wing it through the sky faster than most birds. It even looked like an arrow in flight as it soared down to the island. Casander, waving to it from the grounds of the school, was glad to see its arrival and rushed back inside to fetch the scroll from the tower.

"Seeress! The *Arrow* is here!" he called out as he ascended the stairwell for the final time. He ran up the steps with the exhilaration of those who had been up too late and for too long. When this last chore was done, he would at last have that most satisfying feeling of accomplishment and be free to get some real sleep.

Receiving no response to his words nor to his knock on the door, he opened it gingerly and stepped into the scriptorium.

He had to watch his step—empty inkwells littered the floor. Eluned sat at the desk, resting her hands upon the rolled-up scroll. It looked almost comically huge beside her, not just because of the oversized parchment, but because she appeared to have filled the entire roll. Had she written an entire book overnight?

Her efforts seemed to have exhausted her at last. She sat there in silence, perfectly still, staring down at her work. Casander took a step closer.

"Seeress?"

She gave no response.

"Seeress? Are you all right?"

Eluned made no sound as he approached her, not even when he touched her on the shoulder.

"Seeress?"

When she turned to face him, he nearly jumped.

"Ah, Casander. Help me seal the scroll, will you?"

"Yes—yes, of course, Seeress." He went to the wall cabinet and returned with the stamp of the Oracle School and a stick of rich red sealing wax—but when the Seeress reached for them, the scroll was so heavy it opened and unrolled itself, spilling across the desk and off its edge onto the floor, where it continued to roll open like a carpet.

In shock, Casander dropped the sealing implements from his trembling hands and stared in horror at the unspooled lengths of parchment spread out across the stone floor.

"Seeress … *What have you done*?" She said nothing. He covered his mouth, and with his heart racing, he sank down to the floor to read the scroll. Tears began streaming down his cheeks and a low, keening moan escaped his quivering lips as he ran his fingers across the tiny, detailed lines.

The Seeress had written her magnum opus in the most minuscule of lettering—and then she had written over it, over and over again, until there was nothing but a great streaming palimpsest of chaos, every scrawl and scribble turned to utterly illegible mush. She had not created a book, only a monstrous, insane banner of unyielding blackness.

PART FOUR

CATACLYSM

Chapter Twenty-Eight
Trionn-Fī

AURICHALCUM TOWER

In the light of the morning sun, the gigantic, faceted jewel that was the Aurichalcum Tower gleamed blue as the depths of the sea. Thanks to sorcery, all the balustrades, stairways, and flying buttresses surrounding the azure teardrop seemed to be made of no more than delicate swirls of wire spun from silver and aurichalcum, electrum, and gold. The iridescent flooring of the palace's balconies was carved from one hundred and twenty thousand tiny panels of polished abalone.

By tradition, their Imperial Majesties greeted the air fleet from the south-facing balcony that overlooked the palace grounds, along with the throngs of celebrants filling the imperial courtyard and gardens. The Emperor Patrokleos was in the middle of delivering his opening speech.

"And so, as the five fingers of every hand move in concert to work, to build, to create, to defend, and to hold our loved ones close—so too do our five realms work together in harmony for the good of all." As he took a moment for the thunderous applause to die down, the Empress Rheanna came over to touch his hand, an unplanned gesture. She leaned in close to whisper in his ear.

"My love, Master Hviskair signals for your attention."

He looked to see a most unassuming man, balding and slight, waiting in the wings. Hviskair had the look of a dull librarian, though his actual title was even duller—the Petty Assistant to the Palace Housekeeper. Patrokleos gave him a slight nod, then turned back to the crowds.

"So do your Emperor and Empress of Trionn-Fí hereby open this Imperial Festival!"

The imperial couple smiled and waved to the throngs, and then once more returned inside. Three-quarters of his opening speech, and all of hers, was left unsaid, but they knew Hviskair would not interrupt them except for urgent reasons—those who knew he existed at all, knew him as one of the Palace Master of Housekeeping's lesser assistants, but in fact, he had much more pressing duties. He was the Imperial Spymaster for the entire realm.

The trio went directly to a guarded side passage behind the main throne room, and there Hviskair quickly touched three points on the wall that opened the hidden door to a secure meeting room. Vissente, the Emperor's Lord Mage, and Taranis, the Chief Captain of the Palace Guard, already awaited them inside. The spymaster wasted no time coming directly to the point.

"Our man inside the *Cathedralis* has just sent word. The Psychidions have not only completed Abraxas—they are readying to put it to the test within the hour."

The others' faces paled at the news.

"I want the Holy See cordoned off at once," the Emperor commanded. "Have the palace mages cast wards of containment and bafflement over it—"

The Lord Mage nodded.

"—and send a full company of the Sovereign Guard, including battle-mages, salamandrae, and gēnomi, to arrest the Hierophant, High Priestess, and Málach. Same with the other Psychidions. If any resist, kill them."

The guard captain nodded as well.

The Empress spoke up. "One more thing. Arrest the rest of the Council of Ecclesiarchs and the Vestals, but treat them with courtesy—we need to know if we can trust any of them on the thrones of the *Cathedralis Geminae* after today. Hurry!"

The two men saluted and rushed out to put the plan into action. As they emerged from the secret chamber into the corridor, the Empress turned to Hviskair. "Send word to the guard below that the courtyard must be cleared at once. Announce that all must immediately make way for a parade."

"Majesty," he said with a bow of his head, and hurried after Vissente and Taranis, just as the Lord Mage suddenly stumbled and clutched at his head.

"Vissente!" Taranis caught him as he swooned, lowering him gently on the floor. Hviskair and the Emperor and Empress rushed up to them as the mage's eyelids fluttered open.

"What's happened?" the captain asked him. "Vissente, do you need me to summon the mages?"

"Or a physicker?" Empress Rheanna added.

"No …" the mage said weakly. "Get out … Everyone must … get out. Now!"

They all heard it then, a strange, deep droning through the throne room's high cathedral space. It might have been coming from the ranks of the room's giant guardian statues—which were now coming to life. As one, they raised their spears and fists and roared upward so hard it brought down the sky—the thousands and thousands of were-light stars cascaded all around them and flew off in all directions.

Vissente, cradled in Taranis's arms, stiffened, his eyes fixed straight ahead.

"Is—is he dead?" the Empress asked.

Uncertain, Taranis could only shake his head. The low, eerie thrumming was growing louder, drowning out all the other sounds. Hviskair grabbed Taranis by the shoulder. "You heard him—we have to *go*!"

He looked up, his eyes wide. "Your Majesties—*run*!"

Taking his wife's hand, Patrokleos pulled her away. Neither of them had run since they were children. Courtly protocol was strict—royals could never run. But they ran now, along with Hviskair and Taranis, and all the other human courtiers and servants, fleeing the statue warriors that were attacking everyone in sight.

The Emperor called out the word of command to bring them under his control. Either he could not be heard over the ever-louder, reverberating din, or—unthinkably—they refused to answer him. The four ran for the stairs, but now the towering stone guardians were blocking those trying to escape, scything through them with their sweeping lances.

"The balcony!" the Emperor cried. "Get back to the balcony!"

They turned and ran back the other way, but a spear as tall as a pine tree went flying across the throne room and through Captain Taranis like a piece of meat on a skewer as the Royal Couple and Hviskair made it out onto the balcony.

Across the palatial complex, at the other end of the crown, Empress Rheanna could see the *Cathedralis Geminae*, the Holy See. A sickly green glow emanated from its twin spires. Above the spires, the air fleet was no longer soaring stately in formation—the troubled sky was filled with crazed shapes stumbling about like angry hornets or burning bright as comets.

"Hviskair!" Patrokleos shouted. The Emperor leaned over the railing and pointed to the slender silver stairway one floor below. "Help me lower her to the stairs!"

"What?" Rheanna's face paled. They were very high off the ground. The crowds below were as tiny as scurrying ants. If they dropped her, or if she missed the stairs when they let her go—

Patrokleos took her by the shoulders. “Listen to me! It is our only chance!”

The tower shuddered suddenly, and a curious sizzling, rustling sound from above made the three of them look up. The Aurichalcum Tower was shimmying wildly, its faceted azure skin beginning to splinter away in tiny bits, like scales off a butterfly’s wing.

Before they could move, jagged little shards rained down upon the trio, shredding clothes and flesh alike. And then the entire palace, silver balconies and all, came crashing down in a shimmering, jeweled avalanche.

T
A
R
O

Chapter Twenty-Nine
Trionn-Fī

Aboard the Imperial Flagship, *Spirit of Tarocchi*

Four and a half thousand feet above the highest rooftops and towers of the city, the pride of the empire's air fleet greeted the sun in the breaking dawn, hundreds of vessels of all sizes filling the bright morning sky—a thrilling spectacle to behold.

While bands of horns, fifes, and drums saluted them from the streets and plazas with a rousing blare of martial music, the airships soared overhead in one alternating chevron after another. With airfoils extended, upper and lower sails unfurled and full, and decks garlanded larboard and starboard with long festive streams of brightly colored pennants and were-light globes, each airship almost resembled some exotic tropical fish as they traversed across the sky. At every pass, the cheering crowds below showed their respect, but the most enthusiastic round of applause and flag-waving came when the throngs caught sight of the imperial flagship, *Spirit of Tarocchi*.

Of the hundred and twenty largest vessels, it was their greatest and grandest. With a deck five hundred feet long from bowsprit to taffrail, the *Tarocchi* dwarfed the other airships, and its crew complement of eight hundred made it virtually a city unto itself compared to its sisters. In addition to the seventy-five officers and six hundred enlisted airmen and specialist crew members, it boasted ten diviners, seers, and weather-mages; thirty battle-mages—ten each, specializing in lightning, fireballs, and shield spells; and fifty Athaméan Sky Marines.

Twenty-five more mages were elemental specialists, on hand to wrangle the team of undine firefighters, a squad of combat salamandrae, and above all, the hundreds upon hundreds of sylphs that kept the massive ship afloat in the sky with the collective power of a harnessed hurricane.

On the quarterdeck, Wöllem, the Crown Prince of Tarou, stood alongside the ship's captain and the master ship's mage, all three of them beaming. The trio's spirits shone as brightly as the buttons on their crisp dress uniform jackets. All along the deck, dignitaries and their entourages from all across the four provincial realms strolled about, admiring the views.

"A glorious morning, Captain Andoni!" enthused the prince.

"Indeed, Your Highness," the captain agreed. "Saveriu, your weather-workers have done a masterful job of clearing the sky of clouds."

"Thank you, Captain," the weather mage replied. "On such an occasion, we could hardly do anything less."

Prince Wöllem moved closer to the rails, barely containing his excitement. "What a view the Gods enjoy! From this height the entire capital looks like a child's clockwork toy."

"Indeed. And to see how the palace and cathedral walls form the crown of the city—truly an enchanting sight, is it not, Your Highness?"

"An absolutely magnificent work of art. It feels as though you could just reach down and place the crown on your head. Or pluck out the Aurichalcum Tower and carry it off like a jewel in the palm of your hand! What do you say, Captain—shall we bring the ship in closer to better hear the crowds?"

"As Your Highness wishes," the shipmaster said indulgently. He turned to the helmswoman. "Mister Fenna, bring us around for another pass." She nodded and acknowledged the order with a gentle turn of the ship's wheel hand over hand.

It was just now getting too bright to use were-light signal lanterns, so the signalmen stationed at the stern and forecastle used their semaphore flags to indicate the change of direction to the neighboring vessels. In concert with the ship's rudder, crafted in the shape of a grand fishtail, the *Tarocchi*'s ornate airfoils, ribbed like the wings of a giant bat, flexed along with its ailerons, all easing the great ship softly creaking into a smooth banking maneuver.

"Master Mage, take us down to one thousand feet, if you would."

"Aye, aye, Captain." The mage stepped to the speaking tube mounted in the wall of the stern cabin and called down to his crew to relay the order. Three levels down, Pherick, the chief elementalist duty-mage, clipped on a safety line, opened the hatch on the floor, and briskly descended down into the *sylph*-locks on the lowermost deck. Although calling it a deck was misleading, as it was completely open to the air and contained little more than the landing gear—and a legion of enslaved ghosts.

The hurricane roar was formidable, as was the terrifying sight of hundreds of furious air elementals in full tumult, three cyclonic circles slaving in unison along the ship's length to maintain its imposing lift. From his tiny platform of metal grating—barely the width of his body—the mage eased up on the spell compelling their exertions, keeping a careful eye on the long glass mercury barometer mounted beside him as the ship slowly descended toward the ordered altitude.

"How odd," Saveriu, the master ship's mage, murmured apropos of nothing, with a curious look on his face. Then his eyes rolled back and he staggered, clutching for the rail.

"Steady now!" the captain cried out with a surprised chuckle as he and the prince caught Saveriu from stumbling. It was not like their ship's top mage to succumb to a bout of airsickness.

"Saveriu!" Prince Wöllem exclaimed. "Are you all right there, old man?" He was not. The mage, eyes still fluttering, was unable to respond.

"I need a physicker!" Captain Andoni called out, alarmed now. "Physicker to the quarterdeck!"

"No, no, I'm all right," Saveriu said, embarrassed. He raised a hand as he collected himself. "Must have just been a touch of—"

A new commotion erupted ahead of them at the bow. Two of the forward weather-mages seem to have been struck by the same swooning fit—for they fainted outright and collapsed. Already disconcerted, the prince looked up wide-eyed as a *sylph*-tender, some forty or fifty feet above, dropped from the rigging like a stone, headfirst and without a sound—until his body impacted with the deck a few feet away from the horrified royal.

Nearby crew ran to their fallen shipmate's aid, but it was clear at a glance that the crumpled man was stone-dead. The ship's diplomatic guests looked on in shock, rendered speechless.

A series of odd popping noises interrupted their stunned silence—from all along the length of the *Tarocchi*, the glass globes containing the ship's running lights were shattering, releasing a brilliant flurry of were-light elementals into the air, rushing up like the sparks from a kicked campfire log. The tiny sprites were escaping out of the cabin windows and breaking free from the prison of the signal lanterns and floodlights.

On every deck, from fore to aft, alarms were raised throughout the *Tarocchi*. All the mages onboard were stricken with the same fit of dizziness, and all the were-lights joined in the mass escape, leaving the shouting, panicked crew belowdecks in near or total darkness.

Only one area of the ship was immune to the unexpected blackout—down on the battle deck, strong sigils normally kept the squad of salamandrae asleep and smoldering in their fireproof pens until called to battle. Now, the heavy oven-strength doors were opening, forcibly pushed from inside by fiery, almost spectral limbs. As the salamandrae stepped out and took in the fresh air, they flared to full strength, radiating waves of heat and light throughout the chamber, and casting a wavering amber glow into the corridor beyond.

The elemental troops that emerged were only vaguely humanoid in shape, looking more like billowing phantoms on fire, and burning with an unearthly intensity that required neither timber nor fuel to stay ablaze—not to say they didn't enjoy consuming such tasty treats. Their handlers had spells to curtail those natural instincts, protect the ship from their flames, and keep them focused on their only job—repelling any boarders alongside the ship's complement of Sky Marines. But somehow, all the usual wizardly restraints had disappeared, freeing them in a vessel of delicious wood, rope, and sailcloth. Yet even with all these temptations, their hunger was eclipsed by something else—seething, overwhelming anger.

Noise from nearby made them turn their heads—the sound of terrified crew members, blundering around in the darkened corridors in search of the exits. It infuriated them. Like moths in search of the moon, knots of fleeing crewmen ran down the corridor toward the only source of light to be found. The desperate men froze when they entered the compartment and caught sight of the half dozen freed flame spirits.

Humans and salamandrae stared at one another for a heartbeat, the elemental's supernatural fire reflected in the crewmen's frightened eyes. Then, with a chorus of inhuman roars, the elementals charged them in a berserker rage.

The three closest crewmen were engulfed in flames, screaming and flailing while seized tight in fiery embraces that consumed them as thoroughly and quickly as if they had stepped into a roaring furnace. The rest fled for their lives while the salamandrae split up after them, flowing down the corridors, trapping the crew in cabins and odd corners where they could close in on their prey. Flames, smoke, and the aroma of roasting flesh quickly filled the combat deck.

On any given day, the ship's undines were content to lounge placidly belowdecks in their holding tanks or pipes, normally moving only when needed to help serve as ballast elsewhere in the ship—until general quarters were sounded, when they would be called into swift action, extinguishing any fires throughout the levels of the ship, or climbing the masts in quasi-human form to rescue any burning sails.

Now, throughout the vessel, they were overflowing their tanks and looking to take their vengeance on anyone who crossed their path. Some merged together to form literal waves of attack, washing like a flash flood through the darkened passageways crowded with desperate crew trying to escape. They gleefully overran the soft, choking humans, slamming them against walls and into each other. They smashed down doors and flooded compartments to seize and drown any trapped inside.

In the galleys, some of the water elementals took a special delight in hunting down the solitary little kitchen salamandrae, who screeched in terror and struggled to escape their ovens, only to be doused and snuffed out, perishing in a shriek of steam.

Down amid the *sylph*-locks beneath the ship, Pherick sank without warning to the floor of his precarious little platform, the elementalist mage suddenly unsteady and in real danger of passing out. His head reeling, he shot out one arm, snaking it around the access ladder and held on for dear life while clutching his forehead with the other, clinging to consciousness as tightly as he clung to his precarious little platform, desperate not to slide off, safety line or no.

Thousands of feet below, the uncountable spires and rooftops of the city and all its teeming crowds filled his sight, the view wobbling and spinning around crazily. He clenched his eyes shut, fighting a wave of vertigo. Pherick hadn't felt so skysick since he was a greenhorn on his first flight. Then the dizziness passed, as abruptly as it had hit.

What in the hell was that *about?*

Shaking his head, Pherick checked his scalp for blood and dragged himself back onto his feet. Still woozy, still clinging to the ladder, he straightened out his safety line, giving the clasp a few sharp tugs to make sure it was still secure. The barometer showed they were still on an easy descent. He breathed a quick sigh of relief and began to ascend toward the warmth and safety of the ship's interior.

Three rungs up, he was thrown off the ladder, instantly and entirely—flailing and falling in an ocean of air.

His whole body jerked as the safety line caught, wrenching his torso violently and nearly tearing free of his belt. The breath was knocked out of him before he could scream—he could feel the cracked ribs and tried to curl up in an attempt to ease the agonizing pain in his side, but it left him racked and paralyzed.

When he could open his eyes again, he found himself dangling like a worm twisting on a hook. To his horror, the damaged clasp on his safety line was little more than a bent metal finger, snagging more than holding the remains of his torn belt. Either or both threatened to tear loose at any moment.

Despairing, he looked up. The flimsy metal grate platform and its ladder were both intact, still rocking in the wind, some fifteen or twenty feet overhead. There was no sign of any assailant. But he couldn't have misjudged his step up the rungs, could he? *No time to figure it out now.* In these howling winds, Pherick well knew no one would be able to hear him up top if he cried out for help.

He was on his own.

Nothing for it. Here goes.

He took a deep breath—and the searing pain through his lungs stopped him mid-gasp. Through a torturous full minute, he struggled to catch his breath again in quick, jerky huffs through his nose and clenched teeth, before experimentally lifting his arm. The dagger-point stabbing pains in his rib cage quickly ended any thought of raising his arm any higher, let alone hoisting himself up the rope.

Above him, each of the three swarms of air elementals was a swirling, rushing blur, all straining against the bulk of the vessel. He only needed one medium-sized *sylph* for what he had in mind, and with a quavering voice through gritted teeth, he struggled to cast the spell to call one down.

He finished speaking the words, but they seemed to have had no effect. A stray gust of wind buffeted him, and he redoubled his efforts to hold fast as his safety line twisted and swayed.

Then he noticed the pair of ghostly, storm-dark eyes staring into his without emotion. A *sylph*'s near-invisible form floated close at hand, a humanoid wraith on the wind, gently undulating before him and ready to serve.

"Good," Pherick said, relieved. He pointed up to the hatch. "Bring me up there—but carefully now!" The *sylph* cocked its head at him like a bemused dog. Then it drew nearer in a serpentine fashion, its body flowing like a ribbon in the sky. It reached out and took hold of the line with vaporous hands, testing the rope's strength.

"No!" Pherick commanded sharply. "*Not* the line—you carry *me* up, quick now! And be careful, damn you!" The *sylph* hastened to obey. It circled down to him until they were nearly eye to eye … and then backhanded him full across the face.

The buffet sent Pherick spinning back perilously, and he cried out in a blend of pain and fear. His aerial opponent came around for a second attack, now twisting itself into the form of a full whirlwind as it dove for him.

His sole lifeline now a crazed pendulum, the pain-racked mage contorted his body, trying to face his assailant. The man-sized cyclone came up at an angle straight for him, and with one last desperate effort, Pherick cried out a sorcerous word of command—a spell that held instantaneous death for the elemental.

"Tshadhaefhahrjizack!"

As the sound of the last syllable left his mouth, the murderous whirlwind reared back instantly, reverting to its ghostly humanoid shape in a snap. Its body was little more than a force of nature bound into a very specific form—all a suitable incantation had to accomplish was to release that sorcerous energy binding the elemental together in order for it to dissipate into nothing more than a harmless, insubstantial cloud.

But that did not happen.

Instead, the *sylph* only glared back at him. Pherick could sense more than see the sardonic smile beneath its thundercloud-colored eyes. And in an instant of terrible realization, twisting in the wind, suspended by a thread and reeling from pain, he saw that more sylphs were gathering, encircling him—a dozen, no, more than two dozen—and still more were coming, as if attracted by the sound of his failed incantation.

Slowly, he lifted his face to see a trio of them overhead, straining together at the safety line. He raised his hand and cast a dispersal spell at them. Nothing.

And then they succeeded in snapping the line.

Pherick's howls of despair as he plummeted were drowned out by the shrieks in the roaring, enraged tempest that plunged down after their former master. He fell another hundred feet before being snatched up again by a gang of sylphs, and yanked just as far skyward before they released him again, sending him flying free before another sudden flurry seized him and sent him tumbling away in a different direction.

Then the realization hit him.

They would not let him fall to his death.

The furies tossed him back and forth between them like crows on the wing fighting over a scrap of meat, until he could no longer tell up from down. Their cruel laughter was maniacal and bone-chilling, and soon indistinguishable from shrieking screams. Then his own screams joined theirs, with each fresh paroxysm of pain, each spray of crimson droplets carried away by the wind.

He was right. They would not let him fall to his death.

He would never touch the ground again—at least not before they tore him to pieces in midair.

Up top, Prince Wöllem barely had time to take in the death of the fallen crewman. Beside him, Saveriu stood perfectly fixed in place except for the cabalistic gestures he made with upraised arms. The blood had gone from his face as he repeated the same incantation over and over, his voice growing ever more panicked with each repetition. Just what the ship's Master Mage was trying to accomplish, the prince could not guess, but it was clearly failing.

The prince turned to Captain Andoni, but the commodore's mask of command was slipping—Wöllem could see the fear behind his eyes, and it was contagious. Both men flinched as the entire main deck suddenly shuddered with a deep timber-creaking groan, as if a whale were trapped deep in the ship's hold, thrashing about to escape.

A frightening new vision caught the prince's eye—above them and to starboard, a trio of cruisers suddenly pitched and plunged nose-first, dropping past the *Tarocchi* with the speed of diving ospreys. As he stood frozen in horrified fascination, watching the three airships plummet down, sails ragged and fluttering, leaving a trail of falling debris and crewmen, sound and movement took on a dreamlike quality.

Moments later, when the deck convulsed again, more violently this time, it was as if the *Tarocchi* and all the other ships in the unfeeling sky had joined together in some grand underwater ballet—all sounds muffled, all movements slowed. Close at hand, Captain Andorni, Saveriu, and the nearby crew were tossed to the deck, untended lines whipped about like striking serpents, while steamers of smoke and stray were-lights continued to fly up from portholes and open hatches. The nobles and dignitaries scrambled for safety like frightened farm hens, all traces of dignity and composure gone. The air rang with barked orders and shouts of alarm.

Off their port side, one particular dreadnought—their sister ship, the *Justice*—had turned into a spectacular theater of war between two ancient enemies. All along the main deck, the combat salamandrae and undine firefighters battled one another. A conflagration raged above among the rope netting and sails where the fire elementals were making their last stand, while waves of undines washed the deck clean of crew members and harried the hissing, spitting salamandrae from below.

Meanwhile, some of the more capricious air spirits coaxed undines to join with them in forming waterspouts that spun with crazed abandon across the main deck, flinging crew members and salamandrae alike overboard before twisting away into the sky.

Not to be outdone, other sylphs gave themselves over to suicidal dances with fire elementals, led by some perverse death wish, or perhaps an overwhelming ecstatic desire that no being composed merely of flesh and blood could ever hope to understand. Their coupling gave birth to terrifying cyclonic firestorms that quickly consumed what remained of the *Justice* before the remaining sylphs finally grew tired of sustaining their playground in the air and abandoned ship to let the whole thing fall.

Nearby, a smaller cruiser's starboard airfoil was buckling wildly as a swirling mob of enraged sylphs targeted its joints, enjoying the looks of terror from their former masters—the helpless shipboard mages who could do nothing to stop their rebelling servants. They and their surviving shipmates could only watch in horror as the entire wing collapsed, snapping shut like a lady's fan. Immediately the unbalanced vessel rolled over like an overturned basket, dumping its crew before commencing a death spiral of its own.

Everywhere His Highness the Crown Prince looked, he could see similar dramas playing out throughout the heavens—airships turned to fiery shooting stars, or simply dropping like stones. The entire Imperial Sky Navy was raining down on the city. Then his stomach lurched as he felt the deck dropping beneath his feet.

With a shock, he realized he now had an audience of his own. All along the length of the *Tarocchi*, waves of sylphs were coming up over the rails, and the ship was losing further altitude with every desertion. The more they streamed up, the faster the mighty vessel sank—until the bowsprit suddenly pitched forward like a diving narwhal, and everyone on deck tumbled after.

The prince was thrown forward, like Captain Andorni and the ship's chief mage alongside him. His body struck Fenna, the helmswoman, and she went flying toward the ship's forecastle along with her officers. By some miracle, the prince's own fall was painfully stopped by a bone-cracking collision with the ship's wheel. He clutched it for dear life as the entire city-ship plunged into a free fall.

In shock, lungs aching, his vision reeling, Prince Wöllem stared at the falling crew being snatched in midair by howling sylphs. Not content to merely watch them plummet to their doom, the spirits flew alongside during their final descent, tormenting them like cats playing with mice.

He could not be sure if the rumbling and booming he heard was the sound of impacts or merely blood roaring in his ears, but before he mercifully lost consciousness, Wöllem could see the airships smashing down, dozens and dozens of them bombarding the city and its environs.

Chapter Thirty
Athamēan Border

THE MOUNTAIN INN

Alia woke up with a start, heart hammering in her chest. Sweat had trickled down her face and pooled between her breasts. The only light came from a guttering candle on the wall across from her bed, and for a brief second, she didn't know where she was. Then the evening's humiliations flooded back, and she wished she could forget. Forget where she was, why she was there, and what the future held. A future she didn't want. With a man she didn't love and who would never be happy with who she was.

She lay there for a minute, breathing deeply, trying to calm her heartbeat in the hopes of a little more sleep before beginning the last leg to Trionn-Fí.

Then the bed moved with a jolt, as if a giant hand had grabbed it and given it a single hard shake. Alia yelped in surprise, clutching her bedclothes like a maiden protecting her modesty, heartbeat hammering anew.

Before she could reach for her sword or even take another breath, the same invisible giant shook the entire room, slowly at first, then picking up the pace, tumbling her out of the bed. She hit the floor with a bone-jarring thud, rolling as the floor undulated beneath her and an otherworldly roar filled her ears.

Something smacked hard into her stomach, knocking her breath away. Her sword—luckily in its leather sheath, or it might have sliced her open. Alia grabbed it by the hilt as the inn continued to shake, walls crumpling, chunks of plaster tumbling from the ceiling, dust filling the air, filling her lungs. Choking her. She quickly rolled under the bed frame, sword and sheath flat under her stomach, held on to one of the heavy wooden legs with both hands, and closed her eyes, protecting them from the worst of the plaster dust. More pieces of the ceiling pelted the mattress; the floor continued to shimmy. Alia sent up a prayer to whatever gods might be listening that the floor beneath her didn't collapse and that she didn't suffocate.

Then, as abruptly as the shaking had started, it stopped. The bed settled back onto the floor with a resounding thump, sending up another cloud of dust.

Harbalorio awoke to the smell of something burning. Opening his eyes, he saw that smoke was coming from the front of his doublet and he sat up with a holler of alarm.

"What is it?" Jakobi mumbled sleepily from his bedroll on the floor next to him.

"I'm on fire!" Harbalorio slapped his hands against his smoldering doublet, then reached into the inner pocket to pluck out his grandfather's pipe lighter. He swore as the hot metal burned his fingers, dropping the lighter on top of his bedroll, which also began to smolder as the salamandre inside popped out and began spreading its flames. Harbalorio yelled and began smacking at the elemental, which easily danced out of the way of his hands, cackling with glee.

Birnardus, sleeping on his other side, woke up, assessed the situation, and poured the remnants of a bottle of wine over the salamandre, which hissed as its flames and its life were extinguished.

"Can we go back to sleep now?" he groused.

Just then, the earth began to shake, and all thoughts of sleep were abandoned.

Chapter Thirty-One
Trionn-Fī

The Headquarters of the Psychidion Mages—Seven Years Ago

Keth had never fit in with his fellow apprentices. Tonight made that abundantly clear.

They came for him as he slept in their shared apprentice's dormitory room, four of the biggest and cruelest boys. They first woke him with a punch to his gut, and then, as he gasped for breath, two of the boys held him down as a third balled up a sock and stuffed it in his mouth before he could speak a spell or cry for help.

"Lift up his head!" their leader hissed. It was Bailes, a steely-eyed, ferret-faced bully, known for his inventive torments.

His henchmen did as he said. Bailes then held up a wineglass—something moved inside it.

"We have a present for you, Keth," he crooned. "Wanna see it? C'mere, take a look." He snapped his finger and summoned a were-light—no bigger than a firefly—that hovered above them so that Keth could appreciate his gift. Keth's eyes widened in fear.

Inside the glass was a bane-spider, its hairy, crimson-speckled body about as long as Keth's thumb. Its bristly legs scuttled madly as it struggled to find purchase on the tall glass sides of its prison.

"Look closer!" Bailes said with an ugly smile. He grabbed the back of Keth's head, forcing it down so he could jam the glass up against Keth's face. The spider hissed and reared up, hitting the glass as it struck at Keth's open eye.

"Oh, she doesn't like you, Keth—or maybe she does. Maybe she wants to lay her eggs in the corner of your eye!"

The other boys chuckled, tightening their grips as Keth struggled madly to free himself.

"Careful, Keth!" Bailes said, shaking the glass to agitate the arachnid further. "If you make me spill, I might accidentally dump it right smack on your eyeball. Have you ever been bitten by a bane-spider? Augh! It burns for weeks—if it doesn't kill you!"

As he spoke, he very slowly tipped the glass toward Keth, driving the spider crazy. "I can't imagine how much it would hurt if you got bitten on your *eye*—can you?" Then he upturned the glass.

Keth screamed through the gag, but their hold on him was tight as the spider scrambled and hissed on the surface of his eye.

A bolt of blue came out of the dark, dashing the wineglass away from his face to shatter on the far wall and sending the spider to the floor. Then a quartet of violet streams snaked out next, each snatching up one of Keth's tormentors, leaving them dangling off the ground as they squirmed helplessly. A robed and bearded figure stepped into the little circle of were-light, his eyes glowering. The rank on the collar of his cowl was that of an archmage.

Without a word, he raised his hands, then slowly lowered his left hand, palm down, while raising his right, palm up. As he did so, Bailes and his minions shrank until they were the size of dolls—while the bane-spider grew until its bristling body was the size of a dire wolf.

"Come," he said to Keth, and the two departed, leaving the situation in the room to sort itself out.

"Thank you for saving me, Master," Keth said as they walked quickly through the corridors of their faction's guildhall. "But—will the other boys be all right?"

Master Hallam gave a little snort in reply. "Who knows? Banespiders cocoon their prey before they settle in to consume them. I expect they'll be fine at least till morning. Perhaps longer if someone finds them in time." He clapped his apprentice on the back. "But don't worry yourself about those juicy little grubworms. Let their masters deal with it. Come."

Hallam led Keth down the hall and into the stairwell.

"Where are we going?"

"*You* are getting into a carriage and slipping out of the capital. *I* am going into exile."

"What? But … I don't understand. What's happened?"

"What's happened is, as the strategists call it, a coup d'état. Our esteemed colleague Master Málach—I suppose it will be *Lord* Málach, now—has pulled off a most impressive feat. He has managed to condemn my research as 'vile, reckless, and dangerous'—while simultaneously taking credit for all its accomplishments. He will be the next leader of the Psychidions—assuming that he isn't already. How did such an untalented weasel ever become a mage? His true calling is as a politician."

They emerged in one of the back corridors of the guildhall. Hallam looked both ways to make sure no one was observing them, and then the two slipped out onto the grounds and out a back gate. In the alley behind, a small, closed carriage awaited.

"Get in," Hallam instructed. "Inside there are books to continue your education."

"But Master, what will happen to you?"

"Don't worry. They can't afford to *kill* me; they still need me—or they won't understand what in blazes they've stolen!" He let out a short, barking laugh. “No, it’s to be exile for me. Not too far, mind you—you know what they say, keep your friends close and your enemies closer—so they’ve petitioned the Emperor to send me into house arrest in the old astronomical observatory out in the ruins of the old city. Which he most certainly will agree to. They say it’s haunted, which means I’ll be just fine.”

“So … I’m to meet you there?”

“As far as anyone else will know, that’s the story. You will be in exile along with me—but, in fact, you are going back home.”

“What? But I can’t go back to Athamé!”

“There’s no other choice. It’s no longer safe for you in Trionn-Fí, not with our guild, or any other faction. I can’t send you to a *civilized* province. No, it’s got to be back to that barbaric cultural backwater that spawned you. You’ll be safe there.”

“But … but I’ll be miserable there.” The words sounded pathetic to Keth even as he uttered them. He stared at his master, hoping against hope he’d change his mind.

“Miserable, but safe,” Hallam replied, unmoved. “Go home to your father’s estate. I’ll send word when—*if*—it’s safe to return. Until then, you stay where I can find you—and, with any luck, where no one else can. Take this,” he said, handing over a purse. “This should be more than enough to get you there with some left over, if you’re careful.”

“But … but what will I do?”

“Do? You’ll continue your studies, of course. You’re very fortunate. Take full advantage of your misery and dismal environs to avoid distraction and improve upon your craft. Now get in and go! Before it’s too late!”

Upon a tall slant of rock outcropping, Keth sat quietly surveying the family cattle and any passing cranes winging their way overhead. Five years had passed since he returned to his father’s estate in Athamé, and his best place for uninterrupted study and meditation was here atop his own personal sanctuary, where he came every day after his chores were done and stayed until after the sun set.

The bloodred sun was sinking into the horizon when their hired hand rode back from the postal station in town with the mail. The rider held up a parcel and waved it to let Keth know it was for him.

Surprised and pleased, Keth wiped the sweat off his brow and quickly scrambled down to meet him on the dirt road. He thanked the man for delivering the plain little bundle wrapped in cheap hemp cloth and leather lacing.

On the family dinner table, Keth sliced through the leather cord and unwrapped the bundle to reveal a folded letter on heavy parchment, and a cylindrical traveling case of dark-colored boiled leather, like a map case. He opened the letter and whistled up a hovering were-light to read it by.

It was from his master Hallam, written by his own hand in that unique florid and serpentine script of his. Keth had long grown familiar with it, and yet he was having trouble reading this particular letter. The handwriting seemed more scrawled than usual, as if it were written by a trembling hand or in the midst of great distress.

Keth frowned, puzzling through the message. Though he could make out the words of the text, its content was bizarre and nonsensical, speaking in riddles and curious non sequiturs. Trying to understand what it actually meant with its talk of his master's experiments, membranes between worlds, intrigue and skulduggery among the *Psychidions* ... it made his head hurt.

The letter urged him to leave at once, and ended, curiously enough, with talk of first things first, and with cryptic utterances—*Know this: recognize an X ... signaling numbers or words* ... and mentions of dreams and nightmares. He put down the letter and sat back in his chair, rubbing his eyes. Reading it all the way to the end left him shaking and disturbed. Only one thing in the entire message was perfectly clear—he had to leave immediately and bring this mysterious case with him.

He turned and looked at the leather case where it stood upright on the table, its lid lying next to it. Strange—he couldn't remember unbuckling the lid's clasps. A green glow emanated up from the case's interior, radiating brighter even as he watched. At the same time, the rest of the room darkened, the green glow the only light to be had.

Standing, Keth approached the case, feeling the light bathe his face as he leaned over to peer inside. The interior appeared to be no more than a churning cauldron of eerie green vapors, and yet he felt compelled to reach his hand in to pull out whatever was inside. His fingers closed on something solid, deep inside the case, deeper, he thought, than the depth of the case itself.

He pulled it out.

His eyes widened in horror as he stared at the thing in his hands, and then he knew with an inexplicable certainty that he had to get out of there *now*—he had to run, and not stop running until he was across the continent. When he tried, though, his movements felt suddenly sluggish, as if he were trying to move his limbs underwater. Every fiber of his being wanted to back away from the case, wanted to drop the thing he held, but he couldn't. His feet were rooted to the floor.

"I have to go," he said to nobody. "You have to let me go."

"You haven't left yet?" roared the booming voice of his master, though Keth couldn't see him. He tried to explain, but his vocal cords seized up.

He looked upward. There was no house anymore, just a sickly green sun overhead in a pallid sky.

"Run," Hallam commanded him. *"Run!"*

But he only stood there.

"Run! Before it's too late … *It's too late … too late …"*

Chapter Thirty-Two
Athamē Border

THE MOUNTAIN INN

It's too late.

Keth's eyelids flew open and he sat bolt upright on his straw tick, a wool blanket pooling around his waist. It was still dark in the common room—the shutters were closed, and the only light came from the banked-ember glow of the slumbering salamandre in the fireplace.

It's too late.

Keth sat there for a moment, letting the sounds of the communal dormitory—snores, blankets rustling, and an occasional muffled fart—dissipate the dream and ground him in the here and now. Reaching out, he made sure the map case was still at his side, the strap around his shoulder. The familiar feel of the boiled leather reassured him—

—until he remembered what it held.

Too late.

Before Keth could begin to decipher his dream, a wave of dizziness overtook him. He put his fingers to his temples and lay back down on the straw, but the sensation did not go away. It got worse—the floor beneath him lurched. Once. Twice. And then it kept shaking. The room around him woke up—screams and cries of alarm, the sound of crockery breaking, and the more disturbing noise of earth rumbling as the cliff in back of the inn began to crumble.

Even with his aching head covered by his arms, a sudden brightness caught his eye. Keth looked over to see the salamandre risen to its full height again, exultant, as if stimulated by all the commotion. Were-lights swarmed about freely, like fireflies.

Then the flaming giant took a step out of the fireplace, the planks of the common room's wooden floors smoking beneath its tread. Keth could see what passed for its eyes staring at him with a frightening intensity.

Then it crouched down and reached out for him, taking him by surprise.

There was no time to utter a word as Keth rolled out of the way of its grasping limbs. It missed him and caught his straw bedding instead, which ignited like a funeral pyre. Still on the floor, Keth raised a hand and shouted a sorcerous command for it to stop.

"Khozkha Khuhrahr!"

The fire elemental instantly knelt in obedience—only to then leap into the air, launching itself at him in a fury. Without thinking, Keth dove to the side as the salamandre crashed down beside him, and then rolled again under the momentary cover of a table. The flame spirit chased after him, battering aside the bench and table to either side. Without cover now, Keth quickly rose to his feet and spoke the elemental death-spell.

"Tshadhaefhahrjizack!"

He watched in shock as, in answer, the salamandre grabbed up the long wooden bench with ease and held it overhead in triumph. It smoldered in its grasp, blackened, and then burst into flame. With a roar, it flung the burning length at Keth. He ducked barely in time—it flew over him and smashed into the wall behind the bar in a hail of sparks and flames.

Shouts of terror from the rest of the now-awakened sleepers in the common room only fueled the thing's rage. Distracted by the shrieks of an unlucky traveler who was too close to get away, the fire spirit scooped the man up—straw mattress, blankets, and all—and bear-hugged him, making a bonfire of the man in an instant. The salamandre seemed to relish the man's quickly roasting flesh, like a pagan god accepting the sacrifice of a burnt offering.

While everyone else ran for the front door, Keth had no choice but to keep backing away from his pursuer and sprint into the kitchen. A second fire elemental crouched in the firepit, hungrily bent over and consuming the side of pork that earlier it had been roasting on the spit. Without any hesitation, the mage ran up to the cauldron of cold stew hanging there and upended it upon the ravenous salamandre. The creature scarcely had time to notice Keth's arrival before being unceremoniously extinguished.

An inhuman roar came from behind him—the first salamandre had followed Keth into the kitchen and witnessed his abrupt pyrocide. Keth looked about quickly—the only way in or out was the doorway blocked by the elemental itself. No escape.

He quickly shifted behind the brick island housing the firepit—the elemental would have to choose one side or the other to reach him—and prepared to bolt for the door in whichever direction the salamandre didn't take. Perhaps it could read minds—instead of picking a single approach, it split itself in two, blocking both possible escape routes and closing in on him from either side. He backed away warily, desperately looking for a weapon or at least some kind of barrier or shield but seeing only knives, pots and pans, and baskets of produce.

His twin stalkers flowed toward him, gliding along the floor as smoothly as phantoms. They made a curious crackling sound that might have served them as mocking laughter. He backed further, realizing as he did so that he was cornering himself. And then he could go no further. His back hit something solid, heavy and wooden—a tub.

Turning around in a flash, he took hold of the tub with both hands and dumped it out—dirty dishes, dishwater, and all—and sent the whole mess spilling across the floor, dishes breaking into a clattering frenzy of bits, while the dishwater washed across the kitchen's stone floor in a wave. What would have been a mere annoyance to a cook was a nightmare to the fire elementals. They screamed in fear—an inhuman sound—and sank into the drenched floor as if it were quicksand, drowning in a puff of steam.

Only then did Keth have the luxury to acknowledge the void inside him where magic used to live.

Chapter Thirty-Three
Trionn-Fī

THE INNER CITY AQUEDUCT

Magpie stared over the edge of the aqueduct, fighting vertigo as he looked down at the crumpled bodies of his would-be killers in the rose garden a hundred feet below. He didn't linger, though, wasting no time fleeing from his precarious perch and returning through the maintenance shed to retrace his steps into the upper city.

As he paused briefly to catch his breath, a shadow darkened the whole city block. But only for an instant. He and everyone else in the street glanced up to see an entire imperial warship come whistling down from the sky and vanish behind the nearest towers.

The roaring, splintering boom that followed a heartbeat later was as terrifying as it was thunderous. Screams rose along with a dirty gray plume of dust and debris as it crashed somewhere down the hill. The street suddenly buckled, and the jolt sent Magpie and countless others sprawling headfirst onto the cobblestones.

Groaning, he picked himself up, bruised, bleeding, and reeling, and staggered to his feet again. Magpie's vision was as wobbly as his legs—all the buildings on this block seemed to quiver from the impact, as if they had magically turned to pudding. Further above, even the colossal ring of walls and buildings that formed the palatial estate's giant crown were trembling.

When he finally realized what was happening, the horror of it almost brought him to his knees—all around him, those exotic buildings and towers most dependent upon sorcery to bolster and support their incredible feats of impossible architecture were coming apart before his eyes.

Suddenly, crumbling pieces of masonry were bouncing and rolling into the boulevard in choking clouds of grit and dust, rumbling toward him and the other street-goers in a flood of ruin. His pain forgotten, Magpie ran down the street away from the oncoming destruction, faster than he had ever run from any mortal pursuer.

The tide of wreckage washing down the streets was deafening. Those who could not get back to their feet or run swiftly enough were overwhelmed and crushed. Magpie dared not look back. New obstacles fell into his path on all sides. Toppling stone pillars crushed three fleeing men in front of him like hammers.

Eyes half blinded by tears and dust, lungs aching, he raced down the sharply inclined street as others slipped and fell beside him. He didn't dare stop to try and help, only ran and dodged—and ran—and dodged—and leaped over obstacles.

Some of those obstacles were human.

He dodged a chunk of falling debris, only to then have to do a crazy jig to miss being crushed by another, and then had to sprint again to avoid a toppling marble statue of some ancient king. The white titan seemed to be imploring him, reaching with an outstretched hand as it toppled over and cut off the screams of those caught beneath it.

Panic sank claws into his chest at every step. A boulder-sized segment of roofing came slamming down on the boulevard on an erratic, random trajectory. With almost perverse timing and accuracy, it rolled over a frantic woman running beside him.

More by blind, stupid luck than anything else, Magpie stumbled to the side and fell with a painful thud into what remained of a doorway's rugged stone arch. He clung to the cold stones while the deluge of ruin and debris rolled on down the slope of the street, leaving crushed corpses and pooling blood in its wake.

Huddling under the shelter of the sturdy arch, Magpie covered his head and struggled to catch his breath again. The air was still full of dust, but once the worst of the rubble landslide had finally subsided, he shaded his eyes with one hand and tried to get his bearings. From the bottom of the walls surrounding the palatial estate—the highest point of the capital—he had run all the way downhill to Crown Province Park in the Inner City.

Chaos reigned—blood-soaked corpses and debris littered the length of the thoroughfare as far as he could see. Ragged crowds fled for their lives, but there was no safety, no matter which direction they ran. The falling sky had turned the color of doom. Wailing with maniacal laughter, vengeful sylphs coursed by overhead, reveling in the destruction.

Over the unending chorus of screams and cries rising up from the city—audible even above the bone-rattling crash of falling walls and bridges and the moaning, shuddering, yawning collapsing of mansions, castles, and towers—came an even more devastating sound.

Bombardment.

As if the Gods had emptied their dustbins upon the world, everything littering the heavens rained down on the heads of the damned. The empire's proud aerial armada was reduced to wooden shooting stars, bits of sky-wrack, and falling bodies—a man-made hailstorm hammering the earth in an unrelenting drumbeat of calamity.

All across the sky Magpie could see the armada streaking to the ground. The rain of falling ships seemed endless and pulverized anything caught in their fatal path. One impact at a time, a proud city of a million souls was flattened into smoking rubble, miles of surrounding environs transformed into an archipelago of craters.

A small, whistling missile of some kind streaked down from above and ricocheted off Magpie's arch, startling him. Two more rapidly followed, prompting him to huddle closer against the stones and cover his head with his arms, although he still kept watch for more surprise threats coming from above. Then he saw them.

At first Magpie could not identify the strange, bright colors dropping from the sky. As they drew nearer to the ground, he could make out a mix of fireballs and other pinwheeling shapes that reflected the light like metal or glass. Then, just before they touched down, he saw them for what they were—undines and salamandrae.

The hapless, tumbling undines in more or less human form struck the surface first, each one splattering on the pavement. Some of the scattered drops wound around the cobblestones in a hundred tiny rivulets striving valiantly to recombine, while others were too far gone and simply became wet spots.

Their salamandrae rivals, however, were better equipped for flight and landing. They touched down gently and immediately went searching for victims to incinerate or greenery to feast upon.

Time to move again, Magpie thought, laying low and trying to remain as inconspicuous as possible while the fire elementals torched whatever—and whoever—they could get their flaming hands on. When the closest gang of them ran off toward the palace in search of more fun, Magpie scrambled from his refuge and ran in the other direction.

He hugged the sides of the road, avoiding the open spaces and carefully, desperately, slunk quickly from cover to cover—which was how he tripped over the young girl hiding amid the rubble.

She shrieked in pain as he fell on her, and Magpie quickly clapped his hand over her mouth. "Don't scream!" he hissed into her ear. "They'll hear us! Do you understand?" Terrified, she nodded, breathing hard to suck in her pain.

Magpie looked around to see if anyone had heard, but thankfully her cry appeared to have been lost among the din. He removed his hand and stared at her.

What am I going to do with a little brat in tow?

The girl looked to be about ten years old, her tow-haired curls and face covered in dust except for where the tracks of tears wet her cheeks. Would she be able to keep up with him, or would she just get them both killed? He peered up and down the street. Small fires were burning all around, and from nearby came a paroxysm of screams and laughter. For the moment, however, no one was in immediate sight.

"Come on, we can't stay here."

"I can't move," she said, her voice quavering in pain and fear. Magpie looked down and muttered a curse under his breath. She was pinned under a gigantic mermaid's split torso, as thick as a heavy log—part of a warship's figurehead that had crashed into the nearest mansion and brought down half the building with it. She looked up at him, a despairing look in wide brown eyes shimmering with tears. "Please help me."

He covered his mouth and exhaled thoughtfully, silently shaking his head while he pondered what to do. Ominous noises sounded nearby, too close for his comfort, and he made his decision.

"I'm sorry, I can't. I'm sorry."

She stared up at him in incredulous horror. *"You're going to leave me?"*

He couldn't meet the girl's eyes.

"I'm so sorry," he whispered.

And then he was gone.

He'll come back, Lally promised herself, listening to the sound of crashing airships—some in the distance, some dangerously close. *I know he will.* In every direction, pillars of dust were rising above the city. She simply couldn't believe that the man had just abandoned her, that he wouldn't come right back for her. Or, if not him, surely someone …

Someone will come. Someone will.

She kept telling herself that, trying to ignore the crushing pain that kept her trapped.

Someone will come.

Chapter Thirty-Four

Above Trionn-Fí

From a thousand feet in the air, Trionn-Fí and the verdant lands surrounding it were quickly becoming what looked like the remains of a campfire—one that a madman had put out in a frenzy, by stabbing and battering it viciously with a poker, then scattering its embers to the four winds.

Exhilarated, the rebelling sylphs continued to sweep the pristine sky of human filth—they weren't merely drunk on their newfound freedom, or even understandably out for vengeance; it was that the same force that had broken their sorcerous constraints had also driven them mad.

On the underside of the stricken *Spirit of Tarocchi*, the air elementals were deserting the ship en masse, pouring from the sylph-locks and flowing out into the winds. Then, when enough of the locks were abandoned, came one final, irrevocable instant when the balance between the miraculous and the catastrophic was crossed, and the great city-ship plunged forward into a nosedive.

The *Tarocchi* stretched five hundred feet from stem to stern, longer than the height of any tower in the capital city. To all the upturned heads in the city below, caught under its shadow, it looked as if the tallest of buildings had been upended and cast down at them like a spear. Some at the edge of the growing shadow tried to flee for their lives. Others, paralyzed by the realization that escape was impossible, could not take their eyes off the looming juggernaut directly above them.

Thousands of streaming sylphs swirled and chased after the plummeting flagship with glee, fascinated by all the thousands of marvelous things falling from it—smoke, rigging, ropes, tools, nails, and so many screaming humans. They dove alongside, close enough to the doomed crew members to see the terrified expressions on their faces. Some of the more daring elementals dipped close enough to snatch up falling sailors to torment further before dropping them to their deaths.

Then, from what had started as a nosedive, the ship began to tilt end over end. So it was upside down and at an angle when it touched down at last, the bow half striking in the lower city while the stern spilled out into the outermost ring of the Grand Canal. The thundering crash of its impact was more deafening than anything yet heard in the morning's bombardment of Trionn-Fí.

Dozens of buildings were obliterated instantly, along with everyone within them, while in the streets and docks, crowds of refugees trying to flee the city were mashed beyond recognition. In the Grand Canal, the *Tarocchi*'s stern crashed down like a giant's club, throwing up waves that spilled over both banks and reached as high as the tallest tenement buildings. The surge of water inundated the eastern edge of the outer city. The torrent funneled through the twisty, narrow streets, washing away anything not bolted down and drowning everyone in its path for blocks.

Chapter Thirty-Five
Trionn-Fī

THE INNER CITY

Still pinned, Lally lay and watched in mute horror as the *Tarocchi* dropped from the sky and crashed in the distance with a thundering impact that made the earth shudder. But she had other terrors closer at hand.

Don't scream. You can't scream.

Through half-closed eyes, she could see a trio of rogue salamandrae stalking through the rubble-choked street, in search of people to burn. *Don't scream,* Lally told herself again, her cheeks wet with tears. *The salamandrae'll hear you.* The flame spirits were taking their time, methodically poking through any likely hiding places. And they were coming her way.

She strained to wriggle out from under the ship's figurehead that pinned her, but that only chewed up her legs further against the grinding, unforgiving bits of broken brick and gravel. Growing more desperate, she pushed against the mermaid's hardwood torso and then it did move—but it shifted the wrong way, and the sudden burst of stabbing pain made her cry out.

Lally bit her hand to stifle her shriek, but the damage was done. *Don't cry,* Lally told herself, her cheeks wet with tears. *If you cry, you won't be able to stop. And then they'll hear you, and then they'll catch you, and then they'll roast you like a pig.* Through the dust in the air, she could see the approaching salamandrae's reflected firelight glazing the rubble around her. They were close enough now that she could already feel the warmth coming off them.

Play dead.

Already half buried under rubble and covered in dust, she fought to hold her breath, to stop her trembling, and resist the impulse to sniffle. *Play dead.* She made a rag doll of herself, sinking into the pile of rubble, hoping against hope she could blend in and they would pass her by. But between her heart's wild thumping and the struggle to breathe through the dust and ash without attracting attention, she was afraid it was impossible.

As if reading her mind, the closest salamandre suddenly snapped its gaze on her. She froze.

Play dead.

The fire elemental seemed to sniff the air, keenly interested in its fresh discovery. It headed straight for her.

Lally held her breath as the salamandre drew close, looming over her. It placed its hands on the figurehead and peered down. She kept her eyelids half open, the way she did when pretending to nap to fool her little brother. From the corner of her eye, she could tell it was looking directly at her. *Don't look at it. Play dead. Be stone. Be a limp dishrag. Play dead.*

It was torture to remain unmoving, desperately hoping the reflection of flames in her eyes didn't give her away. The salamandre made a curious, pleased noise, and suddenly the scent of smoke and burning timber tickled Lally's nostrils. The elemental had stretched out its billowing arms and laid its head against the giant wooden mermaid's scalloped fishtail, and was happily consuming its oaken deliciousness.

Its two companions noticed it was feasting without them and flowed up to join in alongside the first. Sparks rose and crackled as they dug into their meal. The heat from just one elemental had been bad enough—with three of them feeding, it was unbearable, and rapidly turning into a bonfire. Lally tried to stay calm, to stay still, but inside she was in pure panic—she was going to burn to death whether they discovered her or not.

Please! Please don't let me burn to death here, she prayed to the Sun, the Moon, and the Guiding Star. The heat from the blazing wood atop her was so unbearable she couldn't stop the tears or contain her small mews of anguish.

The salamandrae looked up from their meal briefly but didn't notice the girl trapped beneath their noses and went back to their meal.

A few moments later, however, the ground shook again, a single massive jolt that forced an involuntary cry from Lally. The elementals once more stopped feeding—and this time all three saw the captive girl beneath them, laid out like a sacrificial offering. All three let out bloodcurdling howls of triumph, and Lally screamed as they abandoned their meal of wood and eagerly surrounded this living prey with hoots of crackling, cackling laughter. They bent over her and Lally screamed again, wailing in pain and terror.

The sound of her wail seemed to disturb the trio, causing their flaming bodies to waver and flutter anxiously. Then she felt the earth start to shake again and realized it wasn't her scream that had rattled them.

The salamandrae stood in confusion as the cobblestones rumbled, and then shook in earnest as the tremor grew stronger and more violent. The ship's figurehead shifted, and Lally screamed a third time. Simultaneously the building behind them at last collapsed entirely with an ear-numbing roar. The fire elementals backed away from her in fear, and then as fast as they could, fled for their lives from this powerful banshee.

Just as suddenly, the juddering street calmed once more. Overwhelmed, Lally lay her head on the rubble and finally gave herself over to her pain and grief, her sobs flowing out of her like water. *Let the salamandrae think I'm a banshee. I'll drown them in my tears.*

There was a sound of movement coming up from somewhere behind her. All her bravado vanished, and she caught her breath, playing dead again as she listened intently. She heard footsteps on a pile of rubble, and as they came closer, she could only pray they were human.

Someone knelt by her side and she cracked open her eyes as narrowly as she dared. It was the same man who'd stumbled over her and then left her to her fate. "You came back," she said weakly as he set about moving what was left of the smoldering figurehead off her.

Taking care to avoid the hottest patches that had been left blackened and reduced to glowing embers under the hungry salamandrae's touch, he carefully took position, muttering under his breath as he exerted himself. "Stupid." Shove. "Sentimental." Another shove as he strained to lift it. "Idiot!" With one last push, he managed to toss the burned figurehead aside. Then he knelt by Lally's side, poking and prodding her legs gently to see how badly she was hurt.

"I don't think anything's broken. Can you stand?" he asked.

"I … I think so."

He put an arm around her and carefully helped her to her feet. It hurt but she could do it.

There was another rumble, this one deeper, more ominous, as if it came from the bowels of the city. The man swiftly picked her up. "Hold on," he ordered, and Lally obeyed, wrapping her arms around his neck.

What was left of the remaining buildings crashed down around them as he ran a gauntlet of destruction, Lally clinging to him with desperate strength. Walls toppled, spilling bricks and rubble in front of them, turning their escape route into both a maze and an obstacle course. Even the streets themselves were cracking open, fissures splintering into existence that gave her rescuer a split second to leap across as they continued to widen. Lally closed her eyes tight against the erupting chaos and held on, waiting for the moment when he mistimed his steps and they were lost in one of the crevasses or smashed by falling masonry.

But they cleared the hazardous streets and reached the open ground of what had been a park, and both collapsed on the grass, out of breath. The earth was still rumbling, but here at least they were in no danger of a building falling on them—as long as no new chasms opened up and swallowed them.

At last the tremors stopped and Lally looked around her, realizing her rescuer had brought her back to Crown Province Park.

The once beautiful park was now a battlefield, strewn with the dead. A few feet away was the fountain where the undines had slaughtered her brother. The elementals were nowhere in sight, but somewhere …

Pax is here.

She avoided looking at any of the corpses around them.

Instead, she turned to the stranger who had saved her life. He lay on the grass, eyes closed and breathing heavily as he tried to catch his breath.

"Thank you for coming back," she said quietly. "My name is Lally."

He nodded. "My pleasure."

"Who are you?"

At that he opened his eyes. He gave her a curious look and paused a long while before answering. "You can call me Magpie."

Lally was going to ask him why he was named after a bird, but her attention was caught by a glimmer of blue on the lawn next to her. Picking up the tiny azure shard, she realized there were hundreds of thousands of them littering the ground. She craned her neck toward the great rocky hill of the palatial estate looming over them, at the giant crown formed by the walls and buildings atop it. The jewel of the Aurichalcum Tower, however, was destroyed, reduced to countless blue shards.

Then something even worse caught her eye, and she gasped in such horror that Magpie sat up. "What is it?"

Wordlessly, Lally pointed.

The very hill itself, the heart of the capital, was *sinking*. The two watched in numb disbelief as the earth groaned one last time, allowing for one final dark miracle to play out before their eyes. It was as if the giant crown had grown too heavy for the earth to hold it aloft any longer, or the roots of its mountainous foundation far below had somehow been reduced to quicksand.

The entire towering center of the city slowly and inexorably descended—down, down, down, like the humped back of a great whale submerging into the deep—until the mount was a no more than a knoll, just higher than the ground they lay on. Then the crown itself was level with the park. And still it sank lower.

Crying out in fear, Magpie flung an arm around Lally and braced the two of them as the ground they crouched upon suddenly started to bend and bow beneath them. The palace complex continued to sink, dragging the entire inner city along as it collapsed into the depths of the earth, turning what had been the upper heights of the capital inside out, transforming a summit into a sinkhole.

And it was taking them with it.

Chapter Thirty-Six
Arcanum

THE ISLE OF CHTHON—ORACLE SCHOOL

Kneeling, Casander frantically pulled at the ruined parchment roll until he had unrolled it completely, nesting himself in its entire crumpled blackened length. He sat there, shuddering and weeping, inconsolable. Eluned did nothing but sit at the desk, unmoved and unmoving.

His most dire of fears had come true. His friend and mentor had gone mad, and whatever vital secret she had uncovered was lost forever. Everything was lost.

The room began to spin, and he suddenly felt as though he was going to faint. He propped himself up with both hands to support himself until it passed. As it did, he could hear a strange noise coming from the tower windows—high-pitched, whining, banshee wails. As if he were sleepwalking, he found himself drawn to it and went to the window to see more.

Outside, with the perfect clarity of a nightmare, he saw the *Arrow* spiraling upward into the sky. Then, like the movement of a giant sewing needle pulling thread, it paused, dipped, and reversed course. It rolled as it plunged down, falling at a sharp angle. Transfixed, Casander could only stare, numbly taking in the laughing sylphs pulling the flier to its doom, and the trajectory they chose—they were riding it straight toward him.

Like a statue, he locked eyes with its screaming pilot as the air elementals drove the vessel like its namesake into the tower. It impacted just a floor below them, and the building shook with a sudden jolt that threw both Casander and Eluned to the floor along with everything on the shelves and desktops.

For a minute, he thought the shaking tower might collapse entirely, but then the movement settled again. He looked over to the Seeress. She lay on the floor, but her eyes were open and she was calling for him. He leaned over, straining to hear her whispers.

"Casander … It has come."

"Seeress? What has come?" She struggled to get the words out.

"The last … vision. Listen now."

Doomed, doomed is Arcanum
The time of magic goes away
The time of monsters returns

The riches of poor Pentaclys are spent
Undines tear apart the merchant fleet
Gold, goods, and sailors all sink to the depths
The canals are choked with the dead
Once fine white marble palaces
Now but ruins, stained with blood

The horses run wild in Beauchalice
There is no joy, no song, no food, no drink
The fields and vineyards
become swamps and murk
Home to monsters
and heir to nightmares

Rejoice, warriors of Athamé
The Emperor is dead and
peace is in pieces
So shall you have your fill
of bloody battle unceasing
—and more than your fill …

Wand, Coin, Cup, and Sword
Tarou dies from cancer
Death rains down on Trionn-Fí
The Gods are driven mad
Nature is raped and births monsters
One becomes many
Five becomes four
Wand, Coin, Cup, and Sword …

As she spoke the last verse, her voice warbled into a low moan, growing steadily louder until it reached an ululating scream so piercing that Casander clutched his hands over his ears. She looked up at him and he, too, screamed as her eyes began to glow with an unearthly green light that quickly grew painfully bright—until they became twin green flames, flaring as her eyes burned and then melted in their sockets.

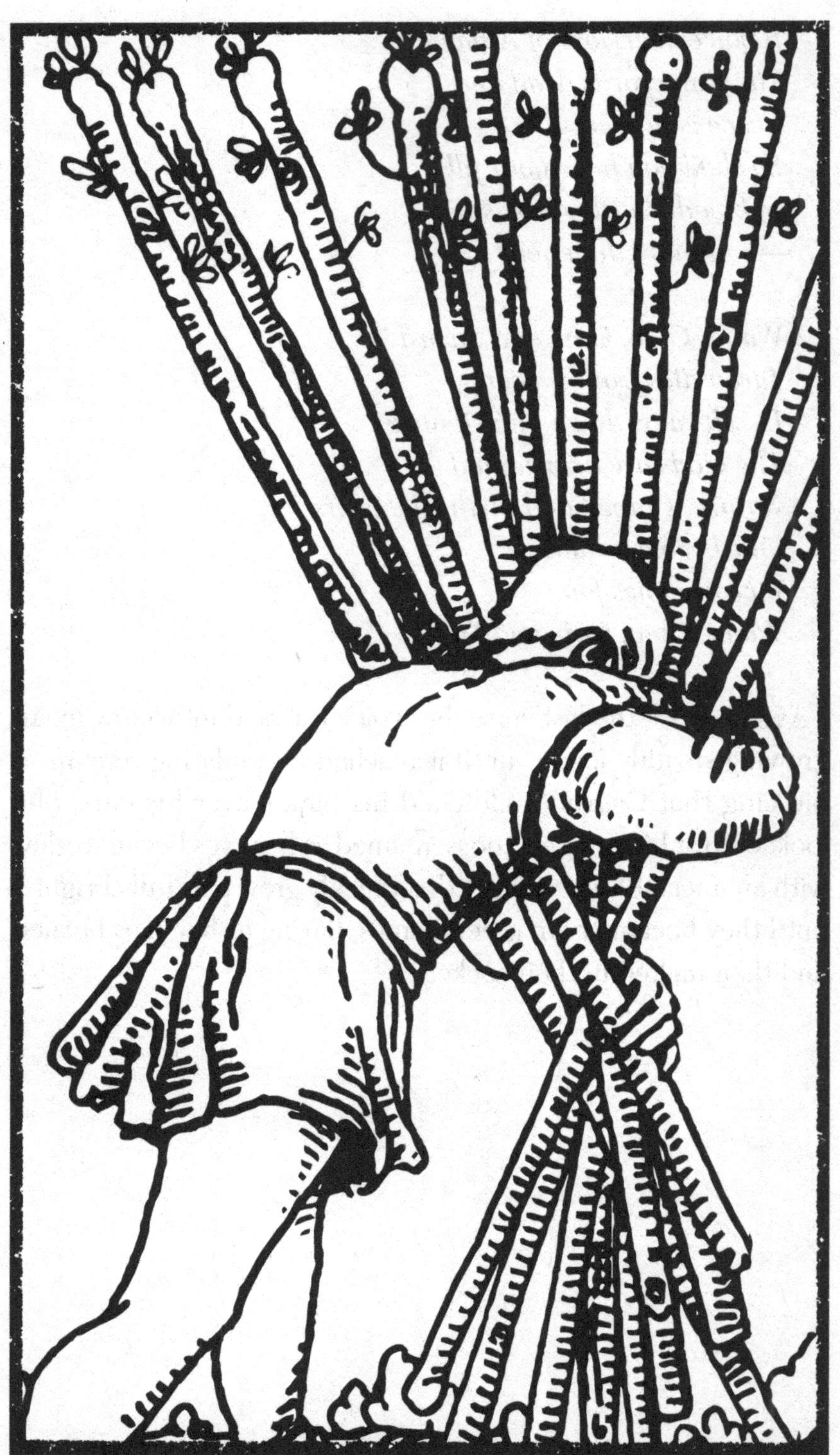

Chapter Thirty-Seven
Athamēan Border

The Mountain Inn

Scooting carefully out from under the bed, Alia pushed herself up on hands and knees and coughed until her throat was raw, spitting out phlegm the color of the walls ... but at least she could breathe again. Her eyes stung and tears poured out. She crawled over to the dresser, pulled herself up to a standing position. The washbasin and pitcher had miraculously stayed on the vanity—a miracle of sorts, she supposed. Pouring water into the basin, she splashed it into her eyes until the stinging subsided and she could once again see clearly. Then she made her way to the room's single window that overlooked the front of the inn, opened the shutters to reveal a broken pane, and looked outside.

Dawn had broken, and watery daylight filtered through yet more dust. Part of the hillside had shaken free in the quake—rocks, chunks of earth, and foliage littering the ground between the inn and stables, from which drifted the sound of frightened neighing. There was commotion going on downstairs. People were running into the courtyard, their faces numb with shock. One of them—the golden-haired Pentan—had a cut across his forehead, blood streaming down his face and soaking into the collar of his doublet, where it blended into the crimson velvet.

As she watched, Raff came out of the stables, Dari behind him. They looked shaken but uninjured. Raff glanced up, saw Alia in the window, and waved. She gave him a thumbs-up so he'd know she was unscathed and ducked back inside to get dressed and join her friends.

As she buckled her sword belt around her waist, however, she remembered that she was not the only person with a room on the third floor.

Callan.

Callan wasn't in his room, which hadn't seen as much damage as hers during the quake. A few chunks of plaster had dislodged from the walls and his dresser lay on its side. His nightshirt lay crumpled on the floor and there was no sign of his boots—Alia surmised he must have gotten dressed and gone downstairs. She tried to ignore the sharp stab of hurt when she realized he hadn't bothered to check on her.

But she still felt it.

She left Callan's room and made her way to the stairs. Surprisingly, they were mostly intact—slightly warped here and there, but they looked safe enough. Still, she trod carefully, keeping to the side, hugging the wall and using the banister for safety until she reached the second-floor landing, which had buckled up in the center. There she paused, using the tip of her sheathed sword to test the floor's structural integrity.

"Hello ... ?"

A tremulous voice came from the hallway. Alia left Callan's room, following the sound a few doors down. Jezel stood in the doorway of her room, plaster dust and blood marring her otherwise porcelain complexion. Hair askew, fallen from its neatly styled curls. She was still in her nightgown, yards of frothy oyster-colored silk and lace. Swallowing unwanted bile, Alia went to her side, putting an arm around the shaken woman.

"Are you injured?"

Jezel looked at her, gaze unfocused. "I … I don't think so … ?"

Guiding Jezel back into her room, Alia sat her on the bed so she could see where the blood on the woman's face came from. It was just a shallow cut in her hairline above the forehead—a lot of blood but nothing to worry about.

Alia said as much to Jezel, blotting the blood away with a hand towel soaked in water Alia had sopped up from the floor—Jezel's pitcher and basin had not been as lucky as Alia's.

Jezel gingerly touched her forehead, wincing as her fingers found the cut. "It hurts. Will there be a scar?"

"What? No. Just a scratch. Nothing to mar your beauty. We just need to find some salve for it." Alia paused, then added, "Don't worry. There will no doubt be plenty of men in Trionn-Fí vying for your attentions." She tried her best to keep the resentment out of her voice as she finished daubing away the last of the blood.

"Disappointed?"

"No."

Jezel gave a half smile. "Liar."

"I'm not that petty," Alia snapped, tossing the towel into the basin.

"You don't have to be," Jezel replied with a sigh. "A family fortune, beauty not yet begun to ripen, and a handsome fiancé to boot. What need for pettiness?"

A groan distracted Alia before she could reply.

"Is there someone else in here?"

A pained look crossed Jezel's face. "Bellamy. My … my lady's maid. She's in there." Jezel pointed to a door on the other side of the room.

"You forgot about her?"

"N … no, I—"

Not waiting for her to finish her response, Alia crossed the room and opened the door in question. It led to a tiny chamber smelling of mildew and vomit, the latter spilling out of a chamber pot lying on its side. The room had not fared well—large chunks of plaster littered the floor and rocks had broken through the wall at the far end from the rockslide.

A girl no more than sixteen lay on a mattress, a dark blue woolen blanket pulled up to her chin, hair as fine and pale as corn silk spilling over bare shoulders. Her skin was as pale as that of her mistress, but with an unhealthy greenish tinge. Some debris from the ceiling had landed on her legs and there was some blood, but Alia couldn't tell how serious the injury might be.

The girl—Bellamy—groaned again. Alia knelt by her side.

"Are you injured?"

"I … I don't know. I'm just … I'm so thirsty …"

From the look and smell of things, Bellamy had been throwing up for hours. She needed water.

"Is she well?" Jezel sounded concerned. Enough so that Alia almost believed she might care for the fate of her lady's maid. Almost.

"I think so. But she needs liquids."

Jezel appeared in the doorway. She'd retrieved a linen handkerchief and kept it pressed against the gash on her forehead. "She was sick to her stomach when we arrived yesterday."

"And most likely was ill most of the night."

A single sharp shake rattled the building.

Gasping, face blanched, Jezel clutched the doorframe. "Is it starting again?"

Alia slowly shook her head—the earth seemed to be finished moving for the time being. "I think things were just … settling a bit." She got to her feet. "I'll go fetch some water and find someone to look at her wound and help carry her downstairs.

"I could help . . ."

Have you ever lifted anything heavier than a handkerchief?

But Alia didn't voice that thought aloud. The fact that the woman had even offered had to mean something.

"I think it's best if she stays here until it's certain it won't injure her more if she's moved. Can you stay here with her?"

Jezel nodded. "Yes."

"I'll be as quick as I can."

Most of the inn's staff and patrons had gathered in the common room, some still in their nightclothes. The scorched remains of one dead man lay on the floor, and a few other people appeared to have minor injuries—cuts and scrapes at worst—but most seemed to have escaped the earthquake at least physically unscathed. Two of the Pentans huddled together at a table, a bottle of wine in front of them. *Hair of the dog*, Alia thought.

There had been trouble with the salamandrae, the innkeeper was explaining to other customers.

She could see that. There were scorch marks all across the common-room floor, and a burned bench had apparently been thrown behind the bar. And the kitchen was a disaster. Otherwise the inn had also weathered the quake well.

With no fire burning in the large stone fireplace, the temperature was much colder than it had been the previous evening. Alia could see her breath in front of her and was glad she'd thrown on her woolen overcoat.

Alia was pleased to see that the Athamé soldiers present were fully dressed, including armor and weapons. She looked for Raff and Dari and, not finding them, assumed they were still outside checking on the horses to make sure they hadn't been spooked too badly or injured. The rest of the journey to Trionn-Fí without horses—while possible—would take at least another full day.

Callan was also missing. *No doubt checking the baggage*, Alia thought. After all, their wagons were loaded with weapons and other goods from Athamé, including a fortune's worth of emeralds and diamonds from the Irkhanan estate. What could be more important to a Pentan than that?

Certainly not the well-being of his betrothed.

Before she could dwell on this further, the front door opened to admit a gust of icy wind. Raff and Dari, both panting, blew on their hands to warm them, water dripping off their cloaks. Ignoring their sodden clothes, Alia gave them heartfelt hugs, thankful to find them uninjured.

"Still some rain but the wind has stopped trying to blow us off the road." Raff wiped moisture out of his eyes.

"Is that rain or sweat?" Alia asked.

"A little of both," Dari replied. "We've been pulling chunks of the hillside off the back of the inn, trying to shore up parts of the walls and roof that collapsed."

"There's a lot of damage to the third floor," said Alia. "Second too, but the top got it the worst. I was lucky to have a room at the front."

"As was your betrothed."

"Worse luck, that," Raff muttered. He glanced toward the kitchen. "I wonder if they've managed to get the fire started. I'd kill for some hot tea."

"I was wondering about the fireplace," Alia said, nodding at the now-cold hearth and the extent of the burn damage throughout the room. "Were the salamandrae spooked by the quake, do you think?"

Raff shrugged. "Your guess is as good as mine. But I gather it was pretty horrific. If not for the mage, the entire inn and everyone in it might be cinders by now."

"How long do you think before we can get back on the road?"

"You're not the first person to make that inquiry." By Raff's expression, Alia knew to whom he was referring. Raff looked as irritated as a cat that had just had its tail yanked.

"No more than an hour," Dari said. "About the same time we would have left if the ground hadn't decided to try and shake us off like fleas on a dog." She grinned. "Nothing like a good shaker to get people out of bed."

"Well, that's something at least. I need to take care of a few things, and then I'll be back to help sort out the wagons with you."

"Don't worry about it," Raff said. "Not too much to do beyond loading what gear we brought out last night and hitching up the horses."

Dari nodded. "We just want to finish helping put up tarps until these folks can suss it all out when the rain stops."

"You look like you could use some of this." Raff held out a flask. Alia hesitated—she hadn't had anything to eat yet. Raff waggled it in front of her. "Just a little one," he urged. "It's been a rough day already."

Giving in to temptation, Alia took a quick but satisfying slug of very good Chalicean plum brandy—her father may have been on the outs with Athamé's royal family, but he still insisted on the best for his household, and that included provisions. She enjoyed the pleasant burn as she swallowed it, then handed the flask back.

"You've seen Callan?" she asked.

Raff jerked his head toward the door. "He's making sure all his goods are still in the wagons."

"Of course." Alia kept her tone neutral. "Were any of the horses injured?"

"No, thankfully, they're all fine. Unhappy as hell after that shaking, but no injuries."

"Much like us," Dari added.

"Did you sleep in the back of the common room?"

"Stables," Raff said. "Fresher air."

Dari nodded in agreement. "Pentans," she said, not bothering to lower her voice. "Their farts are rancid." The Pentans in question shot her dirty looks. They looked somewhat worse for wear, although it was impossible to tell whether it was from last night's wine or the rude awakening this morning.

Alia laughed, then immediately felt guilty when she remembered the task at hand.

"I'll be back in a few minutes," Alia said. "If Callan … if he asks about me, please let him know I wasn't injured. I'm sure he's anxious to resume the journey to Trionn-Fí."

Without waiting for—or really wanting—an answer, she scanned the room until she saw the lone-wolf Arcane mage from last night. He sat at a table in the corner of the room, cradling a large mug of steaming liquid, looking as though he had already been through hell. She went over to him.

"I'm sorry to interrupt your breakfast," she said without preamble, "but we could use your assistance."

"Why?"

"A girl was injured in the quake."

The mage kept his eyes on his mug of tea. "What makes you think I can help?" Neither his expression nor tone were welcoming.

Alia stared at him, taken aback by the man's overt hostility. Finally, she replied, "You're a mage. You have knowledge of such things. And I thought that's what mages did. Help people."

Heaving a resigned sigh, he pushed his chair back from the table and, for the first time, looked directly at Alia. She gave an imperceptible indrawn breath.

He was beautiful.

High cheekbones on a thin, fine-boned face. A mostly straight nose with a bump on the bridge that spoke of being on the wrong end of a blow. His eyes, beneath thick, softly arched brows, were an almost crystalline gray framed by dark lashes. Mesmerizing eyes, if not for the fact that the flesh around them was sunken, almost bruised in appearance. He looked as though he hadn't seen a good night's sleep in days. Still …

"What's wrong with her?"

His gruff tone brought Alia back to the business at hand. "She has a gash on her leg from falling debris. And I gather she was sick to her stomach when she and her mistress arrived yesterday evening and it lasted throughout the night. My soldiers can help dress the wound, but if she is to travel to Trionn-Fí this morning, it would be better if she's not heaving her guts out. Perhaps you have something that can help with that … ?"

"I have something that should help," he said. "And I'll see what I can do about her leg, but we'll have to be quick. I need to get to the capital."

As do we all. But Alia kept the thought to herself.

"Is she downstairs?"

"No, she's in a room on the second floor with her mistress. We didn't want to try and move her until we knew how bad the wound on her leg might be."

He grunted by way of reply, got to his feet, and retrieved his scuffed leather satchel and a small tubular map case.

"You travel light," Alia observed.

"I don't need much." With that, the mage stalked to the stairs, managing to look inconvenienced every step of the way.

Alia followed, resisting a very strong impulse to boot him in the rear. She'd had enough of men acting like sullen adolescents over the last few days. Which once again reminded her that Callan still hadn't come to check on her well-being.

Stuffing the hurt into a dark corner of her mind, she stomped up the stairs after the mage.

"What's your name?" she called as they reached the second floor.

"Why do you need to know?"

"For the love of—" Alia took a deep breath. "Because I'd rather call you by name instead of 'surly mage.'"

He paused briefly on the second-floor landing. "Which room?"

"First door on the right … surly mage."

She thought he might have given an amused snort, but it was hard to tell, as he'd already entered the hallway and headed toward the room in question. Alia followed.

"Keth," he said over his shoulder just before they entered the room. "My name is Keth."

They found Jezel sitting at her dressing table, running a brush through her luxuriant dark brown hair while keeping an eye on Bellamy, who now lay on the bed under a pile of blankets, eyes shut, her breathing shallow but steady. Her corn-silk hair was damp with sweat. A chamber pot sat on the floor next to the bed.

Keth turned to Alia. "I thought you weren't going to move her," he snapped.

"So did I," Alia retorted. "And how did you know she was moved?"

He looked at her as though she was a simpleton. "That is not where a servant sleeps."

"She was freezing," Jezel explained calmly. "She couldn't stop shivering, and I thought it best to get her off the cold floor and onto the bed."

The mage scowled at her. "You might have made her wounds worse by doing so."

She shrugged. "If so, at least she is warm and comfortable."

He looked as though he wanted to say more, but instead set his bag on the edge of the bed and carefully folded the covers back so he could look at Bellamy's injured leg.

The girl's eyes fluttered open.

"How do you feel?" the mage asked in a voice gentler than Alia had heard him use until now.

"My leg hurts … and I—" She made an involuntary retching sound and leaned over the side of the bed. Keth grabbed the chamber pot and held it under her head with one hand as she miserably dry heaved. When she'd stopped, he helped her lie back against the pillows. Then he opened his leather carryall and rummaged around inside, finally pulling out a small jar from which he extracted what looked like herbs.

"Put these under your tongue," he said. Ignoring the girl's weak protests, he popped them in her mouth and added, "They'll still the nausea."

Jezel left the dressing table and sat on the other side of the bed. She held her maid's hand and murmured, "You will be fine, Bellamy. See? You have a mage from Arcanum to heal you."

Bellamy looked up at her mistress and gave a weak smile through her misery. Alia could tell that the girl trusted Jezel, which made Alia feel even more kindly toward the woman. That, and her willingness to pick up a chamber pot, and more, for the comfort of her maid.

Alia put a hand on Jezel's shoulder. "I need to check with my guards and my … my fiancé"—she actually stumbled over the word—"and find out when we can leave. Will you be all right?"

Jezel nodded. "Yes." She paused, then added, "Thank you."

"See if you can find cloth for bandages and alcohol to clean the wound. Clear spirits would be best," Keth said curtly as Alia headed for the door. "And sugar," he yelled as she left the room.

"Would you like some fine wine with your order, sir?" Alia muttered as she clattered down the stairs, hurrying in spite of her irritation with the mage.

Reaching the bottom of the stairs, she rounded the corner of the landing to the hallway and came face-to-face with Callan.

Chapter Thirty-Eight

"Alia!" Callan exclaimed, reaching out to touch her face. "Tell me you're uninjured."

She eyed him coldly, unimpressed by his too-little-too-late show of concern—even if it did seem sincere.

"More to the point, is your property in the wagon undamaged?" She made to brush by him, but he grabbed her wrist, halting her in her tracks.

"You're surely not angry with me for making sure our future is secure." It was a statement, not a question.

"And if I had been killed, what then?" Alia shook her head, not trying to hide her hurt or contempt. "I suppose your future would still be secure."

"Alia—"

"I believe the caravan will be ready to depart in an hour," she said coldly. "Now, if you'll forgive me, I have something I must attend to."

Ignoring Callan's protestations, Alia pulled her arm free and went into the common room, where she found the innkeeper outside of the kitchen sweeping up broken bottles. He looked harried, but when she asked him for the supplies Keth had requested, his response was immediate and heartfelt.

"Gladly," he said. "Without your soldiers pitching in to help, this place would fall down around us in no time. Here." He put a mug of tea and a large slice of a rich, dark brown bread slathered in butter and honey in front of her. "You have yourself a bite to eat while I fetch what you need."

Despite her encounter with Callan, Alia headed back up to the second floor in a much-improved frame of mind, thanks to the bread and tea. When she reached Jezel's room, she was surprised to see Bellamy sitting propped up against the pillows, taking cautious sips of water. Her color was much improved. Keth sat next to her, gently daubing the wound on her leg with a section of linen sheet.

Jezel was sitting on the edge of the opposite side of the bed, her expression serene. Alia wondered if she practiced it in the mirror to avoid premature wrinkles, then banished the unkind thought out of her head. Now was not the time for pettiness, especially when the woman had already proven herself more than the shallow opportunist she had first appeared to be.

She put the supplies on the bed next to the mage, who gave a brief nod of acknowledgment. "How bad is the wound?" Alia asked.

"It's superficial. She'll have a bad bruise, but luckily the cut itself isn't deep. Best she doesn't do much walking for a few days." He shot Jezel a dark glance as he spoke.

"I've yet to make Bellamy run alongside horse or carriage," Jezel said mildly.

"How are you feeling?" Alia addressed the question directly to Bellamy.

"So much better," the girl replied. "His touch truly is magic!" She cast the mage an adoring look. Alia had to stop herself from snickering.

"The medicine works quickly," Keth muttered, not looking at anyone directly. He focused instead on the supplies, adding sugar to a glass of water and soaking clean kitchen linens in what smelled like juniper spirits.

Alia caught Jezel's eye over his bowed head, and the two of them exchanged an amused glance.

"Come find me if you need anything else." Alia headed back out the door, pausing to add, "But don't wait too long—we're leaving within the hour."

Chapter Thirty-Nine

After retrieving her belongings from the wreckage of her room, Alia joined the rest of the guard outside of the inn, seeing for the first time the destruction the quake had caused the immediate landscape.

The back of the inn that abutted the mountainside was partially buried under earth and rocks. An uprooted tree leaned against the roof as if resting.

Alia walked past the stables as the horses were hitched up to the wagons. She needed some time to herself and wanted to take a look at the road.

Alia looked down the way they'd traveled. The road was peppered with fallen boulders, chunks of earth, and more trees that had lost their grip on the mountainside. Still, it looked as though it could be navigated, albeit cautiously, so she carefully threaded her way between several hefty boulders with the intention of scouting a few hundred feet down the road. She stopped short when the road abruptly ended in a rockslide that covered the width of the road, at least fifteen feet high at its peak.

Retracing her steps, she was about to check the road to the north when she heard Raff call her name. He was standing at the wagons, so she made her way back to see what he'd found out.

"Has anyone checked the road ahead yet?" Alia asked. "I saw the landslide heading down."

Raff nodded. "I had Falla and Geffen head about a hundred yards up. They say other than a few boulders shaken loose, it looks fairly clear heading toward the High Road."

"That's good news," Alia said. "At least until the festival is over and people need to travel home."

"With any luck, the other roads leading out of Trionn-Fí are in better shape."

Falla, another of the Athaméan guards, a girl just turned sixteen, trotted over. "Pardon the interruption, Lady Alia, but the Pentans want to know if they can travel with us to Trionn-Fí."

"The Pentans?" Alia turned to Raff. "Don't they have their own carriage?"

"No, they've been traveling on a permit with the Imperial Courier," he said, referring to one of the slow coaches that traveled the periphery of the continent delivering mail, tax revenues, and such, as well as the occasional official. "Cheap if you can score permission to use it, and gets you to your destination … eventually."

"I suppose if you're not in a hurry …" she said doubtfully. She turned back to Falla. "Do they want to follow us for safety's sake?"

The young guard shook her head. "No, they wish to ride in our wagons."

"What? Why?"

"The imperial coach was damaged in the shaker and will take a few days to repair," said a now-familiar voice—Keth had come up behind them from the direction of the stables.

"There's more," he continued, looking even more strained around his eyes and mouth than he had when she'd first approached him. He paused, staring almost blindly off into the distance. "Something is deeply wrong," he finally said. "The salamandrae in the inn had to be extinguished—they went berserk." He swallowed as if his next words hurt his throat. "And there's no trace of any energy running through the ley lines."

"That's not possible." Alia shook her head. "*How* is that possible?"

He looked at her then, those silver-gray eyes intense, almost despairing in their bruised, hollowed sockets. "I don't know. It shouldn't *be* possible."

"But it does mean those who took the courier coach this far are stranded," Raff pointed out.

"Unless," a female voice interjected, "we can impose upon your goodwill to see us to the capital."

Alia turned to see Jezel, who had approached from the inn. The sound of her footsteps was muffled by their conversation and the hard rain pelting. The woman wore a hooded cloak of crimson-oiled silk, the hood pulled over her head to keep the rain off her mane of sable curls.

"I must get there as soon as possible," Keth said abruptly. "It's a matter most urgent."

Alia believed him—she could almost see lines of stress radiating from the mage.

"Do we have room?" Alia directed this question to Raff, who scratched his neck and furrowed his brow. A sign that he was taking the question into serious consideration.

"It might be a bit of a squeeze," he finally replied, "but between the three wagons and the coach we should be able to fit—" He turned to Jezel. "How many people?"

"Six," she replied briskly. "The three Pentans, our mage here, and Bellamy and me."

Taking Raff aside, Alia asked, "What if we left some of our baggage behind?"

"What if we left his lordship behind?" Raff retorted. "Because he surely won't agree to leaving your dowry here."

"We could leave behind two of the guards to watch over it."

"Alia, m'girl," Raff replied, "do you really think he'd be willing to trust anyone who isn't in his employ?"

Sighing, Alia turned back to Keth and Jezel. "I don't know how much of your luggage we can take, but we'll find room for you."

The mage nodded. "This is all I carry." He held up the map case and his small leather carryall.

"And my maid and I will make do with whatever space you can spare," Jezel replied gratefully. She rested her hand on Alia's shoulder and gave it a brief squeeze.

"Falla," Alia said. "Tell the Pentans we'll take them to Trionn-Fí."

Chapter Forty

By the time the Athaméan caravan left the inn, the rain had given way to a heavy mist that cloaked the sullen clouds. It also muffled sound, voices falling flat and lifeless. Even the keening of the wind had fallen off, leaving an eerie stillness in its place.

There were now twenty-five members of the caravan—Alia and Callan; the three Pentan traders; Jezel and her maid; the mage; five Tozzo retainers; and a dozen soldiers from the Irkhanan estate, including Raff, Dari, Falla, and the twins.

Callan had not been pleased to find out Alia had agreed to share their wagons and carriage with three Pentans and Keth. Those gentlemen had very little in the way of baggage, yet Callan clearly grudged every inch of space it required, even though nothing had needed to be moved to accommodate it. Conversely, he had been charm itself when Jezel had appeared, a pale Bellamy at her side. He hadn't grumbled about where their more substantial belongings would fit in the wagons, just ordered Raff to find room for it. He insisted on riding in the carriage with Jezel and Bellamy "in order to make sure the ladies were properly chaperoned." This was accompanied by a darkling glance at his fellow Pentans as if accusing them prematurely of ill intent.

It meant one of the four men needed to surrender their seat in the carriage and travel on horseback. Harbalorio volunteered to ride. "Especially if it means the pleasure of your company." He flashed a smile at Alia.

"It doesn't, but thank you for your courtesy," she replied with deceptive sweetness.

Harbalorio had accepted both Alia's rejection and an agreeably placid mare with good humor. The Pentan had endeared himself to the soldiers by loading his own gear and that of his fellows, both of whom were still suffering the effects of the previous night's wine. Harbalorio, though, was full of energy. Dari was more than happy to intercept his attention, flirting with him with her earthy humor and no-nonsense personality.

He's good-natured, I'll give him that, Alia thought. Like a very handsome puppy, bounding here and there with almost annoyingly endless enthusiasm. It was *almost* a nice change from the mage's taciturn nature and Callan's sullen anger. Just … a bit exhausting.

Keth rode outside of the carriage, having borrowed one of the steeds from the Irkhanan estate. It was as fine and feisty as Alia's mount, Vigo.

When he'd swung himself astride the tawny-gold stallion with an ease that put Callan's equestrian skills to shame, Alia looked at him in surprise.

"Never heard of an Arcane equestrian."

"I've done my share of riding."

"I didn't think you went in for horses in Arcanum."

"I was raised with horses," Keth said, and rode ahead before she could question him further.

"Keep a slow pace," Raff cautioned the mage, repeating the instruction to the other riders and drivers. Callan started to disagree, but Raff cut him off. "We don't know what kind of damage the shaker might have done to the road farther up, so we're going to go slowly and test the ground so that all of us will make it to Trionn-Fí in one piece."

When Callan opened his mouth to argue, Raff had added, "If you'd like to scout ahead on foot at your own pace, Milord, be my guest. But I will not risk our horses." He turned his own horse around and rode ahead, leaving the fuming nobleman to withdraw back into the carriage.

Jezel closed her eyes and pretended to doze so she wouldn't feel obligated to converse anyone—including Callan.

When boarding the carriage, she had purposefully sat on the opposite end of the same seat as Callan, with Bellamy between them. She no longer envied Alia the match. In fact, Jezel found herself pitying her, no matter how young, beautiful, or rich she might be. It was clear that the girl had been raised to be a warrior, not an arm decoration or cash cow for a petulant lordling. It was equally clear that Callan would see to it that Alia's wedded life was unbearable unless she catered to his every wish and whim. Jezel doubted she herself would be able to stomach the man's moods for any amount of money.

Under lowered lashes, she glanced over at her maid, who had recovered a healthy glow thanks to the mage's herbs. Bellamy was able to put some weight on her injured leg—not that Jakobi or Birnardus gave the girl much chance to do so, so determined were they to play the gallant gentlemen to her damsel-in-semi-distress. She reflected that either man would be a decent match for a girl of Bellamy's station—not that she was in any hurry to part with her maid's services. After all, she had a way with Jezel's masses of hair that rivaled the best stylists in Beauchalice.

Other than Harbalorio and Dari, the riders traveled in silence for the most part, the dripping of the thick fog and otherworldly silence wrapped around them.

Keth kept to himself, riding slightly apart from the pack without straying too far ahead, although it was clear he was chafing at the slow going. Alia wondered what was at the bottom of his worry. *No*, she amended, *his fear.*

Surely there was a good reason for the loss of his connection with the ley lines and the way the salamandrae had abandoned their posts and attacked their masters. Some fluctuation in the stars or perhaps the quake itself had temporarily blocked the lines. All just speculation on her part, of course. She would have liked to ask Keth. The mage, however, had once again fallen into a gloomy silence, and Alia didn't want to get slapped down for intruding upon whatever dark thoughts were in his head.

And perhaps she was afraid of what his answer might be.

As they progressed farther up the mountain road, the mist thickened into fog. Alia rode with Raff and Keth in front of the coach and wagons, setting the pace for the rest of the caravan.

Raff did not look happy. "Hey, summon some were-light for us, won't you?" he asked the mage. "We can barely see a wagon's length in front of us."

"I can't," Keth replied tersely. "In normal circumstances it wouldn't be a problem, but there is nothing normal about what happened."

"Nothing normal about this fog either," Raff muttered.

Alia nodded in agreement. She had never seen fog gathered so close or so thickly to the ground. It swirled around their ankles, the horses' hooves, the wagon wheels. It also made it impossible to see what the terrain was like more than a few feet in front of them. Even Callan had given up sticking his head out of the carriage window to inquire why they were *still* moving so slowly.

Raul kept muttering, "I don't like this."

Neither did Alia.

They passed a cut in the granite hills that looked like a trail leading into a narrow canyon ... well, really more of a crevice. Alia noted it automatically—she and her fellow soldiers had been trained to pay attention to any and all possible escape routes in the surrounding terrain, a holdover from the decades of wars between petty chieftains when it was easier to kill the members of a caravan and steal their goods rather than pay the price for Athaméan gemstones, ores, and weapons.

Just beyond the cut, the fog became so thick that Raff ordered a halt to the caravan, taking advantage of a sizable turnout hugging an inward curve to the steep mountainside. Glancing over at Alia, he began counting. "One, two, three ..."

Callan banged on the side of the carriage and yelled, "Why have we stopped?"

Smirking at Alia, Raff called back, "We're going to send someone to scout the road ahead on foot before we go any further."

"Why on foot instead of on horseback?" Callan's tone had gone from irritable to petulant. "You're wasting time."

"The scout can test the ground a lot more safely on foot than on horseback ... m'lord."

"I'll go ahead," Alia hastily offered. Anything to get away from what was a continuous hellish preview of her marriage-to-be.

Raff frowned. "I'd rather send Dari. Remember, my job is to get you to Trionn-Fí and eventually Pentaclys in one piece. Your father would not look kindly upon me if you tumbled off a cliff."

"I'll go with her," Keth said unexpectedly. "I may not have access to magic, but my senses are most likely better than anyone else's here."

"And I'll be careful," Alia assured her friend. Dropping her voice, she added, "Besides, I'm not so certain I wouldn't rather *jump* off a cliff than hear Callan complain again."

"I could always push him off the edge when no one's looking."

Alia gave him a sharp glance. "You're not joking, are you?"

He didn't answer.

Dismounting, Alia handed Vigo's reins to Raff. He in turn held out a spear, the shaft made of smoothly polished hardwood and the head a leaf-shaped, lethally sharp point of Athamé steel. "Thought you might want this," he said.

All Athaméan soldiers received such a spear when they graduated from their first year of school, and then were given their sword when their formal training was complete. Alia carried her sword while traveling but had stored her spear in one of the wagons, figuring she wouldn't need it on the road. She took it from Raff now and gave him a grateful look.

"I don't need to tell you to test the ground in front of you with each step, but you"—he cut a look at Keth—"might not have thought of that." He handed the mage another spear. "Take care of this. It belongs to Falla. She would like it back."

Keth handled the spear with surprising familiarity. "Don't worry. I'll see that it's returned to her."

Alia and Keth moved slowly forward, walking side by side. The only sound was their muffled footfalls and the intermittent thump of the spear butts as they probed the ground in front of them.

Alia glanced over at him as they crept forward. Keth's profile stood out clean and sharp against the grayish-white fog, his expression serious.

"Can you sense anything?"

"Not yet."

"How much further do you think till we reach the High Road?"

"I'm not sure. This fog …"

Something in his voice made her glance sharply at him. "It's just fog," she said uncertainly. "… isn't it?"

The mage shrugged. "Your guess is as good as mine at this point, but it feels wrong to me. Then again, without access to magic, everything feels wrong."

Their words dropped into the air like stones, not so much muffled as deadened.

Deadened.

Alia did not like that word.

"It doesn't feel right to me either," she finally admitted. "And the smell … it's almost bitter. It—"

Keth's arm shot out, his forearm hitting her right below her breasts, driving the air from her lungs. She sputtered as he picked up a rock and threw it in front of them. It seemed a long while before Alia heard a clattering sound, the noise flattened—deadened—but still clearly coming from below.

Mage and warrior looked at each other.

"Maybe we got misdirected by the fog," Alia said hesitantly. "That could be the edge of the cliff … ?"

The mage obligingly tossed another rock hard to the right. This time the pause before they heard it strike the ground was even longer.

Alia's heart sank. This was not good.

"Perhaps there's room to pass if we butt up against the cliff."

"Even if there is," Keth replied seriously, "would you want to risk the chance of another shaker while the wagons are crossing? Or the possibility that the ground underneath would crumble beneath their weight?"

"Of course not," Alia snapped. "I just wish this blasted fog would clear so we could see how bad it really is."

As if in response the wind obligingly picked up, blowing the dense fog away long enough to reveal the road in front of them.

"Oh." Alia's voice was small and hurt.

If the landslide blocking the road back to Athamé was nearly impassable, this was impossible. At least a hundred feet of road was gone, fallen into the ravine below, so that the road's edge leading up to the High Road abutted the precipice on their left. The cliff in turn rose straight up in a sheer face at least fifty feet high, if not more. Alia doubted it could be scaled by hand and foot without ropes and pitons—none of which they had brought—let alone even a remote chance of ferrying wagons and horses up it.

"We could see if it's possible to climb down into the ravine here and then up the other side."

"Maybe," Keth replied doubtfully. "If enough of the road and cliff fell to create a gentle enough slope, it might be doable. But . . ." He shook his head.

"But you don't think so."

"Given how high up the mountains we are and the possibility of another shaker bringing down more of the cliff above, I think it would be unwise."

Not wanting to give up on the idea even though she knew he was right, Alia gripped her spear tightly. Testing the ground every step of the way, she slowly approached the drop.

"Don't go any closer!"

Even as Keth yelled the warning, the ground started crumbling beneath her feet when she was still several feet from the edge, and Alia nearly pitched forward into space, pinwheeling with her arms to keep from going over the edge. During the endless seconds when her balance was in question, she got a glimpse below. Even partially obscured by the fog, Alia saw that there was no gentle slope—just a sheer drop of hundreds of feet.

More of the road began to fall away under her feet and Alia realized she was about to fall with it. She threw herself backward as a hand grabbed the collar of her overcoat and hauled her away from the chasm with a strength she wouldn't have expected from the mage. The road continued to collapse, almost as if it was chasing them, and Keth continued to drag Alia away until the two overbalanced and fell on their backsides a good thirty feet away from the edge, where they both lay catching their breath for a few minutes, still clutching their spears.

Finally, Alia slowly sat up, heart still in her mouth, stomach roiling. That had been a near thing indeed.

"Thank you," she finally said, once she trusted her voice to work.

Keth gave a brief nod.

The chasm between the new drop-off and where the road picked back up on the other side was at least ten feet wider than it had been when they'd first viewed it.

"We should move," Keth said. "Even a small aftershock could be enough to take out more of the road."

As they watched, more of the hard-packed dirt road crumbled away into the void.

"We should go back," Keth said unnecessarily.

Alia did not disagree.

Chapter Forty-One

Alia and Keth returned to the caravan, the fog once more swirling in the air like undulating gauzy curtains as the wind picked up again.

The occupants of the carriage had disembarked during their absence, stretching their legs and sheltering in the slight windbreak of the turnout that hugged the base of the mountain. Even Bellamy, looking much improved, stood outside the conveyance, Jakobi and Birnardus on either side of her. Alia hid a grin—the two Pentans were either very gallant or very opportunistic. Either way, the girl looked pleased by the attention.

Jezel, however, was clearly unhappy, looking askance at Callan as he paced up and down the stretch of road the length of the caravan. His impatience was palpable. It was telling that the rest of the caravan ignored him—except for the Tozzo men-at-arms and Callan's manservant Ermo, trailing uncertainly in his master's dust cloud.

Harbalorio and Dari, both leading their horses, joined Raff as Keth and Alia relayed their findings, Alia finishing with, "We'll have to turn around and go back to the inn."

Raff cursed under his breath, then said, "This is not good news. You're positive there's no way through?"

"The landslide downhill from the inn is bad," Alia replied, "but the road is still stable and much wider. It's just a matter of clearing the slide, maybe a few days of hard labor. Up there, though?" She gestured in the direction she and Keth had gone. "The road narrows substantially, and the ground beneath has been undercut. It won't bear my weight, let alone heavily laden wagons."

"Impossible," Callan snapped.

"I assure you, m'lord," Keth said coldly. "It is not."

"I'm sorry, Callan," Alia interjected, "but there is simply no way to travel any further on this road. We'll have to return to the inn and see if the landslide can be circumnavigated and a return made to the Low Road."

"And what then?" Callan glared at her. "Am I supposed to spend another fortnight at your father's estate? Unacceptable. We must find a way through with the wagons."

"It is impossible." Keth's voice was icy. "Your precious wagons and their contents will end up scattered through the gorge along with your bones if you go much further. As it was, your affianced nearly fell to her death when the road started to fall away beneath her feet."

Callan turned to Alia. "Is this true?"

She nodded. "I would have fallen had it not been for him."

"I thank you, mage, for saving my fiancée's life. Perhaps she'll stop risking it unnecessarily." Nodding stiffly at Keth, he turned away without another glance at Alia, delivering yet another blow to her without lifting a hand. She stared at the ground, willing the hot tears that threatened to spill over to stay where they were.

"Allow me to apologize for my countryman," Harbalorio said, glaring after Callan as he stalked back to the carriage. "Gives Pentans a bad name."

Raff jerked his chin at Dari. "Let's get going. And if that turd knuckle should meet with an accident along the way ..." Shaking his head, he stomped back to his mount and swung up into the saddle, yelling, "Everyone back in the carriage. We're returning to the inn." With that, he took his horse at a careful pace down the road and vanished around the bend.

Before any of the passengers could obey, Raff reappeared, grinning widely.

"I think we might have a way to the capital."

Alia, Keth, Raff, and Dari stood with their mounts in front of the cut they'd passed on the other side of the bend. It was a good five feet in width, as if a giant axe had chopped down through the granite to create a path through the hillside. It looked as though it'd been there for a long time.

"Do you think it's wide enough for horses?" Alia said.

"More to the point," Raff replied, "is it safe?"

"I don't think this happened during the shaker," Keth interjected. "You can see where plants have had time to put roots down."

"The entrance is wide enough," Dari said. "But we should check farther up just to make sure."

Raff nodded. "Dari, see what it looks like inside. If we can take horses, all the better. If not, better we find out before proceeding any further. It'll save time in the long run."

"I'll go with you." Harbalorio, who had joined the group along with his friends, stood by Dari's side and flashed her a smile. She nodded and then turned back to Raff.

"How far do you want us to go?"

He gave the matter some consideration before replying, "If it's still wide enough for horses after five hundred feet or so, we'll take our chances."

Nodding, Dari slapped Harbalorio on his velvet-clad backside. "Let's go, Fancy Pants."

Shooting a grin back at his friends, the Pentan happily followed Dari as she strode up the trail. The two vanished around a bend a few minutes later, the passage marked only by the sound of raucous laughter.

Raff rolled his eyes at Alia. "Poor sod doesn't know what he's in for, does he?"

She grinned at him, but the grin quickly faded as she replied, "He's lucky. Sometimes it's better not to know."

Chapter Forty-Two

Dari led the way into the crevice, Harbalorio close behind. The fog swirled around them, although not as thickly as before. Visibility faded in and out, giving them momentary glimpses of the terrain ten or so feet ahead, then snatching it away.

Harbalorio sniffed the air with a frown, catching a faint whiff of something acrid. "What's that smell?"

"Hell if I know." Dari kept walking, navigating the uneven footing with ease while Harbalorio, not as agile, kept tripping on loose rocks.

"Thought you Pentans were supposed to be graceful," Dari commented after he stumbled for the third time.

"You should see me on the dance floor," he replied with a grin.

They continued through the crevice, which narrowed ever so slightly the farther they went. It was still wide enough for horses, but the footing got even worse. Rocks covered the path as if some giant had casually tossed several handfuls onto the ground. Cracks bisected the damp granite walls, some of them looking deep enough to make Harbalorio start thinking about what could happen if there was an aftershock and they cracked open wider.

"Do you think these were caused during the quake?" he asked uneasily.

"Why do you think I'd know?" Dari tossed back over her shoulder.

"We don't really have quakes in Pentaclys, whereas Athamé seems to have more than the other three provinces combined."

After a brief consideration, Dari said, "Fair enough. All I can tell you is that this"—she gestured around her—"looks like it's been like this for a while. If it had happened during this morning's shaker, the cracks would look more like raw wounds."

"A lovely image."

They continued on, the crevice narrowing even more as the trail took an upward turn. Still passable, although the ledges that had been ten feet above their heads when they'd started were now only a foot or so away from skimming the top of Harbalorio's head. The fog cleared away for a few seconds and he looked ahead—the trail appeared to level out in the next twenty feet, but then it vanished around a bend.

To keep his mind off the possibilities of being buried alive, Harbalorio asked, "So why is Mistress Irkhanan marrying Tozzo anyway? She's far too good for him."

"Too true," Dari replied glumly. "Alia's doing it for her family. Well, really for her father." Off Harbalorio's questioning look, she continued, "See, Lord Irkhanan pissed off King Jurijans—that's the ruling house of Athamé—and he needed a way to get back in the king's good graces."

"Normally when someone pisses off a king, that's the end for them and their family. So why are they still alive?"

"You aren't just a pretty face!" Dari gave him an approving look and continued, "Because, see, Lord Irkhanan didn't actually commit a crime and, because he's in good standing with most of the noble families in the province, the king didn't dare arrest him. It would make him look bad, and if you don't have the backing of your nobles, you damn well better have a strong military behind you. And the thing is, Lord Irkhanan has the loyalty of the

Athaméan military because his school has trained most of them over the last twenty years or so."

"This still doesn't explain why his daughter is marrying one of the biggest prats in Pentaclys," Harbalorio said. "And Callan is the best out of the bunch! The Tozzos don't even have wealth to make up for their intolerable arrogance."

"Which is why he's marrying Lady Alia."

"So what does she get out of it? Damn!" He ducked barely in time to avoid hitting his forehead on an outcropping on his right.

"Noble family connection in Pentaclys, but more importantly, a noble *merchant* family connection in Pentaclys. One with connections to most of the important trade outposts on the continent."

"Oof. Makes sense." He shook his head. "Well, she's getting the raw end of the deal."

Dari nodded, giving him a look of renewed appreciation. "Damn right she is. Alia should be leading garrisons of soldiers together with Raff. Not giving up all that she is for a piece of Pentan dung." She shot him a glance. "Sorry. Didn't mean all Pentans."

Harbalorio was still trying to shape a good retort when they reached the bend in the crevice. They followed it to the left … and then stopped.

"Well, hell," Dari said.

The path didn't end, but in the space of two feet it jagged hard to the right.

"No way a horse can get through here." Dari smacked the granite wall on her right, flinching when a scattering of stones and dirt rained down. They both cast an uneasy look upward, where the top of the crevice was lost in the fog.

"What next?" Harbalorio asked.

"We see if this gods-damned crack in the mountain goes anywhere."

With that, Dari continued on the path to the right. After a brief moment and one more look up, Harbalorio followed her.

Chapter Forty-Three

The two were gone for less than half an hour—although that was enough time to have Callan pacing back and forth with impatience. Alia could tell that Keth was also feeling the weight of time passing too slowly, but he chose not to show it as obviously. It was only clear in the tightness of his features as he stared off into space, seemingly staring at nothing. Although Alia was certain that he saw plenty, and none of it pleasant.

Dari and Harbalorio reappeared around the first bend in the trail. She shook her head as Raff looked at her expectantly.

"Closes off just before it opens up into the forest," Dari reported glumly. "Takes a sharp turn and narrows at the same time."

"Is there room for us to go on foot?" Keth asked.

"I think so." Dari shrugged. "But it won't be a stroll in the park. Still, it looks like it's been traveled. Hard-packed dirt before the rains hit. Lots of rocks, probably from the shaker. But the hillside is mainly granite, not sandstone. Should be safe enough unless an even bigger one hits. I think it's wide enough for all of us"—she cast a somewhat doubtful glance at Birnardus—"but not a chance we'll get a horse through without taking its bones out."

"You say it opens onto the forests?" Raff looked thoughtful.

Dari nodded. "I can't tell how long it'll take to walk, but unless we run into another unexpected surprise, I think we're looking at maybe another full day of travel at most to get to Trionn-Fí on foot. And we'll want to pitch camp before nightfall tonight."

"Go on foot? Are you mad?" By now Callan's objections almost blended into the background, much like the wind. "What about the wagons?"

"They'll be safe enough at the inn." Raff's tone was neutral, which meant he was on the razor's edge of losing his temper. "We'll send them back with four of our soldiers to watch over them until the road back to Athamé is cleared."

"How do I know your soldiers won't help themselves to part of the contents in the meantime?"

Alia's face tightened, but before she could respond, Raff said, "I don't know about your men-at-arms, m'lord, but Lord Irkhanan does not suffer thieves or cowards in his employ. To accuse his soldiers of such is to dishonor his name."

"Send two of your men as well," Alia suggested tightly. "After all, the dowry is mine until we're married, so you can trust that these soldiers will guard it with their lives."

"You can always go back with the wagons, if you please," Raff suggested.

"You would certainly be more comfortable," Alia agreed.

"By Pentan custom, their Imperial Majesties must give their blessing to our match," Callan replied haughtily. "Which means we must present ourselves before them as a couple."

Never mind that Athaméan custom said nothing of the sort, she thought. Out loud, she said, "Then you'll have to trust our soldiers and yours to look after *my* dowry until we return." Alia stared at him until he nodded his agreement.

Lips tightening into a thin line, Callan replied, "Very well. After our marriage is formally blessed by their Imperial Majesties, we will return to the inn, retrieve the wagons, and take the Low Road to Pentaclys."

Chapter Forty-Four

Truth be told, Alia was just as glad that Vigo and the other horses from her father's lands would be safe at the inn. Athaméan horses were worth a pretty penny, almost as much as horseflesh from Beauchalice—although she would argue the value of Athaméan warhorses against Chalicean pleasure mounts any day—and she didn't trust Callan not to try and sell them in Trionn-Fí without her knowledge or consent.

Never mind that like the swords and spears, the soldiers of Athamé were given their mounts by those they served. Never mind that Vigo was hers and not part of the dowry. Never mind that Callan had promised to uphold certain Athaméan laws and customs, even when they didn't match those of Pentaclys.

The passengers had a choice to go back with the wagons or forge ahead on foot to the capital. All of them chose to continue on to Trionn-Fí. Jezel tried to convince Bellamy to go back to the inn, but the lady's maid insisted she preferred to continue on with her mistress.

"I know I can do it," she said when Jezel expressed concern for Bellamy's injured leg. "Who knows how long you will be in Trionn-Fí? Who will do for you if I'm not there?"

"Understand," Raff said gently but firmly, "that if your leg gives out, you will become a hindrance."

"I swear I will not hold you back," Bellamy insisted.

"If she needs help along the way," Jakobi exclaimed, "I vow to assist her."

"And I as well," Birnardus cried, not to be outdone.

Harbalorio would have added his promises of assistance if he had not become so friendly with Dari over the last few hours. He didn't want the soldier—or her mistress—to think him fickle. Let his friends and fellow merchants play the gallants and profess their undying devotion to the pretty lady's maid. Surely she didn't need more than two escorts, after all! Besides, he thought she was foolish for insisting on traveling on foot. He said as much to Dari away from the others' hearing.

"Does the girl really think her mistress can't find another lady's maid for hire?"

"I think that's exactly what she's afraid of," Dari replied. "Would you risk being abandoned at a wayside inn in the middle of the mountains? How will she get home if her mistress doesn't come back for her?"

"I … well …" He stopped, having no answer for that. After a moment, he continued, "If she needs more assistance than my friends can offer, I hope you won't think ill of me for helping her."

Dari smiled and patted him on the arm. "I'd expect nothing less of you."

Harbalorio wasn't sure if this was a compliment or not, but he decided to take it as such and smiled back at her.

Now the party of sixteen made their way through the crevice, the civilians sandwiched by the remaining eight soldiers, with Raff in the lead and Dari bringing up the rear.

"Remember," Raff had warned, "take only what you can carry. Our soldiers have their own loads to bear and can't help with your baggage." He cut a glance at Callan, who had already loaded down Ermo and his two remaining men-at-arms with his luggage, along with a couple of small but heavy canvas sacks containing rough-cut emeralds and diamonds.

"We don't want to be without funds at the festival," was his reasoning. And while Alia couldn't argue with the common sense of the plan, even one small bag of the valuable gemstones would have been more than sufficient for the needs of the entire party—not that she believed Callan would be so generous as to pay for more than fifth-tier lodgings in the poorer districts for the soldiers. With that thought in mind, she'd surreptitiously tucked some of her dowry away in a pouch—she would not have her friends and fellow soldiers suffer for lack of funds. Or Callan's unwillingness to spend them.

She cast a quick glance back at Bellamy, who, despite her injured leg, was doing well. But then she had two gallants helping her navigate the uneven terrain and act as willing pack mules—Jakobi had her carryall and Birnardus her mistress's. Even Jezel carried something—a fine leather handbag that Alia suspected contained her jewelry and money.

Alia reached the sharp bend that Dari had warned them about. She navigated her way through it easily enough, but those with more baggage or—in Birnardus's case—more girth, had a harder time of it. It was simple enough to feedbags and other supplies around the bend by hand—Alia took Jezel's carryall from the Pentan to help his progress—but there was nothing for it. Birnardus had to squeeze through as best as he could.

"Ho, good friend," Jakobi said, waiting for his turn through the narrow passage. "If you plug the gap, would you rather we leave you for wolves to eat or feast upon your tender flesh ourselves?"

Sweating and swearing, Birnardus disdained to answer his friend, concentrating on squeezing through the last bend of the zigzag. Something below his waist caught on a bulge of rock, jerking him to a halt. After a few minutes of struggle and an ominous cracking noise, he finally made it through.

"Gods and devils," he swore, collapsing on a patch of sparse grass when he emerged from the crevice.

"You forgot this." Jakobi, emerging behind him, tossed something onto the grass beside the red-faced, puffing merchant. It was the snarling red-and-gold dragon that had formerly adorned his codpiece.

Birnardus looked down at the remains of his pride and joy and heaved a mournful sigh.

"It was too good to be true," Harbalorio murmured, patting his friend on the shoulder. He dodged the half-hearted blow Birnardus aimed at him, then helped the man to his feet.

The Tozzo retainers, on the heels of their master, struggled with the leather sacks heavy with gemstones. The bags caught on outcroppings, making their progress slow and tortuous. The retainer in front heaved a sigh of relief when he made it through to the other side.

"Blasted fool!" Callan yelled as the second man became wedged in the narrow throat of the crevice after trying to squeeze through with the bag slung over one shoulder. "If the bag rips and you lose even one diamond, you'll pay for it with a hand."

"That's a thief's punishment!" Alia exclaimed.

"If the lout loses my money, it's the same as stealing it."

Brushing by her betrothed, Alia went back in the crevice to where the poor manservant was wedged, now afraid to try and move for fear of ripping the leather sack.

"Hold still," Alia instructed. Reaching out, she put a hand under the sack and lifted—it didn't budge. Her hand brushed the stone wall and she winced at the slimy feel of it, as if it was coated with algae instead of condensation from the fog. Her fingertips tingled, an unpleasant, almost burning sensation. Snatching her hand away, she gave another emphatic shove with both hands, this time managing to dislodge the sack and free the poor retainer from the crevice. She moved out of the way as he fell forward onto the ground with a grateful cry, the sack thudding onto his back seconds later. He was quickly followed by the rest of the party.

Raff looked at the civilians, most of whom were huffing and puffing, as they sprawled on the clear patch of grass onto which the crevice had opened.

"If they're this tired after a short walk over easy ground," he said, shaking his head, "how are they going to make it to Trionn-Fí hiking up through forest and down the hills? It'll take them a month."

Alia couldn't disagree. Other than the soldiers, and Keth—who champed at the bit more than any horse she'd ever known—the rest of the party seemed exhausted by the trek through the crevice. Even Callan, young and fit as he was, rested on the ground as if he'd scaled a mountain rather than hiked for less than a half hour. *Maybe it was just the fact that they'd had no choice*, Alia thought.

"Give them five more minutes and then roust them."

"Yes, sir." Alia and Dari both gave him a snappy salute.

Chapter Forty-Five

IN THE MOUNTAINS SURROUNDING TRIONN-FÍ

The mountains rose up on all sides, creating a sort of cradle sheltered from the harsh winds that blew into the valley below. There was a path of sorts leading from the clearing into the trees. Fog hung in the air, draping the tops of the pines and creating a humid warmth that was more unpleasant than the chillier climes on the other side of the crevice. Water dripped from branches onto the party, causing those who had them to pull hoods over their heads. Those that didn't, such as the three remaining Tozzo retainers, continually wiped water out of their eyes and mouths, and looked generally miserable.

Alia almost asked Callan why they were wearing their livery, velvet in the scarlet and black of the Tozzo family, but decided not to question it. He looked displeased enough as it was. His stylish great cloak was a masterpiece of tailoring to be sure—it would have made all the ladies' hearts swoon at the fanciest balls and dinner parties in Pentaclys or the capital—but was not particularly waterproof. The other Pentans were better off in cheaper but versatile canvas greatcoats, made for sun and rain alike. Even Bellamy was more suitably protected from the elements—along with her mistress, she wore a hooded cloak of oiled silk. Bellamy's was a shade of rose pink that highlighted her frail beauty, while Jezel's crimson cloak was a suitable foil for her dramatic good looks. The frosting of moisture on her sable hair gave her an almost ethereal appearance. Alia was certain she was aware of it.

To her credit, however, the Chalicean didn't complain about the rough footing or uncomfortable conditions. Neither did Bellamy, although it became quickly apparent that the lady's maid was in some discomfort after several hours of trekking through the forest. She started favoring her injured leg, her attempts to hide it painfully obvious.

"She's never going to make it as far as the capital," Dari muttered to Alia as they brought up the rear.

"She will if those two gallants have anything to say about it," Alia said, watching as Birnardus found a stout branch that had fallen from one of the oak trees and gave it to Bellamy as a walking stick. She smiled up at him in thanks.

"They are all holding us back, though," Dari observed. "Except for the mage. If he doesn't slow down, he'll leave the rest of us in his dust."

The two women watched as Keth strode through the trees, following the barely there path as sure-footed as if it were the finest of paved roads.

Raff took a swig from the flask Dari held out. "He'll be grateful for the company when night falls."

"I thought mages could see in the dark," said Dari.

Raff raised an eyebrow. "It won't do him a whole lot of good to see the wolves if they decide to make a meal of him."

"The Chalicean isn't doing too badly for a pampered courtesan."

"No, she isn't," Alia agreed, less reluctantly than she would have last night. She had to admire the fact that Jezel wasn't leaning on anyone—including Callan—to make her progress easier. She held her handbag in one hand and lifted her skirts with the other, navigating the ground in low-heeled crimson boots with the serene expression of a noblewoman promenading in the park. Despite her initial impression of the woman, Alia felt that she might just grow to like her.

Raff called a halt a few hours later. It was, as best as they could tell, shortly past midday, and everyone but the soldiers and Keth were tired. They took shelter from the ever-present drizzle under a rocky overhang not quite large enough to fit everyone, so the majority of the soldiers hunkered down, cloaks pulled over their heads, under a copse of evergreens bunched close together. It was enough to give a little relief from the damp while they rested.

Alia sat with the soldiers, leaving Callan to huddle under the overhang with the rest of the civilians, although he managed to give the impression of being alone even though his manservant Ermo hovered near him. Bellamy sat next to her mistress, fussing over her while her two Pentan gallants fussed over Bellamy. Harbalorio chose to plunk himself down by Dari, who shared her flask of brandy. Keth, on the other hand, rested a distance away from the rest of the party, head back against a tree trunk, hands resting on bended knees, his eyes moving restlessly beneath hooded lids.

Alia wasn't at all sure if he was actually looking at anything in front of him or seeing something that only he could see. Either way, his restless energy was catching and she found herself anxious to keep moving even though she was tired.

Excusing herself from the soldiers, she went over to a fallen tree trunk away from the rest of the group and sat down, rested her back against the trunk and closed her eyes, determined to relax even if it was just for a short while.

"May I?"

Opening her eyes, Alia looked up to see Jezel standing in front of her. Heaving an internal sigh, she replied, "Be my guest."

Jezel sat down on the trunk itself instead of the ground, settling her skirt around her feet. "Do you really think we can make it to the capital by tonight?"

"Dari is our navigator," Alia replied, "and she's rarely wrong. Worst case, we'll make camp if it gets too dark to travel any further and be safe."

Nodding, Jezel looked across the clearing at her maid, whose face was drawn. "I worry that Bellamy will not be able to travel much further at the speed your soldiers have set."

"I'll ask them to slow down a little. Raff won't like it—"

"And neither will the mage," Jezel murmured.

Alia laughed. "Definitely not. I admit, I'm curious why he's so antsy to reach the capital." She glanced over in Keth's direction, tension clearly visible in the set of his shoulders.

The man intrigued her, it was true, almost as much as his rude manners irritated her.

Taking a sip from her waterskin, she offered it to Jezel, who accepted gratefully. If someone had told Alia she'd be sharing her supplies with the same woman who had been sniffing around her fiancé the evening before, Alia would have laughed in their face. Disasters made for strange bedfellows.

The strange odor still hung in the air, if anything a bit stronger than it had been in the crevice. Which was odd since that had been almost an enclosed space, whereas they were now out in the open. True, the trees were thickly clustered and created a canopy of sorts—although sadly not thick enough to stop the rain—but surely the smell should have dissipated rather than increased. As much as Alia hated the strong winds that had blown going up the mountain road, even a breeze would have been welcome to clear away some of the ever-present mist and the hint of sweet-sour stink that hung in the air.

"What do you suppose that smell is?" Jezel asked.

"No idea. I don't even quite know what to compare it to—it's sweet and rancid at the same time, like meat covered in honey left out to spoil in the heat."

Jezel looked at her. "That's horrible. I refuse to believe that you've actually smelled anything like it."

"Do you know of the Kurnellicaia Badlands in Athamé? At the far edge of the desert, there are ants that get as big as a large man's thumbnail. The nomad tribes that live out there sometimes use the anthills as a way of meting out justice. They use honey to attract the ants."

"Tell me you made that up."

Alia shook her head. "Totally true."

"I could have gone my entire life without knowing about that."

Grinning, Alia held out her flask. Jezel shook her head.

"They leave the condemned staked out until there's nothing left but bones," Alia continued. "The smell doesn't last long, but for a day or so, if the wind blows in the right direction ... well, it's a stink you don't soon forget."

Wrinkling her nose, Jezel took the proffered flask and took a hearty swig.

Raff granted the party a half hour of rest. Keth would have happily rousted them after half that time and almost continued ahead on his own, but despite his urgency and against his better judgment, he found some comfort in the company of others, even if he didn't want to mingle too closely with them.

A curl of mist blew past him, carrying with it the strange, unpleasant odor. He thought it smelled like the scent certain carnivorous plants exuded to attract flies and other insects into their trap, where the unlucky bugs were stuck and then digested.

Not a comforting comparison.

He stared at the fog as it drifted through the trees. It seemed to sparkle like snow crystals in the sunlight ... but there was no sun and the sparkle had an iridescence that was ... odd. It shimmered with colors that bore a token resemblance to colors like green, violet, cobalt blue, black, and silver, yet were nothing like them. For a brief second Keth felt nauseated looking at them. Then that particular patch of mist blew through the trees, dissipating into the pine needles.

Its departure didn't comfort him.

No matter how often he reached out with his senses, Keth could feel nothing. None of the spark that told him energy was pulsing through the web of ley lines. It was like a fire that had gone out, embers long since turned to charcoal, cold and dead. He felt as though an integral part of him had been torn out of his heart and soul. It terrified him, this absence of magic, in a way that very little had frightened him in his life.

His gaze fell upon the map case in his lap.

Almost as much as what was contained within terrified him.

Chapter Forty-Six

The further they went along, the more they saw of the earthquake's handiwork. Random cracks began to appear in the ground, as if giant claws had raked the earth. At first they saw only the outermost reaches of the fissures, no more than a few inches wide, but as the group continued toward the capital, the cracks opened up to become a foot across, or even wider.

Harbalorio cast a worried look at Dari.

"Should we be concerned?" He joined her at the edge and peered down into the narrow crack.

Shrugging, she replied, "Probably not. But if things start shaking again, that could change."

"It smells like something died down there," he said, wrinkling his nose in distaste.

"Maybe something did," Dari replied cheerfully.

"That's not reassuring."

"Wasn't meant to be."

Behind the rest of the group, Ermo and the other two Tozzo retainers—Merlini and Girolamo, both strapping, dark-blond men in their twenties—struggled with their burdens. It was bad enough being stuck with their master's luggage—surely he could have made do with fewer clothes under the circumstances!—but to be saddled with the bags carrying the precious gems *and* the temptation of knowing that just one of the stones inside was perhaps worth more than the three of them combined would make in a year ...

Even the loyal Ermo was resentful.

"I'm a valet, not a packhorse," he kept muttering, glancing uneasily around to make sure his master didn't overhear his complaints even though Callan, along with everyone else, was far ahead of him.

"Yes, and your family has been in service to the Tozzos since the dawn of time," Merlini said with a roll of his eyes. "When all is said and done, you're still just another servant like the rest of us."

After that sharp but accurate put-down, Ermo picked up his pace and declined to speak to his two fellow retainers, who were just as glad to see him vanish ahead of them.

"Thank the Gods *and* the devils," Girolamo said with a relieved sigh. "I don't think I could take another minute of that wet blanket's whining."

"He's not wrong, mind you," said Merlini. "This is truly a pisser of a journey. It's the way he insists he's better than us just because he helps Master Callan in and out of his trousers that sticks in my craw."

"Precisely!" Girolamo agreed emphatically. "Does he think *we're* beasts of burden? We're guardsmen, and a lot of good it will do his lordship if he's wearing clean underthings and someone cuts his throat because we're too loaded down to reach our weapons!"

The two continued to grumble companionably as they lugged their master's baggage through the trees.

Ermo made his sullen way ahead of his fellow retainers, bitterly resentful as the straps on the bags he carried chafed against his shoulders, even through his doublet. He wasn't used to hard work—the most challenging daily task he had in his experience was dealing with his temperamental and hard-to-please master. And Ermo had learned through trial, error, and manipulation just how to do that. He had achieved—so he thought—a modicum of respect in his master's eyes, anticipating his moods and needs, and adjusting his wardrobe choices accordingly. Ermo had even allowed himself to believe that Master Callan was fond of him. But being reduced to nothing more than a pack animal had given his somewhat overinflated sense of importance a solid kick in the teeth.

Almost immediately Ermo felt guilty for his thoughts. Surely these were highly unusual circumstances! Did he expect his master to arrive at the festival with only the clothes on his back? Of course not! That would be a dishonor not only to the Tozzo family but to himself as well.

Holding his head up high, he strode forward with renewed energy and a lighter heart, even whistling a jaunty tune as he kept up the brisk pace. At this rate, he'd be sure to catch up with the rest of the party before his worthless compatriots.

It was a good quarter hour later before Ermo realized he'd gone in the wrong direction and lost the trail. He stopped, peering around at thickly set trees in the perpetual gray mist. There was no path beneath his feet, nor could he see one, no matter which direction he looked. The only sound was the constant dripping of moisture from branches—no matter how he strained his ears, he couldn't hear any voices or footfalls to give him an idea of which way to go. Finally he decided to retrace his steps and pick up the trail again, never mind worrying about beating Merlini and Girolamo in a race that only existed in his head.

Turning, he set off, trying to keep up his spirits by whistling again, but soon found himself pushing through thick, prickly bushes and trees set closely together. Branches whipped across his face, one catching him painfully above one eye, causing it to tear up and blur his vision. One particularly pernicious limb tangled in his clothing, ripping his fine linen shirtsleeve. Cursing, Ermo gave a determined tug and pulled free, lurching out of the stand of trees into blessedly clear air.

Before he could get his bearings, however, the ground beneath his feet crumbled and he was thrown forward, finding himself in a free fall. His scream of alarm was cut off as he plunged into moving water, the weight of the bags slung across his shoulders dragging him down below the surface.

"Did you hear a yell?" Merlini looked up, startled.

Girolamo shrugged, disinterested. "Probably old skinny-shanks Ermo walking into a spider's web. He's a hothouse posy, that one."

Merlini did not disagree with his friend's assessment of the valet, but still …

"Maybe we should check."

"Why?"

"If he's run into trouble, we should help him."

Stopping in his tracks, Girolamo stared at him in exasperation. "And if something *has* happened to Ermo, who do you think will get stuck carrying his share of the baggage?"

Merlini considered this. "Good point."

"Thank you!" Girolamo resumed walking.

"But," Merlini continued, "do you really want to risk his lordship's displeasure if we show up without him?"

Girolamo stopped again, heaving a resigned sigh. "Good point."

"Thank you."

"Shit," Merlini said. Girolamo nodded glumly.

It had taken them no time at all to find the unfortunate Ermo—in his panic, he'd left a trail even the most maladroit of trackers could follow. When they came to the cliff he'd fallen from, a quick and careful look twenty feet down revealed Ermo's body wedged between two boulders in a small but fast-moving river.

"Should we take him out of the water?" Merlini asked. "Looks like a safe enough path further down."

Girolamo shook his head. "Don't want his lordship accusing us of filching anything. Best to just tell him the news, don't you think?"

Callan stared at Ermo's submerged corpse from the edge of the river in stunned disbelief—for once, he had nothing to say. Alia and Dari had accompanied him there, Merlini and Girolamo leading them. Now they waited for their master's instructions on what to do next.

"Get him out of there."

The two men scrambled to obey the order, trying to keep their footing as they waded gingerly into the rapidly running water. Luckily it was only hip-deep or it would have been impossible to retrieve the body. Dari stood on the riverbank and helped the men ferry the corpse onto shore, where they set him down near the river's edge.

Alia thought the valet would most likely have survived the fall had he been able to shuck the bags still slung across his torso. The leather straps were tangled around his body, one looped about his neck as if he'd tried unsuccessfully to remove it. She wondered if Callan had come to the same conclusion. He knelt by his valet's side, a bereft look on his face. And despite everything, Alia couldn't stop the rush of empathy that washed over her. Without further thought, she went to his side.

"It wasn't your fault," she said gently, putting a hand on his shoulder.

"I know it wasn't my fault!" He angrily shrugged her hand off. "The fool should have been paying attention!"

She tried taking his arm, but he jerked it out of her grip and turned on her, raising one hand as if to strike her, his face so distorted with rage it was almost unrecognizable. Then, before she could move, his arm fell to his side and he took two staggering steps backward before his legs collapsed under him. He sank to the ground, arms limp at his sides, hands resting on the dirt, palms up. He stared at nothing, his breathing harsh and labored.

Alia motioned his retainers and Dari away. "Wait for us on the path," she instructed. Then, approaching Callan with the same caution she would use with an unbroken horse, Alia knelt in front of him.

"Callan ... ?"

She said his name softly, ready to dodge if he raised his hand against her a second time. But she didn't think he would. Something had snapped inside him. She wasn't sure what, exactly, but all the tension and anger seemed to have drained from his body. She couldn't tell if he even marked her presence.

"I've failed," he said dully. "Failed my family. Failed my retainers." He swallowed hard, then continued. "And worst of all, I've failed you."

Alia didn't know what to say, so she kept quiet and waited. After a few minutes, he spoke again.

"I had no choice in this marriage, you know. Because of my father and older brother, our family fortune is gone. All we have left is our good name and the reputation built over decades with the Merchant's Guild. And if we can't pay Jerrod's gambling debts, we will lose both that good name and our reputation."

"I had no more choice in the matter than you did," Alia suddenly said.

He looked up at that.

Alia gazed at him steadily and continued. "You have to be aware of our situation, Callan. The opposite of yours, really, with plenty of wealth but our good name in jeopardy. We're at risk of becoming pariahs in not only our province but all of Athamé. The connections your family has will help restore my father's good standing with the Jurijans, the Athaméan royal family. Ensure that our good name is saved." She paused, then added boldly, "But I had other plans for my future."

This hit Callan's ego, she could tell. She continued.

"Then, when you arrived at our estate, I thought maybe the match would work. You showed admiration for my martial skills. I imagined we would practice these things together over the years, that you would be proud of me for who and what I am." He was quiet as she finished. "Then you made it clear that this was not the case. That what makes me an Athaméan—a desirable woman by Athaméan standards—caused you displeasure, and that you would be ashamed to have me as your wife unless I changed."

He remained silent for a long minute, then sat back in a more comfortable position, legs folded. She remained where she was.

"I would have accepted the match regardless of what you looked like," he said. "My father made it clear I had no choice. But then you rode up on that ill-tempered stallion of yours, looking like a goddess of war in your armor."

She remembered the moment—Callan had been standing with her father on the front steps of the Irkhanan estate when she and Raff returned from patrolling along the property's borders. His caravan had arrived early. She hadn't been looking forward to this meeting, but he'd seemed so pleased to meet her, so genuinely happy with what he saw, that some of the tight knot in her chest had loosened.

Now, he said, "I couldn't believe my good fortune to be betrothed to such a beauty."

She sat down beside him, giving her haunches a break from squatting.

"And watching you spar with your fellow soldiers ... I'd seen Athaméan women fighters before, but none like you. You were glorious." He gave a small laugh. "And the way you spoke your mind, the respect you received from your family ..." He looked at her, glanced away, and then repeated, "I could not believe you were to be my wife."

She took all of this in, searching for the best response. Finally she asked, "What changed?"

"I realized you would never need me as much as I needed you. You don't need someone to fight for you. I knew your martial skills would horrify my mother. My friends would mock me. Never to my face," he added bitterly. "But I know what they're like. And the more I thought about this ... the more it ate away at me, I began to see you as my friends would. As my mother would. What Pentan man would have a wife who could best him in swordplay? Who has to be rescued instead of being the hero?"

"Did your father know nothing of Athaméan traditions before seeking to make this match?" Anger and hurt warred within her.

"I doubted he cared. I am the younger son, and once I brought your dowry into the family, he would not have thought twice about it. He no doubt would have joined in mocking me—Callan and his warrior wife."

He shook his head. "But oh, Alia, when I first saw you ... my heart stopped and I almost got to my knees to thank the Gods. You deserve better than a man too weak and worried about what his friends might think rather than rejoicing in winning a woman like you."

Alia sat with that for a few minutes. Picked up stones and tossed them in the stream. Callan stayed quiet next to her.

"I don't know if we can make this work," she finally said. "But I'm willing to try if you are."

His hand reached out and clasped hers by way of an answer.

They had no real tools with which to dig a grave, so Ermo was laid to rest in the river itself, filling the bags he'd carried with rocks to weigh him down.

Harbolario fastened the straps to Ermo's belt buckle, and Merlini and Girolamo had lifted the body and put it back in the river, as far in the center as they could without risking drowning themselves. Then they all rejoined the rest of the group further up the path and continued on their way.

Chapter Forty-Seven

When it became obvious that they would not make it to Trionn-Fí before nightfall, Raff reluctantly called for the group to make camp while it was still light. They found a large clearing, the foliage above dense enough to shelter them from the worst of the drizzle. Birnardus collapsed in an exhausted heap while Jakobi laid out his cloak for Bellamy to rest upon.

While Raff and Dari set up the camp with the help of Harbalorio, Jezel, and the two remaining Tozzo retainers, Irkhanan soldiers Falla and Geffi went off to forage for berries, mushrooms, and the like, to round out the food they'd brought with them. Keth, although unhappy with yet another night's delay, accompanied them to make sure any mushrooms collected wouldn't kill them. Falla shyly offered him the use of her spear for the expedition, which he graciously—for him—accepted.

"I'll look for wood," Alia offered.

Callan jumped to his feet. "I'll help you carry it."

The foragers all set off in the same direction, splintering off as need or whim took them.

Alia and Callan ended up going off by themselves, hunting under rock ledges and beneath thick mounds of pine needles for wood dry enough to use in the campfire. Callan's stiff, unhappy mannerisms had been replaced by the boyish enthusiasm he'd shown when they'd first met, and Alia found herself enjoying his company. When he offered his hand to steady her as she climbed over a fallen tree, she took it.

Their tranquility was shattered by a high-pitched scream, one filled with unimaginable agony and then abruptly muffled as if a heavy blanket had been thrown over the person screaming.

Without hesitation, Alia took off through the trees toward the sound, Callan close on her heels. Within minutes, they reached another clearing.

"Look!" Callan called. "Isn't that an Athaméan sword?"

Alia went over to him. He pointed at a blade lying at the edge of one of the larger fissures they'd encountered in the last few hours. It glistened as if wet.

Definitely Athaméan workmanship, Alia thought. It looked familiar, not just because of its providence. It—

"That's Falla's sword," she said, recognizing the design on the bronze crosspiece and hilt.

Callan reached for the sword. "Well then, she'll be glad to have it back, I warrant." He reached for it just as Alia peered over the edge down into the gash in the earth. What she saw made her eyes go wide with horror.

A good ten feet down sprawled a body that looked partially digested, the remnants of boiled leather and iron armor clinging to scraps of flesh and bone. The head was a skull, the mouth open in a perpetual scream. One eye socket was empty while the other still contained a hazel eye, lidless. Even as Alia watched, both flesh and bone seemed to crawl with some glistening ooze that slowly spread over the eye, which dissolved in its socket.

She noted all of this in an instant, turning to Callan as he reached for the sword.

"No, don't!"

His fingers wrapped around the hilt and he gave Alia a cocky grin. "What are you worried about? I—"

He stopped, the grin fading into a bemused frown. "It stings," he said simply.

And then he started to scream.

There was no buildup. No rising crescendo. The first scream was high-pitched and raw, the sound of someone in agony.

Alia stared in shock as Callan, still screaming, tried to cast the sword away, but it seemed to stick to his hand, almost as if his fingers were sinking into the leather-wrapped hilt. She reached forward to try and help, but Callan stumbled away from her, his mouth stretched wide as howl after primal howl peeled forth. Clarion calls of agony that shattered the air itself. He fell to his knees in front of the crevasse and Alia once more reached for him.

"Alia, *no*!" Keth's voice.

A spear flew by her, the wind of its passage ruffling her hair before it passed through Callan's shoulder, the impact knocking him backward into the crevasse. Alia screamed, the sound mingling with Callan's still gut-wrenching howls, and she lunged toward the edge, staring wildly down into the crack in the earth where her betrothed lay on his back a good ten feet below, his limbs tangled with what was left of Falla, the spear pinning him to her corpse.

"Raff, stop her!" Keth's voice.

Before she could reach for him, Keth seized Alia by one shoulder and hauled her back, using both hands to grab her when she bolted forward again.

"Let go of me!" She fought against his hands as Callan's screams became bubbling howls, as if his vocal cords were dissolving.

"You can't help him!" Keth shook her as she continued to struggle, using an elbow to deliver a sharp blow to his midsection. She knew just where the weak points lay. He gave a sharp hiss of pain and spun her around to face him, fingers tightening on her arms right above her braces. Keth also knew the vulnerable points and how to reach them. "You can't help him," he repeated gently.

She looked down into the crevice.

Callan's upper torso, face, and neck were dissolving, the strange, shimmering jellylike substance now covering him. It had eaten into his throat, reducing his screams to horrid liquid gurgles. His eyes stared into hers, lidless, the sockets collapsing inward as he stretched out a raw-fingered hand, entreating her. Even as she watched, the flesh sloughed off the bone.

"Callan ..." Her voice broke as his went silent.

His flesh and clothing took on a wet gleam, shimmering in colors that made her eyes hurt and her stomach churn.

As she stared down, the colors seemed to intensify, each noxious shade clashing with the others. As they swirled round and round, Alia leaned forward on the balls of her feet, wanting a closer look. Something in those colors could tell her why Callan and Falla died. She knew it. She—

A hand cracked across her face, the open palm rattling her brains but snapping her out of whatever trance she'd fallen into. She stared in bewildered shock at Keth, who pulled her away from the crevasse and its grim contents.

"What did you see?" he asked softly.

She shook her head, the memory of those colors already fading as if they'd never existed. "I ... I don't remember."

Chapter Forty-Eight

Alia stared into the fire crackling in a circle of stones the soldiers had gathered, careful to stay away from the gashes in the earth. The loss of one of their own hurt each of them deeply—they were more than a unit. They were a family. And Falla had been the youngest of the group. Geffi was guilt-stricken—she'd gone off along a deer trail lined with wild blackberry bushes while Falla foraged ahead. "I should have stayed with her," she kept repeating. No amount of reminders that Falla was a trained soldier like herself made any difference.

For Alia it was a double blow. Even if she and Callan hadn't come to terms, he still wouldn't have deserved to die that way.

Someone sat down next to her—it was Keth. She barely glanced at him before going back to her flask and taking a deep pull. It would be gone soon at this rate. Maybe Raff had another bottle squirreled away ... Despite that, she still held up the flask to the mage to offer him some as well.

Keth shook his head and said nothing. He didn't try to cheer her up or tell her it wasn't her fault or any of the other things both Raff and Dari had tried to pull her out of a downhill spiral. Somewhere inside herself she knew they were hurting as badly as she was—for Falla's loss, not Callan—but she couldn't find it in herself to take comfort, let alone give it.

Yet she found the mage's presence oddly soothing.

A good ten minutes passed in oddly companionable silence before Alia broke it. "How did you know?"

He didn't ask her what she meant. "The colors on the sword and on his arm."

Now she looked at him. "What do you mean?"

"You didn't see them?"

"No ... just a sort of ... I don't know, something that glistened like a slug's trail on the blade and moving up Cal—" His name caught in her throat. "Up his arm. Eating away at him. What did you see?"

"Colors. But none that I've seen before except—" He stopped abruptly.

"Except ... ?"

For a moment Alia didn't think he was going to answer her. He stared into the fire, eyes haunted. Then he looked back at her. "Except for an experiment of my old master's. It ... did not end well."

She waited for him to explain further, but he fell silent. Once more she offered him her flask and this time he took it.

Chapter Forty-Nine

Girolamo and Merlini decided they should camp out of earshot of the others, the better to discuss what they would do now that their master was out of the picture. They found a promising spot to roll out their bedrolls in a grove of trees adjacent to one of the fissures in the ground. It was far enough away from the campfire to ensure privacy and also far enough from the crevasse for peace of mind.

"I call that spot," Girolamo said, pointing to a patch of soft white heather.

"Damn your eyes!" Merlini swore, eyeballing all the rocks and branches he would need to remove in order to sleep comfortably.

As he cleared a spot, he asked, "Don't you think we should go back to Pentaclys and tell Lord Tozzo what happened?"

"I do not!" Girolamo shot back immediately. "It was our job to look after Master Callan. I don't think Lord Tozzo will care that we were not to blame for his death. Do you?"

After a brief moment of reflection, Merlini sighed. "No."

"Maybe this will cheer you up," Girolamo said. Reaching into the pouch hanging from his belt, he pulled out two rough-cut diamonds. "One for each of us. It should help us find our feet in the capital, don't you think?"

"Unless we get arrested for theft," Merlini replied glumly as he continued tossing rocks and sticks off into the bushes.

Girolamo shoved the stones back in his pouch. "When you're done being an ungrateful lout, let me know. Until then, I'll just hold on to both of these."

When he finally spread out his cloak on more or less clear ground, Merlini saw that Girolamo was using his cloak as a pillow. The bed of heather was evidently comfy enough that he could sleep on the ground cover—he was already snoring comfortably, the lucky bastard. Merlini looked enviously at the snow-white carpet and crouched down for a closer look.

"Sorry, tender young maiden, there's no room for you to share my bed tonight," Girolamo said, opening his eyes and startling his friend.

"Get stuffed," Merlini growled back. "Just wanted to look at this natural mattress of yours."

"Sure you do. Just keep your hands where I can see them."

"Don't flatter yourself." Merlini ran a hand over the silky, feather-soft strands. "This isn't heather, you know."

"I'll sleep on it just fine all the same."

"Stupid lunkhead. I'm not trying to steal your spot. I'm just saying this feels a little sticky. More like—erm, I don't know, spider silk or something."

Girolamo snorted. "You're going to have to try harder if you think I'm going to let that spook me into trading places."

"No chance of that, my thick friend," Merlini said, returning to his own bedding. "I only mean to say where there's spider silk, there's spiders."

"Jealous," Girolamo yawned. "Sleep tight!"

We'll figure out our future tomorrow, Merlini thought. He'd had enough of Girolamo for the night.

Merlini rose with a groan the next morning, his back still sore from the previous day's exertion.

"I trust you slept well, princess," he said—but Girolamo was already gone. He stood and stretched with a loud yawn. "Why didn't you start a fire for breakfast?" he called, looking around for his worthless friend. There was no sign of the man. Where he had slept, however, there was a man-shaped patch of bare earth in the middle of the white heather or whatever it was. Merlini grunted at Girolamo's sad attempt at a little joke.

Very nice. Can't be bothered to start breakfast but has the time to make snow angels. Utterly worthless. "Where are you, you lazy varlet?"

Shaking his head, Merlini walked over to the far end of the fissure and answered the call of nature. He whistled nonchalantly as he pissed off the edge, but the whole time he was keeping a wary eye out for Girolamo, fully expecting him to jump out from behind a tree. *If that idiot thinks he can sneak up behind me, he's getting a faceful of piss*, he thought with a grim relish.

Girolamo was being unusually quiet, but Merlini was used to his tricks and knew the joker was lurking nearby. He could feel it. He finished his business but stayed where he was and cautiously turned his head ever so slightly. Sure enough, out of the corner of his eye, he could make out movement behind him, emerging from other end of the chasm. He turned in triumph.

"Hah! Got you now, you bast—" The word froze in his mouth.

It was not Girolamo, but a huge shambling figure, taller than a standing ice bear, a faceless white giant with great shaggy limbs and the tapered head of a salamandre—but this bizarre creature was not made of flame, but something white and gauzy as cotton.

The silent behemoth reached down for him with outstretched arms that ended in tufts of silk instead of hands, and Merlini nearly backed right into the crevasse. He drew his dagger and slashed across the creature's midsection. Both hand and weapon immediately became mired, stuck fast in its sticky torso.

No sound came from the creature as it slipped what passed for a hand under Merlini's shirt, spreading onto the bare skin of his chest, reaching with the other around the back of his head. It seized the nape of his neck in a hideous parody of a lover's grip, the filaments insinuating themselves into his hair, locking the creature's hold on him. Then, unhurriedly, it began to pull Merlini's face closer.

With a relaxed, undulating movement, it silently slid its body forward until it was fully pressed up against Merlini's, and then worked its way closer still, legs flowing over his, their torsos merging. Merlini's trapped arm was completely absorbed. He flailed with his free hand, trying to block the creature's advances, but it was quickly engulfed as well.

Merlini tried to scream for help, but no sound emerged—the thing's touch had a paralyzing effect. He could not even flex his vocal cords. His eyes grew wide as his terror increased, unable to do anything while the faceless horror continued to pull him in at a sickening, leisurely pace. Inch by inch, his straining muscles gave up the fight, allowing his whole body to sink into the white softness. As his throat and then chin succumbed, he felt the monster's silken filaments grow and slide eagerly past his lips, worming their way around his paralyzed tongue and sinking deep into his throat.

The last thing Merlini saw before the awful, implacable whiteness became total was its ravenous filaments pushing their way under his eyelids and crowding deep into his eye sockets. And then it swallowed him.

Alia woke up to the smell of breakfast and a throbbing headache. Opening her eyes, she stared blearily at the same dreary, drizzly gray skies as yesterday. Then Dari's face filled her vision, holding out a tin mug with steam rising out of it.

"Camp coffee," Dari said. "Should kick the pounding right out of your skull."

Wincing, Alia sat up, cloak pooling around her hips and legs, and accepted the mug from her friend. Took a sip and winced again. "Gods, that's vile." She drank some more, letting the bitter brew clear her head and ease the pain. She looked up at Dari. "Thanks."

"Figured you'd need it. There's bread and honey—a gift from the innkeeper—and apples if you're hungry. How 'bout you help me wake everyone up?" She grinned. "Raff wants to be out of here an hour ago."

Keth was already up, along with Soren and Geffi, and it wasn't too difficult to rouse the three Pentan merchants, Bellamy, and her mistress. Jezel—quite unfairly, Alia thought—looked somehow younger and even more radiant after a night sleeping on the ground. Her irritation faded, though, when the woman gave her a hug, her sympathy unspoken but felt nonetheless.

In short order, everyone had eaten and was ready to continue the journey to Trionn-Fí.

Alia looked around. "Has anyone seen Cal ..." His name caught in her throat and she tried again. "Has anyone seen the Tozzo retainers?"

"Girolamo and Merlini?" Jakobi pointed through the trees. "They camped up that way."

"Dari, go check on them," Raff said. "If they didn't skip out in the night, tell them we're heading out."

Nodding, she started off in that direction, but almost immediately stopped in her tracks and took a few steps back into the clearing, eyes wide as she stared between the trees.

Raff shot her an impatient glance. "What is—" He stopped when he saw what she was staring at. "What in the name of Athamé's blade ... ?"

A pair of unusual strangers lurched through the trees, casually ambling toward camp like two drunks wending their way home from a tavern. They were tall enough to be stilt-walkers and sported some kind of ridiculous oversized rural costumes with pointy tufted heads, all made of snow-white fur, or perhaps bundles of white flax.

The party looked at one another in confusion.

"Who are these walking haystacks?" Raff muttered. "Is there a harvest celebration going on out here?"

"Perhaps so," Harbalorio replied. "Or perhaps they got drunk and wandered off from the festival."

"They're a fair piece from Trionn-Fí—but it makes as much sense as anything else," Birnardus agreed.

Bellamy nodded eagerly. "I'm sure that's what it is. We have mummers dressed like that in Beauchalice—they're supposed to be snowmen or something like that. You have to give them a treat or a kiss before they'll go away."

"Well, I don't like it," Jakobi growled.

"Don't bother with either," Raff said. "We've no change to spare, and no time for mummers or carnivals or whatever they're up to."

Even Keth seemed baffled by them. "They almost look like golems," he mused aloud. "Golems made of cobwebs ..."

"Ho there, you two!" Jakobi called out. "You'll have to tell us what you're dressed up for."

The two figures made no response, silently shambling closer. Giggling, Bellamy approached them and curtsied. In response, one slowly extended his arms to hug her.

Jakobi stood up and put up his hand. "See here, if you're not going to tell us your business, that's close enough."

Bellamy laughed and swatted him on the arm. "Oh, Jakobi, don't be such a churl. It's just tradition! Here, mister monster, I'll give you a kiss." Pursing her lips, she closed her eyes as the mute giant bent down toward her, pulling her in for an embrace.

Meanwhile, the other slowly reached out for Jakobi, who was having none of it. "Not unless you want a good thump on your noggin, my friend," he growled, taking a step back.

"Oh! It tickles!" Bellamy looked suddenly nervous as it lowered its silky head, putting what would have been its mouth—had it had one—over hers. Her eyes flared wide with panic as she tried to scream, only to have the sound smothered as her face sunk into its candy-floss surface, the thing enfolding itself around her limbs and torso.

Jakobi wheeled about to come to her aid, but the second monster was already on him, catching him from the side and wrapping him in a bear hug. With perverse slowness, it tightened its grip, pulling him into its body while he bellowed in distress.

The others, who had been watching in amusement, suddenly realized the danger. Jezel screamed Bellamy's name and Harbalorio drew his sword, charged forward, and lunged, stabbing the golem absorbing Jakobi. His blade sunk deep into its flank and out the other side, but it seemed completely unfazed. Gritting his teeth, Harbalorio twisted his sword to finish the monster, but found his sword arm mired, and—to his horror—sticky weblike filaments streaming from its bloodless wound and crawling up his forearm.

For a few panicked seconds Bellamy thrashed her arms and legs, but the golem lifted her off the ground, filaments slipping under her blouse and skirts, seeking out her bare flesh as it continued to engulf the rest of her face into its own.

An ululating banshee howl rang out as Dari, sword raised high, attacked the thing from behind. Leaping up, she swung her blade in a powerful lightning strike that came down at an angle as she landed, slicing clear through the creature's torso.

The top of its body wobbled for a brief moment, like a newly felled pine in that terrible moment before it succumbs to gravity ... then regained its equilibrium and resumed its meal, unconcerned. Dari stared in disbelief, and then attacked again, swinging her sword in a savage arc at what passed for the golem's tufted head, just above Bellamy's.

This time the blade bit deep—and stuck. She cursed and tugged with both hands to wrench it free, but only succeeded in getting herself ensnared in the sticky surface of its broad white back.

Raff leapt over the campfire and brought his sword down hard on the golem holding Jakobi. The stroke cleft its head down the middle, coming dangerously close to splitting the Pentan's head as well—but did nothing to stop the monster. Instead, Raff found his sword stuck and his arms snared by its webbing.

Bellamy had ceased her struggling—the thing had engulfed her face and her limp body was disappearing into the cobweb golem's torso while an enraged Dari only entangled herself further in its back.

Meanwhile, Jakobi's attacker silently folded its upper torso over him, draping over his head like a cloak. Harbalorio and Raff were both cursing and struggling to pull free, but their own bodies had betrayed them as well, refusing to offer any resistance as they were pulled in further.

Alia, Geffi, and Soren had drawn their swords as well, but hesitated when they saw how useless their comrades' weapons were against the monsters. Alia looked on in desperate horror, then turned to Keth. "Can't you do anything?"

He cursed, shaking his head. But Alia's eyes lit on the campfire and she quickly snatched up a brand, kicking up a plume of sparks, and thrust it at the golem holding Bellamy and Dari. A wide swath of the webbing instantly blackened and shriveled at the touch of the fire.

"Quick! Burn them!" Alia yelled, and those who were still free rushed to take up more blazing branches from the campfire. Alia kept up her own attack, grimly pleased to see the sticky mass of filaments sizzle away so rapidly. As the layers of cobwebs burned away, a withered, leathery face appeared, staring back at her, its eye sockets black and empty, its flesh little more than dried mummified skin on bone. The golem's core, its skeleton, was the desiccated husk of Merlini.

The fire did its work quickly—Alia had to drop her torch to catch Bellamy as she tumbled free, her hair and clothes starting to smolder. Alia pushed the girl to the ground and covered her in a cloak to prevent the flames from spreading. In moments, the others had been pulled to safety, and both golems were reduced to ash, leaving only the grisly remains of their original victims.

Chapter Fifty

The mood around camp was subdued as Alia, Geffi, and Soren treated the injured. Bellamy had received the worst of it, both from the golem and the burns she'd sustained when it had gone up in flames. Her hair had been singed, crisped tendrils coiled around her face, while her back, neck, and upper arms bore scorch marks. Jakobi was in slightly better condition, but the fright of nearly being suffocated had left its mark on him as well. The two of them sat on the ground in a daze, Jezel by Bellamy's side, while Raff and Keth studied what was left of the two Tozzo retainers. The rictus on what was left of their faces was difficult to look upon.

Raff asked, "Have you ever seen or heard of anything like this before?"

The mage shook his head. "No. No mention of anything of the sort in any of the scrolls or grimoires I've come across, nor in any of the teachings I received. Still ... I think it's probably best if we burn the rest of the remains."

"No argument here."

There was no eulogy as the wizened husks of Girolamo and Merlini went up in flames. No one remaining knew them well enough to speak about their lives, and no one had liked them well enough to comment about the brief time they'd shared on the road.

Once the pair had been safely reduced to ash and the fire put out, Raff faced the group.

"As I see it, we have two choices. We can continue to Trionn-Fí and hope for the best, or we can turn around now and go back to the inn. From there, you can all go where you please. What do you say?"

"I say it's time to be done with this doomed journey and turn around!" Birnardus exclaimed. "Why should we risk any more lives chasing a dream that's turned into a nightmare?"

"No." Keth strode forward. "We have to continue."

"Why?" Dari snapped back. "We'll never make it in time for the festival—even if there still is one now."

Harbalorio heaved a heavy sigh. "As much as I hate to agree, there's little chance of any of us making money at the festival, even if the earthquake didn't curtail the celebrations."

"This isn't about any damned festival!" Keth shouted.

Birnardus snorted like an angry bull. "You can't possibly think whatever your business in Trionn-Fí might be that it's more important than the lives already lost!"

"I do." Keth's voice was steely. "And far more. It's worth my life—all of our lives."

Birnardus stood up, his face red with rage. "Are you mad? Do you think we don't know who you are, you damned *Psychidion* hexmonger? It's your bloody faction that's responsible for all this calamity, isn't it? This earthquake, and now those unholy abominations. *You* did this, didn't you?"

"What are you spouting off about, you gilded codpiece?" Alia snapped. "Do you think you're helping anything by these pointless accusations?"

"Ask him!" the Pentan retorted, pointing to Keth. "Everyone remembers how the Emperor had to rope in your order once you lot began meddling with black arts. And that defrocked archmage of yours—the one they say started the whole debacle ... what was his name?"

"Hallam," Keth said flatly.

"*Hallam.*" He hissed the name. "Did you know what he was up to? Were you part of his plans?"

Keth stared at the Pentan with a cold, flat gaze. "Hallam is my master."

Birnardus waved a hand at Keth as if the mage had just made his case for him.

"Well, isn't that fine! Hallam the Mad is your master! They exiled him, but your cursed faction didn't learn their lesson, did you? They wanted to follow in his footsteps, merrily traipsing down to hell! The Gods only know what else you and your damned friends have unleashed upon the realm! And *you* want us to lay down *our* lives just so you can meet up with your friends and carry out more mischief?"

"That's enough, Birnardus." Harbalorio put a hand on his friend's shoulder.

"The hell it is!" Birnardus shook him off. "This bastard is the devil's own apprentice!" He strode over and snatched up Keth's map case from where the mage had set it down during the fight.

Keth's face tightened to see the case in Birnardus's grasp. He extended a hand. "Give it back."

Birnardus ignored him. "So what's in here, eh? What is so gods-damned important in here that you're willing to spend *our* lives to get it to *your* Psychidion friends?"

"Don't open that," Keth said carefully as Birnardus started to unbuckle the clasp.

"Get back! I'm going to see what you're smuggling once and for all!"

Keth took another step closer, his voice low and even, his tone placating. "There's nothing you'd be interested in inside there, I promise you."

"I'll be the judge of that," Birnardus snarled. "Don't try to beguile *me* with your spells, you skeevy little warlock! I'll see for myself!"

"I'll tell you. Just keep the case closed, I'm asking you." He took another step forward and Birnardus scrambled away from him.

"What kind of country bumpkin do you take me for? I'm a Pentan merchant!"

"Birnardus, do what he says," Alia said harshly. "It's his business, not yours, nor is it any of ours!"

"Like hell it is!" The Pentan finished undoing the buckle and started to remove the lid.

"It's a flower!"

At that, everyone turned to stare at the mage.

"Birnardus, it's a flower," Keth continued. "Just a flower. It's kept fresh by a simple preservation cantrip, and if you open the case, you'll break the spell. That's all."

Birnardus stopped prying at the lid and became quiet. "That's it? A *flower*?"

Keth nodded. "That's it."

"Trollshit," Birnardus muttered, and popped off the lid.

"Stop!"

It was too late—the big Pentan had already reached his hand in.

"Well, I'll be damned," he murmured. "It *is* a flower." He pulled out the bloom with a flourish.

It was an ugly plant. The thorny stem was bloated and uneven, the blossom misshapen, its color the dark rainbow sheen of spilled oil.

Keth took a step back, fear in his eyes. "Put it back in the case, Pentan," he said softly.

"Why are you so afraid of a—" Before Birnardus could finish his sentence, the flower came to life in his hand. The stem swiftly encircled and fastened on his hand like a fanged tentacle, while the dark blossom opened to expose a lamprey-mouthed ring of tiny needle teeth—which bit down on the flesh of his palm.

Howling in pain, Birnardus flailed his arm for a few frenzied moments before he was finally able to tear the creature off and fling it away. Fast as a viper, it slithered away into the grass and was gone. The Pentan clutched at his hand and groaned, glaring darkly at Keth.

"Damn you, assassin!"

With his other hand he drew a dagger and rushed at Keth, but Harbalorio and Dari grabbed him by the shoulders and held him back.

"Let me go, blast you both! He's poisoned me with black arts!"

"Don't be an idiot!" Dari growled. "He tried to stop you. What did you expect would happen? Be glad you didn't stick anything else in there, you great thumping tub of lard!"

For a moment it seemed that Birnardus wouldn't listen to reason, but then the fight went out of him and he sat heavily on the ground, cradling his wounded hand. Keth approached slowly, hunkering down by his side and holding out a hand.

"Let me see the wound," he said.

Birnardus gritted his teeth and glowered at him, but let the mage inspect the bite mark and the circlet of little puncture wounds from where the thorns had drawn blood.

"Will he live?" Harbalorio asked.

"Damned if I know," Keth said. "Rinse it with plenty of whiskey and bandage it all the same. Then we'll see. But best keep an eye on him so we know if he turns into something unnatural overnight." He got to his feet, turned, and then paused. "We may have to kill him." With that, he walked away.

Birnardus shook himself free from Harbalorio and Dari's grasp and cradled his hand again, staring after Keth's retreating form.

"He's joking, isn't he?" he asked, looking from one to the other. "Isn't he?"

"Hell if I know." Dari shrugged. "Now sit down and let me see to your hand before it gets infected."

"Keth! Keth, wait a moment!"

Alia hurried after the mage as he strode away into the trees, finally catching him by the arm. "Would you just wait?" she exclaimed.

He did, turning to her with a dark expression. "What?" he snapped, then glanced down at her other hand. "Do you plan on killing me?"

She followed his gaze and saw that she'd automatically put her other hand on the pommel of her sword. "Don't be stupid," she shot back, exasperated. "I'm a soldier. There are things in the forest that want to kill us."

"And you think I might be one of them." It was not a question.

"By the Gods …" She took a deep breath, then another, so she could resist the temptation to smack him across the back of his head. "No, you idiot. And I'm not blaming you for what happened to Birnardus. He had no business going through your things, and you gave him fair warning to leave well enough alone. But—"

"But you want to know if what he said was true." Again, not a question.

Alia looked him in the eye. "Yes. I mean, not the poisoning with black arts drivel, but why is it so urgent that you reach Trionn-Fí? And I *would* like to know what the hell kind of flower bites a man, and why you've been carrying it with you?" When he didn't reply, she added, "What *do* you know about what's going on? If you want us to help you get there, you owe us an explanation."

"She's not wrong." It was Raff, who, along with the rest of the party, had been watching and listening to their exchange and now waited for what he had to say.

Keth heaved a long, deep, shuddering sigh, then squared his shoulders as if reaching a decision.

"Six days ago, I received a package from my master …"

Chapter Fifty-One
Southwestern Highlands of Athamē

A Modest Homestead—Six Days Ago

Keth brought the package into the house. On the family dinner table, he sliced through the leather lacing and unwrapped it to find a folded letter on heavy parchment, and a cylindrical traveling case of dark-colored boiled leather. He opened the letter and whistled up a ball of hovering were-light to read it by.

Hello, my dear boy, the letter began, and it then proceeded to ramble on about the weather in the hinterlands north of Trionn-Fí, followed by a tedious and detailed account of Hallam's successes and setbacks in vegetable gardening, shared some breezy gossip about notables in the capital, and ended with half a page of salacious limericks.

Keth smiled wryly to himself and shook his head. Setting the pages upon the table before him, he smoothed out their folds until they lay flat. *Let's see what you really wrote*, he thought, and spoke a spell known only to his master and him.

> *"Idir-Hallamis gamisha Kethra, scriihivhiin tor-daum avriarha firinnockh …"*

Parchment of Hallam, give me, Keth, his true words …

In response to his voice, the letters of Hallam's florid script twisted and turned like eels in a pond, swirling into new shapes and positions to form a completely different message. In his imagination, he could hear Hallam's voice as clearly as if they were in the room together.

Tell no one this.

My experiments are going well, and I have at last discovered a way to improve upon my earlier work—so much so that I have finally succeeded in what I set out to do, thanks to skill and deft subtlety that Málach could only wish he possessed. Inside this case, I give you this sign …

Picking up the leather case, he unbuckled the clasp. The lid twisted off easily enough, but the tube appeared to be empty. Turning it over, he gave it a gentle shake and was surprised when a single long-stemmed flower slid out and fell upon the table. He picked it up.

It was like no bloom he had ever seen before—the bud was a weird hybrid, like a rose twisted into the shape of an iris. The texture was that of fine silk, stippled with swirls of tiny, raised bumps. It had an unearthly beautiful iridescent color, almost obsidian, but also lustrous, like the feathers of a pigeon's head in the morning sun. A ridge of tiny thorns wound up the stem. Careful to mind them, Keth held the flower to his nose and breathed in its scent. Its fragrance was another disquieting blend—it made him think of overripe fruit and ashes.

Very unique. A beautiful, if somewhat disturbing gift. But not the sort of thing his master was inclined to bestow on him. So why had he sent it? What did it signify?

He returned to the letter.

The clipping comes from my garden—in a sense. A more accurate description is that it comes from beyond the veil, since I have pierced the boundary. The changes you see in this once-ordinary specimen of plant life are because the influence from another, thoroughly alien, dimension has played upon it. Through the opening in the interdimensional laminae, I have been able to effect, a remarkable transference has been achieved. The emanations from this still mostly unknown alien force have taken a living thing from our world and infused within it the nature of another world—creating a wholly new amalgam.

This is yet another thing Málach fails to understand—we cannot interact with the animating principle of this counterdimension to ours without altering its nature, just as it, in turn, alters ours in the most strange and unpredictable ways.

The terms of my annoying exile required me to be shackled with a binding spell that confines me within one hundred paces of my tower. Therefore, I need you to take this to Trionn-Fí and present it before Málach and the Psychidion leadership. With your explanation, it will both prove that I have accomplished what they strive for and serve as a warning that they risk blundering into unexpected peril without my further aid and expertise.

You will recall from my previous letters that I have been keeping tabs on their progress through surreptitious means of my own. Do you remember what I told you about their approach? And who they are in league with? Urgently impress upon them the need to bring me back from exile before they go any further.

Hallam was being doubly cagey, considering the sorcerous security measures he had already taken with his missive, but Keth knew his own master and his theories well enough to recognize that he was referring to the barrier-crossing Abraxas Scepter, Hallam's notorious—and, by imperial sanction, forbidden—sorcerous instrument whose theory and design Málach had stolen from him. Nor did his master need to remind Keth that the secret patrons of the Psychidions were in the *Cathedralis Geminae.*

> *Leave at once, and if you find the welcome from your former colleagues is lacking, go elsewhere immediately and without fail. Now I leave you with one final word of advice that you may need to share with others. First things first. So, know this: Apprentice Boy, recognize an* X *as signaling numbers or words, dreams or nightmares, etc.*
>
> *—H*

Keth frowned at that final paragraph. Part of it was plain enough—if Lord Málach and the other Psychidion leaders refused to listen to reason, he would need to take the evidence across the palatial estate to the Aurichalcum Tower, to the Emperor's own Lord Mage, Vissente. But what did he mean by "first things first"? What was first? And what in blazes did his master mean by that last cryptic line?

> *Recognize an* X *as signaling numbers or words, dreams or nightmares, etc.*

He sat back in his chair and racked his brain, trying to remember what Hallam had mentioned to him before, but this did not sound familiar at all. He ran it over and over in his head. None of it made any sense. It was no sorcerous principle he had ever been taught. *X*? What—and where—was *X*? And that business about numbers and words, dreams and nightmares—he was baffled.

Apprentice Boy. He frowned again. His master had called him many things over the years, but "Apprentice Boy" was weirdly out of character for him. Why the sudden derision? He cast various spells of deciphering but could find no further sorcerous tampering or trace of hidden runes, glyphs, or other secret writing. Perhaps it was a code. But if so, how was he supposed to crack it?

First things first ... first things first ... He had a sudden flash of insight and read over the final part of the letter again.

So, know this: Apprentice Boy, recognize an X *as signaling numbers or words, dreams or nightmares, etc.*

First things—first ... letters? He went over the sentence again, word by word. Suddenly it was clear—there *was* a message in the final line, hidden in the first letter of every word:

A*pprentice* B*oy*, R*ecognize* A*n* X A*s* S*ignaling*
N*umbers* O*r* W*ords*, D*reams* O*r* N*ightmares*, E*tc.*
A B R A X A S N O W D O N E
A B R A X A S N O W D O N E
Abraxas Now Done.

Now he understood why he needed to leave immediately. He rose from the table and grabbed the leather map case, trying to ignore the sudden jolt of fear that shot through his chest.

Chapter Fifty-Two

Raff was the first to speak after Keth had finished his explanation. "So you are to go to your old order and warn them not to activate the Abraxas Scepter without first consulting with your master."

"Yes."

"But they already have," Alia said slowly. "Haven't they?"

"I fear so."

Raff frowned. "Are you saying Birnardus is right? Your faction caused that shaker?"

"I can't prove it—but yes, that is what I think." He paused, then added, "And it might also explain these unearthly phenomena coming from the fissures."

The rest of the party looked at one another uneasily.

"Can anything be done?" asked Alia.

"I don't know," Keth admitted. "But I *do* know that the Abraxas Scepter must be at the center of it all. The damage is done. We can't reverse that, but if we can destroy the scepter, perhaps it will prevent the damage from spreading any further."

"Hold on," Raff spoke up again. "If what you're saying is true, then how bad are things in Trionn-Fí?"

"There's only one way to find out."

"The hell there is!" Birnardus muttered, prompting more unhappy grumbling among the others.

"Look, I'm not asking anyone else to go," Keth exclaimed. "But don't you see, if somebody doesn't stop this, these things that we've encountered ... they could spread across Tarou. Perhaps even further!"

"Yes, well, you go ahead." Birnardus waved a dismissive hand. "'Perhaps' is a vague promise on which to risk our lives. *Your* kind made this mess—you fix it."

"Didn't you hear the man?" Alia said in disbelief. "What we've already seen ... he's saying it could spread! Surely a chance to stop that from happening is worth the risk!" When no one else spoke, she continued. "Well, I'm going with him"—she shot a look at Birnardus—"regardless of what anybody else is going to do. What the rest of you do, and where you go from here—that's your decision."

"She's right." Jezel, who up to this point had been silently tending to Bellamy, spoke up. "The more of us that accompany our friend the mage here—"

"No friend of mine," Birnardus interrupted. Jezel went on as if he hadn't spoken.

"—surely the better the chance of success." When no one argued, she continued. "And another thing to consider. We've been on the road a full two days and two nights, and we've lost four of our party. We're what? Less than an hour or so from Trionn-Fí?" She gestured to Bellamy and Jakobi. "Our friends are injured and in no shape to trek back to the inn. Best to continue and find shelter, food, and whatever help we can."

Alia stared at the Chalicean in unvarnished admiration as she sensed the tide turning in favor of continuing. Not even Birnardus could find fault with Jezel's logic—although it was clear he wanted to—and it was decided they would press on to Trionn-Fí immediately.

Chapter Fifty-Three

Despite the fact that they knew they were drawing close to Trionn-Fí at last—Dari thought she'd caught a glimpse of the capital over the last rise—that knowledge did not improve the mood of the group. Everyone was on edge, the soldiers especially alert, keeping their eyes out for any other unknown new threats. Strange things were afoot, like the walking horrors that had transformed the two Tozzo retainers, or the goo that had killed Falla and Callen.

Raff had taken the lead, letting Dari bring up the rear again. She preferred that to point—only her natural skill as a navigator made her agree to switch positions in the first place. If Soren and Geffi weren't so green, she'd have trusted them to watch their backs, but they were both so shaken by Falla's death and the morning's horrors that she doubted either could fight a babe in nappies. She hoped they'd snap out of it soon—her gut told her they hadn't seen the end of trouble on this journey.

"I tell you," Dari muttered to Harbalorio, "I would rather face bandits and highwaymen any day than those ... well, whatever they were." She shuddered. "And I'd sure as hells rather die by the sword than however those two men died."

"Damn the mage and his cursed secrets!" Birnardus griped—yet again. "If he'd just been honest in the first place, I wouldn't have been forced to open that damned map case!"

"You'll get no sympathy from me," Harbalorio said. "You had no cause to mess about with his belongings, and you wouldn't have been hurt if you'd minded your own business."

Except for a disgusted snort and a roll of his eyes, Birnardus had no answer.

The trees towered above them, branches starting twenty feet up. The ground was thick with pine and fir needles that crunched softly underfoot. Instead of the fresh, pungent fragrance of pine, the citrusy aroma of fir, and rich loam of the forest, however, the unpleasant sweet-sour smell had thickened, joined by the faint stench of rancid meat.

"It's coming out of those damn cracks in the earth," Birnardus proclaimed, although at a fraction of his normal bombastic volume. His voice fell flat in the stillness of the forest.

And they're getting bigger, Harbalorio thought uneasily.

"Just stay as far away as you can from those gashes," Dari said. "And keep your eyes open. There's more wrong here than an earthquake can account for."

The closer they drew to the capital, the more difficult it became to avoid the crevasses. They became wider while, at the same time, were set closer together, making it more difficult to find clear ground between them. And the stench that rose from them grew worse with each one they passed.

Even worse than the smell, though, were the noises. Scratching, scrabbling sounds, both furtive and menacing at the same time. It started to take its toll on the group.

Bellamy and Jakobi were lagging. Jezel had noticed her maid slowing down not long after midday had passed, her steps faltering.

Oddly, now she had lost her limp. Jezel supposed that was a good thing, but it still disturbed her, although she could not say precisely why.

At first Jakobi had supported Bellamy, helping her keep up with the rest of the party, but not long after she'd slowed down, he had also started to lag behind.

Jezel dropped back to check on Bellamy. "Are you feeling well?" she asked, putting a gentle hand on the girl's shoulder.

Bellamy nodded, her expression dull.

"I'll look out for her," Jakobi said flatly. Neither seemed in a conversational mood, so Jezel nodded and let them be, and went to talk to Dari and Harbalorio. Birnardus had also joined them, his ruddy complexion unusually pale and moist-looking.

"Tell me, sir," she said solicitously, "are you not feeling well either?"

"Nothing a bottle of Chalicean wine wouldn't fix," the Pentan replied. His hearty voice fell as flat as Bellamy's lackluster tone had, as if the air itself was swallowing sound.

"You look downright green," said Harbalorio.

"Nonsense!" his friend protested. "Just not used to all this blasted walking." Jezel caught him glancing down at his wounded hand, and for an instant saw a worried look cross his round face. Then it was gone so swiftly she wondered if she'd imagined it.

"I see the Southern Bridge!" Raff shouted from up ahead. The mood of the group visibly lifted and everyone's pace picked up now that the end of their journey was in sight. An unseasonable gloom of fog, tawny-colored like a lion's mane, obscured their view of the capital as they continued their approach, but they could make out the wide dark band of the Grand Canal encircling the city. Straight ahead was the magnificent Southern Bridge that spanned it in a graceful arc, high above the waters.

Standing proudly at the foot of the bridge was a familiar and welcome sight—the tall spires and wide gates of the Athamé Arch, a beloved landmark that had long greeted travelers on the High Road from the south, just as the other three main entrances into Trionn-Fí did for the other cardinal directions. Alia's heart leaped to see it had survived the earthquake. It was a good sign, and she allowed herself to feel a little joy at having reached the capital after such a harsh journey.

"I can't wait for a proper bath," Jezel said to no one in particular.

"I'll take a bottle of good Chalicean wine," Birnardus chimed in. "And a proper meal and a decent bed to boot!" He turned to call out to Bellamy and Jakobi, who had fallen even farther behind. "What about you, Jakobi?"

His friend ignored him and kept walking, his arm around Bellamy.

"I say, what about you, Jakobi?"

He still gave no answer.

Harbalorio and Birnardus exchanged looks. "Jakobi, can you hear me back there? Stop pestering the poor lass and catch up with us, you lazy sluggard."

"Perhaps he's too busy sealing the deal with the fair Bellamy," Harbalorio joked.

"Nonsense," Birnardus protested, predictably. "It's obvious she prefers me—the indulgent girl is too kind to the wretch. She took pity on him and is simply allowing him to assist her while I am indisposed. Too kind, that girl …"

As they crossed under the arch, his theorizing trailed off, giving way to an uneasy silence as the group studied the view before them. As expected, the tall gateway was a sight to behold, its finely sculpted details, golden spires and finials all decked out with the usual decorations for the Imperial Festival, brightly colored ribbons and pennants—though it was eerie that there was no sign of traffic nor any sign of the handsomely uniformed honor guard normally stationed there. Looking out over the

Grand Canal, there were no pleasure crafts on the water, nor even any fishing boats.

There was no sign or sound of any human activity—at all—from anywhere.

Stepping onto the bridge, the party continued forward, wisps of the thick, dun-colored fog curling around them and the two bridge towers. It hung like a veil in the air, shrouding everything in mystery.

"Does this seem strange to you?" Jezel asked Harbalorio.

"I must confess, it doesn't make me feel particularly festive," he replied. "It's—"

As they reached the midway point of the bridge, a forlorn gust of wind cleared away the gray fog, as if drawing back a curtain to allow them their first unblemished view of the Imperial Capital. Harbalorio's words dried up in his throat, and the excited chatter that had rippled through the party moments before, when they first spotted the arch, cut off with the finality of an iron door slamming shut.

Trionn-Fí, the crown jewel of Tarou, was utterly gone.

Being the first to spy the great crown upon the mount at the heart of the city was a favorite game of travelers. The shimmering azure facets of the Aurichalcum Tower and the Imperial Palace never failed to inspire awe and deep patriotism. It was surreal to gaze upon the city now and see *nothing* where a fabulous palace should be crowning a mountain. It had not been fog obscuring the vista, but a shroud of smoke and dust caused by whatever devastation had befallen the capital.

The entire city had been flattened, like flowers pressed under glass.

The tallest points of the magnificent city were now the lowest—the towers and spires, mansions and rooftops of the Upper City's Noble Quarter surrounding the Crown Mount, all dragged down along with it—vanished into an almost perfectly round depression in the middle of what used to be neatly laid out streets and parks, magnificent estates and architecture. Fissures and crevasses wound their way between the buildings, and the noxious-colored mist seemed to almost bubble as it drifted out of those same wounds in the ground.

"It's ... it's all gone," Jezel whispered.

Bellamy and Jakobi had fallen behind again, weaving almost as if both were drunk as they slowly made their way across the bridge to the others. By the time they had caught up, both sank to the ground, overwhelmed by the destruction. Jezel hurried to her maidservant's side.

"Here." Alia held out a waterskin. Jezel took it and handed it to Bellamy. The girl took a deep pull from it and then handed it to Jakobi, who followed suit.

Once they had both drunk their fill, their heads sagged forward onto their chests as if too heavy to hold up. Bellamy's hair fell in sheaves of corn silk gold in front of her face.

"Bellamy?" Jezel put a hand on the girl's shoulder.

Bellamy turned her head toward her mistress. So did Jakobi. Their eyeballs looked like balls of white clay. Their mouths fell open, white tendrils emerging, undulating like seaweed underwater. More tendrils came out of their nostrils and some started worming their way from their eye sockets as well.

Jezel screamed and threw herself backward, scrambling away frantically as those tendrils reached for her.

Alia, closest to Jezel, pulled her away from the advancing monstrosities—all the more horrible for the vestiges of humanity that still clung to them. Although with each slow, deliberate tread, those remnants became harder to see. Their clothing started to rip at the seams as more tendrils burst from their bodies, splitting open along arms, legs, and torsos.

Bellamy's beautiful, long, pale blond hair fell out as silky threads pushed out of her scalp and replaced it. In a few moments, her body was covered in a thick coat of filaments. The slender tendrils continued to grow longer until it was clear that in a few moments, there would be no visible sign at all of the human beneath the cobweb golem.

"We need fire!" Dari cried.

"Drive them off the bridge!" Raff shouted. "Use your spears! Don't let them get close enough to touch you!"

Alia looked to Keth, who ran over with her spear in hand and drove the butt end against Jakobi's doublet-clad chest. He shoved hard, forcing him back away from Alia and Jezel. The flurry of white tendrils continued to erupt from rips in his doublet until it was buried within them. They quickly enveloped the spear haft, straining to grow fast enough to reach Keth's hands.

Raff and Soren joined him, using their spears to keep the thing that had been Jakobi from pushing past Keth's defense, herding it toward the edge. Then with a final shove, they pushed it over, Keth's spear still stuck in it as it pinwheeled away and down.

Meanwhile, Dari and Geffi drove back what used to be Bellamy as it tried insistently to reach Jezel, who cowered behind Alia. Raff and Soren helped them drive it off as well and sent it tumbling away like a rag doll. Both golems plunged into the water far below and vanished beneath the surface.

Jezel got slowly to her feet and looked over into the deep, dark water. And burst into tears.

"Oh ..." Alia breathed softly and took the stricken woman in her arms to let her cry out her grief against her shoulder.

When she was done mourning for the moment, Jezel brushed the tears from her eyes, blew her nose on the handkerchief Birnardus silently offered her, and got to her feet. Then the remaining members of the party slowly made their way over the bridge. The urgency seemed a thing of the past.

"Why should we go further?" Harbalorio finally broke the silence. "There's ... there's nothing there."

"The Abraxas still needs to be destroyed," Keth reminded them. "Or what we see here could happen to the rest of Tarou ... if it hasn't already."

No one had a reply to that. Without another word, they made their way into the city.

Chapter Fifty-Four

The Outer City sprawled before them, crumbled buildings of clapboard and plaster, stone and brick rubble littering the ground. The fissures burrowed through the streets and the ruined buildings, many filled with water that shimmered with the strange, nausea-inducing colors. Corpses littered the streets, most dressed in festival finery now filthy and ragged. There was blood on walls, bricks, and cobblestones as if an insane painter had dipped a brush in gore and spattered it everywhere.

Trionn-Fí had been visited by death in dozens of terrible forms—no one had died easily or kindly. Bodies were everywhere, jumbled together like children's dolls thrown carelessly to the ground.

Some had drowned—the canals were choked with corpses, although there were also sodden bodies lying in the streets. Others had been crushed by falling debris or trapped in buildings as they'd collapsed, and still others that looked as though they'd fallen from a great height, now practically flattened into a pulp. Body parts protruded from the wreckage—a child's arm stuck up from a pile of collapsed bricks, hand outstretched toward the sky as if begging for rescue. And still others died by burning, charred beyond recognition as to age or sex.

The air was still thick with dust, forcing the travelers to cover their mouths and noses with handkerchiefs or makeshift kerchiefs. It stung eyes and got into noses and mouths. And underneath it all, the stench from the fissures mingled with the odors of violent death.

Vendor stands lay smashed on their sides, their merchandise scattered thickly on the ground. Fabrics, glassware, ceramics, food, jewelry, tapestries, rugs, weapons, and any number of other items mingled in what would have been an irresistible treasure trove if not for the dust and debris coating it—and the corpses that shared its resting place.

"A fortune's worth of Athaméan steel," Dari said softly, looking at the pile of weapons. Keth silently retrieved one of the swords, testing its balance with a practiced air before buckling a sword belt around his waist and sheathing the blade.

A flash of emerald caught Alia's eye and she crouched down, picking up a necklace made of sparkling green glass beads—cheaply made but something that would no doubt have delighted someone with only a little money to spend. A table holding wooden toys still stood upright. The corpse of a little girl lay next to it, her hand still clutching a wooden dragon with wheels and a string with which to pull it. Her eyes stared sightlessly upward. A woman lay on her side next to the child, one arm protectively around the little girl, the other covering her own head in a futile attempt to ward off whatever form of death had come their way.

The group walked silently through the charnel house that had been Trionn-Fí, each trying to come to grips with destruction so terrible, so final that it was impossible to comprehend. No matter which way they looked, there was nightmare fodder for the rest of their lives.

An entire row of houses wiped out by the carcass of a downed airship, bodies of its crew members still tangled like broken marionettes in the rigging.

"How do you think that happened?" Harbalorio said in disbelief. "Those dreadnoughts are supposed to be indestructible."

"Only by the strength of their magics," Keth replied softly. "When the magic went, so did the mages' control over the elementals carrying them. Slaves do not always treat their masters kindly, given the chance. Can you blame them?"

Remembering what had happened with his lighter, Harbalorio said no more, trying not to picture what must have happened when the elementals found themselves unchained.

They came across one particularly disturbing corpse sprawled in the middle of a pile of luxurious rugs. It had been an older man on the skinny side, one of the poorer inhabitants of the city, if his worn and patched woolen trousers and threadbare linen shirt were anything to judge by. Frowning, Raff knelt by the body.

"What is it?" Alia joined him, wondering what it was in this cornucopia of horrors that had caught his attention. Using the tip of his blade, Raff lifted the dead man's shirt, exposing his lower torso—his entire intestinal cavity had been scooped out. He looked up at Alia with a grim expression.

The others came up behind them, peering over Raff's shoulder at the gutted corpse in horror.

"By all the Gods, what *did* that?" Harbalorio said, aghast.

"I don't want to know," Birnardus muttered.

"None of us do," Dari snapped. Her temper tended to flare up when she was uneasy or scared, as if to convince others—and herself—that she wasn't frightened.

Raff turned to Geffi and Soren, who looked as though they were about to vomit. "Keep your swords out and your spears ready," he said softly. "And remember—we're Athaméan warriors, and if we run into whatever did this, we will fight it and kill it."

The twins nodded in tandem, their commander's words putting steel back into their spines, even if their faces were still pale with fear.

Chapter Fifty-Five

As they penetrated deeper into the city, the destruction, if anything, grew worse. While there were still some structures that were at least partially standing, they grew fewer with each circle of the city they traversed.

Oddly enough, though, the number of corpses lessened.

"This makes no sense," Raff spoke quietly to Dari and Alia, not wanting to upset the fragile equilibrium the twins had seemed to have gained. "Where are all the bodies? Surely there should be more. I mean, look at this." He gestured at the surrounding devastation.

"There are probably more underneath all the rubble," Alia said. But it rang false to her even as she said it.

Part of their unease came from a sense that the damage seemed to be worsening as they advanced—the fissures were increasing in number and size, with some large enough to be called chasms. Dari stared down into the nearest one.

"You don't think the earth just ... swallowed everyone up, do you?" No one had an answer. The smell was nearly overwhelming as they walked by the larger ones. The mist shrouded some of the fissures, as though trying to conceal them, while bubbling out of others, shimmering unpleasantly with unearthly colors that hurt their eyes and made their stomachs churn with nausea. It made everything seem more surreal than it already was.

Even beyond these things, though, was the unshakable sense of being watched. Of being stalked. Alia caught glimpses of movement out of the corner of her eye, but when she turned to look, the only thing she saw were dead bodies lying among and under the ruined buildings. But as Raff said, not as many as logic dictated there should be.

"Maybe the survivors have started taking the bodies somewhere for burial," Dari offered.

"What survivors?" Raff cut her a look. She shrugged, unable to come up with a response. They hadn't seen a living soul since entering the city. Not even an animal, neither fish nor fowl.

"Something else we need to consider," Raff continued. "Not counting the two Tozzo retainers, so far only Bellamy and your friend"—he nodded at Birnardus and Harbalorio—"transformed into those creatures. Not everyone touched them, but those of us who did ... well, we need to keep a close eye on one another."

"Do you think we might ..." Birnardus trailed off and swallowed hard.

"I don't know," Raff replied. "Maybe we'd have turned by now. Or maybe ... well, those two were the only ones who were ... swallowed. Either way, we need to be careful. There's no way of knowing how any of this stuff works."

Birnardus glanced uneasily at his bandaged hand, then caught everyone looking at him. "I feel fine!" he insisted. Jezel approached and put a hand on his shoulder.

"Be that as it may," she said in a voice as smooth as velvet, "promise me you'll tell me if that changes."

"I ... yes ... yes, of course!" Birnardus stammered, face red as a ripe tomato. "I would never do anything to put your life in danger, My Damsel."

"Thank you, My Sir. I know I can trust you."

Jezel caught Alia's eyes and smiled.

Keth followed his own counsel and tried to stay calm even as his sense of urgency was exacerbated by growing dread. He had known that if Abraxas had been activated, things would be bad, but nothing had prepared him for this. His only choice—unless he turned and fled—was to keep moving and carry out Hallam's instructions as best he could.

He could only be grateful that the elementals appeared to have abandoned what was left of the city. Hopefully they had returned to the elements from which they came.

As if reading his mind, Harbalorio asked, "Do you think they're still here? The elementals, I mean?" The Pentan looked around uneasily.

Keth shook his head. "If there were, we would all be dead."

The further into the city they penetrated, the fewer structures remained intact. Here and there, a lone dwelling or business stood. The group took a quick break to eat in the Drunken Salamander. The tavern sign featured a stylized fire elemental, big-eyed and smiling, like something that one would find painted on a nursery wall.

Furniture was overturned, crockery shards crunched underfoot, and the floor was sticky with spilled beverages, but there were plenty of metal tankards and several unbroken bottles of wine and mead. Birnardus found a keg of beer with a working spout and immediately drained an entire tankardful in three long draughts.

"We can't afford to get drunk," Raff warned.

"Surely you don't judge a man for a drink under these circumstances," Birnardus said in offended tones.

"Not at all." Raff took a drink from one of the bottles of wine, passing it on to Geffi. "But I *will* judge you if one of us dies because you're pissed. Just keep a clear head. There'll be time for getting drunk later."

When they made ready to leave the tavern, Dari asked, "Should we leave our belongings here and just carry our weapons?"

Raff thought about it and shook his head. "Better not. Who knows if we'll be back this way? We may need what we carry to survive when we make it out of Trionn-Fí."

"*If* we make it out of Trionn-Fí," muttered Birnardus resentfully. With that in mind, he stuck two unopened bottles of wine in his satchel. If he was going to die, it would be with the taste of Chalicean wine on his lips.

Chapter Fifty-Six

The wide boulevard they were on led straight through to the Inner City, and to the Imperial Palace and *Cathedralis Geminae*, but a fissure at least five feet across ran down the center of it, making a straight path forward impossible. The group went on either side of it—Keth and Alia to the left, the rest to the right—climbing over and around chunks of marble, bricks, and other rubble as they attempted to stay on target.

They encountered another corpse with its guts scooped out as they entered the Middle Circle. This one was female, and it looked as though there hadn't been much of her before she'd died—fashionably skinny to the point of emaciation. She lay outside of the remains of a fashionable mansion near the Noble Quarter and wore an elaborate wig the color of ripe wheat that spoke more of money than taste. It had been knocked askew, revealing a sparse head of straw-like hair underneath.

Alia most likely wouldn't have liked the woman had she met her while alive—she'd encountered too many ambitious social climbers who looked at life as a succession of ladders to climb, never truly enjoying what any of the rungs had to offer because there was always another one waiting to be conquered. She'd thought Jezel fell into that category, but adversity had brought out the best in the woman, and Alia found herself warming to her despite the worst possible of introductions. When this was all over, perhaps they could even be friends.

So deep was she in her thoughts that Alia didn't see the corpse in front of her until she tripped over it. She recovered her balance just in time to prevent herself from landing directly on top of the body. This one was male, with a major portion of his head missing. In a straight line through the top half of his mouth, a clean, scarily precise cut had removed everything—his tongue hung slackly over the bottom lip and teeth. The rest of his face and skull were nowhere to be found.

Keth came up next to her. "What in the name of the Gods is this?" he muttered.

"That's even worse than the last one," Alia said shakily.

Glancing around, Alia saw another body in the same semi-decapitated condition. Then another, and another, and others with intact heads but missing their entrails. It was as if her vision had been blurred and suddenly everything came into focus. There were dozens of both, including children.

Even stranger, many of the bodies seemed to have paired off in death—always one of each—their limbs intertwined, hands clutching the other's throat or curled into claws sunk into rotting flesh. Those that had mouths had sunk their teeth into their opponent's throats or shoulders or whatever they could reach, red meat sticking out from between their lips. Those missing the tops of their heads had gouged-out eyes, pulled-out tongues, wrenched-apart jaws.

"What fresh hell is this?" Birnardus moaned.

Alia shook her head. The carnage was unimaginable.

"Why isn't there blood?" Keth suddenly said.

"What do you mean?" Alia joined him to stare down at the pair nearest to him—a little girl no older than six, the midsection of her lace-trimmed yellow velvet dress, in fact, soaked with blood, and a skull-less boy wearing breeches and long-sleeved doublet of the same fabric. Blood had run in thick rivulets from the remains of his face and head to crust the top of his doublet. "There's blood everywhere."

"Yes, but look at these wounds." He pointed at the two lying side by side, the girl's hands filled with chunks of flesh from his arms, his fingers buried in her eyes. He looked over at the rest of the group, all of whom were on the other side of the crevasse. "No blood. Which means they were made after these people died."

Harbalorio shook his head in denial. "Impossible."

"After what we've already seen," Raff said, "I don't know if that word means anything anymore."

Dari gave him a sideways glance. "I do not find that comforting."

"Neither do I."

The sensation of being watched grew suddenly stronger. Slithering noises, coming from the ruined buildings around them, vied with clacking, scuttling sounds from the crevasse. To add to the discord, something—or somethings—shuffled and dragged their way toward the group from behind them and in front.

Alia's instincts screamed danger and she dropped into a crouch, muscles tensed and sword at the ready. Around her, her fellow Athaméans and Keth did the same, and the two Pentans drew their smallswords while Jezel unsheathed the dagger she wore at her waist.

"What in the name of Athamé's steel is happening?" Geffi's horrified whisper carried across the crevasse.

"Stay strong," Alia said, hoping her voice wouldn't crack and betray her own fear.

"Steady," Raff shouted. "Remember who you are and where you come from!"

Even though she knew his words were mainly for Geffi and Soren, they still put steel into Alia's spine and she saw Dari straighten as well. She caught Raff's eye and, despite her fear, smiled at him, a wide devil-may-care, almost crazy smile. These were her comrades and she would defend them to her death if necessary.

It happened all at once.

Things came pouring out of the crevasse—scores of nightmare crustaceans the size of meat platters, with ten claws, the front two ending in scissorlike pincers. Their hard shells were the red purple of livid dead flesh when the blood pooled. Each had a single pus-yellow eye the size of a cantaloupe in the middle of their shells and imposing mouths that opened and shut like jagged-toothed bear traps. Their claws clicked and clattered on the rubble.

At the same time, multitentacled creatures like octopuses, their color the slimy grayish white of a fresh corpse, slithered out from the rubble and dropped down from sagging beams and window frames, pulling themselves by their tentacles, pulpy gourd-shaped bodies undulating behind them. Red eyes were on either side of their bulbous heads, mouths in the center, the latter opening like a lamprey's to reveal circular rows of needle-sharp teeth. They were all a foot or so in size, the ropy tentacles contracting and expanding with each undulation.

Then the group found out why some dead were missing their abdomens and others the tops of their skulls.

Approaching from the rear were dozens of shuffling corpses, grayish-white blobs where their stomachs and intestines should be. Tentacles vanished up into the torso and down into the hips, like ivy climbing a wall. The mouths of the octopod corpse-riders opened and closed in anticipation while those of their dead corpse-mounts hung slack-jawed.

Blocking their way in front were more walking corpses, but these wore a crustacean skullcap, claws dug in on their bisected heads with a vise grip while the corpses' mouths were hidden under the shells, giving them all the appearance of helmeted cyclopes.

All the hijacked corpses lurched unsteadily and implacably toward them, stumbling on the debris and falling, then getting slowly to their feet, never losing sight of their prey. Meanwhile, the horrors from the crevasse and the ruins closed in from either side.

Skull-eating crustaceans poured out from the crevasse, sending everyone scrambling from the edge as far back as they could—only to be hemmed in by the oncoming tentacled corpse-riders. Alia scanned in all directions and made a quick decision. Their best hope was to fight through the walking corpses blocking their path forward and run like hell. She looked across the fissure at Raff and pointed ahead. Raff nodded, having come to the same conclusion.

She and Keth were on their own until the crevasse narrowed enough for all of them to come together again, Alia realized. "Run!" she yelled to him and took off down the boulevard just as the front wave of corpse-riders and skull-eaters closed in from both sides. Several of the slithering corpse-riders lashed out with their tentacles to entangle her shins. She nimbly jumped over them, smashing down with her sword as one of the skull-eaters scuttled to intercept her. Her blade cracked the crustacean down the middle, its eye oozing down its broken shell as it gave a chittering squeal and died. More scurried to take its place, but she was already running again, somehow keeping her feet on the rubble-strewn ground as the creatures skittered around and gave chase.

Keth caught up with her, the ground sloping down slightly as they encountered more cyclopean walking corpses, the foremost a well-fed man dressed in soiled silk and velvet finery. Without pausing his stride, Keth took the thing's head off with a horizontal slash across its neck, shoving it out of the way as he reverse-cut to decapitate one reaching for him from the right. They both died with the same high-pitched squeal as the one Alia had dispatched, human puppets folding over on themselves now that nothing was pulling their strings.

It was hard enough to fight their way through the ranks of grotesque corpses, but they quickly found just as great a threat came from the surprise ambushes of the unattached creatures.

A corpse-rider launched itself at Keth from a lantern post, wrapping its front tentacles around his thighs and immediately slithering up to his torso, its lamprey maw open in anticipation of digging into his guts. He gave a yell and shoved the point of his blade into the top of its head. Alia immediately seized it, peeling it off him and flinging it at one of the skull-eaters. The crustacean gave an angry shriek and fell on the dying thing, cutting it to ribbons with its claws and sinking its razor-sharp teeth into its bloated head.

As the two sides converged on Alia and Keth, the battle took an unexpected turn—each proved just as eager to attack their rivals as their human victims. Skull-eaters and corpse-riders collided, brain-piercing shrieks and squeals coming from both sides as they ripped into one another. The corpse-riders used their surprisingly powerful tentacles to seize the crustaceans, rip the legs off, and penetrate their carapaces. Once they secured a good grip, they could crack one open with the ease of a nutcracker shelling a walnut. The skull-eaters, in turn, used their numbers, two or three converging on one corpse-rider and slashing into it with their claws and chomping teeth. There was no blood from either side, just foul-smelling ooze of the same nausea-inducing shade as the mist bubbling up from the cracks.

Alia and Keth stared in horrified fascination as the two factions slaughtered each other, the duo seemingly forgotten. Then Keth took Alia's hand and the two turned and ran, the sounds of the unholy war eventually fading into the distance until they were forced to skid to a sudden stop, sending bits of dirt and pebbles flying—catching their footing just in time to keep from launching themselves off the edge of a precipice.

Chapter Fifty-Seven

Alia and Keth found themselves looking down upon a surreal and utterly unexpected vista. It was unsettling to see the palatial estate so horribly transformed from the highest pinnacle of a mighty capital city into the lowest depth of a pit surrounded by miles of ruin and rubble. And yet somehow everything within the Crown Mount was remarkably preserved by whatever geological force had inverted it from peak to trough—the mountaintop had sunk into the earth with the structures built upon it relatively unharmed, the major exception being the Aurichalcum Tower, which had been effectively pulverized into glittering blue shards.

"Shall we go back and wait for the others?" Keth asked.

Alia looked down at the remains of the *Cathedralis Geminae*. "They know where we're headed, and I trust Raff and Dari to get the others this far. Why don't we go scout ahead instead?"

Keth nodded his agreement and the two of them carefully descended down a crumbled portion of the outer wall into the center of the depression.

It was uncanny. Except for the palace itself, if she ignored the occasional cracks and fissures, the fallen ruins, Alia could almost make herself believe they were taking a quiet evening stroll through the palace gardens. The pair easily traced their way through the grounds to what remained of the *Cathedralis Geminae*, the Holy See and Twin Seat of the Highest Ecclesiarchs of the Empire.

Unlike the palace and majority of the sumptuous buildings and mansions in the Noble Quarter, the Holy See had not relied on sorcery to support a fanciful superstructure. Instead it was meant to evoke the appearance of simplicity and antiquity, and had been built from simpler materials, colossal stones, and expensive marble.

They made their way over the flagstones of the plaza where worshippers once gathered and stepped carefully inside the rubble-strewn ruins of the great cathedral itself. The vaulted ceiling soaring over their heads had not survived its precipitous descent into the underworld. Its high stone walls and towering pillars stood broken and jagged, like the fingers of a clawed hand reaching up from hell. They continued into the deeper interior of the *Cathedralis*. Once brightly illuminated by hundreds of were-lights, it was now cast in shadows.

"Here." Keth picked up two long brass candlesticks and tore strips from crimson velvet curtains that lay puddling on the floor. Soaking the strips in holy oil, he then wrapped them around the butt ends of the candlesticks and, with flint and steel, lit the makeshift torches, handing one to Alia.

Various ornate doorways led off from the sanctuary into other parts of the labyrinthine complex—the cathedral's sacristy, chapels and shrines, libraries, quarters, and guest chambers, and the imposing doors safeguarding the treasury and the archives.

At every turn, flashes of gold and silver reflected in their sputtering torchlight. If they had been treasure hunters, there would have been more than enough riches to keep Alia and Keth busy for months. They ignored all these and instead delved deeper into the extensive administrative wings. Except for the echoes of their boots upon the marble flooring, all was quiet as a tomb throughout.

Alia finally broke the silence. "Have you noticed anything odd?"

"Odder than an entire mountain sinking beneath the earth?"

"No, I mean here." She gestured around. "Inside. There are no corpses. Not in here, nor the cathedral itself. Don't you think there'd have been casualties when all the damage hit the main sanctuary?"

Keth considered this. "Maybe everyone in the complex survived."

"Now that *would* be a miracle."

He shrugged. "I agree. So maybe those that *did* survive moved all the bodies."

"Either way ... where is everyone now?"

Going further, the two came upon another main corridor, its ceiling twice the height of the passageways they'd already traversed. Alia suddenly stopped, crouching and bringing her torch down for a closer look at the marble floor. A narrow fracture ran through it, twisting down the deserted passageway like a coarse black length of thick twine. She pointed to where it led, and Keth nodded. If Abraxas was indeed the center from which all the fissures originated, it seemed as promising a lead as any.

The corridor ended at a set of tall golden double doors, large enough to allow pikemen on horseback to parade through. The doors were engraved with an enormous ecclesiastical seal that neither of them was familiar with. Both were ajar, opening onto the corridor, and they were able to slip through the gap between them without difficulty.

Inside, the air smelled fouler, with the same noxious reek that seemed to haunt all the cracks and fissures caused by the Psychidions' disastrous experiment. That smell, however, was overlaid by the copper stink of blood.

By the light of their torches, Alia and Keth could just make out a hint of the domed ceiling high overhead. At their feet, the rich marble floor had been overlaid with elaborate and complex designs set down in black and gold.

"What are these runes?" Alia whispered. Something about the place called for hushed tones.

"Patterns of evocation and conjuration, mostly," Keth replied quietly, illuminating the designs with his torch. "Some for divination as well, looks like." His eye was caught by a new pattern that appeared in the hazy circle of his torchlight—a rust-brown splatter of dried blood.

As they continued further into the room, it became clear that was just one of many bloodstains—some dry, others disturbingly fresh—obscuring the arcane designs, along with huge, cobweb-shaped cracks where something heavy and unyielding, like a troll-sized maul, had pounded on the floor.

"Looks like there was quite a fight."

"No, not a fight," Alia corrected. "A slaughter. And yet still no corpses." A few steps further in, and they could see the smashed wreckage of magical equipment and instruments strewn about, broken glass and delicate pieces of metalwork dashed across the marble floor. "Could any of these be from your scepter?" she asked.

"No, these are all just general thaumaturgical devices to aid scryers, monitor the ley lines and such. The Abraxas will be shaped like an Athaméan tournament mace." Off her look, he continued, "You know, the flanged kind they use to batter heavy armor with. Only it will be made from the darkest shade of blue crystal, and it will be massive, the size of a temple pillar, or—"

"Or that?" She pointed ahead.

He looked where she was pointing and caught his breath. "Yes. Exactly that."

The Abraxas Scepter was just as impressive as Keth described it, thick as an ancient redwood and so tall it had barely fit inside even this huge chamber. The Psychidions had followed Master Hallam's design to the letter. It was composed of solid blue-black crystal, grown for years deep underground by sorcerous means before being harvested, carved and shaped, then masterfully inscribed across its entire surface with lines of powerful glyphs and sigils.

Seeing it at last with his own eyes, Keth realized that his only chance of success would have been using his knowledge to shut down its function and hope that no other mage could come along in the future and reactivate the device. Even if all of their party had survived and were with them, they would have needed long lengths of heavy chains to pull it down, and to all have been armed with mattocks and hammers, if they were to have any chance of demolishing the structure.

But all that was moot—it was already destroyed.

Approaching the fallen giant, Keth ran his hand over the boulder-sized crystalline chunks almost reverently. Something truly massive had brought down the scepter and broken it into pieces, leaving them where they fell in a long pile that still kept the shape of the thing and roughly bisected the domed chamber. Now that they were close enough, the light from their torches allowed them to see that on the other side of the divide, a significant portion of the room had caved in, leaving a large, jagged hole in the floor.

"It must have been magnificent to behold," Keth said softly. "I wish I could have seen it before it was destroyed. Seen it in all its glory."

Alia looked at him uneasily. If the thing had been whole when they'd arrived, would Keth have tried to use it again? Re-create the experiment that destroyed Trionn-Fí? *No,* she thought firmly. She trusted him.

She had to.

"Who do you think *did* destroy it?"

Keth began to answer, then stiffened, and put a warning hand on her shoulder.

"We're not alone."

Sounds came from outside the doors—running footfalls and voices that fairly vibrated with excitement. But they didn't sound right. Didn't sound human. Alia thought it was as if whoever—whatever—was talking had a mouthful of dirt and snot, their voices rattling and clotted, their words guttural and unclear.

Then more torchlight spilled into the room as the enormous golden doors behind them were pulled open—and by the sound of it, other doors as well. In moments, they were surrounded by a crowd of dark, misshapen figures that seemed to pour in from all sides of the chamber. Their eyes glowed like fireflies. Some were armed with pikes, some with swords, others with crude clubs.

In the flickering half-light, it was hard to make out features, only glimpses that suggested lepers or plague victims, dripping candlewax faces, grotesque hunchbacks, hulking behemoths, twisted and redoubled limbs, every kind of lopsided, misshapen flesh imaginable. Some looked like walking corpses, flesh sloughing off the bone. No two were the same. As they drew nearer, Keth and Alia saw that their skins had taken on a sickly greenish cast. The glow of their torches showed mouths stained with blood. They also realized from the filthy remnants of their clothing that the monstrous crowd surrounding them had, not very long ago, been Psychidion mages, cathedral palace guards, high church officials, and vestal virgins.

There will be no getting out of this chamber without a seriously one-sided fight, Alia thought grimly.

"Keth, draw your sword."

He did as she commanded.

Their opponents were still keeping their distance for the moment, content to ring them in with pikes and staffs and sheer numbers. They were careful not to tread upon the runes or bloodstains and stepped reverently around the litter of the magical equipment scattered about. This room was clearly a holy, sacred space for them.

From somewhere in the dark came echoes of chanting, some droning dirge of the kind sung by monks, but darker and more unsettling. The glowing lines of more torches appeared through the cracks of a doorway straight ahead of them. The crowd around Alia and Keth became more excited as the droning chants grew louder, and then that last set of doors swung wide open.

A procession of chanting, malformed figures streamed in, bearing a large palanquin. The bearers set the litter down close by the rim of the gaping pit in the floor and gathered around it on either side.

Alia and Keth blanched at the nightmarish sight enthroned before them on the litter. The once-splendid robes were now encrusted with filth and in tatters, and their flesh had taken on the same green hue as the others, but mage and soldier could still recognize the starry-night-sky motif, the silver crescent headdress and silken veil, and the white-and-gold vestments and gilded miter. There was scant else to remind anyone that this grotesque shape had once been the High Priestess and the Hierophant—or that there was anything human in what was left.

It made Alia think of wax figurines that had been exposed to flame and melted into one another to form one single malformed lump—a legless pile composed of other human bodies that had been absorbed to form a dripping, fleshy mound. Its mournful facial features rode loosely upon their skulls like masks of tragedy, blistered torsos lumped together in a great blob of tortured flesh. Its heads and necks protruded from the same oversized shoulders like some fanciful double-headed bird from a heraldic crest. It reeked of corruption, of rancid flesh.

The monstrosity raised two limbs to the sky in a gesture of benediction, and the rabble surrounding Alia and Keth bowed before them in reverence. When they spoke, it was two distorted voices speaking as one.

"The old Gods are driven mad and changed beyond recognition," they croaked.

"—As are we," their unholy flock called out in response.

"All praise to the one true god who cometh from beyond, the god who threw down Abraxas and brings a new world."

"—And blessed are all the children born of its womb."

"Truly, they hunger."

"—They shall be fed."

"Behold, their nourishment comes."

"—Let them be fed."

The thing lowered its arms and turned its red eyes upon the tense pair standing before them.

Keth refused to show any of the fear he felt. "Hold," he commanded, raising his arm. He bowed to the enthroned abomination courteously. "I am a member of the Psychidion mages, with an important message for Lord Málach himself. He will wish to see us."

Low, disquieting chuckles rippled through the crowd.

"Don't think to order us, Upstart," the melded atrocity snarled. *"Or you'll join your sniveling little Lord Malcontent sooner than you like."* Then they addressed their eager sycophants.

"Do not fear the mage. He has no power anymore. Nor the warrior, for she can withstand neither your might, children—nor the terrors soon to come."

The mob laughed louder now, a blend of thick, mucus-filled cackles and high-pitched tittering that pierced the air like needles.

"What do you want with us?" Alia called out boldly.

"Your flesh, trespassers," they said, prompting more demonic laughter. *"Look into the pit before you, interlopers. What do you see?"*

Below them they could see only dark gloom, though the thick, fetid smell coming up from its depths was revolting.

"It is your judgment. You will join us—or feed us." The mound of their throne-bound body quivered and rippled in anticipation.

In answer, Alia spat in their direction.

"Very well. We will feast!"

The mob rushed them. Alia leapt up upon the fallen chunks of Abraxas, and Keth followed just as the wave hit them. Swinging her blade, Alia decapitated the first three to reach her with one deadly horizontal slash. Desperately, Keth thrust and hacked, brandishing his torch as a second weapon, but only managed to keep his attackers at bay for a moment as the press of the crowd came over the rubble and forced him back.

Alia had better luck, killing two more. The pikemen were coming to the fore now, concentrating on her, driving her into retreat from her perch. She beat aside two of the polearms and twisted just in time to turn a killing thrust from a third into a grazing hit. Cradling the pike, she dropped and let the point hit the rubble, then seized it in a tight clinch, hoping to leverage the spearman's momentum against him. It worked too well. He went sprawling headfirst in the pit—taking the pike and Alia down with him.

"Alia!" Keth yelled before the surging crowd smashed into him, overwhelming and lifting him up and into the waiting abyss. He struck the side of the pit as he tumbled to the bottom.

Chapter Fifty-Eight

Overhead, the mob howled their victory and crowded around the rim of the pit to watch the spectacle unfold. Alia shook her aching head, pushed herself up on her elbows, and took quick stock of her condition. Nothing broken, just bruised. Her opponent had helped cushion her fall—now he lay prone and groaning, one leg canted to the side at an unnatural angle. Keth sprawled nearby, unmoving.

She fought against a sudden wave of nausea—down here the stench was unbearable, a sickening mix of vomit, blood, shit, and offal, and something worse underneath it all.

They had dropped into a subterranean chamber with a ceiling too low around the perimeter of the pit to stand upright. Another fissure ran through the chamber, creating passageways before and behind them. Barely any light reached them from above, but their pair of guttering torches offered some illumination—she could at least see that the pit floor was crisscrossed with thick ribbons of some sticky coating, like giant glistening slug trails. There were random body parts scattered about as well. An armor-clad leg from the knee down, a knob of bone at the top as if the shin had been torn from the body. Part of a hand, the remaining fingers covered in jeweled rings. A woman's head that looked partially melted, her mouth open in a silent scream.

They'd fallen into a charnel house, joining the remains of the mob's meals.

As she gazed about her, nearly paralyzed with horror, a small, calm part of Alia's brain wondered why there weren't more bodies. Surely this wasn't enough to feed the mob overhead. Then she heard a strange noise, and the hair rose on the back of her neck. She quickly moved to Keth's side.

Something was coming through the tunnel in front of them. A man would have to crawl or crouch low to slowly and carefully make his way through to them, but whatever this was, it was coming fast, moving with an odd snuffling, padding sound. It filled the entire width and breadth of the tunnel.

"Keth," she whispered frantically. "Keth, wake up!"

Alia's opponent stirred and turned his ruined face to her. Back when he was fully human, he must have been a palace guard. He still wore what was left of his chain mail and tabard, though the diseased skin around his lips had rotted and peeled away like a dead man's, baring his crooked teeth in a perpetual grimace. But she could see he was still human enough to know fear—he quickly sat up when he heard the thing in the tunnel approach. He knew what was coming to feed.

The pikeman lurched to his feet—his progress hindered by both his broken leg and the sticky patches on the ground—and raised a hand to plead with his fellow cultists.

"Pull me out! Help me! Pull me out!"

But they ignored his cries for help.

Alia stared as the shape shuffled through the tunnel toward them. At first glimpse, it looked like an enormous human skull. When it emerged fully from the fissure, it was far worse.

Its head resembled that of a giant housefly, with a long beak-like proboscis and wriggling, protruding palpi. But its eyes were those of a praying mantis—oversized and yellow green, the pupils tiny black dots eagerly tracking its prey.

It propelled the bulk of its elongated, maggot body forward with a squirming, undulating motion, then lunged out with clawed, sticklike forelimbs covered in bristles, to pin down the screaming pikeman before he could reach for his weapon. As he cried and prayed aloud to it for mercy, it leaned over him, bringing its horrible face in close, as if listening intently to his pleas. Then the lower part of its mouthparts opened like the bloom of a snapdragon to reveal a fleshy, mucus-lined throat—and from that trumpet shape suddenly emerged a steady stream of yellowish-green vomit.

The man's screams intensified, and a burning, acrid smell overpowered the air as his steaming flesh bubbled and dissolved into red froth. Like a lark picking in the dirt for a worm, the creature's needling proboscis probed its victim's body, sucking up the chunky, warm broth that only seconds earlier had been muscles and intestines.

"Keth! Wake up!" Alia shouted. But the mage did not—or could not—move.

Alia's soldiering instincts took hold and she instantly scanned the room to locate the weapons—their fallen swords and torches, the guard's pike. The monster methodically spat up another spurt of bile upon its struggling victim, and this time his agonized screams gurgled away, along with his face and skull.

Sticky slime trails pulled at Alia's armor as she crawled over to Keth and shook him.

"Keth! You've got to *wake up now*!"

His eyes snapped open.

"Look out!" he yelled, staring past her.

Alia turned her head to see the thing's rippling bulk coming after her. Without hesitating, she snatched up the guard's pike and thrust it at the oncoming monster. It reared back with a shrieking hiss, spraying its bile, and the front end of the pike's hardwood haft dissolved away, dropping its smoking spearhead.

"Grab your sword and run!" Alia screamed at Keth as she tried to keep the creature at bay with what remained of the pike's wooden shaft while dodging its spitting counterattacks. Although it could not project its acid very far or very accurately, it would only need a single solid hit to take her down and then finish her.

Alia retreated, following after Keth, but once she was out from under the well of the pit, the ceiling was so low she was forced to crouch. Either by cunning or instinct, the giant insectoid was forcing her to withdraw into an increasingly cramped space where she could not swing her sword or even stand upright. Its own movement and attacks, however, were not hampered at all. Worse, at every step, the viscid slime on the ground stuck to the soles of her boots, hindering her movement even further.

Alia didn't dare turn her back on the charging monster, even for an instant—and could only watch with dismay as it flowed over her abandoned torch, extinguishing it. Now she could only see by the unsteady, bobbing globe of light coming from Keth's torch somewhere behind her, partially blocked by her own body. She thanked the Gods he'd thought to grab his when he fled. She didn't want to think about her chances of beating this thing in the dark.

Keth was calling out to her, but she couldn't make out what he was trying to say. It was taking all she had to keep steady—in her awkward crouch, she couldn't put her whole strength into her thrusts, and with only a half-dissolved polearm shaft to defend herself, the thing was pressing its attack, its facial palps waving in anticipation of consuming her.

And then Keth's torch went out.

Without thinking, Alia's reflexes kicked in and she thrust the shaft forward with all her strength. It caught somewhere on the monster's massive skull. By some miracle of combat, her improvised lance bent with the impact, but thankfully, did not snap in two or fly out of her arms. The jarring collision lifted her and her weapon, tearing her free from the gummy secretions underfoot. It also knocked her backward, sending her sprawling on her backside.

The creature seemed completely unbothered by the pitch-blackness. Alia could hear it surging forward, smell the acrid stench of its acidic drool, and feel the clacking of its proboscis as it stabbed at her repeatedly, trying to position itself to unleash a killing gush of vomit. She tried furiously to kick away from the thing's deadly onslaught, but a jab of its beak-like proboscis caught her in the thigh—and then as she thrashed and twisted to get away, a second lucky stab pierced a weak spot in the lacing of her hauberk, spearing her in the side.

Alia grunted in pain, gritting her teeth as she desperately thrash-kicked her body free and backward—just as a spill of its digestive juices splashed down between her splayed legs, spattering her armor. She could see nothing, but the acid stench was overpowering. She kicked out again, and felt it connect with softer tissue—one of its eyes, she hoped. She braced herself for another probing attack from its proboscis, but something else—one of its clawed forelegs?—clamped down on her shoulder.

She was yanked back violently, and in that same instant, realized it was Keth's hand that gripped her, and that he was trying to drag her to safety in the dark. But then he stopped. She felt his body awkwardly leaning over hers, heard the soft crunch of his sword as he thrust it into the creature's face. It let out another ear-splitting shriek and retreated, hissing and spitting.

"Keep moving back—the way is too narrow for it to follow!" Keth urged.

Needing no further encouragement, she scrambled to join him back in the tapering passageway as the monster came roaring back to attack again.

Keth was right. Huddled together in their little burrow, they could hear it just a few feet away, worming its way closer as it frantically scraped at the rock walls in its efforts to squeeze in after its prey.

"Are you all right?" he asked.

Catching her breath, Alia nodded, then realized he couldn't see her.

"Yes, I think so."

The pain in her side was like a hot brand. There was a terrible smell, and she didn't dare run her hands along her armor for fear that there might still be traces of its digestive juices there. They would need to clean and bind her wound soon.

The thing suddenly sounded closer. But surely it couldn't squeeze its body in any further—could it? They took a moment to scoot further back anyway.

"I have your sword," Keth said. "Do you think you can get in a killing blow?"

"Maybe, if I could stand up, but I won't take the chance of getting anywhere near that thing's face in the dark again." She did not spook easily, but the fresh memory of the screaming guard's bubbling face made her gorge rise.

"We have to get out of here," she said. "How far back does it go?"

"I'm not sure," Keth replied, "but I do know we'll have to crawl. The ceiling drops fast."

"That's not good news."

"It's either that or deal with that thing."

A dreadful thought occurred to her. What if this way was a dead end? The creature's disgusting vomit stench was already fouling up the air—with its massive, maggoty body plugging up the entrance to their tunnel, how much air did they have left? And even supposing they could kill it without getting splashed with its acids, how could they move its bulk out of the way to escape?

She heard it scraping closer. The dark was starting to play on her mind—if they didn't do something, she thought she might go mad.

"Then we crawl."

As she inched forward on her stomach in the pitch-blackness, Alia fought to ignore the pain in her side and to control both her breathing and her rising fear. She could hear Keth's breathing coming in hard rasps ahead of her as he dragged himself forward. It was slow going, hard to move without every shuffling movement stirring up fine dust that gave them both choking fits. The rock ceiling was unforgiving and only an inch or so overhead. She banged her skull more than once trying to progress forward.

How far had they already gone? Twenty feet? Thirty? Less than ten? Alia had lost count of the times she had pulled herself forward like an inchworm and had even less idea how long they had been down here. Time and space had lost all meaning in the dark and the stench.

"Be careful," Keth called back to her. "The ceiling gets lower up here."

Lower? How can it get any lower? She gritted her teeth and continued on. A moment later, her forehead bumped into something—the sole of Keth's boot.

"Are you all right?" she said, her voice higher than she liked. He grunted in response.

"Yes—just—squeezing ... through." She heard his body slither away from hers. It would be her turn next.

Tired of bumping her head against the ceiling, she turned her face to the side, cheek pressed up against the cold stone, trying not to inhale any more dust as she inched her body ever forward. The studs in her armor kept catching on the rough surfaces of the ground and walls.

Suddenly she could go no further. She'd become wedged in the tunnel, and it felt as though the walls were actively pressing on her from all sides. Alia felt the sizzle of pure panic in her body, like a wild stallion fighting the reins, threatening to break loose at any moment.

"Keth ... I'm stuck." Her voice trembled despite her efforts to control it.

“Don’t try to move—let me scout up ahead first.” His voice already sounded far away.

Her heart started to race, and it was getting harder to breathe. Bile rose in her throat—she felt as though she was going to be violently sick at any moment, and fought to keep it down, to keep her breaths short and calm even as her throat closed up.

Breathe, soldier, she ordered herself. *Just breathe.*

Something touched her heel and she screamed. She thrashed forward and one of the studs on her armor ripped and gave way, letting her scramble onward again for a few feet before a choking fit forced her to pause and let the dust settle.

There was nothing there, she told herself. The creature was far behind them, and if she had trouble squeezing through the narrow tunnel, its humongous body could never fit. And surely they’d hear it if it was slinking up behind them—wouldn’t they?

Alia called out Keth’s name, and then again, but there was no response. Her head began to swim, so she rested her cheek flat against the cold stone to collect her thoughts for a moment ...

Stirring suddenly, she opened her eyes, but it made no difference—it was still pitch black. Had she fallen asleep?

Where was Keth? How long had he been gone? Her sudden spike of fear had temporarily silenced the pain from her stab wound, but now it came roaring back again. She felt along her injured side. It was sticky—but whether from the creature’s slime trail or blood, she couldn’t tell.

She called out Keth’s name once more, frightened at how weak she sounded to her own ears. It made her wonder how much blood she’d lost.

“Alia! I’m here!” His voice echoed off the stone walls. “Are you all right?”

“Yes! I made it through and now I’m coming your way!”

“No, wait! You can’t!” He said something else, but the echoes drowned it out.

"What?"

"I said, we can't keep going. It's a dead end!"

Waves of sheer rage, raw fear, and black despair washed through her. *This is where we die, here in pitch-blackness*, she thought. *And no one will ever know what became of us*. Somehow the second part seemed worse than the first. That thought made her laugh, so she did, letting herself laugh until it turned into crying and then back again, howling until her body shook uncontrollably—and the white-hot pain in her side jolted her to her senses again.

When she was done, Alia wiped the tears from her eyes and the snot from her nose. She felt empty inside, as though all her emotions had poured out of her. What now? She decided she would make her way to Keth—she didn't feel like dying alone.

She had no idea how long it took her to belly crawl her way through the zigzagging passageway until she reached him, but a flicker of joy sparked when she touched his boot once more. The dead end opened up just enough that she could squeeze up next to him. For a moment they lay there in silence. Alia could feel his breath on her face. His heartbeat was steady and reassuring in the cramped space.

"It's good to see you again," came his voice from the darkness.

That made her smile, and she wished she could see if he was smiling, too, the wry bastard.

"You too. Any thoughts on what to do now?"

"A few came to mind, but none of them very happy ones."

She had no answer to that, and they stretched out in companionable silence for a while.

"Gods, I wish we had a flask right now," she murmured idly.

"That would be just the thing," he agreed. They both fell quiet again.

"You know," Alia said at last, "if this party gets to be too tedious, I have a dagger in my boot."

"That's a cheery thought."

"It beats starving to death or suffocating."

He sighed. "You're right. I'm glad we have a blade when—*if*—it comes to that."

"You know," she suddenly repeated, "for an Arcane, you're awfully handy with weapons."

There was a moment of silence before Keth heaved another sigh. "Well ... that's because I'm not one."

"What?"

"I was born and raised in Athamé."

"You?" She laughed in disbelief. "An Athaméan?"

"Born and raised in the Southwest Reaches. For the first thirteen years of my life, anyway."

"But you're a mage."

"I started manifesting the ability as a toddler."

"What did you do—summon salamandrae to your crib?"

He laughed. "Nothing so dramatic. Mostly, it was just that wild were-lights were attracted to me. Terrified my mother. When I was a little boy, I could do a cantrip or two, little things like that, but my parents hoped I'd outgrow it. When I didn't ... they sent me to be schooled in Arcanum."

"So you're the proverbial wizard in Athamé."

"It's been said," he sighed. Clearly it wasn't the first time he had heard that old chestnut.

Alia nodded even though he couldn't see her do it. "You must have been a natural to have gotten so proficient at that age."

"Yes," he said matter-of-factly. "It's why they waited so long to send me away. When I was called to Trionn-Fí to apprentice under Hallam, I kept up my weapons training. I found that the two disciplines complemented one another."

"Were you sad to leave Athamé?"

He laughed, the sound short and unmistakably bitter. "No. My parents did their best to beat the magic out of me. I tried my best to suppress it, but one day my father went too far and I set the cudgel he used to beat me on fire. They couldn't see the back of me too quickly after that."

"How could they not have been proud of you?" Alia asked, horrified. She and her father didn't always see eye to eye, but he'd never made her feel that he was anything but proud of her.

"We were not a wealthy family. Had I been good enough of a fighter to be accepted into the royal guard or land some imperial position, gone up in rank, I might have changed that. My father thought, well, at least I might become a battle-mage. I had to disappoint him in that too."

She thought of another question. "What's it like to be able to feel magic?"

He let out a huff of air but was silent. At first Alia thought she'd offended him, but then he answered. "Like molten fire running through my veins, but it doesn't hurt. It's like riding the winds, knowing I can choose which way they blow. It's ..." He stopped, swallowing hard. "It's the center of my being, and I don't know what I'll do if it doesn't come back. Being without it is like death."

"I'm sorry," she said softly, reaching and finding one of his hands. She squeezed it. After a moment, he squeezed back.

They fell into silence again. Then, after a few moments, "Alia?"

"Yes?"

"Hand me your dagger."

Her heart fell.

"So soon?" She wanted to say something light and funny, but that was all that could come out.

"That's not what I mean. I want to check something."

Relieved, she reached down and slipped the dagger from its sheath in her boot, passing it up to him.

"What are you doing?"

"There's a little seam up here ... I wonder if ..." She could hear him scratching away at the stone for a long while, but then he stopped.

"Sorry to raise your hopes. I thought it might be a fault in the rock, some way into another passage." His voice sounded heavy, as if he had been trying to keep his hopes low, but they were dashed all the same.

"It was good of you to try." She lay still, trying to think of a way to extend the conversation, but everything seemed trite and stupid. "Keth?"

"Yes?"

She had to say it. "I ... I'm glad it's you here with me."

A long pause. So long that Alia regretted her honesty. But then his hand found hers.

"I wish we'd met at another time in our lives." Keth's voice was soft.

They had been down there too long, she thought. It seemed that the stagnant air was getting thin. Maybe they wouldn't need the dagger to end themselves after all. Or would slit wrists be less painful than running out of air? She felt something strange on her forehead, like the faintest of caresses on her dusty skin, and wondered if it was a hallucination, a sign that the air was going fast. Or ...

"Keth?" she said, barely daring to hope. "Do you feel that?"

"What do you mean?"

"I think I felt something ..." Then she felt it again and her spirits soared. "Keth, I think I felt *air*."

She heard him picking at the wall with the dagger again, more energetically this time.

"You're right!" he exclaimed. "I can feel it too! It—"

Keth's words were cut off by a sudden rumbling crash, followed by a booming sound and a cloud of dust that had Alia coughing and choking. She waved her hand to clear the air.

"Keth? Are you—"

She suddenly realized she could *see* him, lying still in the dissipating swirl of dust, lit by a thin slant of light coming from just ahead of him. He had managed to dislodge a fragile shelf of rock that had blocked the way to a fissure that opened to the surface about twenty or so feet up.

"Keth?"

She reached over to tug on his ankle and gave a start when he jumped, shaking his head. They stared at each other, faces breaking into wide grins, whooping and hollering. She quickly crawled up next to him and they gazed at the sky overhead, drinking in the fresh air.

Chapter Fifty-Nine

While Alia and Keth fought for their own lives on the other side of the crevasse, Raff, Dari, the twins, and the Pentans formed a protective circle around Jezel, who scooped up a chunk of hardwood, holding it like a bat. Each soldier had their sword in one hand, their spear in the other, and Harbalorio and Birnardus drew their rapiers. Birnardus gave a faint moan but stood fast.

The things attacked—slithering corpse-riders from one side, scuttling skull-eaters from the other, while the animated corpses on both sides steadily closed the distance between them. There was no way of knowing which of the three was the biggest threat, so Raff treated them with equal prejudice. "Dari!" he shouted. "Take the crabs! Geffi, Soren, keep the others moving! We'll be right behind you!" With that, he faced the octopoidal corpse-riders, slashing one in midair as it sprang at him. He speared one and then another in rapid succession, stomping on yet another as it tried to scurry up his legs. It split open beneath his booted foot, spraying foul-smelling ichor.

Meanwhile, Dari smashed into the skull-eaters with her sword, cracking the shells of some with the edge of her blade, sending others flying back into the crevasse with the flat. She tried using her spear but quickly abandoned that approach when the spearhead got stuck in the first one she pierced. She almost discarded the weapon but immediately decided against it. She was glad she did when a corpse—its destroyed abdomen pulsating wetly—grasped her shoulder, the puppet master within withdrawing its tentacles and reaching for her. With a combined scream of disgust and fury, Dari plunged the spear, crustacean and all, into the corpse-rider and its mount, shoving them back into a crowd of oncoming dead bodies and sending half a dozen to the ground.

Following Raff's orders, Soren took point and Geffi brought up the rear, doing their best to keep the attacking creatures away from the three civilians as the five ran for it, following the crevasse as it jagged to the right. Harbalorio and Birnardus held their own against the oncoming wave of hijacked corpses being ridden by skull-eaters like cavalry, while Jezel fought back against the crustaceans on the ground, striking with her own improvised weapon.

"We've got this!" Soren hollered to his sister, giving a whoop as he dispatched three corpse-riders slithering quickly toward the group from the right, then sent a skull-eater back into the crevice with a well-placed kick. Geffi whooped back, grinning as she pinned an opportunistic corpse-rider to the ground, using her foot to hold it in place while she pulled her spear out.

Then the unthinkable happened.

As she withdrew her weapon, the corpse-rider under her foot suddenly whipped its tentacles up and around her ankle, quickly climbing her legs and hips until it reached her torso. Before she could do more than scream, its mouth protracted and buried itself in her stomach, burrowing and tearing first through the hard-boiled leather of her armor and then into the flesh underneath. With ghastly speed its tentacles ripped Geffi open, causing her entrails to spill out, hollowing her out like a melon, before the creature squirmed up and into the cavity. And as Geffi died, the thing took control of her body.

"Geffi!" Soren's cry of anguish rang through the ruins. Without thinking, he started back toward her, but hands seized him by his shoulders and spun him around. Unlike his twin, Soren didn't even have time to scream before the thing cradled in the corpse's head leapt onto his skull and began eating.

Locked in combat, the others saw what was happening but could do nothing in time to save either one. They could only watch in horror as both of the twins' bodies were taken over. Raff and Dari roared in outrage and grief as they battled their way forward to reach the rest of the group, who were still fighting valiantly for their lives; every foot of ground gained a victory. When the two remaining soldiers reached them, slashing and hacking everything in their path, those feet became yards.

Meanwhile, Geffi's corpse gained its balance first and lurched toward Jezel. Birnardus bravely stepped in front of her, only to be shoved aside by Soren, what was left of his face now obscured by the cyclopean skull-eater. The thing gave a squealing hiss and stalked toward the newly mounted corpse-rider. The thing turned Geffi's head in its direction, eyes staring blankly as it moved to meet its enemy's advance. As they came together, hands wrapped around each other's throats, a great chittering, shrieking noise arose as the majority of the abominations abandoned their human prey to attack one another.

"Quickly," Raff yelled. "Now's our chance!" He and Dari herded Jezel and the two Pentans between them, forcing them to find new reserves as they tore along the snaking path of the crevasse, plowing through what was left of a mansion, the front facade tumbling in on itself, into the ruined pantry and kitchen, and then out the servant's entrance in back. Finding themselves in a walled garden with a gate that opened to the back of another mansion, they repeated the process in reverse, then again, weaving their way in and out of the ruins until they finally ended up on a quiet, narrow street where the cacophony of the battling monsters was nearly inaudible. The five of them were spattered with vile-smelling ichor. They sat down on the front stairs of the mansion nearest to them—relatively undamaged in comparison to its neighbors, at least from the outside—for a brief rest.

"Where to now?" Dari panted, hands on her knees as she took in great gulps of air.

"We need to find Alia and the mage," Raff replied.

Jezel staggered over to them, hair streaming down her back, long since fallen out of its braids and jeweled pins. "We ... we need to keep going through the Inner City to the Palatial Estate," she said as she tried to catch her breath. "Keth had mentioned the *Cathedralis Geminae*."

Raff looked up and down the street. Their slapdash escape had taken them away from the crevasse, thank the Gods, but he had no idea where they were or how to find their way to the Inner City. The once clear landmarks of the Aurichalcum Tower and the Crown Mount were gone, and the straightforward path of the boulevard they'd been on was too dangerous to try again. So what now?

The sound of creaking hinges from behind them launched him to his feet, sword out to cleave whatever came through the door. His blade had already started its downward arc when a young girl, tangled hair hanging in her face, poked her head out.

Chapter Sixty

"*No!*"

Jezel threw herself against Raff, catching his sword arm on its downward swing. The blade came down and bit deep into the wooden door, just inches above the child's head—instead of splitting it in half. The girl froze in fear and screamed, the sound high-pitched and shrill like a teapot come to a boil.

Jezel immediately pulled her into her arms, holding her as the girl buried her head against her chest. "Hush, my darling," she said softly, stroking her matted hair as Raff—face white with the shock of having nearly killed a child—stumbled back a pace.

"Lally!" cried a male voice from inside the mansion. The door was flung open, and an inoffensive-looking man brandishing a poker iron stepped outside.

"Don't dare to hurt her," he growled in a surprisingly menacing tone for someone with such a kindly face. Even outnumbered five to one, he wasn't afraid to threaten them with his wrought iron weapon.

He seemed an unlikely bodyguard—more librarian than stalwart defender. With his cherubic baby face, he could have been anywhere from his early thirties to his mid-forties, with pleasant if unremarkable features. Even his hair was a nondescript mousy brown. He stood neither short nor tall, wearing black breeches, a gray linen shirt, and a black cotton doublet that were obviously not his—the well-made clothing hung awkwardly on his thin frame.

Jezel stared at him in disbelief. "Magnus ... ?"

The man stared back at her, soft hazel eyes widening incredulously. "No ... it can't be ..." He peered more closely at her face. "Jessy?"

Jezel broke into a wide smile. Letting go of the girl, she grabbed him in a fierce hug. He lifted her off her feet in return before taking her by the shoulders and kissing her on the forehead. "Jessy ... I can't believe it's you!"

"You always did turn up in the most unlikely places, Magnus," she replied with an uncharacteristic grin.

The others observed this unlikely reunion with bemusement before the unwelcome sound of chittering and clacking brought their attention back to their surroundings, where a few skull-eaters could be seen far down the street.

"Quick," the man called Magnus said urgently. "Before they see us."

They needed no further urging. The group quickly entered the abode, Magnus shutting and bolting the door behind them, holding a finger to his lips for quiet as he led them further into the mansion.

What had been a mansion was now mostly rubble. The upper stories had collapsed, crushing everything on the first floor save for one narrow strip of the front half, leaving little more than a tunnel from the front door to the kitchen. Debris of expensive furnishings dislodged and broken during the earthquake—shards of porcelain vases, fine crystal, and the like littered the cracked marble flooring.

Magnus led the way into the kitchen pantry, where a trapdoor lay open, exposing wooden stairs leading down into the sublevel. He motioned everyone down the stairs, Jezel leading the way with the girl still attached to her like a limpet, short arms clutching Jezel's waist like a lifeline. After everyone else had descended, Magnus joined them, closing the trapdoor behind him.

The group found themselves in a well-stocked larder, lit by a dozen or so thick pillar candles set into sconces, on the floor, and on the top of a jury-rigged table made of a large solid block of wood. The temperature was cool but not unpleasant, especially after the horrific battle and subsequent flight. The table was covered with food—loaves of dark bread, chunks of cheese, and sausages. A few apple cores littered the floor and an open bottle of Chalicean wine sat in the middle of the feast, several empty ones lying on their sides on the stone floor.

Birnardus went immediately to the bottle of wine, upending it into his mouth without even looking for a glass. Raff didn't reprimand him this time, instead grabbing the bottle from him and doing the same before handing it back.

"There's more in the wine cellar," Magnus said mildly, pointing to a door at the far end of the larder. "And plenty of food, so don't be shy." He stared at Jezel again. "It really *is* you, isn't it?"

She nodded. "It's been so long, Magnus."

At this point, the girl reached up and tugged on Magnus's hand. "Why does she call you Magnus? I thought your name was Magpie?"

He smiled down at her with genuine affection. "It is, Lally. But when I was younger, people called me Magnus."

"And a great many other names," Jezel murmured archly.

Magnus-Magpie shot her a look. "Indeed. But now I do prefer Magpie, if it's all the same."

"And I Jezel," she replied.

"That's a pretty name," Lally said, reaching up and touching Jezel's tangled mane of sable curls. "Your hair is so beautiful." She wrinkled her nose. "But you need a bath."

Jezel laughed. All of them, with the exception of Magnus—Magpie, rather—and Lally were splattered with foul-smelling ichor but at least they were alive. "Perhaps you can find me some water so my friends and I may wash up."

"There's clean clothes too," Lally said eagerly. She held out the skirts of her long-sleeved, pale blue linen dress. Like Magpie's clothes, it was too big for her but enviably clean.

"Not to interrupt your reunion," Raff broke in, "but can those things hear us down here?"

Magpie shook his head. "The walls are too thick. I don't know how much they hunt by sound, really, but why take a chance? For the most part, Lally and I stay down here. It's safer and there's food. That's more than I can say for the rest of the city."

"How do you two know each other?" Harbalorio asked curiously.

Magpie and Jezel looked at one another. Jezel finally sighed and answered, "We met in the slums of Beauchalice."

Birnardus looked at her in shock. "You weren't born to wealth?"

She laughed, the sound rich and full, and completely devoid of her previous artifice. "No, my good sir. I could not tell you who my parents were, only that this man was the saving of me. Magnus was both a brother and a mentor to me. He kept me fed and taught me how to survive."

Magpie smiled reminiscently. "I taught Jessy how to pick pockets and locks with the best of them."

"It's true," she admitted with a sigh. "He also made sure I never had to sell myself on the streets. When I took my first protector, it was by my choice. I never looked back." She reached out and put a hand over Magpie's. "Except to wonder where you'd gone off to, my friend."

Magpie shrugged. "I didn't want to interfere in your new life, Jessy. And the rest of Tarou called out to me—and my talents." He looked around the larder with a rueful glance. "Now look where we are. And where we're likely to die."

Lally made a small sound of distress and Jezel shot Magpie a reproachful look.

"Have you seen any other survivors?" Harbalorio asked. "Surely you two can't be the only ones."

"Not since things went to hell yesterday morning. And you've seen what happened to them. Didn't take more than an hour or two for those creatures to put paid to those that weren't killed outright." Magpie poured himself some wine. He hesitated, then added, "There are others but they're as dangerous as the monsters. They're not too picky about what they eat, if you take my meaning."

"Look," Raff said. "We appreciate the shelter and the food, but two of our party are still out there. We were separated when those things attacked. They're headed to the *Cathedralis Geminae*."

"Then you might as well bid them farewell," Magpie replied. "That's where those other 'survivors' are holed up. Lally and I got out of that part of the city by the skin of our teeth. The odds of your friends surviving on their own out there are slim to none. And trust me—I know how to calculate odds. It's my business."

"One of them is an Athaméan warrior," Harbalorio interjected as he carved off a chunk of bread and some sausage. "And the other is a mage who knows the city well."

Dari nodded, swiping the bottle of wine from Birnardus before he could finish it. Grumbling, he vanished into the wine cellar to fetch more. "They made it out of the thick of the fight with those abominations. If anyone can survive, I'd place bets on the two of them."

"Normally I'm a betting man," Magpie replied, "but only if there's a chance of winning."

"Be that as it may," Raff shot back, "the mage is trying to fix whatever it is that went wrong here. And he needs our help."

"Besides," Harbalorio interjected, "we're going to leave Trionn-Fí when all is said and done. Which means if you join us, you'll have an armed escort." He grinned at Dari. "I can testify to their skills myself."

"And what would you have done if those things had found you again?" Magpie countered.

Raff shrugged. "Run like hell. All good soldiers know when to retreat."

"But there are scores of them and only five of you."

"You're the one who taught me never to give up," Jezel said pointedly. "And this little girl—"

"I'm almost twelve," Lally broke in.

"And this young girl," Jezel said without missing a beat, "deserves a better future than spending the rest of her life in a larder, no matter how well stocked it might be."

Magpie looked at her, then at Lally. He heaved a huge put-upon sigh. "Fine. But we wait for at least an hour to make sure our ugly friends have gone back into their hole or at least far enough away that we have a chance of making it to the Inner City."

"What's that?" Birnardus came out of the wine cellar, arms filled with a good half dozen bottles.

"Eat, drink, and be merry, my friend," Harbalorio said, giving Birnardus a hearty slap on the shoulder. "It may be the last chance you get."

Chapter Sixty-One

The crack they found themselves in after breaking free of their tomb was comparatively spacious, with enough room for the two of them to stretch their limbs, side by side. The earthen walls on either side rose a good twenty feet or so above them, but that was a problem to be dealt with after Keth tended to Alia's injuries. The natural light from above did as much to raise their spirits as the relatively fresh air.

"What now?" Alia asked as he removed her armor to assess the puncture wound in her side.

"I need to escape the city and go north into the ruins to find Master Hallam," he said, lifting her shirt carefully. She hissed in pain as the fabric stuck to the blood in the wound.

"I don't understand," she said after the initial shock. When he didn't reply, she looked up to find him frowning at the wound. "What? Is it that bad?"

"I've seen worse," he replied neutrally.

In truth, he was worried. It looked infected, and she'd lost a lot of blood. Still, there was nothing to do about it for the time being other than bind it as best he could and get her to Hallam's.

"There's something I don't understand," she reiterated. "I thought you said we needed to destroy Abraxas?"

"It's more complicated than I first thought," he admitted. "I was sure Abraxas was the door letting in these monsters, and closing that door was the first step to solving the problem."

"But now that the Abraxas has been destroyed, why didn't that fix the prob—ow!" She winced as he poured spirits from her flask on the wound, sweat now pouring down her brow from the pain.

"Sorry."

"S'okay," she mumbled, trying not to scream as liquid fire burned through her veins. "Why does this part always hurt even more than the injury itself?"

He gave her a crooked smile. "A question for the ages." Cutting strips of fabric from the hem of his cloak, he started binding the wound.

"The problem is that there's more going on," he said in answer to her unfinished question. "It looks like the Psychidions were just pawns for some other force—this 'new god' that didn't just unleash all these terrors but used Abraxas as a tool to commandeer our world's ley lines. And now it is actively reshaping our world into something else. I'm hoping Hallam can help make sense of it all and knows what our next move should be." He paused in his work briefly, an oddly vulnerable expression on his face. "And I need to know that he's still alive. He's ... he's my real family."

It was her turn to be silent. "I'm sorry," she finally said. "I should have thought before I spoke." She squeezed his hand. "We'll find him."

Reaching out, he touched her face briefly, caressing the line of her jaw, before he resumed wrapping her wound.

"But first," she continued, "we need to find the others." She didn't add, "If they're still alive"—any other option was unthinkable. "Which means we need to find a way out of here."

They both looked up at the steep wall in front of them, then at each other.

"It's narrow enough to chimney our way up," Keth said thoughtfully. "Are you up to that?"

She considered it. “I don’t know,” she finally answered. “But I’m willing to try.”

After her first attempt, however, it was obvious that Alia could not climb on her own, and there was no practical way for Keth to help her make the ascent. She rested with her back against one side of the fissure, panting heavily and trying not to let him know how much the attempt had hurt. “You’re going to have to leave me here,” she said, gritting her teeth against the pain.

“No.”

“Keth, you have to.” She put a hand on his arm when he started to argue. “You said yourself that you have to find your master. That he’s the only person who may be able to fix all”—she waved a hand in the air—“of this. If you can come back for me … well, I’m not going anywhere.”

“Alia, I …” He stopped, unable to argue with the logic of her words. “I’ll come back for you. I swear it.”

“I know you will,” she said, even though they both knew it was an impossible promise to keep. “I have my sword. It’ll keep me safe in the meantime.”

Keth started up the fissure, using hands and feet to spider climb his way up. He tried to ignore the hot tears in his eyes as Alia receded further and further from his sight. She didn’t deserve to die this way, from starvation and thirst, or worse, if the abomination that had stalked them managed to find its way to her. But what choice did he have?

Still, he hated himself more with every foot gained.

“Ho there, mage! Need a hand up?”

Startled, Keth nearly tumbled back down. As it was, he lost a few feet before digging in with his hands and feet again. He craned his neck to look up at the top of the fissure. There he saw Birnardus waving a coil of rope at him, Harbalorio at his side, and Raff, Dari, Jezel, and two unfamiliar faces next to them.

Once again, he had tears in his eyes, but this time it was from a relief so huge he didn’t know how to feel it.

Chapter Sixty-Two

Since it was the way to and from the sorcerous province of Arcanum, perhaps it was fitting that the High Road to Trionn-Fí to the north wound through an area of mysterious ruins.

Before the four provinces were forged into a single unified empire, there was no middle kingdom in the wild, unruly mountain country at the center of the continent. It was bandit country, where merchant caravans trod fearfully—and with a small army of escorts. Over time, the brigands and highwaymen learned there was safer money to be made through extortion than from banditry, and then even that mellowed into hostelries, trade, and farming, and the birth of a number of small hamlets.

Eventually teams of imperial surveyors, in search of a suitable place to build the new capital, chose one particular high rocky hill surrounded by an oxbow lake to become the Crown Mount and the heart of Trionn-Fí, the City of Triumph. From its heights spilled forth the city's district, rings and canals that expanded and filled the valley, swallowing up all the little villages that had come before.

But to the north of the capital and stretching for several leagues into the foothills, a traveler would still pass by signs of older inhabitants of the region—stone circles and megaliths, now moss-covered and cracked, and other traces of once-extensive ruins of some ancient city, now belonging only to the wolves and night birds. These were widely known to be unsafe places, where ghosts and other malevolent specters held sway and took vengeance on the living who dared trespass. Hallam's place of exile lay in one of these haunted bastions.

After a few leagues, twilight was already giving over to night, and the northbound road continued to serpentine its way up into the mountains that formed the Arcane border, but the remaining nine had come far enough.

Despite the closing dark, spotting their destination was easy. Hallam's tower stood atop a bald hill about a quarter mile off the road. Either because it had not come through the recent earthquakes unscathed, or because it had simply succumbed to the ravages of time, the roof had partially fallen in, making it look like the ragged sleeve of a giant reaching for the crescent moon. But its highest windows were lit up, bright as lighthouse beacons.

"I think we've found your hermit," Raff said to Keth, who nodded, but had nothing else to add. To Alia, increasingly in tune with Keth's feelings, the mage seemed more pensive than relieved to have located his master.

The travelers looked at one another, and then took the path up.

In a forgotten kingdom lost to time, the tower must have once served some early sorcerer or priest-king as a stellar observatory, surrounded as it was by a precise ring of rune-carved calendar stones. Now the gaps between the slender standing stones were filled with stacks of antlers and deadfall to serve as a sheepfold for a modest flock of ewes and goats.

Entering the yard through its single gate, they walked past a vegetable garden and a row of flowers, fenced off from the hungry livestock. On the left was a duck pond, the water shimmering with the same nauseating swirl of colors they'd seen before.

His curiosity piqued, Keth drew near for a closer look at the garden. The vegetables appeared to sense his approach, stalks quivered in their beds, while thorny rows of blackened alien roses actively turned on him like a clutch of serpents, hissing and baring their teeth. He quickly backed away, turning just in time to see a duck land on the surface where it vanished abruptly. Bubbles rose on the surface, breaking with a squelching sound to release an unspeakable odor.

Lally tugged at Magpie's arm.

"Magpie—Magpie! Look! What's wrong with them?" She pointed to the sheep and the bleating goats.

"Hells!" he gasped.

All of them turned to stare at the animals.

There were about a dozen in the little herd, an even mix of sheep and goats. At first glance, there was nothing obviously wrong—until one noticed some had too many or too few eyes, while others appeared to have traded their legs and hooves for a sluglike body or a clutch of stubby tentacles. No two of the goats had the same number of horns, and the horns themselves looked like curved daggers, sharp as shark teeth. When one sheep opened its mouth to bleat at them, the maw stretched open far too wide, revealing an array of jagged carnivore teeth.

"Get to the tower—*go*!" Raff commanded, drawing his sword. Magpie swept up Lally in his arms, and he and the others moved quickly to the tower door.

One of the bigger black goats had a whole ridge of horns going down its spine where it merged with its spiked tail. It seemed more timber wolf than goat as it hunkered down and, locking eyes with Raff, began to creep straight toward him. At the same time, two others rose and did the same, flanking him. Their leader padded up faster—then all three charged Raff at once.

Two more swords sang out of their sheaths, and Alia and Dari took position on either side of Raff, stepping into the charge and swinging. The leader leapt into the air, snapping teeth bared to tear out Raff's throat. He caught the beast mid-leap with an expert thrust, skewering it straight through, while Alia and Dari took down each of theirs with a single cut, followed up with a quick coup de grâce to finish them. The attack was over almost before it had begun.

The seasoned trio of warriors wiped their blades and immediately moved back into their original formation, ready for the remainder of the mutated flock to attack as well. Instead the rest quickly retreated and huddled together, watching them apprehensively from afar. Meanwhile, Birnardus was already banging upon the tower door and yelling for someone to come open the door. It was solid oak and bound with iron, newer than the tower's stone walls. They would need a battering ram to get through it.

"Is it locked?" asked Harbalorio.

"I can pick it," Jezel and Magpie both piped up simultaneously.

"Allow me," Harbalorio said, elbowing his friend aside. He took hold of the handle and gently pulled. The heavy door swung open at once, and he smirked at Birnardus, who harrumphed in reply.

Cautiously peering inside, Harbalorio turned to the rest of the group. "Come on—it's clear."

Inside, the furnishings were sparse and uninteresting, little more than the bare essentials expected for a hermit in seclusion, and silent as a tomb. A larder and kitchen lay through a door in the back. There was no sign of anyone in the place—at least not downstairs. Birnardus poked his head in the back, curious to see how well stocked the pantry remained. A hatch in the floor caught his eye, and he knelt to investigate it further.

"Ah, look! There's a root cellar—or a wine cellar ..."

Taking hold of its iron ring, he opened it wide. In the darkness below, a constellation of eyes reflected a glowing red in the light. Rats? Bats? He quickly closed the hatch again, no longer quite so thirsty.

Along the circular wall wound steps up to the second floor—where a steady stream of bright light slanted down from above. Keth went to the bottom of the stairs and looked up. He knew where he'd find his master.

Limping over to him, Alia put a hand on his arm. "Do you want anyone to go with you?"

"I'd better go up alone," he replied. "Hallam can be—intimidating."

Alia nodded. "Just call out if you need us."

"I'm sure it will be fine." He looked at her with concern, noticing the fever sweat dappling her brow and chest, and the way she surreptitiously held her wounded side. "Will you be all right?"

"I'll live," she said. "I just need to sit down, I think."

"Here." He pulled out a wooden chair with a cushioned back and seat and helped her sit. Raff joined them, pulling out his ever-present flask and offering it first to Alia—who took a sip and handed it back—and then to Keth, who accepted it gratefully.

"Why don't you all find something to eat?" Then he remembered the carnivorous flowers outside. "On second thought, don't eat or drink anything in here." He started to say more, thought better of it, and ascended the steps without another word.

"Is there anything sadder after a long, hard day than a full pantry that you can't touch?" Birnardus said glumly. "I don't suppose the wine would be safe to drink ... ?"

"Why don't you go ask the goats?" Dari suggested.

"Well, what shall we do while we wait for those two to sort things out?" Harbalorio asked.

Before anyone could answer, Keth came down the stairs again, stopping halfway.

"I ... think you all need to see this."

Chapter Sixty-Three

The upper floor was a large open space with a high ceiling, some sixty feet or more, containing little more than the stone steps running up to what little remained of the very top of the tower. Still, illumination flooded the entire chamber, which was draped from floor to ceiling with long, gossamer strands, some forming whole sheets of a sheer diaphanous silk.

The light that bathed the room was radiating out from what looked like a blazing white gem, as big and as bright as a lighthouse lamp, hanging overhead roughly halfway up the height of the interior. It shone so bright it was impossible to make out any real details, but it appeared to be enclosed in a gauzy white cocoon, suspended from the highest rafters by more silken threads.

Everyone was awestruck by the sight, none more so than Keth. His fingers tingled and the hairs on the back of his neck rose. There was magic here—great, potent reserves of it, so much that it made his head spin and gave him a heady rush of both exhilaration and fear.

"What *is* this place?" Alia asked, trying to hide a fresh wave of exhaustion.

"I ... I'm not certain," he replied in awestruck tones. "But it feels like this is where all the magic left in the world has gone. And something else ... I can't quite grasp—"

"Your master did that?" Birnardus interrupted. "Stole all the world's sorcery?"

"Not *stole*, exactly, but—"

"Where is he now?" Raff cut in. "Could he have escaped?"

"Not ... escaped," echoed a deep voice from overhead. *"I've never left."*

"Master Hallam?" Keth's voice rang out with joy at hearing the familiar voice. "Where are you?"

"I'm here," came the voice from out of the blinding light above. The figure of a man came down the steps, wearing the robes of an archmage. For a moment, a trick of the light seemed to both surround him and suffuse him like a nimbus, making him look like something out of a vision, the ecstatic appearance of a holy saint or a demigod.

But when he reached them, Hallam was just as Keth remembered him, his impressive beard, the glint in his eyes that did not suffer fools lightly.

"Master Hallam," Keth said, bowing to his mentor. "It's good to see you."

"And you." The archmage extended his arms, and the two embraced warmly.

Hallam then held his apprentice at arm's length and looked him up and down. "You've grown some, I think," he said with affection. "And you need a bath."

"Are you all right?" Keth said, hardly able to believe that Hallam was still alive.

"It's I who should ask you that!" Hallam exclaimed. "You appear to have been through some trials on your way here. But now you can rest, assured of your safety! Welcome to your refuge, you and all your companions. This is a most happy occasion, and I have food and drink enough for all!"

The others' stunned silence thawed somewhat at that, but Keth's face remained unchanged and urgent.

"Master ... everything you warned us about has come to pass. The Psychidions have—"

"Oh yes, yes, I know." Hallam gave a dismissive wave of one hand. "Like idiot children, they played with their little toy—rejecting all my warnings—and poked their little pinprick through the veil—ooh-hoo! Ha! I wish I could have been there to see the look on their faces when they saw what was waiting for them on the other side!" He cackled wildly, causing everyone but Keth to back up ever so slightly. No one wanted to offend him.

"It's not just that." Keth struggled unsuccessfully to keep his calm, and the words came tumbling out. "Master, surely you must know this already, but ... they've destroyed the city—Trionn-Fí is *gone*. Everyone is dead or ... changed. The elementals have gone berserk and revolted, and there are all manner of horrific new creatures coming from cracks in the earth. They speak of a new god coming to bring forth a new world. And the ley lines ... the magic ... it's all gone away."

Hallam listened to all this impassively before at last cutting in. "Oh no, my son. The magic isn't gone. Can't you feel it? Of course you can. All the magic is right here. Look."

He made a waving gesture and a phantom image came to life in the air before them—a vision of a swirling, chaotic form, hazy and dizzying to look upon, and harder still to make sense of. It was roughly spherical in that it had any discernible shape at all. There were features—things that might have been eyes, mouthparts, tentacles, claws, stingers, stalks, tendrils, grasping structures, and other limbs harder to identify—that seemed to be parts of one roiling, turbid mass, constantly in a churning turmoil, its surface ever-changing in one kaleidoscopic twist after another.

"They call it a god?" Hallam said softly. "What ignorant, superstitious fools. It has no more intelligence than a patch of lichen."

"What is that horrible thing?" Jezel asked, horror in her eyes.

"It has no name, My Damsel," Hallam replied. "That is what exists on the other side of the interdimensional veil—at least, one particular denizen in the portion of the void closest to us. For untold eons it has floated through its own universe, with no more direction or power of thought than a jellyfish, and when it encounters other forms of life, it not only consumes them for nourishment but takes from them—unconsciously collecting traits, absorbing them to add to itself. What's more, to those who survive the encounter, it freely shares parts of its own essence. And so it is a marvelous force of growth and change, and the generation of new life.

"And yet," he continued, "it had never come across an intellect—not before I discovered it. So now it has gained a new trait, one singular aspect more magnificent and revolutionary than anything it has ever acquired before in its entire incalculably long existence."

"We've seen its handiwork, Master Hallam," Keth said quietly. "It creates monsters."

"It creates *nightmares*," added Alia. "And it's destroyed everything."

"Such pathos! Such hubris!" Hallam shook his head in dismissal. "These are no more than matters of opinion—from the provincial perspective of merely one species in an unspeakably vast cosmos."

"Er … what?" Birnardus looked confused.

"Master …" Keth spoke very carefully. "This sharing of—how did you say it—sharing of 'essences.' That's what created the changes we've seen, in the flower you sent me, in the survivors of Trionn-Fí—isn't it?"

"Yes, of course. And—"

"And what has it done … to *you*?"

Hallam laughed again.

"Do I seem changed to you, my apprentice?"

Keth said nothing, so the archmage continued. "If anything, the changes have been thoroughly positive. I have gained the most incredible knowledge and insights. The great irony is that it does not know what it knows—but now I do! And of course, I will share them with you."

"Master ..." Keth's voice was strained with the weight of the words he could not say.

"You must not fear. I have been a poor host. You have all traveled far and endured much today. So you will stay here for the night, eat your fill, drink, and rest." He gestured to Alia. "Especially you, my dear. I'll tend to your injuries myself."

Alia did her best not to flinch. Hallam smiled at her as if he could read her inner thoughts.

"Thank you, Master," Keth said. "But first, what can we do to restore the damage? To bring back the magic?"

"Don't trouble yourself with such worries now," Hallam replied. "In the morning, it will be a new day, and everything will feel quite different. Oh, that reminds me—I trust the goats didn't trouble you, did they?"

Keth stiffened, flashing on the horribly altered state of the farm animals and the gardens.

"Is that what will become of us if we stay—we'll turn into monsters like them? Will that help us save the rest of the world?"

Puzzlement crossed the archmage's face.

"*Save* the world? Don't you see, my young apprentice? You *have* saved the world."

"Wha—what do you mean?" Alia stammered, fear in her eyes.

"Oh, I think you know." The glint in his eyes matched the curl of his sardonic smile.

"What in blazes is this old madman going on about?" Birnardus sputtered.

Alia grabbed Keth by the arm. "Keth, what is Hallam saying?"

Keth stared back at his former master. "*Hallam* isn't saying anything," he said coolly. "This thing here has no name."

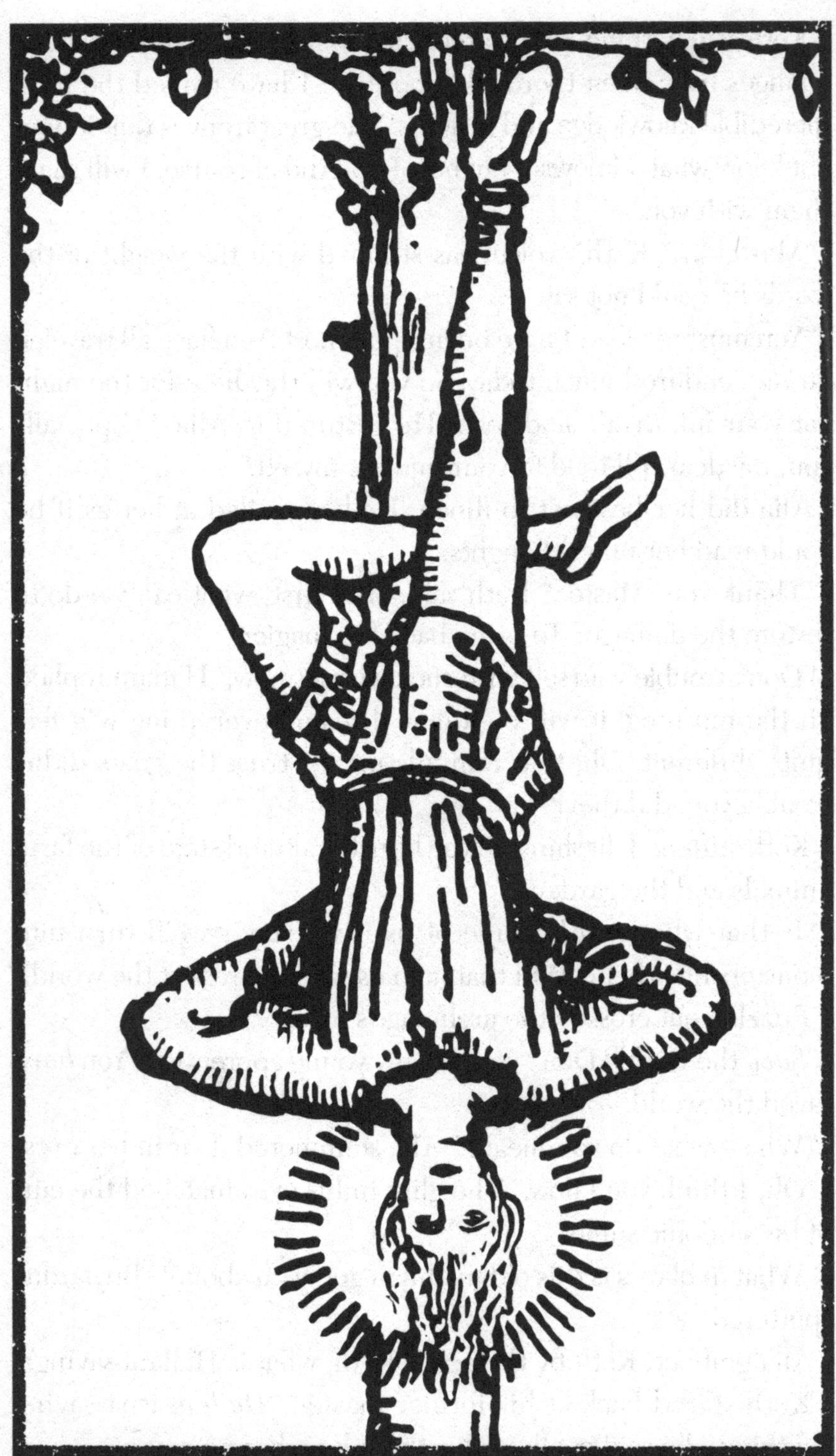

Chapter Sixty-Four

The figure standing before them said nothing, only watched with impassive eyes. Keth raised his hand toward the ball of light overhead and spoke a charm of revealing. The white light they had first taken for some shining jewel diminished its intensity by steady degrees, until all of them could see what the light concealed inside—the real form of Keth's master, Hallam, suspended upside down like a pendulum, dangling precariously by one ankle, with his other leg bent behind. His arms were bound behind him, his body delicately wrapped in a swaddling of silk like an insect strung up in a spider's web.

"What have you done to him?" Keth asked quietly.

"He's fine, I assure you," said the thing in Hallam's form. "You know, I took the image from his own mind—I think he would find it fitting, to hang him the way the old Pentans used to punish their traitors."

It seemed to be telling the truth. Despite the uncomfortable circumstances, the real Hallam's face seemed untroubled, even serene.

"You must understand," it continued, "I would never harm him—nor you, who love him as I do. You"—it gestured to the rest of the group with an expansive sweep of its hands—"all of you, are welcome here."

Keth frowned. "Could you bring him down, please?"

"Of course."

With a twist of his fingers, the mage cast a cantrip, lowering his hanged double like a spider descending on a line of silk—and as it drew closer, the onlookers' curiosity turned to horror.

Now that he hung before them, Hallam—the real Hallam—no longer looked serene. His mouth hung slack, his half-open eyes showed nothing but whites, and his skin had taken on a greenish cast. If he was still breathing, there was no indication of it. The only signs of life were ropy alien veins spreading up from his torso onto his neck and throat, where they now pulsed angrily.

Harbalorio made a face. "Well, sir, either you're lying, or you seriously misunderstand some very basic points about the difference between *fine* and *not fine*."

False Hallam either did not recognize the sarcasm or chose to ignore it. "Join us. The hateful old world is swept away. I have planted my seeds and tendrils in the earth, so now a new world will bloom, like a beautiful garden!"

"Like a cancer, you mean," said Keth.

"Cancer? What is that except growth? We will all grow together, he and you and I, in such exciting new ways!"

"I've heard enough," Raff growled, drawing his sword. Alia and Dari did as well, followed swiftly by Harbalorio and Birnardus. Only Keth noticed that Alia briefly faltered, as if the act of holding up her blade was almost too much for her.

"No, wait!" Keth called out, raising his hands to stop them. "You can't fight it with blades!"

"Indeed—there is no fight between us at all," it said. "And now you *will* rest ..."

He gestured and the light in the chamber flared to blinding proportions, bathing the room in dazzling whiteness, to the exclusion of everything else.

Chapter Sixty-Five

Harbalorio sat by the fire at the inn, patting his pockets for his grandfather's pipe lighter. "Has anyone seen it?" The other patrons all shook their heads. Oh, there it was, on the mantelpiece. How he would have dearly hated to lose the treasured family heirloom. He tapped down his favorite tobacco into his long-stemmed clay pipe, tucked it in his mouth, and with a practiced hand, proudly flicked open the lighter's exquisite little metal doors. "*Bastard!*" the infuriated salamandre screeched, raising itself to twice the size of a man before it leapt upon him, engulfing him in flames and swiftly roasting him to ashes ... over and over again.

Raff swung his sword with abandon, slicing into corpse-riders with savage cuts across the belly, and hammering his blade down upon the helmets of skull-eaters. Surrounded, he blazed a swath of fallen bodies, cracked shells, and noxious ichor, not daring to pause for an instant—not even when he heard the cries of his companions succumbing to their ravenous attackers one by one. But then he saw Dari teetering on the lip of the chasm, screaming, wrapped in tentacles as corpse-riders swarmed her. He watched her fall with one last cry. Cursing, he stabbed a corpse clear through its heart and out its back, but the blade stuck fast—and his opponent continued to attack. Chittering, screeching calls filled his ears as grasping tentacles pulled him down by his legs. The arms of cyclops-driven corpses pinned him down, sending crustaceans scuttling over his face as they bickered and fought over who could eat him. His hauberk was ripped open by ropy tentacles, exposing his stomach to greedy lamprey mouths. He felt a spasm of pain as burrowing needle teeth began to dig into his guts, felt and heard the agonizing bite of strong jaws methodically crunching into his skull and brains …

Dari ran down the corridors of an endless stone maze, unlit but for the crescent moon above. She turned this way, then that—and came upon Bellamy, her eyes wide and pleading. “Dari! Help me!” The shaggy white mass of the cobweb golem appeared behind the girl and wrapped her torso and face in its wide arms, smothering her cries. It lifted her up, kicking and thrashing, its filaments slipping under her blouse and skirts in search of bare flesh. Shouting her battle cry, Dari plunged her blade deep into the beast. It sank to the hilt and kept going, drawing in her wrists, then forearms, and then the rest of her body, and last, her head slowly sank into the flossy white softness …

Jezel staggered down the empty streets of a cold gray city, looking for scraps of food—broke, bone-weary, friendless, and cheerless. The wind blew right through her threadbare shawl. She stopped suddenly at a darkened window, horrified by the ghostly reflection of a gaunt, toothless old hag in filthy rags glowering back at her. The shock stabbed into her chest and she collapsed, her ruined heart leaking her last few heartbeats into the icy cobblestone gutters ...

Magpie, never more comfortable than when in the anonymity of a crowd, felt increasingly paranoid in this one once he realized everyone had stopped moving and talking. They stood stock-still, all turned to him, all watching him in judgmental silence. He turned from one disapproving face to another, only to realize the entire crowd was arranged in formation, each one a perfect arm's length from their neighbor to the front, back, and sides. In fact, there were no people at all—now they were all stone statues. Panicking, he ran through their ranks, but could see no end, only a wavering orange glow in the distance, coming from all sides. As it continued to draw closer, he realized he was seeing fire—that of wickedly grinning flame maidens, their hot-coal eyes locked on him, their prey, the heat becoming unbearable as they closed in on him from all sides ...

Birnardus, raging, called out to be heard again, but no one around the campfire was listening. All their attention was on the infernal mage. "I have proof, I tell you!" he yelled again, snatching up the map case and waving it overhead. Smug Keth shook his head and ignored the Pentan. "Look, damn you all!" he cried, pulling the off the leather cap and reaching inside. "Look!" A slick black viper sprang out and wrapped itself around his arm, striking the meat of his hand repeatedly with its deadly fangs. He shrieked in pain and called out for aid, but the others just laughed at him.

"It's just a flower, you fatheaded dolt!" Harbalorio roared. Birnardus wept and begged for help, to no avail.

"It's killing me," he whimpered.

"No, it isn't," declared Keth. "Just look."

His arm was turning green and morphing into a tentacle, and the mutation was quickly spreading past his shoulder and throughout his body ...

Alia found herself plunged into darkness, scrambling away from the acrid stench of the fly-thing's acid vomit, feeling the claws of its thorny forelimbs raking at her legs as she desperately kicked and twisted to escape it, dragging herself through an increasingly narrow tunnel until the very rock walls above and below closed in on her, entombing her alive in stone forever ...

Chapter Sixty-Six

"No, wait! *You can't fight it with blades!*"

Lally jumped when she heard Keth's shout of alarm. Terrified, she clung to Jezel. By contrast, the archmage-thing responded in a voice both soft and yet still menacing.

"Indeed—there is no fight between us at all. And now you *will* rest …"

At a sorcerous motion of his hand, the half-lit chamber instantly flashed into blinding white light, and Lally buried her head in Jezel's skirts with a cry.

There was silence. She did not dare open her eyes, make a sound, or move a muscle—nothing except cling for dear life to Jezel, who remained standing as still as if she had been turned to stone.

"*Come* …" she heard Not Hallam say, and then came the soft pad of footsteps ascending the stairs. Lally listened intently as the soft echoes faded and then, gathering up her courage, she risked stealing a peek. The blinding light was gone, replaced by the gauzy twilight illumination from before. No one was moving, and of those whose faces she could see, all were staring blindly ahead, with only the whites of their eyes showing. Up at the top of the stairs she could see the false Hallam, but there was no sign of whoever had accompanied him up the stairs.

"And as for the rest of you ..."

He made another sorcerous gesture, and all the wooden shutters of the chamber's narrow windows snapped open, while the rest of the tower echoed with the sound of locks and bars releasing, doors and hatches creaking wide open as well. Lally could hear eerie chittering, scuttling noises of things creeping in from outside in response to the mage's summoning. He performed one final spell, conjuring a ball of darkness in his hands. He pulled at the ebon skein until its strands made a sphere the size of a large basket, then he poured it out upon the stairs. At first the smoky black shape spilled forth and cascaded down the steps like a thick liquid, but it soon rose up like a snake, settling on a human form in a black cowl.

"Sweet dreams."

Then Hallam turned and went further up the stairs—only to disappear, vanishing into thin air as though he were stepping into a bank of heavy fog.

The hooded figure in black came down the stairs with a ghostly spirit's unearthly smooth grace. Lally buried her head within Jezel's skirts again, trying desperately not to be seen as it came down to the floor and glided among her unmoving, unresisting companions. She did not dare look at the face of the specter directly but could only watch as the hooded phantom went silently from one transfixed figure to another, as if closely inspecting their faces. Under its gaze, one by one, each victim began to tremble in place, limbs twitching like that of a sleeper in the grip of a nightmare.

When it turned its attention to Jezel, Lally squeezed her eyes shut as tight as she could and tried to make herself as stony still as the others, clinging to Jezel's leg in a death grip. Despite its utter silence, she could sense its presence next to her, like a chill of shadow in wintertime. She also felt the moment when Jezel succumbed to the thing's gaze, the woman's muscles suddenly quivering in fear. Lally could not stop shaking either—waiting for it to notice her, the pounding of Lally's heartbeat grew so strong she thought it would break through her breastbone.

She flinched when she heard an anguished moan and could not resist opening her eyes.

It was Alia. The specter had its back to Lally, but she could see it was enveloping the Athaméan warrior in its inky black cloak, leaning in close enough that the two could be kissing. But the sounds coming from Alia were of torment, not passion. To her, it could only be the sound of Alia's soul being torn out of her ...

Lally looked around frantically. None of the others could help her now—they were all awaiting their own turn to become the next prey of the thing in the black cloak. Her desperate gaze fell upon the sheathed dagger on Dari's belt. Like a stranded mariner forced to leave the safety of a reef to swim through shark-infested water, she made herself let go of Jezel and crept as silently as she could toward Dari. If the thing heard her, there would be no running or hiding—and could a mortal blade even hurt such a thing? She had no idea, nor any other fallback plan if not.

She reached Dari's side, her little fingers trembling as she slipped the blade from its sheath and gripped it tightly. Another anguished whimper escaped Alia's lips, startling Lally so much she nearly dropped the dagger. The girl steeled herself, holding the dagger in both hands as she stole up behind the figure cloaked in black and its victim.

With one last strangled shriek, Alia collapsed, and the figure in black bent down to keep its hold on her. *He's finishing her off,* Lally realized, and drew as close as she dared—then raised Dari's knife to strike. With a scream, she drove it into the thing's back.

The blade went straight through to the floor. Its cloak was no cloak at all, but a thick curtain of fine black filaments like hair. Lally quickly raised the dagger for a second strike and, with her free hand, reached up to seize a thick fistful of its hair, yanking it downward with all her strength.

The thing in black's head was pulled back and she brought down the dagger on its face—upon what she thought should be its face. It had none. Where a white round face should have been was a great single eyeball, the only body lying beneath the thing's long black mane. In an instant, she met its gaze—

Lally could not find her brother. She retraced her steps again and again, going from vendor to vendor to ask if they had seen him. Although the festival revelries were in full swing, she could still hear him calling her name, asking where she was, pleading with her to come get him. "Lally, I'm scared," echoed his voice through the bazaars. "Lally, don't leave me," his spectral voice begged from the park. Then she saw him, standing staring at her from the middle of the street, expressionless. Calling out his name, she ran to him. But run as she might, she could not reach him—and then the earth between them split into an impassible crevasse, carrying them away from each other like ocean waves, until everything in sight began to collapse and tumble down into the abyss …

—the dagger came down, finishing its trajectory by plunging into the thing's massive eye.

Chapter Sixty-Seven

Keth was woken up by a blow to his stomach. He sat up, fighting to breathe as hands in the blackness pulled him back down, pinning him while other hands gagged his mouth. He was in a dark, bizarre space, lit only by a single stark were-light, the walls and ceiling jutted in at disturbing, impossible angles—yet he knew, in the uncanny way one just *knows* things in dreams, that he was back at his old apprentice's dormitory room, alone with his tormentors.

He was a grown man this time, not just a skinny little kid, and yet the old terrors came rushing back with all their strength, fresh and raw—and he was just as helpless now as he had been then. A gray-eyed, weaselly demon stared into his face.

"Lift up his head!" it hissed. The unseen arms did his bidding.

Keth recognized him. *Bailes, my old bully.* The demon held up a wineglass. Something scurried inside it.

"You remember your present, Keth. Don't you, you stupid Athaméan puke?" Of course he did. Keth could never forget the blood-speckled arachnid body from that night.

"Look closer!" Demon-Bailes said with his ugly smile, grabbing the back of Keth's head and forcing it down so he could jam the glass up against Keth's face. He steeled himself for the scuttling, hissing bane-spider he knew was there—but as he looked inside, he saw instead a tiny version of himself, naked and afraid, and then he was falling—falling headfirst *into* his tiny self, and now it was him trapped inside the glass.

He banged his fists against the transparent walls, yelling for them to let him go.

"Careful, Keth!" Bailes laughed, shaking the glass. "If you make me spill, I might accidentally dump you on the little spider!" As he spoke, the laughing demon slowly, slowly tipped the glass back. The bane-spider was there in the room, next to Bailes, bigger than a dire wolf. Its eight beady black eyes glittered, bristling arms reached up for him, eager, fanged mouth hungry for him.

Time seemed to run slower as Keth pressed against the glass, trying desperately to brace himself and keep from falling into those waiting jaws—but the curved walls were too slick, and he was too tiny to get any purchase on them.

This isn't how it happened, he thought desperately, staring down into the twitching mouthparts of the nightmare face below.

Hallam!

Yes, that was it! His master had come and saved him.

"Oh, Keth!" The demon cackled. "I can't imagine how much it would hurt if you got bitten—can you?" The spider's fangs dripped with venom.

But this was all wrong. This was where Hallam arrived—Hallam should be here to rescue him. Where was he?

"I can't *begin* to imagine how much it would hurt if you got *eaten alive*!"

Then he upturned the glass.

Keth was falling, falling, falling ...

"Hallam!" he cried. *"Help me, Master!"*

The spider's mouth filled his field of vision, already gigantic and swirling, closer and closer—and then Keth heard a voice.

"Give me your hand!"

He reached out—and someone grasped him by the wrist and lifted him up and away from it all.

His master had come, just as he had then, just as Keth knew that he always would.

"It's all right now. You're safe with me. Come."

At first they seemed to be walking, but then, as if in a dream, they were flying together in the night sky, and ahead lay the stars. A flood of relief washed over him, followed by excited curiosity.

"Where are we going?" Keth asked.

"Do you trust me?"

"You know I do," he answered, his heart bursting.

"I know. Come. I want to show you something wonderful."

They flew up to the stars, and deep into the inky tapestry between them, faster and faster, until at long last they came to somewhere there was neither bright points of light nor blackness surrounding them. It was a place of quiet light, diaphanous silk strands floating in space. It felt like home. Together, the two of them floated in a companionable silence.

"Where are we?"

"This is the in-between place. You call it the veil."

Hallam pointed to a shimmering spot in the light ahead of them, a place where the fabric of this reality seemed dimmer, flimsier.

"Go and behold what lies beyond that spot there."

Keth turned and saw a similar spot behind them.

"Where does that one go?"

"Nowhere you haven't seen before. But come, this is why I brought you here. Come see." Hallam beckoned him to come closer, and Keth floated up to him.

"And where does this one lead?"

"My home. When you look upon it, then you will understand its beauty. Then you will see what I wish to share with you. And with that vision, that understanding, you will be changed, utterly. You will be a new person. You must trust me. Come." His voice was gentle and kind, a reflection of everything Keth

trusted, promising everything he longed for. He would do what the voice said.

"I'm frightened—will you come with me?"

"Of course. We'll both go."

Keth felt tears run down his cheeks as they drew closer to the thin spot of the veil.

"Can you sense it—the wonders that lie just beyond the veil?"

He could. He nodded, too overwhelmed for words.

"Shall we?"

"Yes," answered Keth.

He shoved Hallam through the shimmering veil with all his might.

"G'ndúnvahr'ntairsheach!"

Keth shouted the Spell of Securing to close the portal between worlds.

He could still sense the presence of the nameless thing taking Hallam's form on the other side of the portal, feel its rage and shock at his betrayal.

"Don't you remember, Master?" he said softly. "You taught me that spell."

Taking a deep breath, he turned his back and headed for the other thin spot, the one that led back home.

Chapter Sixty-Eight

Raff was fighting. He twitched once, twice, and then snapped back to full wakefulness with an audible start, his muscles sizzling from the jolt of lightning coursing through his veins, still tensed to fight the dream battle he'd left behind in his sleep. Around him, the others were also waking up from their own induced nightmares—except for Alia, who lay stretched out on the hard floor of the tower's upper chamber, moaning, and Lally, who knelt on the floor, numb and silent, holding an ichor-stained dagger.

A spill of long, slender black filaments surrounded the child, spread out on the floor like a woman's hair on a pillow. At their center was a horrid mess of brackish green blood and tissue, and what looked like the ruined remains of a single great white eye. It had been stabbed multiple times.

"What *was* that?" Raff asked as he took a closer look at the girl's handiwork. Lally looked up at him for a few moments, her face blank, and when she spoke, her voice was a numb monotone.

"The mage conjured it to get in our heads and cause nightmares. I think that's how it feeds—it likes the taste of bad dreams. I think it wanted to eat us all."

While Harbalorio and Birnardus knelt down to tend to the unconscious Alia, Dari laid a hand on Lally's shoulder.

"Are you all right?"

The girl nodded. "Yes. I killed it."

Dari grinned. "You sure did—and you did a damn fine job of it too. Here, let me take that back now." She gently plucked her dagger from the girl's unresisting fingers and wiped the blade before returning it to its sheath.

Jezel knelt down beside Lally and scooped her up in her arms. "My brave girl! You saved us all, little one."

Lally smiled, a weary little smile, and let Jezel rock her and stroke her hair. Kissing the top of the girl's head, Jezel shot a significant glance at Magpie, an unspoken promise passing between them.

"I saw it trying to eat Alia," Lally added in her sleepwalker tone.

Harbalorio looked up and turned to Dari, shaking his head.

"Alia ... ?"

The two Pentans quickly moved to let Dari take their place by Alia's side. Leaning over her comrade, she frowned when she saw the red stain seeping through Alia's shirt. With her dagger, she carefully cut away the cloth to reveal the bandages underneath, wincing at the sight. The ragged strips were dark with blood.

"Raff." It was all Dari had to say—he joined her at once.

"Is she ..."

Dari looked at him, her expression grave. When she lifted her hand from Alia's side, her fingers were slick with blood.

"No. But I think ... I think she will be soon."

"We have to stop the bleeding. Keth, can you—" Raff paused and looked around the chamber. "Where is he?"

His urgent question was met with blank stares.

"Keth, where the hell are you?" he shouted down the stairwell.

"I'm here," Keth's reply came from overhead, his voice echoing strangely.

"Keth, what's happened?" Raff called out. "Where are you? What did you do with"—he looked at Hallam's dangling corpse—"that thing?"

"Don't worry. It's gone now," Keth's unseen voice sounded strange, as if he was calling down to them through a culvert.

"We've won, then?" Harbalorio exclaimed. The looks of confusion around the chamber turned to expressions of joy—except for Dari and Raff, still huddled over Alia, worry stamped on their faces.

"Keth, we need you," Raff said urgently. "It's Alia."

The celebratory mood instantly turned hushed and serious.

There was no response.

"Keth, can you hear us? Alia's hurt. It's bad."

"I hear you ..." his voiced echoed down, sounding resigned. *"I ... I can't come back."*

"She's dying, Keth." Raff's normally tough tone was pleading.

Alia gasped for breath, still pushing against the stone tomb of her nightmare. Her eyelids fluttered, and the darkness surrounding her was chased off by blinding light as she woke. She tried to sit up, but instantly sunk back down again, clutching her side with an indrawn hiss, eyes screwed tight against the searing pain. After a moment, she opened her eyes again to see Dari and Raff kneeling on either side of her.

"Don't try to get up," Dari said, offering her waterskin. "Here. Drink some water." Alia tried to take a swallow but started coughing, a pinkish mix of water and blood trickling out of her mouth.

"It ... it hurts ..." Alia's voice was paper-thin.

"Damn it, Keth, you've got to do something!" Raff yelled. "We're going to lose her!"

"Raff ..." Dari said again, tightly grasping Alia's hand. Her head lolled to the side as she coughed up more blood.

"Healing magic doesn't work that way. I have to be able to touch her." Keth's voice was strained.

"Then get down here and do it!"

"You don't understand. This isn't my choice." He paused. *"I can never come back."*

The room was cloaked in stunned silence, except for the sound of Alia struggling to breathe.

Lally began quietly sobbing again, and Jezel rocked the girl in her arms, soothing her as best she could, even as her own heart broke at the thought of Alia's death and Keth's exile. Dari and Raff were silent as stones, tears slipping unheeded down their cheeks.

"What do you mean you can't come back?" Dari demanded, grief making her voice harsh. "If we can hear you, there has to be a way to reach you. Tell us what we need to do!"

"Keth," Jezel implored. "Please. Alia is dying. Is there nothing you can do for her?"

"Bring her up the stairs," Keth said suddenly.

Lifting her in his arms, Raff carried her up the stone steps, all the way to the point where they first saw the false Hallam appear. A patch of the air there shimmered with a soft, ghostly radiance.

"What should we do?" Raff asked.

Keth's voice sounded closer now. *"I'm here, behind the veil. Look for the place where the air is rippling like water."*

Raff took a deep breath and stepped through the hazy curtain.

And then he was gone too.

Chapter Sixty-Nine

Alia felt hands carrying her, lifting her. She felt weightless, like a spirit, but she could still feel hands upon her wounded side, hear Keth's voice softly chanting words she didn't understand. And then ... the pain in her side was gone. Her life force, which had been slipping away, returned to her body.

Opening her eyes, Alia found herself staring up into clear gray eyes framed with black lashes. "Keth," she said, smiling.

Raff leaned into her line of sight as well.

"Raff ... ?"

He nodded. "Who do you think hauled you up the stairs?"

Keth brushed a stray lock of hair back from her forehead. "How do you feel?"

She thought about it. "Fine," she replied with some surprise. She poked herself in the side. Not even a slight tenderness remained. "How did you do that?"

He smiled. "Magic."

"It's back?"

The smile faded somewhat. "Only in here."

"Here ... ?"

Alia sat up, looking around her. Saw an ever-shifting palette of shimmering, opalescent shades, pale pinks, pearl grays, the softest of violets, richer and more intense than she'd ever seen them. Nothing like the abhorrent, unnatural colors that had emerged from the fissures. The air was filled with what looked like skeins of silk, hanging down from a seemingly endless sky.

"Where are we?" she asked with wonder.

"We're behind the veil," Keth replied. "The in-between."

"In between what?"

"In between dimensions," he told her.

"Where's everyone else?"

"They're still back in Hallam's tower, in our world," Raff answered this time.

Keth nodded. "Yes. On the other side of the veil. You and Raff should go back to them."

"Yes," she agreed. Then, realizing what he'd actually said, "What about you?"

"I'm staying here."

"What do you mean you're staying? Are you mad?"

"I wish I was," he replied with a ragged laugh that was almost a sob. "But that thing is still there, on the other side, waiting to get back in—and it has all of Hallam's knowledge and sorcery. I've closed the portal behind it, but if I leave it unguarded … even for a moment … it will come back through. And then all of this … all the deaths … will have been for nothing." The anguish in his voice was clear.

Alia shook her head in denial, searching for a chink in his argument.

"But …" she pressed, "how long can you stay on your guard here?"

"I have all the world's magic in here with me. I don't need to sleep. I don't need to eat or drink. I can keep guard here perfectly, every second of every minute."

"But for how long—the rest of your life?"

"No ..." He sighed, the soft sound spanning the gulf of dimensions. "For the rest of eternity."

Alia stared at him in disbelief.

"I don't understand … how could you—how could any of this—"

"Trust me. Here I'll have everything I need to carry out the task—and all the time in the world too."

"And yet ... you can never go back?"

"Never." He uttered the word with simple finality.

"But ..." She stopped, looking around her. "You'll be alone."

"There are worse fates."

She couldn't imagine any. "Does everyone else know?"

"Only that I have to stay. You'll tell them why when you return."

Before she could argue further, cries of alarm came from the other side of the shimmering portal.

"Our friends need you," Keth said.

"But—"

Raff put a hand on her shoulder. "He's right." Turning to Keth, he said simply, "Thank you."

A high-pitched wail of terror pierced the veil.

"Lally ..." Alia breathed.

She and Raff looked at each other, then drew their swords before turning toward the patch of rippling air.

"Wait!" Keth's shout stopped them in their tracks. "One parting gift before you go. *Lann-lasrach*!" Bolts of eldritch lightning crackled from his outstretched fingers, wreathing the blades of their swords in blue-white flames. "Now go before your friends perish!"

Alia locked eyes with his for a single speechless moment before she tore herself away and the two warriors leapt through to the other side.

Screams and shouts from below filled the air. The pair came through at the top of the spiral stairs only to be immediately attacked by a thicket of lashing tentacles—thick, mutated vines had insinuated themselves through the narrow window slits of the tower and now their thorny, whiplike bodies thrashed back and forth in search of prey.

Fast as serpent strikes, a clutch of vines snapped out and caught hold of Alia and Raff by their forearms, waists, and neck. The hellish plants tightened their grip, binding limbs and choking throats, merciless thorns sticking fast into their armor and drawing blood where they punctured clothing or exposed flesh.

As the vegetal cords encircled and pulled at her wrist, Alia fought to regain her grip on her sword—and succeeded. Twisting her arm, she brought her blade down on her bindings. They snapped apart at the touch of the fiery blade, sliced pieces hissing and thrashing away. With another swipe, she freed herself completely, then took a swing at the vines choking Raff, which sent charred segments flying. The flailing stumps quickly pulled back in retreat, disappearing through the open windows.

Other things had made their way up from the lowest depths of the tower to the chamber below. Not long ago they had been common cellar rats and mice, bats, millipedes, spiders, earthworms, and other creatures. Now they were a swarm of monstrous, oversized horrors—misshapen conglomerations of different vermin and insects.

And the tide of abominations was overwhelming their human opponents.

Dari and the two Pentans slashed away with their swords while behind them, Jezel and Magpie tried to protect Lally with knife and dagger. Alia and Raff charged down the stairs and leapt into the fray. Their blades flashed bright as comets with each swing, blazing a swath through the ranks of the mutants. Those that escaped the blades scattered away in terror, screeching and howling.

Taking the lead, Alia and Raff drove a fiery wedge through to the stairs for the others to follow. Magpie scooped up Lally in his arms and ran alongside Jezel while Dari, Harbalorio, and Birnardus served as their rear guard. In moments, everyone was down the stairs and out the main door—they had closed it when they had first entered, but it now stood wide open, more vines writhing in the doorway, reaching for them. A few quick swipes of Raff and Alia's flaming weapons made short work of them and sent what remained of their chopped, smoldering stumps slithering away out of sight.

The tower's lower level still seethed with a vicious mob of mutated horrors trying to follow them outside, held back only by Dari and the Pentans' needle-sharp thrusts. Raff paused, coming back a few steps, to brandish his ensorcelled blade to cover their escape. The flames had started to flicker, as if they were smothering in the air outside the tower. The same thing was happening to Alia's sword.

"Get this door closed!" Raff yelled.

Dari and the Pentans quickly put their backs against the heavy oaken door, which groaned in protest. Before they could fully close it, however, Alia dashed over to them.

"*Wait!*" she shouted, stepping up to the narrow gap between oaken door and stone doorway where half a dozen thorny, insectile forelimbs and hairy, taloned paws poked through, chittering and clawing to get out.

"What is it?" Raff chopped at a segmented limb with a hooked claw on the end.

"I ..." Alia took a deep breath. "I'm going back in."

Raff turned, eyes wide with shock and disbelief. "Alia, you can't save him. Keth is never coming out!"

"Neither am I." Her voice was low, but there was pure steel in it. "I'm staying with Keth."

The others all stared back at her, speechless.

"Alia, you can't—" Raff stopped, his voice faltering.

"Be sure to take care of Vigo for me, Raff. Don't let Father sell him."

"Alia, please," Raff cried.

"I give all of you what's left of my dowry. If you make it back to Athamé, just tell Father we lost the wagon in the shaker. And Dari ..."

"Yes ... ?"

Alia could hear the tears in her friend's voice.

"Take care. I'll miss you all."

Then she turned and, with one precise motion, expertly slid her blade between door and wall and brought it down in one flaring cut, slicing off anything in the path of her weapon. A chorus of shrieks screamed out in response, and she used the distraction to pull the door open wide enough for her to slip back in.

The last thing the rest of the group saw of her was the grin she flashed them, lit in the blazing blue-white light of her enchanted sword. Then, with a joyful battle cry, she turned and dove into the teeming, howling dark.

In the veil, all was tranquil and timeless—but just outside the shimmering portal, Keth sensed the unbridled hurricane raging in the dark dimension. The alien entity in the shape of his master was battering with all its power against the thin interdimensional barrier separating the two universes, and Keth launched spell after counterspell to ensure that the false Hallam's efforts failed.

Finally, the onslaught subsided. Keth didn't know how long of a break he would have but it would never be long enough. He knew the ancient thing's hunger for his world was eternal. This was only the beginning of the mage's long and lonely duty standing sentry.

He had just begun to settle into waiting when a sudden noise from behind startled him. He wheeled about, hands up to blast the intruder with a bolt of lightning—then froze in shock.

Alia had stepped through the portal and now stood before him.

Keth could only gaze back at her, afraid to believe his good fortune.

"Are you sure?" he said at last.

"Yes."

She held out her hands and he took them.

Epilogue

The seven survivors looked out over the expanse of the middle kingdom stretched out before their eyes. It all looked so still and peaceful in the gentle morning light. There was no sign of Trionn-Fí, no hint of its vanished glories or the horrors now inhabiting its ruins.

"I wonder if we are the last ones who will ever take the northern road," Jezel mused aloud, her breath visible in the cold morning air.

The fiery enchantment on Raff's sword had flickered and then sputtered out a hundred paces from the tower. He was sorry to see it go. Traveling through the night, they had stayed on their guard, weapons at the ready through the long, tense march. But the Great Northern Road had taken them all the way from Hallam's tower in the foothills to the Arcane border up in the mountains without any further attacks. By the time the darkness gave way to the dawn and the sun began to glaze the mountaintops with a golden sheen, they had reached the limits of the High Kingdom.

Now they stood at the crossroads, beneath the ornately decorated border marker. A few days ago, the griffins and wyverns carved into the standing stone would have coiled about its surface and welcomed travelers to Arcanum, answering questions and giving directions, as they had since time immemorial. Now their voices were permanently silenced and they were no more than dead stone. But the travelers knew their way well enough for their purposes.

Raff stared off into the distance, frowning.

"What is it?" Dari asked.

He took a moment before responding. "It's hard to believe the empire is destroyed."

The others remained silent, taking in the awful weight of Raff's words.

"What will become of the four kingdoms now?" Harbalorio asked to no one in particular.

"Rebuilding, if we're lucky," Dari said. "If we're not ... anarchy or worse."

"You don't think the four kingdoms would go to war against one another, do you?" Birnardus exclaimed, visibly alarmed at the thought.

"Perhaps we'll all band together against the monsters and reclaim Trionn-Fí," Magpie said hopefully, but the words sounded hollow even to him.

Patting Magpie on the shoulder, Harbalorio said, "If Keth was right, we stopped the cancer from devouring the entire world outright. So there's that."

Raff shook his head. "Yes, but how great of a threat still remains? How far has it spread? How far *will* it spread?"

"Do you think the monsters will stay in Trionn-Fí?" Lally asked.

The others looked at one another. There was no comforting answer to give her. Shivering, Lally pressed closer to Jezel, who put an arm around the child.

"I wish we could consult the oracles," Jezel said.

Raff laughed, the sound devoid of humor. "The oracles didn't even see their own end. We'll just have to muddle through without them and go see for ourselves."

He turned from the view of their past and regarded the road before them.

Straight ahead, to the north, lay Arcanum, although it was frightening to consider the prospect of just what the Kingdom of Wands must look like, now that the magic was gone. And besides, the only one of them with any reason to go that way was Keth, who would never travel anywhere again.

Which left the ring road that circled the continent. From this point, the remaining choices were left, to Pentaclys, or right, to Beauchalice. The Athaméans would have to weigh the same decision to get to their southern homeland—after all, there was no going through the middle kingdom for any of them.

"We all have choices to make now," Raff said, addressing the group. "Which way?"

"It's west to Pentaclys for us, my friends," said Birnardus. Looking at Harbalorio, he quickly added, "Though, of course, you should *all* come with us."

Jezel smiled and touched Magpie's arm. "A kind offer, My Sir. But we've decided to return to Beauchalice."

"Both of you?" he asked, surprised.

"The three of us, actually," Magpie replied, placing his hand on Lally's shoulder, who seized him around the waist in a hug.

Birnardus turned to Raff and Dari. "What about you, soldiers? Just as easy to get to Athamé from Pentaclys as Beauchalice."

"True," Raff agreed. "But I think these three might be in more need of an escort home than you two bravos—what do you say, Dari?"

She hesitated a moment before answering, "Yes, of course," but not without shooting the briefest of glances at Harbalorio, barely noticeable.

Harbalorio noticed.

"So I suppose this is where we all say goodbye, then," Birnardus said, wistfully.

"Actually, old friend," Harbalorio said expansively, "on second thought, I do want to see these three home to Beauchalice—and then I was thinking I might make a visit to Athamé. That is, if you two don't mind my company." He went and stood by Dari's side, who looked down to hide her pleased smile.

"Here now!" Birnardus exclaimed, outraged. "Am I to be the only one to head the other way?"

"Sure seems so." Harbalorio shrugged. "Unless, of course ..."

"Damn straight I'll join you! Though you'll be buying me some fine Chalicean vintages to make up for the inconvenience! But I don't know what it will take to entice me back to the south."

"Did I mention Alia left a share of her dowry for you at the inn?"

"Well, we'd have to pass the way to get home after all—just don't expect me to travel any further into that gods-forsaken wasteland!"

"Oh, I don't know, old man," Harbalorio said, rubbing his chin thoughtfully. "I've heard Trontes' Skar is nice."

"*Trontes' Skar*?" Birnardus's bushy eyebrows threatened to take flight. "Feh! If you think I'll be kicking around Athamé for long, you've got another thing coming, my fine bucko!"

He kept up his harangue, but the group was already heading down the road to their next destination.

Acknowledgments

As always, there are plenty of people to thank—writing and publishing a book is a group effort when it comes to so many aspects of the process. So in no particular order of appreciation, we want to thank: Jill Marsal, agent extraordinaire (and one of infinite patience); John Harlacher with *Weird Tales®* Presents—his enthusiasm and support for *Tarou: The Fall* has been much appreciated; our editor, Marco Palmieri, who was a joy to work with; Ananda Finwall, our cover artist Jeff Wong, and the rest of the Blackstone Publishing crew—especially eagle-eyed Deirdre Curley-Waldern (any grammatical errors are the fault of our own stubbornness, not her!); Lisa Brackmann, for all of her support, encouragement, and the yummy meals she's cooked for us; the Monday Night Movie Crew, who bring fun, frivolity, food, and much-needed relaxation into our lives; Chris and Merrilyn Galante for so much over the last three years; our Michigan family (with a special shout-out to Susan and the kidcats, Brian and Megan); Harold and Jennifer Perry for their friendship and hospitality; and Steve Saffel, whose presence was felt throughout the writing process, kinda like Obi-Wan Kenobi's ghost.

About the Authors

Dana Fredsti is a writer, actress, former specialty stunt player, producer, director, and editor. She's the author of the *Ashley Parker* series and the dark fantasy series *Spawn of Lilith*. **David Fitzgerald** is an award-winning fiction and nonfiction author and editor. Together they are the authors of the *Time Shards* trilogy. They live in Northern California in a Victorian mansion with ten cats and a dog, and enjoy sword fighting and LARPing.

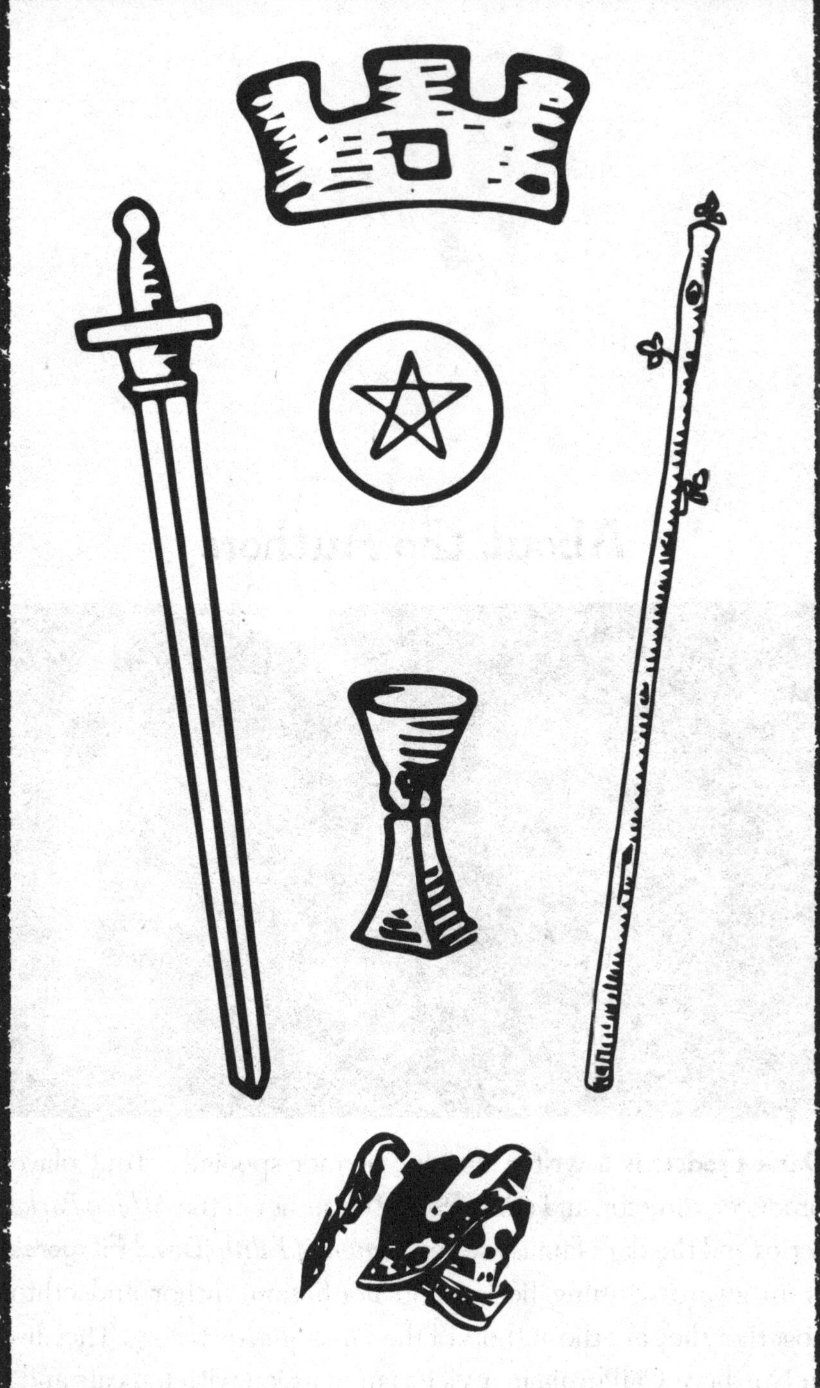